W9-AUY-210

KING'S
SHADOW

THE SILENT YEARS BOOKS IN CHRONOLOGICAL ORDER

Judah's Wife

Jerusalem's Queen

Egypt's Sister

King's Shadow

THE SILENT YEARS

KING'S SHADOW

A NOVEL OF KING HEROD'S COURT

ANGELA HUNT

BETHANYHOUSE
a division of Baker Publishing Group
Minneapolis, Minnesota

Published by Bethany House Publishers
11400 Hampshire Avenue South
Bloomington, Minnesota 55438
www.bethanyhouse.com

Bethany House Publishers is a division of
Baker Publishing Group, Grand Rapids, Michigan

Printed in the United States of America

Library of Congress Cataloging-in-Publication Data
Names: Hunt, Angela Elwell, author.
Title: King's shadow : a novel of King Herod's court / Angela Hunt.
Description: Bloomington, Minnesota : Bethany House Publishers, 2019. | Series:
    The silent years
Identifiers: LCCN 2018058911 | ISBN 9780764233364 (trade paper) | ISBN
    9780764234156 (hardcover) | ISBN 9781493418596 (e-book)
Subjects: LCSH: Courts and courtiers—Fiction. | Herod I, King of Judea, 73 B.C.–4
    B.C.—Fiction. | GSAFD: Christian fiction. | Historical fiction.
Classification: LCC PS3558.U46747 K56 2019 | DDC 813/.54—dc23
LC record available at https://lccn.loc.gov/2018058911

This is a work of historical reconstruction; the appearances of certain historical figures are therefore inevitable. All other characters, however, are products of the author's imagination, and any resemblance to actual persons, living or dead, is coincidental.

Cover design by LOOK Design Studio
Cover photography by Aimee Christenson

Author is represented by Browne & Miller Literary Associates.

19 20 21 22 23 24 25   7 6 5 4 3 2 1

In the Christian Bible, one turns the page after Malachi and finds Matthew as if only a few days fell between the activities of the prophet and the arrival of Jesus Christ. In reality, however, four hundred "silent years" lie between the Old Testament and New, a time when God did not speak to Israel through His prophets. Yet despite the prophets' silence, God continued to work in His people, other nations, and the supernatural realm.

He led Israel through a time of testing that developed a sense of hope and a yearning for the promised Messiah.

He brought the four nations prophesied in Daniel's vision to international prominence: the Babylonians, the Persians, the Greeks, and the Romans. These powerful kingdoms spread their cultures throughout civilization and united the world by means of paved highways and international sailing routes.

God also prepared to fulfill His promise to the serpent in Eden: "I will put animosity between you and the woman, and between your descendant and her descendant; he will bruise your head, and you will bruise his heel" (Genesis 3:15).

King's Shadow closes the gap between the time of the prophets and the coming of the promised Messiah.

PART ONE

37 Years Before the Common Era

CHAPTER ONE

Salome

If my brother had been marrying anyone else, I might have been happy for him. But the seventeen-year-old girl at his side was Mariamne of the Hasmoneans, and nothing would please me more than never having to see her again. But now the war was concluding, so Herod was free to take his promised throne and marry his betrothed. In a few moments, Mariamne and I would be joined as sisters-in-law for a lifetime.

The thought made my stomach churn.

Mariamne, the esteemed bride, was the daughter of Alexandra and Alexander, the closest thing to a royal family the Jews possessed. Alexandra, the bride's mother, was the daughter of Hyrcanus II, the eldest son of King Alexander Jannaeus and Queen Salome Alexandra. Alexander, the bride's father, had been sired by Aristobulus, the second son of Jannaeus and his queen. Though most people would find it difficult to keep track of that family's intertwined lineage, they were more than royal names to me. My father and grandfather had served those kings, so my brothers and I had visited the royal palace many times.

I had long since grown weary of them all.

I thought Herod would be weary of them as well, but Mariamne had blossomed into an exquisite beauty, and my brother was thoroughly besotted.

A murmur of approval rippled through the crowd, followed by fervent whispers.

"This will silence the wagging tongues who say our king is not of royal blood."

"The Jews cannot criticize our king now—not with a Hasmonean queen on the throne."

"I hear he is truly smitten with the girl. Some say she might already be with child."

"About time! Their betrothal has lasted how long? Six years?"

Five, I wanted to shout. I had endured five long years of living with the girl at Masada, five years of hearing her complain about the food, the clothing my brother provided, and the furnishings in her chamber. Never mind that Herod had emptied his personal treasury to provide her with the best of everything. Never mind that Mother had urged me and my other brother to be on our best behavior in her arrogant presence.

Never mind that I had been placed in charge of arranging this tiresome royal wedding. I would do almost anything to make my brother happy, but I would have preferred to endure a full day of torture rather than spend a full week arranging the marriage between Herod and that spoiled hellcat.

I forced a smile as the priest—an ordinary Levite, the best I could find, as Herod had not yet appointed a new *cohen gadol*—lifted his hand and offered a quiet benediction.

When the priest had finished, my brother turned to face the assembly, a wide smile overtaking his tanned face. "May I present to you," he said, a note of childlike wonder in his voice, "my bride and your queen, Mariamne."

The bride, who fairly dripped in jewels and gold chains,

inclined her head in a regal nod and allowed Herod to lead her off the elevated platform. Then she paused beside a servant carrying a pillow and turned to her new husband.

Beaming like a grateful boy, my brother lifted a golden diadem from the pillow and placed it on Mariamne's head.

Beside me, eight-year-old Antipater snorted. I elbowed him, then nodded toward the king. "Mind your manners, nephew. Your father will not be pleased if he sees you smirking at his bride."

"If given a chance, I could make real trouble," the lad replied, his dark brows rushing together. "Should I step forward and ask Father how my mother feels about this? He has cast her off like a worthless old shoe, and yet—"

"Does she not still live?" I frowned and lowered my voice. "You are here, and you are the king's firstborn, a position no one can take away. So mind your tongue and watch your step. You must tread carefully if you wish to remain in your father's favor."

"In the king's favor." Antipater arched a dark brow, revealing a wisdom beyond his years. "A precarious place to be."

"Would you rather be ignored?" I nodded toward the departing newlyweds. "Herod would never forgive me if I allowed you to make a scene at his wedding. So go to the feast and adopt a pleasant expression. Behave yourself. If anyone asks for your opinion of the bride, say you admire her and look forward to getting to know her better. Because you do *not* want to be overheard complaining about your mother's situation."

Antipater scowled, but he was smart enough to know I would not give him bad advice. As the crowd surged toward the reception tent, I waited for my other brother. Pheroras stood at the rear of the expansive chamber, looking pleased. He had supported Herod's plan to marry the Hasmonean girl and did not seem to view her as I did.

Perhaps it took a woman to fully understand another woman. What did men know of our ability to intuit the secret desires hidden behind painted lips and polished faces? To read another female heart through sly glances and tight-lipped smiles? Why could neither Pheroras nor Herod see Mariamne and her mother as I saw them?

Ten minutes after I met Alexandra, I knew she had agreed to this marriage for only one reason: to keep her grip on power in Judea. The Hasmoneans had been pushed off the throne because they could not share power among themselves. Rome stepped in to maintain the peace, and the Senate's edict established Herod as king of Judea. But due to this marriage, Alexandra's grandchildren would be royal heirs, and within a generation Judea would again have a Hasmonean king . . . if Herod allowed Mariamne's children to replace Antipater, his firstborn.

Alexandra's ambition was as obvious as the stars on a cloudless night, yet Herod was so addled by the daughter's beauty he honestly believed she loved him.

In the great pavilion Herod had erected outside the city of Samaria, dozens of dignitaries lounged on couches, drank wine, and shouted congratulations to the king. I walked in with Joseph, my uncle and husband, and scrutinized visiting Roman senators, wealthy merchants, and Malichus, the Nabataean king with his entourage. Were they pleased with the wine? Had we provided enough food? Some guests had come from miles away, and Herod would not be happy if anyone left hungry.

Once I was certain everything was in order, I relaxed and tried not to be too obvious as I drank in the details of dress and jewelry on the Arab women. After being safeguarded for so long at Masada, I felt a keen interest in current fashions and hairstyles. My handmaid, Nada, was set in her ways and for years had been arranging my hair in the same boring style. Now that we had been freed, perhaps Mother and I could finally look like royal women . . .

A bright, eye-catching crimson blazed among the chitons and flowing himations. What did they call that shade, and how did the dyers achieve such brilliance? And silver must have gone out of favor, for I had never seen so much gold jewelry encircling male and female necks. Herod would want Mother and me to look like these women, to show that we were not common but as regal as any noble lady.

"So many important guests have come to honor my nephew." Joseph spoke to me but smiled fondly at Herod. "I never thought I would see such a day."

"Neither did I," I remarked, though my reasons for doubting the marriage likely differed from my husband's.

I nodded toward the wide couch reserved for us, and Joseph led me through the crowd while acknowledging those who respectfully inclined their heads in our direction. Though I was not the focus of attention—the central elevated couch had been reserved for Herod and his new bride—everyone knew I was the king's only sister and my husband the king's uncle. No one wanted to slight us, for my brothers and I were as close as a tree and its bark. Our father taught us to be dependent on each other and to support, protect, and elevate one another whenever possible. To insult one of us was to insult *all* of us, and no one wanted to face our combined wrath.

I should have been overjoyed on this day, yet when I looked at the bride, whom everyone called "the Hasmonean princess," my gut clenched. Mariamne was beautiful, even I could admit that, but she seemed to believe herself superior to everyone around her. Alexandra, her mother, had to be the source of the girl's imperiousness, for even I had heard the woman boast that Mariamne had been born into a chosen race and a chosen family.

I caught my husband's arm. "What do you think?" I jerked my chin toward the bride's mother. "Friend or foe?"

Joseph released a dark little laugh. "Clearly a foe." He grinned at me. "But the sort you keep close so that you may keep a sharp eye on them."

"She's always talking about the heroic Maccabees," I muttered, walking close to him as we threaded our way through the gathering. "Constantly reminding me of the ragtag army that saved Israel from the Seleucids."

Joseph snorted. "Judah Maccabee might have been a hero, but if she mentions her ancestors again, ask her about Alexander Jannaeus, who crucified hundreds of Pharisees on a single night. Or Aristobulus, who murdered his own mother in order to seize the throne. For that matter, ask her about John Hyrcanus, who invaded Idumea and forced us to become Jews."

My husband spoke in a soft voice, but I heard the resentment in it. If Alexandra had been close enough to hear, she would have been alarmed.

The woman despised me; I knew it as certainly as I knew the sun would rise on the morrow. Both Alexandra and her daughter displayed a palpable revulsion when presented with anything—food, garment, or servant—from Idumea, which caused me to wonder how Alexandra had reconciled her disdain for Idumaeans with her desire to see her daughter well married. Throughout the years of our forced togetherness, I had been able to formulate only one reason: she wanted her offspring to reclaim the throne of Judea. If that meant Mariamne would have to marry an Edomite, then so be it. Alexandra, I had come to believe, would marry her daughter to a toad if it meant her grandchildren would be kings and queens.

Both women were always clever enough to veil their innermost thoughts and opinions when seated with Herod or any of his counselors. When we women gathered for a meal or an afternoon's entertainment, however, the veils came off.

"I know why Alexandra wanted Mariamne to wed the king," I whispered as Joseph and I approached our couch. "What I can't understand is why Herod wants to marry that arrogant girl."

"That, my dear—" Joseph tossed a grin over his shoulder— "is because you are not a man."

As the musicians I had chosen played in the corner of the decorated tent, I pressed my lips together and reclined on our couch, positioning my head near my husband's. Joseph had never been the love of my life, but I was reasonably certain Herod arranged our marriage because he thought I needed a mature advisor.

Though Joseph did not love me, I knew he had developed a certain fondness toward me. At twenty-eight, twenty years his junior, I could rarely hold his attention for more than a few moments because he claimed our conversations exhausted him. His concubines attended to his physical pleasures, so he did not need me for physical or emotional satisfaction. But with our marriage he won a role he had greatly desired, that of advisor to the king. Now when Herod sent for me and Pheroras, he included Joseph, which pleased my husband immensely.

I smiled as a sudden thought struck. Perhaps my brother married me to our uncle in order to control me indirectly. If so, his ploy had worked—to a point. But I still could not figure out what he saw in Mariamne. She was lovely, yes, but he could fill a harem with beautiful concubines. She was not particularly bright or clever, and she came with a mother who would vex the patience of a stone.

Yet only Mariamne could give him legitimacy. Rome might have given Herod the throne, but only a Hasmonean would satisfy the Jews of Jerusalem. Still . . . would her so-called legitimacy be enough to make the marriage work? The Jews would not be happy if he married this girl and later set her aside . . .

I pressed my hand to my husband's arm and nodded toward the bride. "What do you think? Will she make Herod happy?"

Joseph followed my gaze. "She has already made him delirious with joy. She is everything he ever wanted—beautiful, intelligent, Jewish by birth, and Hasmonean. If she proves fertile, he will never find fault in her."

"I would not be surprised if she is already with child," I murmured, tilting my head to study the bride's belly. "Five years is a long time for a betrothal. Surely Herod has visited her chamber—"

"Not likely, with her mother hovering about." Joseph smiled. "Alexandra guarded her daughter's purity as if it were more valuable than jewels. No, the girl cannot be with child. But after tonight . . . we shall see."

I looked to the edge of the tent, where young Antipater sat on a bench, his face marked by resentment. "Antipater cannot be pleased by this union."

Narrow-faced Antipater who, along with his mother, had been unceremoniously set aside, did not appear to be enjoying the wedding, but Herod wanted him to witness the new marriage. Herod had banished Doris and would soon send Antipater to his mother. The next time Doris saw her son, she would undoubtedly pepper him with questions about the event.

Herod would approve if the boy told his mother everything.

"What will become of the lad?" I wondered, studying the young prince. The boy looked nothing like my brother. He had inherited his mother's thin face, frail frame, and sparse brown hair. His voice was yet high and reedy, far more suited to a girl than a boy. But since he was Herod's firstborn, he had been indulged from birth until the day Herod decided to marry Mariamne.

"Next week he will leave us," Joseph said. "He and Doris will be well cared for, but Antipater will not be regarded as the heir apparent. Today Herod begins a new chapter in his reign. He has his Jewish queen, and soon he will have Jerusalem. Already our men have surrounded the city, and the Romans are on their way to support us."

"I hope nothing happens to Herod," I whispered, hardly daring to speak such ominous words at a wedding. I should not even hint of such a dark possibility, but I had watched my brother ride away too many times and take too many risks. One day, surely, the tide would turn and he would not be victorious . . . or so lucky.

I had already lost two of my brothers. I did not want to lose another.

"Nothing will happen to Herod," Joseph answered, his voice brimming with confidence. "He has a gift for being in the right place at the right moment."

"But so did Phasael. And Joseph."

My husband shrugged. "Then, considering the world we inhabit, our new queen should produce a son as soon as possible."

I brushed the troubling thought of Herod's death aside and peered across the crowd to where our mother sat on an elevated chair. She held her chin high, a silent rebuke to all those who thought our family unworthy of marriage to a Hasmonean, and then her gaze crossed mine.

Yes. Her eyes sent a silent message. *Your brother will be pleased with your efforts here.*

I sighed and felt the tension leave my shoulders for the first time in a week.

Chapter Two

Zara

"Come, Zara. Show your *abba* what you have learned today."

I left my clay doll in the corner and hurried to greet my father, who had just come through the doorway. I lifted my arms for the usual hug, but his dark eyes were shadowed, and his mouth did not curve in his customary smile.

Not to be put off, I embraced his knees and felt his hand drop to my head.

"They are building war machines," he told my mother. "Outside the walls, an entire camp of carpenters. Towers and battering rams."

I glanced up in time to see Ima place a finger across her lips, and then she gave him a tight, false smile of upper teeth. "Let Zara show you what she has learned today. You will be so proud of her."

As my mother sank to a low stool, I kept my eyes on Abba, who had not looked at me since coming through the door. But when his gaze crossed mine, his mouth relaxed. He leaned against the wall and crossed his arms. "I am watching, little one. What did you learn?"

"This." I turned to my mother, who had untied her hair and let it tumble down her back. Biting my lip, I separated the long hair into three sections, then drew them into my fingers and began to lift and cross, cross and lift, lift and cross. "See, Abba? I'm braiding!"

My father lowered himself to my level. "Ah! You are, and you are so young! How did a seven-year-old girl learn to do that?"

"She taught herself." Mother turned her head, nearly pulling a section of hair from my hands. I made a *tsk*ing noise with my teeth—the same noise Mother made when I was too restless on the stool—and Mother obediently stilled.

"I suppose she's been watching me all these years," Ima went on. "Still, I've never heard of a child learning how to braid on her own. But then I never taught her to tie her apron, either. One day she just did it."

I shook my head. "Tying is not hard. It is easy."

"Not for everyone," Abba said. He caught my arm and squeezed it. "HaShem has given you quite a gift, Zara. I wonder what He will have you do with it. Perhaps you will braid my hair one day."

I gaped at him. "*Your* hair? It is not long enough."

"It might be—soon. I will not want it getting in my face."

I frowned, confused, while Abba stood and gave my mother a serious look. "I have decided to join the men, who will defend the Temple Mount. When the time comes, I will probably stay there for the duration. I may not see you or Zara for days, even weeks."

Mother stood too, gently pulling her hair from my fingers. "Then let us not waste a single moment of our time together."

CHAPTER THREE

Salome

As tribal leaders, senators, and courtiers stood to congratulate Herod on his marriage, my attention shifted to the empty chairs behind the newly married couple. Those seats should have been occupied by Phasael, firstborn of our father, and Joseph, our father's third son. They should have been celebrating with us. Instead, they lay moldering in their graves. Joseph, whom we lost only a few months ago, had not been returned to us, so we had no idea where his body was buried or if it had been buried at all.

My husband followed my gaze. "I miss them, too," he said, his voice a low growl beneath the murmuring of the restless crowd. "They should have been here."

I dashed a tear from my cheek. "I cannot believe we have lost both of them."

"They both disobeyed Herod. If they had not—"

"We should not blame them for doing what they did," I interrupted, settling my elbow into the curve of our couch. "The people were starving when Herod went away, and Joseph was desperate to procure food. And if Phasael had not taken his life,

20

the Parthian commander would have used him as a pawn . . . which would have placed Herod in a bad situation."

Joseph lifted his cup toward the empty couch. "Phasael was probably the most honorable of us all. And the most pragmatic."

I searched the crowd for my eldest brother's wife. I spotted her sitting with a group of highborn Idumaean women, a baby at her breast. The child, a boy, bore his father's name. "May Phasael's son live to follow in his father's footsteps," I said, lifting my cup.

We drank, then looked toward the platform where yet another visiting dignitary had stood to congratulate our brother with a speech. I did not catch the man's name, who unfurled a long scroll, the sight of which made me groan. Would this day never end?

"Live forever, King Herod of Judea." The man lifted his voice to the high oratorical pitch the Romans favored. "Know that your friend and my master Mark Antony sends his congratulations and best wishes. Antony congratulates you not only on your marriage but on your future victory in Jerusalem. You will eliminate Antigonus, the king who would bleed his people dry, and his Parthian allies."

"Antony would have done better to come in person," I whispered.

"Antony would do better to send the promised reinforcements instead of congratulations." Joseph lowered his cup and crossed his arms. "I grow weary of these long-winded messengers. Surely we are near the end."

"You know Herod." I dropped my hand to Joseph's shoulder. "He never tires of hearing how much he is loved. But look." I pointed to a richly robed and bearded man in the back—a Pharisee, by the look of him. "At least some of Herod's future subjects have come to celebrate with him."

Not many Jews were among the crowd, and only two or three

Pharisees. Then again, we were celebrating in Samaria, and the few Jews who had joined us were probably consoling themselves with the knowledge that none of their friends would know they had attended the wedding of their unpopular Idumaean king.

"Samaias." Joseph grunted. "I know him. He is a leader among the Pharisees."

"So did this Samaias come here to congratulate Herod or to curse him?"

"Let us see."

My husband and I waited as the old man walked toward the dais, where Herod and Mariamne reclined on the bridal couch. He did not carry a scroll like so many others but simply folded his hands and bowed his head. "My king," he said, and at those words a stunned silence filled the tent.

I lifted a brow and looked at Joseph. This was the first time we had seen or heard a Pharisee acknowledge Herod as king. Our brother had won more than a bride today—he had won an ally among a group that could hold the keys to the kingdom. Unless this man would later prove false.

I leaned back on an elbow and surveyed the room, studying the faces of the guests who watched Samaias. The Nabataeans and Idumaeans wore expressions of pleased surprise, but the religious Jews . . .

A clutch of them huddled near the doorway—another Pharisee, a man who might be a Sadducee, and a white-robed Essene. What were they, a representative body of religious leaders? They did not seem surprised by Samaias's greeting, unless they had donned dour expressions to hide their astonishment.

I sank back and reached for a bowl of figs on a nearby tray. "For a moment, I thought Herod had won the day," I murmured, keeping my voice low. "But apparently Samaias speaks for himself alone."

Joseph fingered his beard. "Or he does not speak honestly."

I peered over Joseph's shoulder to study the sour-faced men at the back of the tent. Was it not bad enough I had to suffer the arrogance of my new sister-in-law and her overbearing mother? Must Herod suffer the same from every leading citizen of Jerusalem? Herod had earned every honor Rome had bestowed on him, including the crown on his head. None of the Jewish kings had been able to accomplish as much as he had, and once he took Jerusalem, he would accomplish more.

"Will the religious leaders ever accept our brother?" I looked at my husband. "He would be a good king if they but gave him a chance."

"The key to holding Judea," Joseph said, his eyes crinkling as he looked over the crowd, "is subduing the Jews, and that cannot be done overnight. Herod has a long road ahead of him."

"The religious leaders forget we are as Jewish as they are." I crossed my arms. "We keep their Law. We study their Torah. We circumcise men before we allow them to marry into our family."

"Oh, they know those things," Joseph answered. "But they forget, just as they have conveniently forgotten that your grandfather served their esteemed Salome Alexandra, and your father served her son Hyrcanus. They look at all Idumaeans as though we were rats who should not be allowed to tread on the tiles of Hasmonean palaces."

I sighed. "Sometimes I wish I did not bear Salome's name. When I meet the people of Jerusalem, I know they will hear my name, think of her, and decide I will never be as pious as their beloved queen."

Joseph pressed his lips together. "You must be patient, dear wife. Herod has yet to take Jerusalem, and the city will experience the pangs of adjustment after he does. But the people of Judea will grow to love their king, and they will come to admire his siblings, including his sister. And when he saves them from annihilation by the Parthians or some other enemy of Rome—"

"An annihilation they would have already experienced if Herod had not interfered on their behalf!"

Joseph lowered his chin in an abrupt nod. "One day they will appreciate him. That day, however, is not likely to be today, tomorrow, or even next year."

Again I eyed the group of bearded religious leaders, who continued to drip disapproval and disdain. "You may be right," I said, sighing, "yet that day had better come quickly, because our Herod is not a patient man."

Finally, the enthusiastic praise for Herod ended. Though I am certain Herod could have listened to a stream of compliments for hours more, his young bride appeared to be falling asleep at his side.

Seeing that Mariamne was weary, Herod stood, took her hand, and led her out of the tent, vanishing into the garden beyond. They would spend their wedding night in the finest house in Samaria, as the king had no official residence in the city.

I sat up, shook off the stupor of lethargy, and placed my hand on Joseph's arm. "Shall we go to our chamber or do you need to speak to some of the guests?"

A small smile creased his face. "Someone might need to speak to me, but they can find me later. I can tolerate this crowd no longer."

We left our couch, and I sighed with satisfaction as small groups of people parted and bowed as we made our way toward the exit. Though the Jews might not approve of Idumaeans, they dared not show their disapproval to our faces.

As Joseph and I strode through the crowd, a deep and quiet joy filled my heart. *Yes,* I wanted to shout, *I am a daughter of Esau, not Jacob, and yet tonight you look to me for recognition and approval.*

The feeling soured, however, when I realized the men and women around me would soon return to their homes, where they would stop smiling and start criticizing. Though Joseph seemed optimistic, I feared the people of Jerusalem would be like Mariamne and scorn their new king. Their unwillingness to accept Herod might lead them to find fault with all of us—my husband, my brother, and even my mother, who had watched the day's proceedings with wary eyes. Our mother, Cypros, had dressed in somber colors and worn no jewelry, for she was still in mourning, having recently lost a son.

My heart constricted in pity. The past few years had held far more sad than happy occasions for our mother, but I hoped this day had brought her some comfort.

We had not taken ten steps outside the wedding tent when I noticed a woman—a Jewish woman, for she was with one of the Pharisees—whose features hardened in a stare of disapproval when she realized who I was. I had done nothing to earn her disdain, but there it was nonetheless. I should probably become accustomed to such looks.

How I wished I could show the Jews how I felt about their superior attitudes! Herod was fortunate—he could freely speak his mind, though he was wise enough to hold his tongue when he needed to placate the Jews on some point. But Rome had invested him with power and authority, and most of the Jews who came to him had realized he could—and would—execute them if they proved treacherous or disloyal. I, on the other hand, did not hold or desire such power, and yet I would be deeply pleased if I were granted an opportunity to tell the Jews exactly what I thought of their attitude, starting with my new sister-in-law . . .

"You seem perturbed." Joseph leaned toward me, intently focused on my face. "Was this not a happy day for you?"

"Happy?" I barked a laugh. "How can I be happy when I

spent the day worrying about the Levite, the guests, the slaves, the food, the musicians, the men who cared for the horses and camels at the stable—"

"Let me rephrase," Joseph said, cutting off my words. "Was this not an occasion for celebration?"

"How can I celebrate when my brother has married that girl?" I snapped. "Now she and her mother are part of our family."

"Herod hasn't married the mother—"

"He might not sleep with Alexandra, but Mariamne speaks Alexandra's words, voices her desires, and acts upon her wishes. Mariamne is yet a child; the mother controls her. In time she will seek to control Herod, as well."

"You control me," Joseph said, his voice light. "You know I would move the sun and stars to please you."

I blew out a breath. "I do not control you any more than I control Herod or Pheroras. Besides, I have never wanted to control my brothers."

"If you had the power, who would you control?"

"The Jews!" I spat out the words. "Particularly the Hasmoneans. Alexandra and her kind despise us. And Herod is so in love, he cannot see it."

"He is not as blind as you might think."

"Isn't he? Then why did he pull me aside last night and forbid me to be sharp with Mariamne? I am commanded to bite my tongue and bridle my thoughts, swallowing them until I choke, if necessary."

Joseph patted my hand. "You do not have to swallow them in my company."

I halted and turned to him. "I cannot allow this girl to come between me and my brother." I frowned as I considered the ramifications. "I did not believe it possible, but Mariamne, that imperious child . . ."

"Herod would never allow anyone to come between you two.

You are his only sister, and Herod is devoted to you. But hear me in this, Salome: be kind to his new wife and wait patiently, for the bloom *will* fall from the rose. Time will solve your problem. You have only to exercise a little patience."

"Patience does not come naturally for me."

Joseph chuckled. "Of course not, my impetuous wife."

He caught my hand and led me to the house he had rented for the wedding. Before we crossed the threshold, he planted a kiss on my forehead. "You are so like your brother. Your passions run high, and your patience is shallow. But Herod has learned self-control. If you want to be happy in your brother's palace, you should follow his example."

CHAPTER FOUR

Zara

I remember childhood as a time of sweetness, gentleness and laughter, joy and love . . . until death arrived with Herod's army. One day I was the happy daughter of a mother and father; the next I was cowering beneath a table with my mother, praying HaShem would send angels to hide us beneath their wings.

If I had been older, I might have discerned more portents of the disaster to come. But even as a child, as the days grew longer and the buds on the trees burst into golden leaves, I noticed that Abba spent more time away from home and Ima stopped smiling, even when she spoke to me. When the neighborhood women leaned over the courtyard fence, they did not talk of the weather or Shabbat baking, but murmured secrets in the tone reserved for dreaded things. Whenever this happened, my mother would tell me to go practice my braiding, so I did. I braided straws from the broom, Abba's leather belts, and the spun wool my mother used for weaving.

While I practiced braiding and tying knots and anything else my hands found to do, I overheard things:

"They say our Antigonus has been declared an enemy of Rome. That will prevent Roman generals from coming to his aid, no matter how much he offers to pay them."

"Who needs Romans when HaShem is on our side?"

"How can HaShem be for us when Herod now has a Hasmonean wife? Antigonus, Mariamne—are they not sprung from the same tree?"

"Herod is the king, not his wife. And Herod is an Idumaean, a half Jew."

"He will fight hard to win Jerusalem. He cannot rule Judea without its capital."

"Our people will fight harder to defend it."

"If ever we needed our Messiah, this is the time."

I could not see outside the walls, but I knew the attack had begun when all the fathers and sons in our neighborhood went out to fight atop the walls or to stand guard around the Temple. I had heard enough to know what the invaders would do if the walls collapsed, or if they managed to dig a tunnel beneath the mighty stones. The enemy would enter the Holy City with swords in their hands and murder on their minds. One of the neighbors said they would make their way to the Temple, stabbing anyone who stood in their path, because like so many invaders before them, they would be determined to steal the precious gold and silver vessels we had dedicated to Adonai.

"It has happened before," Ima told our neighbor. "Pagans have come to the Holy City and ransacked the Temple. Our men must be strong, and we must ask HaShem to gird them with courage. It is the best way we women can help."

So we prayed, and Ima helped in other ways, too. Every day, after our prayers, she made me sit beneath the table while she covered it with a woven blanket. Then she packed a leather pouch with bread, cheese, and water flasks. She would peer

beneath the table to tell me good-bye and to warn me not to
come out until I heard her return.

"The men have to eat," she told me every time she packed a
bag. "And we women have to make sure they remain strong."

While Ima was away, I waited beneath the table and tried to
be brave. Sometimes, when the wind shifted and the thumping
sounds of the war reached our house, I pushed my fingers into
my ears and prayed so loudly the sound of my voice drowned
out the noise. Ima said the thumping came from Roman battering rams, and though I had never seen one, I imagined them as
great hairy beasts with horns the size of tree trunks and hooves
as big as a house. On the nights Abba was able to come home,
he was always grimed with sweat and dirt, which the huge rams
must have kicked up as they struggled to knock down the walls.

On such nights, my father would sit on a stool while Ima
bathed him with a wet cloth. "Never worry, little Zara," Abba
would say, smiling. "HaShem is with us. Though Herod and
the Romans have armies that far outnumber ours, they do not
have God on their side. And they do not have His promise to
send a Messiah to deliver us."

"What will the Messiah do, Abba?"

"He will defeat our enemies," Abba said, looking to my
mother. "He will restore justice and demonstrate mercy. He
will bind up our wounds and bring peace to the earth."

I believed my father. And as spring warmed into summer,
I continued to believe and look for the Messiah, even though
the sound of the fierce Roman rams sent me scurrying under
the table every time I heard them.

CHAPTER FIVE

Salome

"Any word from the battle today?" My gaze caught Nada's in the looking brass. "Have we breached those cursed walls yet?"

My handmaid clicked her tongue as she braided my hair. "You should not care so much about what happens in war. It is unfeminine for a woman to know about such things."

I chuffed in disagreement. Nada was old and had outdated ideas about what women should and should not do. And she had not been reared with four brothers.

"I care about my family." I lifted my chin. "Father always said we should pull together, so if my remaining brothers—" my throat tightened as fleeting thoughts of Joseph and Phasael passed through my mind—"are at war, then so am I."

Now that Herod had his Jewish bride and two Roman legions at his disposal, he decided the time had come to take the throne the Romans had promised him. The Roman commander Sosius had positioned his legions on the northeast side of Jerusalem where the Temple sat behind thick walls. Before his wedding,

Herod had dispersed his fighting men around the city and directed them to build defensive walls with lookout towers.

Roman reinforcements had arrived by the time Herod rejoined his men. From reports Joseph shared with me, I knew my brother's force consisted of two generals, eleven divisions of foot soldiers, six thousand cavalry, and hundreds of Syrian auxiliaries. The Parthians had supported Antigonus, but in the face of Roman opposition they vanished from the region.

"If rumors can be trusted," Joseph told me over dinner, "the Parthians consider Jerusalem and Antigonus a lost cause."

"Are the Romans doing all they promised?"

Joseph nodded. "They have brought up battering rams and catapults. The Romans are skilled at siege fighting; the legionaries know how to wield a hammer as well as a sword."

"But the men inside—how can Herod rule a city if he has killed hundreds of its people?"

"The men of Jerusalem do not have to die. All they have to do is surrender Antigonus, and the siege will end."

"They will never surrender. They are fighting for the Holy City, for the Temple, for HaShem. They are fighting for the man they believe to be their rightful king."

Joseph's brows knitted. "I thought *we* were fighting for HaShem, the Holy City, the Temple, and the rightful king."

"The *legal* king. Rome has given Judea to Herod because the Hasmoneans could not stop making war against each other. But the people in Jerusalem will never accept Rome's decision."

"Distance . . . brings a balanced perspective."

"But the Jews do not have the benefit of distance. They have been living with the situation for generations." I reached for a slice of salted beef and chewed it slowly, then swallowed. "So how goes Herod's siege?"

Joseph snorted. "Exactly as you would expect. The men

of Jerusalem stand on attack platforms on the walls and pick off Herod's men at their leisure. Others crawl through hidden tunnels and appear in the middle of the Roman camp, swords swinging."

My mouth twisted in a reluctant smile. "You have to admire their spirit."

"Yes. A shame Herod will have to kill the bravest of them."

"As our enemies have killed our family's bravest, as well."

"Ouch!" Nada's heavy hand brought me back to the present. "My scalp is tender there."

She widened her eyes in pretend innocence. "Did I hurt you? Sorry, my lamb."

I glared at her, but as always she ignored my displeasure. She had tended me since the day I came into the world, so she probably felt as if she owned me. Perhaps she did. She had certainly spent more time with me than anyone else, including my own mother.

"Where is my husband?" I asked, certain he would not have ridden out to watch the battle. He had told Herod he was too old to mount a horse, so he would oversee operations from Samaria.

"Your husband is with a Roman messenger. I understand your brother is to meet with them."

Herod was leaving the siege? I could not imagine any reason for him to depart from an ongoing battle.

"Finish quickly," I told her. "I want to see why Herod has come."

"Is it such a mystery? The man has a beautiful bride waiting here."

"Bah! It has to be more than that, so hurry."

"Would you go half dressed? I need to choose a chiton and the proper himation—"

"Do what you must, but be quick about it."

I found my husband, Herod, and the Roman commander standing in the center of the reception hall, a map of Jerusalem on the table between them. The Roman stood with his jaw set and his arms crossed while Herod faced him, a look of implacable determination in his eyes. Joseph wavered between them, one hand fluttering helplessly.

Perhaps I could help solve this obvious impasse.

"Good morning, gentlemen." I spoke in a soft tone, with a feminine lilt Nada would have approved. "How goes the siege of Jerusalem?"

While the Roman's scowl deepened, Herod's face brightened. "Salome! Perhaps you can talk some sense into our friend Sosius."

"The commander?" I gave him one of my brightest smiles. "I was so pleased to hear Mark Antony had decided to send you to Judea. Your brilliant reputation, sir, has preceded you."

The commander flushed at the flattery.

"I have just suggested," Herod said, noticing the sign of weakening in his opponent, "that we stop bombarding the walls and furnish the Temple priests with herds of oxen, bulls, and lambs. Pigeons too if we can find enough."

I shot him a puzzled look. "Are the priests starving?"

"The daily sacrifices," Joseph murmured, tactfully reminding me of the rituals I had forgotten. "We received word that the priests are about to run out of animals for the daily sacrifices."

"Ah." I tilted my head toward my brother. "And you want to supply them with the appropriate beasts."

"Are we not Jews?" He arched a brow. "These things are important to us—and to our people in Jerusalem."

"Of course." I ran my fingertips over the table, admiring Herod's strategy. Though I knew he personally cared nothing about daily rituals, he would need the support of the priests when he entered the city. And if he had taken great pains to ensure that the Temple rituals would not be hindered, the priests would be more likely to support him. They might even be grateful.

"When you retreat from a siege," the Roman countered gruffly, "you give your enemy time to rest, eat, and renew their courage. How do you know our enemies will not devour these cattle and oxen and lambs? How do you know they will not launch a renewed attack an hour after we pull away from the wall?"

"We do not have to pull away," Herod answered. "We have only to let a few shepherds drive the beasts through our lines and into the city. The risk is small, but the potential benefit is great. We need the goodwill of the people, Sosius—especially the priests and religious leaders."

The Roman scowled again, but when he turned from Herod to me, I knew he had decided to relent.

"All right," he finally said, uncrossing his arms. "Have some of your people commandeer an appropriate number of beasts and assemble them behind our lines. But we will not allow the shepherds to enter the city—we cannot afford to enlarge the number of defenders on the wall. Your men will herd the animals through the gate. At that point, your priests will have to take charge of them."

Herod bowed his head. "A good point, Sosius. As you have said, so it will be done."

I gave the commander a grateful smile, hoping my brother's gamble would not make him appear foolish in the eyes of the Romans.

⁓⁓⁓⁓⁓

"Why do they refuse to surrender?" Herod tossed his gnawed chicken bone over his shoulder. "I sent the animals they wanted.

The people have to see I am one of them, that I care about the Temple and the rituals."

"They *do* see," Joseph replied, ever the peacemaker. "They are simply too stubborn to admit it."

I said nothing, but sipped from my goblet as the men complained about the length of the siege. A month had passed since Herod sent animals for Temple sacrifices, yet the defenders of Jerusalem were as resolute as ever.

I was growing impatient with the siege too, for while the men waged war, I had nothing to do. After the whirlwind of wedding preparations, I found myself pacing in my room, desperate to go riding, to argue, to pick a fight with someone.

But I could not, as Herod had ordered me to remain in Samaria with Alexandra and Mariamne. I had to sit and smile and ignore their many provocations and insults. Whenever we three were together, the mother and daughter complained about the food, the weather, and the accommodations. I would not be surprised if Mariamne complained about her inattentive husband when I was not around.

The Romans had also grown irritable with waiting. The defenders of Jerusalem had resisted far too long, and delay would not work to their advantage. Sosius reported that surly soldiers were apt to be merciless when they finally entered the capital city. "Sensible defenders would realize they were surrounded and surrender," he said. "Anyone with half a brain would try to save lives and resources. But the fools behind that wall seem determined to waste every life and spill every drop of blood for a city that has been conquered dozens of times. The place is not impregnable, so why do they keep fighting?"

"Because they are stubborn." Herod pressed his lips together, then lifted his finger. "And blind. But primarily because they believe their God will save them."

Sosius's jaws wobbled. "*Their* God? Is He not yours, as well?"

"He is."

"Then how can a God be on both their side and yours?"

Herod sighed and leaned forward on the table. "Years ago, the Jews—under their high priest John Hyrcanus—invaded Idumea. He told our fathers and grandfathers that we had become Jews so we could be part of his kingdom. But a good many of our people continued to worship Qaus, the god our people had worshiped for generations. We learned how to worship one god in name and another in practice."

Sosius picked up his cup. "And you?"

"I worship—" he lowered his voice—"the god of the realm. In Rome, after the Senate declared me king of Judea, I left the chamber with Octavian and Mark Antony and went immediately to a Roman temple to offer sacrifice. If I had refused . . ." He shrugged. "But that was Rome, and this is Judea. Here I worship HaShem, the God of the people behind the walls of Jerusalem. You would too if you wanted to rule over the Jews."

Sosius finished his wine, then set his cup on the table and smacked his lips in appreciation. "If you expected their determination to waver after you sent in the animals," he said, "your ploy did not work."

"I had hoped it would." Herod gave me a wry smile. "I did not *expect*. One never knows what to expect of the Jews."

"Arrogance," I said, the word slipping from my tongue. "One can almost always expect arrogance, particularly from the Hasmoneans."

"Salome." Joseph shot me a warning look. "Let us not forget our queen."

"Herod knows how I feel about her people," I said. "They believe they are more important than anyone else."

The Roman glanced at Herod as if he expected my brother to explode in anger, but Herod and I had always understood each other.

Now he sighed and leaned toward me. "I understand how you feel, sister, but consider my feelings. One of Mariamne's uncles stands in Jerusalem now, encouraging his men to kill me. If I can tolerate him, surely you can tolerate the women who have become part of our family. Mariamne is your sister now. Love her as I do, Salome. For my sake. Please."

I drew a deep breath and slowly shook my head.

Herod gave the Roman a resigned smile. "If Salome were a man, I would send her over the wall to personally open the gates of Jerusalem for us. She has the unflagging heart of a warrior."

The Roman's gaze fell to the open expanse of my neck, and my flesh warmed beneath his admiring attention. I glanced at Joseph, but my husband seemed to be studying the dew-drenched grapes in his hand.

I met Sosius's gaze and smiled.

In June, only four months after my brother's wedding, we celebrated Herod's entry into Jerusalem. Joseph and I marked the occasion in Samaria because Jerusalem had been heavily damaged by the fighting and Herod wanted to restore order before bringing his family to live in the royal palace.

My husband gave me a complete report when he returned from a visit to the siege camp. "It was only a matter of time," he told me, reclining on his couch while I poured him a cup of wine. "Some of Herod's elite fighters scaled the walls and crept into the city under a cloak of darkness. They found their way through the twisting streets and killed anyone they met. When they reached the city gates, they threw them open and"—he grinned—"the siege ended."

Over a light supper of bread and cheese, he told me the Roman commander sent squadrons into the city, effectively cutting Jerusalem in half and scattering the defenders. Some of the fighters for Antigonus took shelter in the Temple while others hid themselves in the upper section of the city. After the Romans entered, they found a weakened, exhausted populace—they had only to search for and destroy those who resisted.

Joseph lifted a warning finger. "But Herod had underestimated the fury of the Roman legionaries. He wanted to enter the city and claim it as his capital, but the legionaries wanted rewards for all they had endured in the siege. They stormed through the streets, slaughtering anyone who got in their way."

"Even innocents?"

Joseph shrugged. "The legionaries are paid a paltry wage, but they are usually allowed to loot conquered cities. Herod did not want the city looted. He called off his men and pleaded with Sosius, begging him to restrain the legionaries before Jerusalem had been routed. He said—and I have never heard him say anything wiser—he wanted to rule a kingdom, not a desert. He then offered to pay the commander and his men if they refrained from looting the city and the Temple."

I caught my breath. "Did he . . . did Sosius agree?"

Joseph nodded. "He called off his men, and the rioting ceased. Most important, Herod stopped the Romans from going inside the sanctuary. That would have been an unforgivable sacrilege."

I sank onto a nearby couch and felt a knot of tension fade from my neck.

"Fortunately," Joseph went on, "Antigonus was captured before he could escape. As he waited with guards in the tower, Herod went to meet him."

"Herod cannot let him live." I spoke with quiet, resolute firmness. "He is a Hasmonean, a descendant of the Maccabees, heroes to the people of Jerusalem."

"But Herod cannot kill him," Joseph countered. "The Jews would never forgive such an act. And what about Mariamne? How will she feel if Herod kills her kinsman?"

I blinked. "So what—?"

"Herod is clever enough to know his throne will never be secure as long as Antigonus lives." Joseph lifted his cup. "So he is sending him to Mark Antony."

I took a moment to absorb the news. "That is good. The so-called king will be far from Judea, far from his supporters. And Herod will not be guilty of his murder."

"But what of Jerusalem?" Joseph asked, tilting his head. "The city has not welcomed Herod as king. They prefer the king he is sending away, and they will not like having a Roman legion stationed here."

"A Roman legion? In Judea?"

"In Jerusalem. Antony thought it wise, and Herod agreed. If even a hint of trouble arises, Herod will be able to use the legionaries to snuff it out. Rome wants Judea to be profitable and peaceful. They want a king who can keep that peace, no matter how he maintains it."

"Herod can keep the peace." I inhaled a deep breath, thinking about how easily he sent his first wife away. My brother had always been pragmatic.

"Still . . ." Joseph hesitated. "The people of Jerusalem suffered greatly under the siege, and many of them lost family members in the slaughter afterward. Many of their homes were burned, their men killed, and their city has been flooded with Gentiles."

"Herod sent animals for their sacrifices," I pointed out, "and he paid the Romans to stop looting and to respect the Temple."

"That news will not help if the people do not believe it," Joseph said. "And people do not like to believe good reports about their perceived enemy. For even though the Torah says, 'You are not to detest an Edomite, for he is your brother,' most of them detest us for reasons that have nothing to do with our forefathers. They see Idumaeans—all of Herod's family—as puppets, controlled by the Romans."

I felt a flush burn my cheeks. "My brother is *not* a puppet."

"An extension then," Joseph said. "I do not think you can deny he is a tool in the hand of Rome."

"Perhaps," I admitted slowly. "But he is more than one man. He has Pheroras and me. Together we are formidable, just as Father wanted us to be. Rome may think Herod is only a tool to wield, but together we are much more—and we are stronger than they know."

"Indeed you are." Joseph smiled, but in his eyes I thought I saw a spark of worry . . . or perhaps fear.

CHAPTER SIX

Zara

After so many days of war, hunger and privation stamped the faces of everyone I knew. Skin sagged, eyes retreated into facial caverns, and mouths went thin. Ima no longer packed a bag for my father, for she had no bread, cheese, or meat to give him.

Abba did not come home at all anymore, and neither did the other men in our neighborhood. We killed and ate our goat, just as our neighbors ate their chickens and lambs. When I asked why we could not go to the market to get more food, Ima said no one could do their usual work, because everyone in Jerusalem was either defending the Temple, carrying water for the fighters, or caring for those who had been injured on the wall.

On a hot summer evening, with little warning, life as I had always known it ended. I did not learn why until Ima told me some of Herod's soldiers climbed the walls and allowed the Romans into the city. The men who fought with my father—determined, righteous men, all of them—were pushed back to the Temple where they took refuge inside the sacred walls.

But the Romans did not care about the sanctity of the Holy

City. Wave after wave of them poured into the streets where they killed any man who stood in their path, even those who threw down their swords and begged for mercy.

"They were angry," Ima said, her expression vacant. "They said we should have known we were certain to be defeated. They did not believe HaShem would save us." And then, in a voice so low I could barely hear her, she added, "I cannot believe He did not."

My father died that day, struck down, so they told me, on the steps of the altar, one of the last men to give his life in the Temple.

After the Romans had cleared the holy sanctuary, they marched into the city where they attacked the crowds jammed into its narrow streets. Many of those who had taken refuge in the Temple and fled when the invaders entered were now trapped between buildings. They fell before the Roman swords—old men, women, children, and babies in their mothers' arms.

A sword struck my own mother. A Roman cut her across the back, the blade slicing through the bones of her spine. She collapsed as if dead, with others falling on top of her. She was saved only because the Romans did not stop to examine the dead but kept surging through the Temple region, stabbing and slashing at anything that moved.

Though Ima's wound did not appear fatal, the injury left her unable to use her legs. A physician taught me how to anoint her wound with healing oils, then shook his head and said my mother would never walk again.

The physician also told me the Romans had captured our king, Antigonus, and sent him to Mark Antony, one of the Romans responsible for placing an Idumaean over us. "Apparently," he said, speaking more to my mother than to me, "this so-called king is afraid to kill our rightful ruler. He will make the Romans do it."

Ima turned tear-filled eyes on the doctor. "Will the Romans not have mercy? Antigonus is from the family of Judah Maccabaeus."

"Neither the Romans nor the Idumaean hold any regard for that noble family," the physician said. "Instead, we have been given a man from people as common as the earth. Herod and his like are men who should be subject to kings, not kings themselves."

Years later I would learn that Mark Antony had Antigonus beheaded, the first time the Romans had ever executed a captive king in such a fashion. They said Antony hoped such a squalid execution might make the Jews more agreeable toward Herod and less fond of Antigonus.

If that had been Antony's plan, he did not understand human nature. The news of Antigonus's murder only deepened the people of Jerusalem's sympathy for their former king and increased their loathing and suspicion of Herod.

CHAPTER SEVEN

Salome

I shall teach these people who and what I am." Sitting in the great hall of the Hasmonean palace in Jerusalem, Herod straightened and thrust his shoulders back. "I will not give them time to organize opposition. Any and all who have been critical of my government or supportive of the Hasmonean king shall be eliminated at once."

Joseph and I had just arrived from Samaria. We still had dust on our faces, but when a servant said Herod wanted to see us, we only asked where he could be found.

Pheroras pulled a sheet of parchment from a leather pouch and set it before our king. "I have on good authority composed a list of Jews who have ties to Antigonus or other Hasmonean sympathizers. Most of these are members of the Sanhedrin."

"That hotbed of hostility?" Herod picked up the list, his eyes narrowing as he studied the names. "I remember him." He pointed at a name. "When I was summoned before the Sanhedrin to account for my actions in Galilee, this man gave me trouble." His finger shifted on the parchment. "And this one spoke to me as if I were an imbecile. And that one. Ah, the sons of Baba, Hasmonean supporters, all of them. I remember them well."

A shadow of alarm crossed my husband's face. "Would you execute the entire Sanhedrin?"

"Of course not." Herod pointed to another name. "This Samaias—he supported me even before Rome named me king. And this man, Jonias, told the people not to resist the siege." A smile quirked my brother's lips. "He said the armies outside the walls were the instrument by which God was punishing the people for their sinfulness."

"These are wealthy men." Pheroras crossed his arms. "And since they are traitors—"

"God has smiled on us," Herod finished. "Confiscate their property and collect anything of value. After the expense of this siege, my coffers need to be refilled. I have been king in name only for three years and have spent everything to take the throne Rome promised."

"When do we move?" Pheroras asked.

Herod set his jaw. "Immediately. These people must understand that I am king and I will not tolerate opposition."

Herod proved every bit as pragmatic as I hoped he would be. Within days of that meeting, forty-five of Antigonus's surviving supporters had been executed. Few escaped, but although Herod's men conducted a diligent search throughout the city, no one could find the renowned sons of Baba, a group of men who had been Antigonus's staunchest supporters.

While my brother took a firm hand with those who had opposed him, he was generous with his defenders, especially those who had supported him since his days as a commoner. He gave special rewards to the Pharisees Pollion and Samaias because they had glimpsed greatness in him and predicted his rise to power. After confiscating the treasure of the men he had executed, he sent most of it to Mark Antony, calling it "the spoils of war."

Only a few members of the Hasmonean family remained:

Alexandra and her children, Mariamne and Aristobulus, a mere teenager, and Hyrcanus II, a former king and now disfigured old man living in a Jewish community in Babylon. When our father served Hyrcanus, the soft-spoken king had named Herod governor of Galilee, where my brother quickly distinguished himself by capturing and executing Hezekiah, a notorious brigand.

Within weeks after Herod's installation as king, he received a message from the former ruler that Hyrcanus wished to return to Jerusalem. Herod sent for me, Joseph, and Pheroras. We met him in his bedchamber, and after a quick look around, I relaxed. Neither Mariamne nor her meddlesome mother was present.

"What shall I do about Hyrcanus?" Herod asked, his eyes darting from me to Pheroras. "He will undoubtedly expect favors because he promoted me in my youth."

"Let him stay in Babylon," Joseph replied, stroking his beard. "So long as he is away, the people of Jerusalem will think of him as a tired old man. They will not think of him as a king."

"What do you want to do?" Pheroras held up his hands as if weighing options. "Surely there are advantages to either choice."

Herod opened his mouth to speak when I interrupted, "You should bring him back." I gave a firm nod. "The people will think you considerate and kind, and even your wife may appreciate your compassion for her grandfather. But more important, if Hyrcanus is here in Jerusalem, you can keep an eye on him. Give him an apartment near the palace and give him servants from your household—servants who will warn you if he is planning anything traitorous. Be generous with him and keep him close. That is the only way to treat a potential enemy."

Herod's eyes rested on me, alight with speculation. "Thank you, sister." He smiled. "I was thinking the very same thing."

I returned his smile, comforted to know that even as a woman and a younger sister, I could prove valuable to the king.

CHAPTER EIGHT

Zara

I rose with the sun, then stepped outside to let the chickens out of their pen. Their irritated squawking turned to contented clucking as they ran toward the grain I tossed on the ground. Several hens ignored the grain and waddled to the watering trough to ease their thirst after a long night.

Sighing, I leaned against the courtyard wall and studied the narrow street beyond. My mother and I had been living with my aunt Rimonah ever since what Ima called "Herod's war." My aunt lost her husband in that bloody siege, so now the three of us worked together to stay alive. My job was to take care of Ima, feed the chickens, and collect the eggs. My aunt milked the goat and made cheese, and on market days she would take eggs, cheese, and freshly plucked chickens to sell. She would return home just before sunset, exhausted but thankful for the few coins in her hand—even when those coins bore the image of an eagle, the hated symbol of Rome.

Jerusalem had become a different place under our new king. People did not speak to strangers as freely as they once had, and men who met on street corners often spoke in low voices. When

48

I asked Aunt Rimonah what they were whispering about, she placed her hand across my mouth and pulled me close. "You must be careful what you say," she murmured. "People who speak ill of the king usually end up dead."

"But I did not say anything about the—"

"Shh. Whenever you see men talking together like that, do not draw attention to them. Act as if you hadn't seen them at all."

I nodded as a chill gripped my bones. "Would the king kill them?" I whispered.

"I do not know. But someone does, so watch what you say. You would not want to get anyone in trouble, would you?"

I shook my head and backed away.

In those days I was desperate to be a good girl. After Abba died and Ima lost the use of her legs, I wondered if I had done something to displease HaShem. Had I forgotten to keep His name holy? Had I coveted our neighbor's goat? Had I been jealous of another girl or told a half-truth to keep from getting in trouble?

I couldn't remember, so I begged HaShem to forgive me and not let me slip again. But despite my frantic promise, Abba did not come home and Ima did not get better. She seemed to grow weaker, in fact, for every day her face seemed a little paler and her breathing a little shallower.

When I looked at Aunt Rimonah, I saw my fears reflected in her eyes. She depended on Ima to take care of me while she worked at the market, and if something happened to Ima . . .

I knew she did not want to think about the possibility. Neither did I.

One bleak day, however, I saw something so unexpected, so dazzlingly beautiful that the world seemed to shift on its axis. I was sitting in the courtyard, using a clay shard to scoop up chicken dung, when I heard the sound of horse hooves. We did not often see those beautiful animals on our narrow street, so

I looked up in amazement. The horse coming toward me was large, graceful, and as black as the night sky. I must have sighed in admiration, because my sigh was answered by the sound of masculine laughter.

My cheeks burned as I stared at the rider. A young man sat on the horse, an almost-grown boy of fifteen or sixteen. Dark curly hair blossomed around his head, and brown eyes danced above his white smile. His face was so perfectly formed that for a moment I thought HaShem had sent an angel to answer my prayers.

Then the boy spoke. "Have you never seen a horse before?"

For an instant I did not realize he was speaking to me—why would he? But when I did not respond, he leaned forward in his saddle, lowering himself until his head was only a hand's breadth above the horse's thick mane. "Little girl, have you never seen a horse?"

I closed my eyes, then opened them again to make certain I had not been imagining him. I then answered honestly, "I have never seen anything so beautiful as you sitting on that horse."

The young man laughed again, then pulled a coin from the purse at his belt and tossed it to me. "Thank you," he said, grinning. "Be well."

The coin landed in the dust at my feet, but I did not pick it up until after he and his magnificent mount rode away. When he had disappeared, I found the coin, saw an anchor and some sort of writing on it. I rubbed my thumb over the inscription.

Though deception might be wicked, I decided not to show the coin to Ima or my aunt. They would want to spend it, while I wanted to keep the coin forever.

Never had I been given anything so precious by anyone so beautiful.

CHAPTER NINE

Salome

One afternoon I grew weary of being penned up in the palace. Because the place held too many unpleasant memories for me, I summoned Nada and asked her to call for a litter. "We are going out for fresh air," I told her, covering my hair with a veil. "I would like to see how the inhabitants of Jerusalem are adjusting to life under a new king."

Nada crinkled her nose. "Are you certain, my lamb? Some people might not welcome the sight of Herod's sister in their neighborhoods."

"I will not go as the king's sister." I draped the end of the veil over my face. "I will go as an anonymous woman with her servant. No one will know who I am."

Nada sighed heavily, but she obeyed. I was strapping on my sandals when she returned and told me a litter waited for us in the courtyard. "If you want to be anonymous"—she eyed the necklace at my throat—"perhaps you should leave the jewelry behind. Few citizens of Jerusalem walk around with such treasures on display."

I was about to answer with a sharp rejoinder, but then I

realized she was right. And what would it matter? I pulled the heavy necklace over my head and tossed it onto the bed. "Let us leave this place."

We went down to the courtyard. The man who carried the front of the litter asked where I would like to go, and I hesitated for a moment. "To the Temple," I finally said, knowing that area was always busy. "And you may take the longest route—I am in no hurry."

He grunted in reply and gripped the carrying handles, as did the servant at the rear. Nada and I climbed in, and I drew the curtain but left a small crack—enough for me to examine any sights that might catch my interest.

Litter bearers usually moved through the streets at a slow jog. This man, however, had apparently taken me at my word, for he walked, albeit with long strides. We left the palace and ventured into the upper city, moving through the center of the narrow streets. A dazzling white blur of sun stood high in the blue sky, yet the air was sweet with the promise of autumn to come. I breathed deeply and sighed. "Isn't this better than sitting in that old palace?" I nudged Nada's arm. "Don't you agree?"

She made a noncommittal sound and folded her hands, clearly unhappy to be out of familiar surroundings.

Voices reached us through the curtain, and I frowned as people grumbled and moved out of our way. They might not have known who occupied the litter, but judging from their resentful tone, they surmised that we were outsiders. Who but an outsider could afford to hire a litter in such desperate times?

I peered through the opening in the curtain and watched life in the streets glide by. Here, a woman with a crying baby on one hip and a stack of cheeses on the other. There, a Pharisee, his hands folded as he bellowed his prayers by the marketplace. Here, a carpenter, his sweat-stained face lined with weariness as he struggled beneath a heavy beam. There, a merchant, offering meager baskets of grain for sale.

Then a robust masculine voice pierced the curtain. "He was a mere slave in the house of Hasmon," the man said, his voice thundering with the conviction of an ancient prophet, "and he killed all the royal family but for one princess, who preferred suicide rather than to marry him. Does not the Torah say, 'You may not put a foreigner over you, who is not your brother'? Yet we have an alien over us as king, a commoner and an Idumaean, one whose mother was an Ishmaelite."

The litter bearer must have realized that the preacher's words would offend me, because he broke into a jog, hurrying us away from the street corner. I clung to the armrests as the litter bumped and swayed, staring at the fabric ceiling as the conveyance passed through a gate in the ancient wall and approached the Temple Mount.

Nada must have read my thoughts, for her gnarled hand fell upon mine. "Pay that man no mind," she said. "He does not understand anything."

"He knows the Torah," I replied, meeting her gaze. "And the people will believe him because he quotes from the Torah and seems a righteous man. But my father was never a slave. Mariamne did not commit suicide, she married my brother, and Alexandra lives willingly in our household. How can he say otherwise?"

"People ignore the truth when it is convenient. And when they do not like the truth, they invent their own version." Nada released my hand and looked to the opening in the curtain. "Time will prove that man wrong, and the people will open their eyes."

"He called my mother an Ishmaelite."

Nada shrugged. "She *is* Nabataean. Practically the same thing."

"But it sounds so *wrong* when he uses that word. The Jews will think of Ishmael, the slave's son, and they will believe the implication that Mother—and Herod—have taken what rightfully belonged to someone else."

Nada did not reply, and I knew she remained quiet because she did not want to remind me of what I already suspected. The people in Jerusalem felt that Herod had stolen the Hasmonean throne from the former king, Hyrcanus, his daughter, Alexandra, and her children, Mariamne and Aristobulus.

"Why does that man stand on the street corner and proclaim such lies?" I asked, seething. "Look outside—everyone else is busy working, rebuilding, putting their lives back together. Yet that man stands on a corner and preaches against the king? Why would he do that? Has he no house to rebuild? No wife to mourn? No children to care for?"

"I do not know, my lamb."

Of course she did not. Nada was trying to placate me, to calm me, and probably wished she had convinced me to stay at the palace and exchange gossip with Pheroras or Joseph.

I probably should have.

I drew a long, quivering breath, then commanded the litter bearers to return to the palace.

Back in my chambers, I sent Nada to find Eurus, a guard who had been assigned to us during our three-year sojourn at Masada. Though he had never attempted to be overly familiar with me, I felt a bond with him, perhaps because we were about the same age. Like me, he had lived through the days when Judea became a Roman province, and like me, he had known more days of war than peace.

Nada returned about an hour later with the guard, who smote his breast and bowed when he saw me. "My lady Salome."

"It is good to see you, Eurus. How do you like your post in Jerusalem?"

His broad cheeks lifted as he grinned. "Better than the heat of Masada, mistress."

"Indeed it is." I gave him a smile, then came straight to the point. "This afternoon Nada and I took a litter into the city. As we rode through the streets, I saw a man standing at a street corner. He was shouting lies about the king—lying even about our mother. I would know more about this man."

A muscle flicked at Eurus's jaw. "Do you want him removed?"

"No—people would notice, and that might only cause problems for my brother. I want to know why he has time to stand on the corner while everyone else is busy rebuilding. How does he eat? I was given to understand that food is still scarce in the city. Is someone paying him to say those things or is he some new kind of religious zealot? If that is the case, is he Pharisee, Sadducee, Essene? Or some sort of convert we do not yet know about?"

Eurus nodded. "I will find out at once."

"One more thing." I held up my hand. "I would go in a plain tunic, if I were you. You're not likely to find answers if you venture into the streets wearing Herod's uniform."

He flushed, then nodded again. "I will return as soon as I have an answer."

CHAPTER TEN

Salome

As the trio of Egyptian dancers leapt and twirled before us, I found myself wishing that kings did not require entertainment at banquets as small as this one. But Herod was still adjusting to his new role, and after three years of being king in name only, he seemed determined to enjoy every royal advantage at his disposal.

When the last dancer landed his final leap, I led the others in applause. "Bravo, thank you, that is enough," I called, giving my brother a pointed look. "Please allow us time for conversation."

The head dancer hesitated, looking from me to Herod, and my brother waved the dancers away. "What is this sudden need for talking?" he asked, turning to me as the dancers scampered out of the room. "You know you have only to find me if you have something on your mind."

I looked around the chamber to see who still remained. We were an intimate group, only family members, but even though we had lost Phasael and Joseph, we could still fill a room. Our mother occupied a couch near the door, Pheroras reclined next to Herod, and Mariamne shared the king's couch. Alexandra,

56

Mariamne's mother, shared a couch with Aristobulus, her fifteen-year-old son, and Joseph and I completed the circle on a couch next to my mother.

I would have liked to send Mariamne, Aristobulus, and Alexandra away, yet I did not want to offend Herod.

So I drew a breath and launched my question. "I wanted to know if you've heard about the prophecy."

"Prophecy?" Herod barked a laugh. "Which one? If I had an army for every prophecy I've heard, I could conquer Rome."

"Herod." Mother gave him a reproachful look. "Those words, if repeated outside this room, would not please the Romans."

Herod ignored her and grinned at me. "What prophecy is that, sister?"

I sat up straighter. "I did not catch all of it, but it was something about the Temple: 'He who restores it to the glory of Solomon's Temple will have the blessing of HaShem, even to the fourth generation.'"

"Four generations, eh?" Herod scratched his bare chin. "An appropriate divine reward."

"Let us focus on surviving our first year in Jerusalem," Mother said, her eyes flashing another warning. "These are uncertain times for Judea. Mark Antony has given you a role to play, but only time will reveal if you can make it your own."

Herod smiled and looked at Pheroras. "And there you have it—another encouraging witticism from our mother."

Pheroras laughed. "If every bushel of grain held but a single rat turd, you can be sure she will find it." He went on, talking about some incident from his childhood, but the sight of Eurus coming through the doorway distracted me. He stood inside the room, looking around, then spotted me and nodded.

Adrenaline coursed through my veins as I slipped from my couch and followed the guard into the hallway. "Forgive me for interrupting," Eurus said, "but I thought you might want to have this information immediately."

"Indeed I do. What did you learn?"

The guard looked around, then stepped closer and lowered his voice. "Your suspicions were correct, my lady. The man you heard is a shoemaker by trade, but someone paid him a great deal of money to stand on the corner and shout lies about the king. They even provided him with a script." Eurus pulled a scroll from his tunic. "After I gave the man a few coins to surrender this, he was happy to give it to me."

"Did he say who gave it to him?"

"He said it came from a servant employed by a wealthy patron. He never learned the identity of the man, but it had to be someone in Jerusalem."

"Or course."

I unfurled the leather scroll and saw inked writing. The message had been written in Aramaic, the language of the people, and the handwriting was remarkably fluid. The author—whoever it was—had been well taught, for I could see no unevenness in the writing or the words.

"I will keep this." I rolled the scroll and tucked it into a fold of my himation. "And here. For your trouble." I undid the clasp of my gold bracelet and pressed it into Eurus's palm.

"No, my lady, I cannot—"

"You had to pay for the scroll, so consider this a reimbursement—and a sign of my deep appreciation." I smiled. "Thank you again."

"I live to serve you, lady."

"I appreciate it, sir. Now go in peace."

I returned to the banquet, but as I made myself comfortable on my couch, I could think of little but the scroll pressed against my chest. Who hated Herod so much that they would pay a street preacher during a time when every denarius was precious? A wealthy person, obviously. Someone from Jerusalem. An educated person with servants. Jewish, naturally, not Idumaean.

I sighed. Though I had just eliminated thousands of Herod's subjects, the person I sought was one of hundreds more.

~~~~~

Later that night, I left my cozy fire, wrapped a mantle around my shoulders, and stepped out into the hall. No one stirred in this hallway, so I walked to the end and climbed the narrow stairs that led to the palace rooftop. Guards stood at the far ends but no one walked along the low stone wall that rose over the grand entrance below. I walked toward it, running my hands over the top of the stones and smiling at the memories they evoked.

This palace, which used to house the Hasmonean high priest kings, had occasionally been my playground. John Hyrcanus lived here when he conquered Idumea and annexed our land, making Jews of our people. John Hyrcanus's heirs, all of them bent on destroying each other, reigned from this house, as did Salome Alexandra. My grandfather served her husband, Alexander Jannaeus, and my father served her son, Hyrcanus. Whenever Phasael, my father's eldest son, assisted him in some task, Herod, Joseph, Pheroras, and I came up to this rooftop to play, running along the escarpment and tossing pebbles over the edge. I used to watch the pebbles bounce off the stones below while Herod tried to spook horses tied in the courtyard.

But not all my memories of this place were happy ones.

"Imagine finding you here."

I startled at the sound of Herod's voice and turned. He was coming through the doorway, our mother on his arm.

"I thought you would be with your wife," I said, teasing as he nodded at the guards. "Or have you grown tired of her already?"

"I adore her." He gently guided our mother to the stone wall.

"But she is not feeling well. We think—we hope—she may be expecting a child."

"Well. Congratulations." I looked at Mother. "Are you pleased with the news?"

"I'll be pleased when the baby is born." She released Herod's arm and straightened, holding her chin high. "I asked Herod to bring me up here. I wanted to talk to him alone."

"Very well." I turned toward the stairs. "If there is nothing you need from me—"

"Stay, Salome. By *private*, I meant without any of Mariamne's people around. They are like little mice, always listening in the shadows."

I frowned, not understanding but willing to remain.

"Now, Mother—" Herod began.

"Son." Mother turned to face him. "Your father taught you to work with your brothers and sister, to support them in all things."

"You did not bring me up here to talk about Father. What is on your mind?"

Mother grimaced. "I want you to tread carefully around your wife. I do not trust her or Alexandra. I've always believed the Hasmoneans had something to do with your father's death."

Herod sighed. "We've been through this. Malchus poisoned Father. And now he is dead."

"But the poison was administered at Hyrcanus's palace. Who gave Malchus permission to speak to the king's servant? For that matter, who arranged the banquet, if not Hyrcanus?"

Herod threw me a frustrated look, so I stepped closer. "That happened six years ago, Mother. Malchus is dead. Hyrcanus has been exiled. The chapter is closed."

"Is it?" Even in the cold light of the moon, I could see the flush on Mother's face. "Hyrcanus's daughter lives in our house. His granddaughter sleeps in your bed. And I hear you want to bring the old man back."

"He is harmless," Herod said. "And his granddaughter may be carrying my son, your grandchild. This baby will bridge the gap between our houses. This union will heal the rift in Judea. Look here, Mother." He pulled a scroll from his tunic, then unfurled it and spread it on the top of the short stone wall. "See how the house of Hasmon combines with the house of Antipater."

I glanced at the scroll, now silver in the moonlight. Someone had drawn a family tree with Herod's family on one side and Mariamne's on the other. A blank space had been left at the bottom, presumably for the coming child.

"She says you are common," Mother said, stiffening. "She says you are alien and not really Jewish."

For a moment I felt a surge of memory, a momentary epiphany. Something surfaced in my mind, then disappeared. Something I'd remembered? Something I'd forgotten . . .

My eyes fell on the parchment, where a neat hand had written the names of Hasmonean kings and queens. The pieces fell into place. I placed one hand over my garment and felt the small scroll beneath my fingertips.

I tapped the diagram with my other hand. "Who wrote this?"

Herod looked at me. "Why does it matter?"

"Who wrote this, brother?"

He blew out a breath. "Alexandra. She was thrilled with the news about the baby."

I took a deep breath and felt a dozen different emotions collide. "She called you *common*. Alien."

"Salome." Herod gave me a warning look. "I'm sure Mother misunderstood—"

"I'm not referring to what Mother said." I pulled the scroll from my himation and unfurled it. "I heard a street preacher denouncing you with those same words. I sent Eurus to investigate, and he learned the man was paid to rail against you, to

61

lie about you. The person who paid him sent these words to use in his denunciation."

Herod glanced at the scroll, then looked at Mother. She seemed to have grown taller in the moonlight, her eyes gleaming as if to say, *Do not doubt what you cannot deny.*

"The handwriting, Herod—it is the same." I tapped both scrolls. "Alexandra wrote both of these. On one scroll she plans your future, and on the other she condemns you."

Herod scoffed. "This makes no sense. Why would she do both?"

"Because," Mother answered, "she wants another heir. She has a son and daughter. Why not have a grandchild? She will place one of them on the seat of power."

"Bah!" Herod turned away. "I will not listen to this."

Mother gave me a quick look, then walked toward her son. "You do not have to listen to us, but do not be blind to the danger. Enjoy your wife. Celebrate your son. But do not trust Alexandra—the woman neither loves nor supports you."

Herod looked back at me. "You agree with her?"

"I do." I took a step closer. "And know this, brother—even though you do not believe me, with my last breath, I will protect and defend you. You may not be willing to see the danger, but I have nothing to lose by being vigilant. So I will be. I will not let any of the Hasmoneans take what is rightfully yours."

Mother shook her head, a question in her eyes. "Why, daughter, would you do what your brother will not do for himself?"

I sighed. "Because he once did it for me."

As a little girl, I loved visiting the palace. I would often go with my father and my brothers on festival days, or other days when Father had work to do and the king and his family were occupied at the Temple.

One day—I was around seven—I was wandering the wide halls of the palace alone when I spotted Alexandra, who must have been nearly old enough to be wed. She was with a young man about her age, probably a servant, and laughing with him in an overly familiar manner. Then she turned her head and saw me.

Though the passing years have dulled many of my memories, this one remained as sharp as a needle. Alexandra stared at me, her eyes narrowing, and then she said, in a voice dripping with disdain, "It is only one of the Idumaean brats."

The servant looked at me. "She's a pretty little thing."

"Really?" Alexandra cocked her head. "You must have un-refined tastes."

Something in the servant's eyes made me want to run, but fear immobilized me. Father always warned us to stay out of sight and not to interfere with the king's family or his servants. If I ran to Father, he would know I'd done something wrong, yet to stay in the hallway felt dangerous, especially with that odd gleam in the young man's eyes.

The servant laughed again, and the sound of his laughter sent a chill up the ladder of my spine. "It is only a little brat."

Alexandra blew out a breath. "Do whatever you want, but make her disappear afterward."

As Alexandra strode away toward the staircase, the servant gave me a smirk. I lowered my gaze, afraid to look at his face, but I heard the slap of his sandals on the tile and then I saw his feet in front of mine, blocking my way. Keeping my head down, I stepped to the right, but he quickly moved in front of me. I stepped to the left, and he did the same. When I turned to run, his hand gripped my upper arm. Then his other arm hoisted me onto his hip. I dared not scream, for the noise would attract attention and displease my father, and though I kicked and squirmed I could not escape his grip, not even when he propped me in a wall niche and his hands gripped my knees and pried them apart . . .

Before I knew what was happening, Herod appeared behind the youth, his hand clapping the servant's shoulder, spinning him around. Herod's fist landed on the servant's jaw, snapping his chin up and back, and I heard a crack as the youth's head hit the hard floor. He rolled over, groaning, and Herod kicked his ribs until he made no more noise. My brother then looked at me, his eyes swimming with concern. I threw my arms around his neck and clung to him as he lifted me out of the niche and carried me into the courtyard. He placed me in our wagon, then said something to Joseph and Pheroras. Pheroras, being the youngest boy, stayed with me while Herod and Joseph walked back into the house.

I sat in the wagon, silently crying, until Pheroras gave me a cloth to blow my nose and wipe my face. I had calmed myself by the time Father came out with Phasael. He looked around, his brows crinkling with concern. "Where are Herod and Joseph?"

Before we could answer, my missing brothers appeared, walking naturally, smiling and flushed, appearing as though they had been having great fun in the barn or elsewhere on the property. Father grunted and gestured for them to climb in the wagon. We went home without speaking a word to Father about what had happened.

We never spoke about that incident, and later, when I was older, I often wondered if it had been nothing but a bad dream.

But whenever I saw Alexandra and the hard light in her eyes, I remembered her cold cruelty. Though she probably had no recollection of that afternoon, and probably had no knowledge of what happened after she left, I would never forget it.

Nor would I ever allow her—or *any* Hasmonean—to hurt my brother Herod.

CHAPTER ELEVEN

Salome

Two years passed—years in which Herod welcomed his first two sons from Mariamne, extensively renovated the former Hasmonean palace, and put me and Pheroras to work. The king placed Pheroras in charge of Alexandreion, a fortified palace that had been built by the Hasmoneans and razed by Mark Antony and Gabinus when they fought against Alexander, Alexandra's husband. Situated on the northwestern border of Judea, the fortress had been a defensive tower, but Herod told Pheroras to make sure it offered appropriate living space. Defense was not the priority it had been in the days of the Maccabees, for Rome had brought peace to the world. Herod wanted his fortresses to be lavish and livable.

My brother asked me to take charge of furnishing the three towers he was building at the northernmost point of his future palace. Named Phasaelis, Mariamne, and Hippicus, the lower part of each tower was designed to house soldiers and weapons. The upper part of each would be outfitted like a palace, no expense spared. I was thrilled with the opportunity to serve my brother and determined to make those rooms as luxurious as possible.

Herod's primary concern in those years was laboring to make his people love him. He laid out plans to improve the lives of Jerusalem's citizens with a theater, a hippodrome, extensive aqueducts, and beautiful shopping areas. All his architecture would feature Corinthian and Doric columns, lavish interior decoration featuring painted walls and mosaic tiles, and open spaces for public entertainment. But no matter what he built, he would not ignore the Jews' religious sensibilities—no graven images would exist in his buildings. Though he was a Hellene to his core, many of his people were not.

Pheroras, Joseph, and I were his chief counselors and the only people he trusted without reservation. Not even Mariamne, who had borne him two handsome sons and was expecting again, could advise him on political matters. Yet our family had been students of royal politics since the first Antipater served Alexander Jannaeus.

In those days I believe Herod trusted me even more than Joseph or Pheroras. Joseph tended to be conservative in his opinions; he wanted to remain steady even when a situation called for moving forward. Pheroras had a different sort of weakness—he never seemed to have opinions of his own but would poll the table and then pretend he had agreed with the strongest plan all along.

While Joseph and Pheroras focused on small issues, Herod and I kept our eyes on the larger picture. I was keenly aware of how carefully my brother maneuvered under twin threats: the unspoken and ever-present pressure from Rome, which did not look favorably on client kings who could not keep peace in the provinces, and the pressure from the Jews, who did not look favorably on kings who were not sons of Jacob.

To keep the peace in Judea, Herod had to rely primarily on his own forces, for involving the resident Roman legion meant the authorities in Rome would hear about whatever trouble had arisen. Still, Herod's men, most of whom were Idumaean, were never well received by the people, for they saw Idumaeans as ill-begotten outsiders. Whenever Herod's men marched through the streets, the women of Jerusalem spat at them, children ran in terror, and old men thrust out their wizened chests and dared the king's men to strike them. Herod cautioned his men not to respond to such taunts because he wanted to win the people's goodwill, a task that was proving as impossible as counting the waves of the sea. The Jews saw Herod as many things—a stranger and usurper, a son of Esau, a puppet of the Romans—none of them good.

To further complicate Herod's early days, nearly every family in Jerusalem had either lost someone during the siege or had their home looted or destroyed. Months passed before the rebuilding and the mourning ended. "The Jews might call themselves the chosen people," Herod quipped one day, "but they do not choose to forgive."

I must admit, Herod did not help his cause when he took possession of the gold and silver vessels in the Temple. He had prevented the Romans from looting the sacred objects, but when he took them himself, I feared the people would riot. With Herod ignoring my advice, I voiced my concerns to Joseph, who advised Herod by expressing a similar caution.

Herod would not be dissuaded. "Who paid the men in my army for three years?" he retorted. "Who fed you and your servants during that time? Who rewarded Mark Antony and the underlings beneath him? I did. And now that I am king, the people must repay me for all I have sacrificed to govern them. In time, they will thank me for the privilege."

I had vowed to protect Herod from those who would harm him, but how could I protect him from himself? In truth, he had a point—he had spent everything he owned to claim the throne, but Rome was not likely to reimburse him. So the money had to come from the people of Judea.

In those early months of his reign, Herod spent a great deal of his time weeding out dissenters, at least those who were brave enough to speak against him publicly. He established a web of spies, informers, and captains and charged them with reporting anyone foolish enough to openly speak ill of Herod. Within days, perhaps hours, such a man would be executed before the king or on his way to the dungeon. Dissent, Herod declared, would not be allowed.

He continued to reward those who had been loyal to him and our father before him. He sought the few residents of Jerusalem who had been supportive of his cause and gave them a place in the king's court. He vowed to surround himself with people he could trust.

One afternoon I answered a knock at my door and found a stranger outside, his back turned toward me. His garment was rough, his sandals made of papyrus, and his hands unadorned.

I gasped when he turned, and I recognized Herod beneath the tattered head covering.

"Come," he said, his face lighting as he gave me a sly smile. "Let us go into the streets and hear what the people have to say about their new king."

I blinked. "Go out—like that?"

"We cannot go as the king and his sister; we must go in disguise. Quickly, Salome, pull on a rough garment and cover your hair. I want to walk the streets as the people are returning to their homes."

I brought him into my apartment, then bade him wait while I opened a trunk and looked for something simple. I finally found a plain tunic and a rough length of woven wool. I covered my curled hair with the wool, removed my jewelry, and stood before my king.

"Scrub your face," he said, examining me. "You must look like an ordinary woman."

Grumbling beneath my breath, I took a towel from my dressing table and scrubbed the color from my cheeks, lips, and lashes. When I looked as plain as a milkmaid, Herod grunted his approval. "We will go out through the servants' entrance," he said. "Only Eurus will go with us."

And so we went out. Eurus had removed his uniform, so we looked like three ordinary people as we passed through the gates of the palace and into the street beyond.

I had never walked through Jerusalem before. Even as a child, my father brought us to the palace in his cart or wagon, so walking among the people was a new experience. I pulled the edge of the woolen scarf over my nose and mouth, ostensibly to block the dust, but mainly to disguise my features as I stared at the city's inhabitants with wide eyes. For some reason, I had expected to see expressions of dislike and arrogant superiority on every face. Instead I saw life in all its forms: the sweat-streaked faces of working men, the furrowed brows of middle-aged women closing up their market booths, the tired smiles of young mothers carrying their toddlers on their hips as they trudged toward their homes.

We stepped aside for donkeys laden with baskets, mule-drawn carts, and a line of blind men, each man holding tight to the shoulder of the man in front of him. Their free hands held tin cups, still hoping for a coin or two as they made their way to wherever they would spend the night.

At one point, Eurus thrust out his arm, halting Herod and me as a woman flung a bowl of human waste out the window onto the street below. I crinkled my nose as the fecal matter splattered over the cobblestones, mixing with the mule and donkey dung.

"That is horrible," I said, pressing my hand over my nose.

Herod tossed me a wicked grin. "Aye. But they do the same thing even on the streets of Rome."

Herod bade Eurus stop at a street corner. A few feet away, a couple of black-robed Pharisees stood together, their lined faces taut with intensity. Herod edged closer to hear what subject had captured their attention, then turned his back to the men so he could pretend he was talking to me. I went along with the charade, quietly whispering nonsense so Herod could hear the men's conversation. I exhaled in relief when I realized they were not discussing the king but whether or not the Law permitted a woman to put extra logs on her fire after sunset on the Sabbath.

Herod listened, shook his head, and moved on. We walked for nearly an hour, traversing the city streets and walking through narrow alleys as we listened at doorways and open windows, until the sun disappeared behind the rooftops and the streets emptied. During that time no one stopped us or remarked upon us in our hearing. My heart warmed to know that this time at least, Herod had heard nothing to upset him.

He told Eurus to lead us back to the palace. I lengthened my stride to keep up with the two men. "Have you done this before?"

Herod grunted. "Only when necessary."

I snatched a breath as we climbed uphill. "Whatever makes it necessary for you to disguise yourself? You are the king!"

"A king can trust no one." His frown relaxed when he realized to whom he was speaking. "Except, perhaps, his sister."

"I suppose I can understand why you do this, but surely it is not wise. You will not always like what you hear."

"Do you think I don't know that? I need to hear what my people are saying about me. A clever man knows what his enemies are thinking. Such knowledge is priceless."

I stared at him, recognizing the irony he refused to see. Did he know what his wife and mother-in-law were saying about him in the palace? Was he aware of the disdain at the core of their hearts, or would he simply not accept it?

70

One day I sent for my handmaid in early afternoon because the king was giving a banquet and expected his family to attend.

Nada, who had grown slower in the last two years, found me at my dressing table, trying on earrings. Because I'd grown weary of waiting, chitons and himations covered the bed behind me.

Nada took in the mess with one sharp glance. "Has my beautiful girl decided what she will wear?"

I gave my reflection one last appraisal, then lowered the earrings I'd been holding up to my ears. "No. But Herod insists we all be on our best behavior, so it's important I look like a king's sister. We have a guest—an old friend of Mark Antony."

Nada pulled the comb from my hair, allowing it to tumble over my shoulders. "Have you met this guest before?"

I shook my head. "He's a soldier; apparently he and Antony fought together once. But Herod fears this Quintus Dellius has come to spy on him, so everything must be perfect. Including the king's family." I regarded the chitons on the bed, then pointed to a gown of ivory linen. "What do you think of that one? I could wear the blue-and-green himation. And the green earrings."

Nada squinted for a moment, then nodded. "And how will you wear your hair?"

I turned to consider my burnished image in the looking brass. "Down, I think. With the top drawn back and braided. Something artistic, to catch the man's eye."

"Something old-fashioned."

I bit my tongue as sharp words leapt to my lips. In truth, Nada did not know how to create any modern styles, yet I did not want to chide her. Not tonight.

"Something simple," I said, hoping Quintus Dellius would be charmed by a plain hairstyle.

Nada picked up a comb, her hand trembling as she ran it through my hair. "The color is holding nicely, do not you think? The henna makes it feel stronger, too."

"Umm." Her comment barely registered because I was no longer thinking about hair but about our Roman visitor. I caught Nada's hand and turned to face her. "When the banquet is finished, I would like you to follow this Quintus Dellius and tell me what he does."

She blanched. "Follow a Roman?"

"He will be pleasant and genial at the banquet," I said, releasing her. "But after dinner, he will perform whatever tasks his master has asked him to perform. I'm quite certain Antony did not send this man all the way to Judea to report on the king's banquet."

Though I had never asked such a thing before, I knew Nada would do anything I asked.

⌇⌇⌇⌇⌇⌇⌇

The next morning I was not surprised when Nada told me what happened after the banquet.

"Alexandra," she said, drawing out the woman's name. "The stick in your brother's throat. She met Quintus Dellius after dinner and invited him to her chamber."

"Did they know each other before last night?" I asked.

Nada shook her head. "It matters not. What matters is the man paid more attention to Alexandra than to you, my lamb. The man is either blind or he has no sense."

I blew out a frustrated breath. While I appreciated Nada's loyalty, she had always had trouble seeing beyond the latest gossip about who was bedding whom. She was oblivious to the powerful currents swirling around us now that we were swimming with Romans.

"What *matters*," I corrected her, "is that Quintus is a friend to

72

Antony, and Antony is enamored with Cleopatra. And Cleopatra and Alexandra are close friends."

Nada stared, openmouthed. "I . . . I did not know."

I plucked a piece of bread from the tray she had brought from the kitchen. "Apparently those two are united in their dislike of my brother. Fortunately, Antony is not so infatuated with the Egyptian that he allows her to have her way in everything. Now, let me think." I took a bite of bread and stared out the window. "What did Quintus Dellius discuss with Alexandra?" I turned back to my maid and lifted a brow. "I know how you servants talk. Have you heard rumors?"

Nada drew a wheezing breath. "I did speak with Mava this morning. She served them last night."

"Mariamne's handmaid?"

"Yes."

"Mariamne was with Alexandra and Quintus Dellius?"

"Mava said nothing untoward happened; the queen's virtue was quite safe. Quintus Dellius behaved like a noble man. He did not sleep with the queen or the queen's mother."

I snorted softly. Adultery was not on the long list of concerns I had about Mariamne. "Apparently, Dellius has heard of my brother's unforgiving jealousy. So what did they talk about?"

Nada drew another breath. "Nothing untoward, mistress. The Roman complimented Alexandra on her children's beauty. According to Mava, Alexandra was most pleased."

"Of course she was." I gritted my teeth. "What else did they say?"

Nada leaned against the wall as if my questions had wearied her. "The Roman suggested Alexandra hire an artist to paint two portraits, one of each of her children. He said he would take them to Antony, or, if such paintings could not be hastily arranged, she should have them sent to Antony. He was certain Antony would be favorably impressed."

An inner alarm lifted the hair on my arms. "Why would she send their portraits to Antony? This can't be about marriage, for Mariamne is already married and Aristobulus is too young to be wed."

"The Roman . . ." Nada hesitated.

"Go on."

"The Roman said Mark Antony had an eye for feminine *and* masculine beauty. And while he would never attempt to take Mariamne from Herod, if Herod were killed in battle or if he should befall some misfortune—"

"Enough." I closed my eyes and pressed my lips together. So this was about marriage—or rather, about getting Alexandra's royal children on a throne as soon as possible. The Hasmoneans would be kings again when Alexandra's grandsons took the throne, but apparently Alexandra did not want to wait. I turned back to Nada. "If you can, find out if Alexandra is having these portraits painted."

"She is, mistress. I met an artist in the hall this morning. He was excited to be working for the queen's mother."

"By all the gods, that woman is impossible." I clenched my fist and stood, then paced at the foot of my bed. "This will come to no good. Alexandra is trying to usurp Herod's authority, and she is using her friendship with Cleopatra to do it. Antony would have no use for that arrogant woman if not for his pagan Egyptian lover."

Nada remained silent but wiped a trickle of perspiration from her forehead. "Mistress?"

"Mmm?"

"May I leave you now? The morning is hot and I did not sleep much last night."

I waved her away, too perturbed with Alexandra's scheme to worry about my handmaid.

CHAPTER TWELVE

Zara

I sat perfectly still on the bench, minding my manners as my aunt served honey water to the Torah teacher and our guest, Etan Glaucus. Ima sat on the floor near the fire, propped up with pillows, her thin legs covered by a blanket. Her face shone with sweat, and a pearl of perspiration trickled from her hairline. She looked at me and tried to smile, but I knew she had been dreading this day.

"Thank you." Etan Glaucus took a cup and sipped, then nodded his appreciation. He looked at the Torah teacher and pointedly cleared his throat. "Shall we discuss the reason we have come tonight?"

"Yes." Aunt Rimonah sat on a stool. "I understand you would like to arrange a betrothal."

Etan Glaucus nodded. "I have a son, aged fifteen years. He is a good boy, a solid scholar, and he is learning more every day."

"What trade will he pursue?" Rimonah asked.

"Sandal making." Etan Glaucus spread his callused hands, displaying dirt in the creases. "Already he can count goods and manage the books. When he is ready to be married, I will put him in charge of my shop and help him build a house on the roof."

My aunt dipped her chin in a brusque nod. "And you would like your son to take my niece as his bride?"

"Not so fast, Rimonah." The Torah teacher waved his age-spotted hand and pulled a parchment from a pouch at his waist. "I have brought the standard *ketubah*. It is customary to negotiate for the bride before the agreement is signed."

My aunt took the document and stared at the writing on the soft leather. I do not know how well she could read, but I had been taught in one of the schools founded by Queen Salome Alexandra.

"Would you like me to read—?"

Rimonah cut me off with a sharp look. "Everything appears to be in order." She turned to my mother. "Unless you have an objection."

Mother clutched her arms so tightly that her knuckles whitened. "I do not know what—"

"Do you wish to betroth your daughter to this shoe-seller's son?"

Mother blinked, a frown forming between her brows. "When you put it so bluntly . . ."

"Come now." Aunt Rimonah stepped between Ima and our guests and bent to look directly into my mother's eyes. "Without a husband, you will do well to betroth your daughter to anyone. Surely this is an acceptable match."

"But—a shoemaker!" Ima whispered the word as if it were a cursed thing. "Zara is from a fine family! Her father was a Levite—"

"Your husband is gone, and someone must see to his daughter's future. I am willing to help you, but only if you give your consent. I will not have you saying I forced you into this."

"Zara is still so young."

"So is the shoe-seller's son, but that is customary. The betrothal will stand until they are old enough to be married."

Mother threw me a worried glance, then slowly lifted her gaze to meet Aunt Rimonah's. "I would not agree if I had any other choice."

"I know." Understanding and pity mingled in my aunt's eyes. "But you can be at peace, knowing you have made a good plan for your daughter."

"All will be well, Ima." I squeezed her arm. "We must trust HaShem."

The smile my mother gave me seemed distracted, but she nodded to my aunt. "Let us proceed," she said, her voice quivering. "I will agree to the betrothal."

I looked past my mother and studied the firelit face of the man who would one day be my father-in-law. How much did my future husband resemble him? I squinted, trying to mentally erase the age lines from the man's mouth and eyes, and decided my future husband must be a very ordinary-looking fellow.

That would be fine. Because if a simple shoemaker was the only man to come knocking at our door, then I must be a very ordinary-looking girl.

CHAPTER THIRTEEN

Salome

I said nothing to my brother about Alexandra's plan to place her children's images before Mark Antony. Herod did not need to know his mother-in-law wanted to dangle his beautiful wife to bait another man, nor did he need to know she was doing the same thing with her attractive son. I had heard that Antony desired men as well as women, but even if the rumor were false, in the handsome face of young Aristobulus, Antony might well see a future king—a Jewish king, a Hasmonean, a king who would be a friend to Rome *and* have the love and support of his people.

Several weeks passed without incident, and I hoped nothing had come of Alexandra's plan. Nada heard no news of further developments, and as far as she knew, Alexandra had not heard from Antony. All seemed calm . . . at least on the surface.

Until one afternoon when Herod sent for me. I had been sitting in my chair so that Nada could style my hair, but when the messenger said I was to come at once, I rose and flew down the hallway, leaving my handmaid with her hands uplifted and a stunned expression on her face.

As I entered my brother's private reception room, I found him sitting at a table with Joseph and Pheroras.

"We are all here, then," I said. I gave my brothers quick kisses on their cheeks and sank into a chair. "What is so urgent?"

Scowling, Herod gestured to a scroll on the table. The seal had been broken, and I could see the thick smear of wax that had been heavily imprinted with a signet ring.

"Antony has written me." He glanced around the circle. "He has asked me to send Aristobulus to Alexandria. Do any of you know why he might make such a request?"

I drew a sharp breath. "He asked you to send the boy?"

Herod's eyes darted toward me. "What do you know of it?"

I caught my breath as Joseph and Pheroras stared at me with blank faces. Clearly they were as uninformed as Herod.

"I have not said anything because I did not believe Antony would respond," I said, locking my fingers. "But if you remember Quintus Dellius—"

"I do," Herod snapped. "I know he came here to spy for Antony."

"Yes, I had my handmaid follow him. After your banquet, he had a private audience with Alexandra. She told him that your refusal to make her son high priest had dishonored the family of Hasmon."

Herod's brow pulled into an affronted frown. "How do you know this?"

"My handmaid spoke to the maid who served wine in Alexandra's chamber. She heard everything."

"Your mother-in-law whines constantly." Pheroras leaned back in his chair. "Perhaps you should send her into exile."

Herod ignored the comment. "Go on, sister. What did she hear?"

I folded my arms. "Quintus Dellius suggested that Alexandra send portraits of her beautiful children to Antony. I know she engaged an artist, so apparently she did as he asked. Now I gather he wants to meet them—or at least he wants to meet the youth."

Herod sighed heavily, then slammed his fist against the table. "By all that is holy, I cannot make headway with this family! Just when I think we have come to a peaceful arrangement, they meddle in my relationship with Antony. If Alexandra convinces him I cannot control Judea, or that her son would be better at keeping the peace—"

"Surely she cannot do that," Joseph said. "She is only a woman, with no real power."

"A woman's chief power is her influence," Herod said, wagging a finger. "Never forget that."

He pressed his hands over his eyes, then shook his head and released a weary sigh. "I have to be tactful when I respond to Antony, and I cannot send Aristobulus to Egypt under any circumstance. If Antony sees how agreeable the youth is, he might well befriend him . . . and make him king the first time he doubts my grip on Judea."

"So." Pheroras's thin mouth clamped tight as he swallowed. "What do we do?"

Herod tented his hands for a moment, thinking. Finally he dipped his chin in a resolute nod. "Antony said I was to send Aristobulus to Alexandria if it would cause me no trouble. I will explain that sending the boy might cause quite a bit of trouble, especially with his mother."

"How would . . . ?" I began.

"If I ordered the boy away, the Jews might believe I was sending him into exile," Herod said, the grim line of his mouth relaxing. "Yes, that's believable. I will tell Antony that the people love Aristobulus and want to keep him near. If I send the lad away, the people of Jerusalem might erupt in unrest."

"So Ananel will remain high priest?" Joseph asked. "The people seem to approve of him."

"He will," Herod agreed. "Because if Antony sees Aristobulus as a possible high priest *and* king, we are finished."

〰〰〰

"May I see that one?" I pointed to a gold necklace on the jewelry maker's tray, and the man's smile broadened.

"A good choice, my lady. A very good choice. This is the finest gold in the world, mined in southern Egypt."

Nada took the necklace from the man and placed it around my neck. I studied my reflection and ran my fingertips over the large pieces of gold. The necklace was probably worth a king's ransom, yet I could not ask Herod for money now. He had been far too quick-tempered of late.

"This is lovely, Hector, only I do not want to buy it. I have already spent my allowance this month."

The man's face twisted. "But you alone can do it justice. I cannot imagine it around any other woman's neck."

"Unless you are prepared to let me borrow it indefinitely, you will have to improve your imagination."

Uncertainty crept into the jeweler's expression. Then he smiled again. "But of course you may borrow it, my esteemed lady! Keep it, wear it as often as you like, and if anyone asks who made such a stunning piece—"

"I will give them your name, of course." I lifted a brow. "Unless I forget."

His smile faded. "How can I make sure you will not forget?"

"You might want to remind me," I replied. "Visit me every few weeks and let me look over your latest creations. And be assured, even if I do not buy these wonderful treasures, you will be honored by their appearance on my person . . . or perhaps even the queen's."

An even broader smile gathered the wrinkles around his lined mouth. "The queen? Do you think Mariamne—?"

"I'm surprised she hasn't called for you herself. She and her mother both have an eye for beautiful things."

"I have tried to see her, but they say she already has a favorite jeweler."

"All the more reason you should let me display your creations before the king."

"Ah, thank you, lady. Thank you. Thank you a thousand times over."

The man picked up his tray and slipped out of my chamber, leaving me alone with Nada. I fingered the heavy gold necklace again and squinted into my looking brass. "Is this too heavy? Too gaudy?"

Nada shook her head. "I saw something similar on one of the Roman women who visited last month."

"Good." I smiled at my reflection, then motioned for Nada to remove the jewelry. "While you put that away, tell me—have you heard any interesting news from the other servants?"

The corner of Nada's mouth twisted as she undid the hasp. "They say Alexandra has written the Egyptian queen again. She complains about being watched and suffering many humiliations."

"Humiliations?" I shook my head. "I should be so humiliated. What else?"

Nada pressed her lips together. "Her maid says Cleopatra wrote Alexandra and told her to come to Egypt at once, bringing her son with her."

I laughed softly. "Are we really to be rid of her so easily? The queen's mother is going to Egypt?"

Nada shook her head as her shoulders slumped. "There is more, but if you are to hear it, I must sit."

I leaned forward, gripped the edge of a stool, and slid it toward her. "Sit at once. And tell me everything you know."

Nada sighed as she sank onto the stool, resting her hands

on her knees. "After receiving the Egyptian queen's invitation, Alexandra sent a message to the cook."

"Why the cook?"

"If you keep interrupting, you will never hear all of it."

"That is no way to speak to your mistress, but continue. Please."

"The cook's husband," Nada said, breathing heavily, "is a carpenter. Alexandra asked him to make two coffins and have them waiting at the port. Alexandra and her son planned to slip away from the palace and meet him, then board a ship while they lay in the coffins." Nada tilted her head and looked at me. "I know it sounds mad, but it's the truth. Can you imagine how she would have felt if they'd been discovered in those boxes?"

I straightened my spine. "Does my brother know of this? Does the captain of the guard?"

"What do you think? If the story reached me, you can be sure it also reached the captain of the guard. Yes, the king knows, and yes, the plan has been uncovered. Alexandra's coffins were confiscated, and now she is being watched even more closely."

"How angry is my brother? Will he—?"

"The king has done nothing." Nada coughed and pressed a hand to her chest. She finished in a strangled voice, "The queen's handmaid says he is trying to make peace with the queen's mother because of the great love he bears for Mariamne."

I rested my chin on my hand and considered this astounding news. Why hadn't Herod told me about this? He might not want me to know such embarrassing news. He might have been humiliated by the lengths to which his mother-in-law had gone in order to escape his custody. He kept trying to protect her from herself, yet she insisted on making his life miserable. Alexandra complained to Cleopatra, who complained to Mark Antony, who complained to Herod. And Herod had so much more at stake than Alexandra. She suffered—if life in a palace could truly be called suffering—only because her seventeen-year-old son had not been made high priest. But Herod could suffer the loss of his kingdom, even his life, if Antony ceased to support him.

Alexandra's escape plot might have been discovered, but I knew the woman well enough to realize she would not stop meddling until she had achieved her goal.

Reclining on my couch at another royal dinner, I sipped wine from a goblet and studied my brother over its rim. Herod seemed in a good mood, despite the distressing letter from Mark Antony. He had replied, of course, and made it clear he could not send young Aristobulus to Alexandria. Flying in the face of his mentor's wish was taking a risk, but Herod was determined to take this one. Obeying Antony would be a far greater gamble than disobeying.

My poor brother—I could almost feel sorry for him. Mariamne, his greatest love, was also his greatest liability, for her family could undo him with very little effort. Alexandra, who still enjoyed favor and high regard from the Jews of Jerusalem, had done nothing but plot, plead, and complain ever since Herod appointed Ananel the Babylonian to the office of high priest. Why could she not understand why he could not appoint her son?

The boy's age also worked against his appointment to the high office. At seventeen, Aristobulus did not meet the age requirement, for no Jewish high priest had ever been younger than twenty. When first faced with the problem of Alexandra's determination on behalf of her son, Herod had written Hyrcanus, who had once been high priest himself, for suggestions, and Hyrcanus had nominated Ananel, a member of a priestly family in Babylon. The recommendation pleased Herod and so Ananel had been appointed.

Still, a far stronger reason lay behind Herod's reluctance to place Aristobulus in that role, and that unspoken motive was what fueled Alexandra's passionate desire to see her son in the lofty position. Like my brother, she knew Aristobulus would win the people's hearts if he were placed in any position of authority. Though the Judeans had not always loved the Hasmonean kings and priests, the passing of several years had clouded their collective memory. They no longer remembered how the high priest and king Alexander Jannaeus had crucified eight hundred Pharisees on a single day, or how Judah Aristobulus had starved his mother to secure the throne.

Instead, they chose to recall the temperate reign of Salome Alexandra and the heroics of her ancestor, Judah Maccabaeus. They spoke wistfully of John Hyrcanus, who had conquered rich territories to the north and south, and of Simon, the first official prince of the Hasmonean dynasty.

Instead of remembering the later Hasmoneans as men who could be bloodthirsty, ambitious, and arrogant, the people memorialized them as wise, gentle, and strong. Instead of pointing out that the Hasmonean high priests had not come from the priestly line of Zadok, they told themselves that HaShem himself had chosen the Hasmonean priests and bestowed His blessing upon them.

Instead of praising Herod for bringing Hyrcanus II, Alexandra's father and a former high priest, out of exile and back to Jerusalem, they reviled my brother for killing forty-five traitors in the Sanhedrin.

Certain my disdain was visible on my face, I covered my expression with my cup and drank again. My brother could be resolute and firm when he had to be, but he was not without feeling. Indeed, sometimes I found myself convinced that he suffered from an almost womanly excess of emotion. His love for Mariamne was dangerously volatile, and his desire to be loved by his people a constant torment to his soul.

For years I had advised him to cloak his deepest feelings. I had cautioned him yet again, just before we entered the triclinium for dinner.

I took a small loaf from a servant's tray and nibbled at it, looking around to see who had not yet joined us. The heavily pregnant Mariamne was present, as was her elderly grandfather Hyrcanus, his remaining hair grown long to hide the deformity of his missing ears. Pheroras and Joseph had stretched out on couches facing each other. The captain of the guards stood by the door, ever alert.

I lifted my head when Alexandra entered the room, followed by a pair of servants who carried the train of her gown. They helped her arrange her garment on her couch, then backed away, their hands on their knees as they bowed before her.

I felt the corner of my mouth twist. No one else forced their slaves to bow before them, especially not when the king was present. But even now, Alexandra insisted on behaving as though she were royalty.

Herod clapped for a slave, who stepped forward with a steaming chicken carcass on a plate. My brother grimaced as he broke off a leg, then used two hands to crack the breast. He grunted in satisfaction, handing half of the dripping breast to Mariamne, who gingerly accepted it with two fingers.

Now that the king had commenced eating, the rest of us took food from various trays and began our meal. When Herod almost immediately lowered the breastbone and wiped his hands on a linen square, however, I couldn't help but wonder what occupied his thoughts. He usually ate his fill before speaking, so something important had to be on his mind. Was it the business with Antony? Had he already received a reply?

Without warning, Herod sat up and braced his hands on his knees. "Alexandra," he called, his voice ringing in the room. "Stand and face your king!"

In that moment, I felt reluctant admiration for the woman. Despite the iron in Herod's voice, she did not flinch, tremble, or even look up at him. She simply lowered her food, wiped her fingers on a towel, and stood slowly in one smooth motion. Then she looked at him with an expression as blank as a sheet of parchment.

She was either utterly fearless or completely false.

"Alexandra," Herod said, holding her firmly in his gaze, "I have shown great forbearance toward you because of the great love I have for my wife, your daughter. But I have asked these men here—" he gestured to several guests, including Joseph, Pheroras, and Ananel, the current high priest—"to act as a tribunal. Let them hear what I have to say, and let them judge you, for I cannot."

The unlined face showed no emotion, but Alexandra seemed to pale in the flickering torchlight.

"I accuse you," Herod went on, his voice like iron, "of conspiring to dilute my royal authority, granted by the Roman Senate, in favor of your son, Aristobulus. I also accuse you of plotting with Cleopatra, queen of Egypt, to drive me from the throne so that she can extend her territories into Judea. Do you deny either of these charges?"

Silence fell over us like a heavy blanket. Alexandra lowered her gaze. If not for a trembling of her lower garments—I believe her knees were shaking—I would have thought her completely unafraid.

When she looked up once more, the eyes staring out at us had gone wide with terror. "I have not sought to unseat you, my king," she said, her voice tattered. "How foolish I would have been to undertake such a thing because my family is safe with you. I and my children have rested beneath your protection for years, and you have not allowed us to be harmed in these times of turmoil and unrest."

Herod harrumphed and crossed his arms. "You would be foolish to undertake rebellion against the anointed king. So how do you account for the reports that have recently reached my ears?"

"Reports?"

"From Mark Antony, who asks about your children."

The woman glanced around the room as if she could find a fuller explanation on another face. When her eyes lit on me, they narrowed as if to say, *So you know. But you have not won.*

She looked back at Herod and sniffed as tears slipped from her lashes and rolled over her cheeks. "I admit I have tried to gain advancement for Aristobulus, but only because he is a suitable candidate to be *cohen gadol.* To ignore him—to pretend he does not exist—is to dishonor him, my king. It is to dishonor the young man you profess to love as your own brother. But if my actions have offended you, I am sorry and beg your forgiveness."

Herod drew a deep breath, then shot me a warning glance.

I wanted to caution him, to tell him Alexandra was cleverer than he suspected, but I knew I should not give sisterly advice in a public place.

Herod did not wait to hear from his hastily appointed tribunal. His generous nature, coupled with the anxious look from his beautiful and pregnant wife, resolved the matter. "I accept your apology and extend my forgiveness to you." Herod uncrossed his arms and settled into a more relaxed posture. "Let us be content with where we are and be perfect friends again. I will grant your request and appoint Aristobulus high priest, for I have no desire to dishonor my wife's brother. Consider your wish granted."

I glanced at Ananel, who sat blinking at this sudden and unexpected turn of events.

Herod turned to the high priest, as well. "Ananel, you are

to return to your former post in Babylon. Thank you for your service to HaShem and to your king."

The old man opened his mouth as if to protest, but the saving grace of second thought must have restrained him.

I looked over at Hyrcanus, whose nominee had just been rejected. The old man was staring down at the cup in his hand. He would say nothing. He had given Herod good advice, while Alexandra outmaneuvered both of them.

I took another bite of my bread and chewed slowly, amazed that the woman had managed to sway my brother from anger to generosity in less time than it took to drink a glass of wine. Did she understand my brother's generous nature as well as I, or had she stumbled into his mercy purely by chance?

I tilted my head and quietly studied our new queen's mother. Tall, elegant, and quick-thinking, Alexandra was not the sort of woman to be underestimated.

I found my brothers in the spacious reception room, where Herod received visitors. Joseph, my husband, was with them.

"Did you mean it?" Joseph was asking, his face flushed. "You will appoint Aristobulus as high priest?"

"He's only a child," Pheroras grumbled. "A handsome boy, but still a boy."

"He is seventeen," Herod snapped. "Kings have been crowned at younger ages."

"But he is a Hasmonean," I inserted, daring to jump into the conversation. "Have you forgotten how they hate us? Even now they treat us with disdain. Especially Alexandra—"

"I am married to a Hasmonean." Herod's eyes flashed at me. "I will not have you criticize my wife's mother."

"No? Nor her brother? Pheroras is right; Aristobulus is too young to be high priest. He is barely a man."

Herod set his jaw. "He has other priests to guide him."

"The other priests will teach him to hate us," Joseph said, his dark eyes locked on Herod. "They will teach him to despise you. And when he is old enough to figure out that he has the people's support, he will lead a revolt against you."

"The people will understand that I am doing this for them—and for my wife." Herod sank into a chair, then shifted so he could stretch his muscular legs. "They will see that my love for Mariamne is so great that I am willing to give her brother the title of *cohen gadol*. They will support this action and love me for it."

"Will they?" Joseph folded his arms. "Is that a risk you can afford to take?"

We stood in a silence so thick the only sound was the rumble of Pheroras's belly. Then Herod sighed, leaned forward on his knees, and pinched the bridge of his nose. "Truth be told, I am not appointing the lad because of Mariamne," he said, a note of defeat echoing in his voice. "A king is not commanded by his wife. I am appointing the boy because I know the action will please Antony."

I lifted a brow. So . . . a king might not be commanded by his wife, but he can be commanded by his master.

Pheroras and I looked at each other without speaking. Herod did not have to explain further; we understood his relationship with the Roman. Herod served Mark Antony as any slave serves his master—filled with hope that his hard work and dutiful obedience will result in reward and greater freedom. Our father served Hyrcanus and Julius Caesar, and now Herod served Antony, who was part of the triumvirate that ruled the world from Rome.

"Why does Antony care so much about the position of high priest?" Pheroras asked. "I have never known any Roman to take anything more than a passing interest in our worship."

"Our God doesn't interest him," Herod replied, "but Cleopatra incites his lusts."

"I still do not understand." Pheroras looked from Herod to me. "Why should Antony care who holds the office?"

"Have you forgotten?" Herod shook his head. "Alexandra is a friend to Cleopatra. Apparently my mother-in-law has written the queen, who asked Antony to grant her request regarding Aristobulus. So whether the action pleases me or not, Aristobulus shall be our high priest."

Herod's weary eyes came to rest on mine as he smiled. "Ah, you women . . . you wield your powers unfairly."

"And you do not?" I teased him in an effort to hide my displeasure at this turn of events, then sank to the footrest at my brother's feet. "How fares your pregnant wife?"

"She is content." Herod stared at an empty patch of air as though he were imagining something in its place. "She believes this child may be another son, and she is thrilled to know her brother will be high priest. So even if she gives birth to a daughter, she is a happy woman. For now."

I lowered my gaze, respecting his weariness. Herod did not share everything about his marital relationship, yet I was certain he shared more than most brothers. Our father had always stressed family unity, constantly reminding us that we needed each other, so we should put family first in all things. We did, usually, and trusted each other implicitly.

"I am certain Cleopatra would love to be rid of me," Herod added, abruptly lifting his head. "That is why I must remain Mark Antony's friend, be the one who pleases him in all things. If that means I must keep Cleopatra happy, then . . ." He shrugged.

Pheroras shook his head. "Even appoint Aristobulus as high priest? When you know the people will adore him and despise you?"

Herod slammed his fist on the chair's armrest. "You are wrong about that. I have married a Hasmonean heiress, I have brought her mother into the royal house, and I have placed her brother in a high position. I have brought Hyrcanus back to Jerusalem, where he can live out his life in peace. What more can I do to satisfy their hunger for the Hasmoneans?"

"Die," I whispered, lifting my gaze to meet his. "That is the only thing that will please those stiff-necked people. The Jews will never accept you, Herod, and it has nothing to do with what you have done or not done. They despise you because you are a son of Esau and their God said, 'Jacob have I loved, and Esau I have hated.' So they hate you, as well."

"You are wrong, sister." Herod wagged his finger at me. "In time you will see how wrong you are."

"I would love to be wrong," I answered, standing. "But I do not believe I am."

CHAPTER FOURTEEN

Salome

"You there! Girl!"

The flustered slave turned at the sound of my voice and squeaked like a frightened mouse. "Did you speak to me, mistress?"

"Do you see anyone else in the hallway? Nada is late. Have you seen her?"

The girl's eyes widened. "Who?"

"My handmaid. Her rooms are the largest in the servants' quarters, so you must know her. Have you seen her?"

The girl shook her head.

"Then fetch her at once. Tell her that her mistress grows weary with waiting."

The girl scurried away, her sandaled feet slapping the tiled floor. I sighed and retreated back into my chamber, then sat and stared into my looking brass. My hair was a riotous mess, dark circles ringed my eyes, and I desperately needed wine to soothe my headache. Where was that woman?

I stood and paced back and forth in the room. Nada had not been herself the past few days. She had been slower than usual, slower even than the cook who brought me fruit and cheese every morning. Several times I saw Nada clutching the bedpost as if she were feeling dizzy, but then she straightened when she caught me studying her.

Nada couldn't be sick. I would not allow it.

Where was that idiotic slave? She'd had time to find Nada and return with a report.

I picked up a comb and swiped at my curly hair, then gave up and threw the comb across the room. Only Nada had ever been able to make my wild hair obey. Only she knew how I liked things. Only she knew everything about me, so what would I do if she were ill? I'd have to send for a physician, of course. And find someone to take care of her while she recovered from whatever ailed her. Perhaps, as a kindness, I might go to the servants' quarters and spoon soup into her mouth, as she had always done when I fell ill . . .

I stepped into the hallway, looked left and right, and screamed in frustration. "Girl! Where are you?"

No answer.

I threw a cloak over my nightdress and strode down the hallway in my bare feet, not caring who saw me. Let the servants talk. Let Mariamne's ladies gossip. I was Herod's sister, and he would never rebuke me for something as foolish as this. And if I found Nada asleep, I would pull her off the bed and whip her myself.

I stepped outside and headed toward the stone building with plain walls. The entry hall was narrow, dimly lit, and smelled faintly of urine. I crinkled my nose and nearly turned back, but frustration drove me forward. The slaves lived on the ground floor, with the hired servants occupying the floor above, so I crept up the stone staircase and counted doors as I moved down the hall. Nada slept in the fifth room, one of the largest and most pleasantly furnished. I opened the door and nearly ran headlong into the frightened slave I'd sent to find my handmaid.

"Mistress! I—I was just about to return to you."

I ignored the girl and walked to the bed, where Nada lay with her head on a pillow. Her jaw was slack, her mouth open, and her yellow teeth visible because the skin had receded. Her pale eyes stared fixedly at the beams in the ceiling.

The sight was a bucket of cold water poured over my anger. Though I had been perspiring all morning, I felt suddenly slick with a different kind of sweat, the sour, cold dampness of dread. Nada was dead, and had probably been dead for some time.

I knew she was gone—no one could look like that and live—but I couldn't help whispering her name. "Nada?" I touched her shoulder and felt sharp bone through the thin nightdress. No warmth lingered in her body, no softness. Only cold skin and rigid limbs.

"By the crud beneath Qaus's toes." I pulled away, recoiling from the sight. How could death have come so unexpectedly? She should have been sick, bedridden, and given me a chance to care for her, to demonstrate that I had learned to care for others from her example . . .

"Nada," I whispered from a safe distance, "why did you die without warning me?"

No reply from the corpse, only squeaky words from the slave girl. "Death comes for all of us, mistress."

"Hmm?"

"Death comes—"

"I know, girl. Be quiet." Blinking back tears, I looked around the room, hoping the gruesome thing on the bed would vanish and I would turn to find Nada sitting up, her hands warm, her voice sharp as she scolded me for venturing into the servants' quarters.

But when I looked back again, the corpse was still there, accompanied now by a discernible odor.

An unexpected fount rose in my chest, a geyser of hysterical laughter and grief, and my knees gave way beneath the increasing pressure. I sank to the floor and sobbed with my hands over my face, unwilling to look at the thing on the bed . . .

One thought ran through my mind, over and over. Why hadn't I come to check on her last night? I had heard her coughing, I saw her weakening, I should have known she was not well. But I was focused on other things and simply did not take time for her, when it would have been so easy to do so. While she lay here dying, I had been sleeping, or eating, or doing nothing. If I had come, if I had sent for a physician, if I had taken a single moment to think of her, she might not have died.

I do not know how long I wept on the floor, but when the wellspring ceased to flow, I dried my face and stood. The slave girl remained with me, crouched in the corner. Her eyes widened when I looked her way.

"Call the guards," I told her, my voice broken. "Have them prepare Nada for burial. Tell them she is not to be treated like a slave but embalmed and prepared for a royal tomb. She will sleep with me for eternity, but until I am ready to go, she will have to wait."

I moved to the door, feeling as though I had aged ten years in the last hour. On reaching the doorway, I turned to take one last look at the woman who had cared for me since the hour of my birth. How old was she, sixty-five, sixty-six? She never had children, never married. I had been her child, her family, her life. She had never failed me . . . until today.

But I had failed her when I left her to die alone.

That afternoon Herod entered my chamber unannounced and seemed not to notice my red eyes or that I was completely alone and sleeping.

"What do you think?" he asked, sinking to the edge of my bed. Facing away from me, he spread his hands in a gesture of confusion. "I have given them what they want, but still they look at me as though I have slighted them somehow."

I lifted my head from my pillow and swiveled my eyes toward the looking brass on my dressing table. "Who are we talking about?" I asked his blurry reflection. "Your wives or your people?"

He grunted. "Both. I have announced Aristobulus as our next high priest. I have sent the Babylonian back to his people. Before he left, Ananel reminded me that he was from the line of Zadok, but Aristobulus is not. I know Ananel's lineage works in his favor, but what could I do? Alexandra will give me no rest until she sees her son offering sacrifices in the Temple."

"Then let it happen sooner rather than later." I got out of bed and went to my chair so I could sit and face him. "My hand-maid has died. The one who has been with me since my birth."

Herod's frown made me wonder if he was trying to remember Nada or trying to forget I'd mentioned her. "Can't you get another?"

I sighed. Herod cared nothing about servants, especially women's handmaids. "I will get someone else. Eventually." I pushed my unruly hair out of my eyes and wearily regarded him. "I should have cared for her. She died alone in her room."

"Care for her now by giving her a fine burial." He crossed his arms. "So what can I do to win the hearts of these Jews?"

I closed my eyes, my mind thick with fatigue and guilt. "Has Alexandra written Cleopatra with news of her son's appointment? The news should pacify the Egyptian woman—and her lover."

"I do not know. But even if she has, I can't forget that I have done something I did not want to do . . . the thought discomfits me."

"You are the king. You can change your mind. Or postpone the boy's appointment."

"If I change my mind, Alexandra will inform Egypt. Cleopatra will run to Antony, and Antony will write me again—and this time he may insist that I send Aristobulus to Alexandria. If I do, and if Antony finds the lad agreeable, he may decide to make him king. And all these things would happen while I am here, unable to speak to Antony or do anything to reassure him."

I leaned forward and grabbed my brother's wrists. "Stop tormenting yourself," I muttered through clenched teeth, my grip tight on his arms. "*You* are the king, not Alexandra."

His eyes bored into mine, narrowed with rage. He jerked free of my grasp and stood. For an instant I felt raw fear—had I gone too far?—but then he turned and began to pace, his hands locked behind his back. "And—" he drew a ragged breath— "there is the matter of how Alexandra has been working against me for months. She and Cleopatra are more treacherous than Eve, for they conspired without my knowledge. At least Eve went to Adam and spoke plainly to him!"

"Herod, calm yourself. Antony trusts you. Rome trusts you."

"Rome trusts me, yes, but I do not trust Rome. The Senate can be moved in any direction on any given day, depending upon which silver-tongued orator stands to speak. You have not been there, Salome, you have not seen these men in action. I have, and it is both fearful and marvelous to behold. Rome is filled with skillful, manipulative men, and one man does not hold all the power."

"Yet Antony holds one third of the power," I reminded him. "Octavian holds another third, and Lepidus—"

"Octavian and Lepidus do not concern themselves with

Judea." Herod shook his head. "And if Antony believes I cannot hold Judea peacefully, he will appoint another king and we will all be exiled, if not worse." He stopped pacing and looked me in the eyes. "The stakes are high, sister. If he believes we have not been just in our dealings with the Hasmoneans, Rome could demand our lives. Antony would be pleased to confiscate our property."

"Then you must do what you can to keep Alexandra from working mischief. And I will help you."

"Truly?"

"Herod." I stood and squeezed his hands. "You are my brother, and you know I would die for you. You are also the king, so you have every right to control Alexandra's actions. Place a man at her door and tell her she is being guarded because you fear for her life. Make arrangements so that any message she sends is first delivered to someone you trust, so you can be aware of her activities. Do not let her leave the palace or receive any guest except for those you have approved. In this way you can minimize her meddling."

Herod tilted his head. "Alexandra is not a fool. She will know my true reasons."

"Then invent a credible threat, dear brother. Surely one of your men can find some zealot who is upset because Alexandra allowed her daughter to marry an Idumaean. Have someone report on his raving and furnish her with a reason for submitting to your protection. Then protect her with every resource you have."

Herod stared at me a moment, and then his wide mouth split into a grin. "I should have known a woman would best advise me about how to defeat another woman."

"Naturally." I turned back to my dressing table. "Now let's talk about what you can do for me."

"Anything, sister."

I stared woefully at my tangled hair. "I need a handmaid—someone young, skilled, and quiet. Someone who will stay with me for years, so I do not have to go through this again."

"Shall I ask Mariamne? She might have a girl who would be capable—"

"No! I will not have one of her castoffs."

Herod frowned, then nodded. "I will put someone on it right away."

CHAPTER FIFTEEN

Zara

I had just pulled a square of linen from the loom when I heard a man's voice at the courtyard gate. A shadow of alarm crossed my mother's face. "Could that be Etan Glaucus? What if he has brought his son? Zara, wash your face and cover your hair. I do not know why he's come, but we should greet him properly."

I set the linen aside and went to the pitcher and bowl, where I splashed water on my face and glanced out the window. The old man who stood outside the courtyard did not look like a seller of shoes, for he was dressed in expensive robes.

"Hello!" he called, spotting me. "I have an important message for your mother."

Aunt Rimonah walked up to stand beside me. "He is well dressed," she said, her brows lifting as she peered out the window. "And he looks important."

Ima frowned. "What would an important man have to do with us?"

"I do not know, but I will see." Aunt Rimonah pulled a scarf over her hair and stepped outside. She nodded at the man, then tilted her head and gave him a questioning look. "Do I know you? Or perhaps you have come to the wrong house."

The man shook his head. "I have come on the recommendation of your Torah teacher. He remarked on your young daughter's virtue and steady nature."

My aunt grimaced. "I am afraid, sir, you are mistaken. I have no daughter. I live with my sister and her daughter, but the girl has been betrothed."

"I have not come to discuss marriage for the girl, but something else altogether." He pointed at a bench in the courtyard. "Please, may I enter?"

My aunt blinked, and her mouth fell open. Men did not come to the house to see widows, but at least this stranger had the decency to suggest they sit outside, in full view of the neighbors. Aunt Rimonah hesitated a moment before opening the gate.

The man did not sit but pulled off his hat and gave my aunt a confident smile. "I am here to discuss the little girl, so perhaps we should include her mother in this conversation. I understand she cannot walk."

"True." Aunt Rimonah's voice hardened. "She was injured when the king had his Romans storm the city."

Behind me, Ima gasped, and for the first time I realized that this visitor—who wore more expensive garments than anyone I had ever met—might be associated with the palace. So why had my aunt spoken so brashly?

The man did not take offense. "If you would bring the mother out, I should speak to her, as well. Please."

Aunt Rimonah stared at him, and I suspected she would like nothing better than to tell this man to leave. But it seemed she was curious and desperate to know more . . . as was I. "I'll get her," she finally said. "Wait here."

She came into the house, closed the door, and leaned against it. She glanced at me, then looked at Ima, her eyes shining with interest. "Did you hear?"

Ima nodded.

"Shall we listen to what he has to say?"

"About Zara?" Ima's voice cracked. "What could he possibly have to say about a nine-year-old girl?"

"We will never know unless we hear his proposal." Rimonah walked toward Ima, her hands twisting. "What say you? We can hear his proposition and respond as we please."

"What would a rich man want with my child?" Ima's voice vibrated with dread. "It is the king's doing. He has brought wealthy Edomites and Ishmaelites into the city, and they are not like us. Besides, we have made an agreement with the shoe-maker. Zara is no longer eligible . . . for anything this man might suggest."

Rimonah pressed her lips together, silently conceding my mother's point, and then she sighed. "Still, the man has been well mannered thus far, so perhaps his intentions are honorable. Let us at least hear what he has to say."

Ima exhaled slowly, probably realizing she could not argue with her sister. Rimonah moved to Ima's left side and I to her right, and together we carried her to the bench in the courtyard. The moment we passed through the doorway, I felt the pressure of the stranger's dark eyes on me. He watched intently, as if weighing my attitude, and I suspected anything I might say or do in this brief encounter would be of great importance to my future.

"Thank you, Zara," Ima said, lowering herself onto the bench. "You may go back inside."

I bowed my head out of respect, then hurried back into the house and sat beneath the open window where I could hear every word.

"Where do I begin?" the man said when my mother and

aunt had settled to listen. "I am Joseph, uncle to the king and husband to his sister, Salome. My wife has long been attended by a woman who recently died, and she has grieved for days. The king asked me to find her a new handmaid, and when I asked around, many people mentioned that your daughter is exceptionally skilled with styling hair."

Ima groaned, and in that instant I knew she regretted bragging about my skill. If she'd said nothing, this man would not be standing in our courtyard.

"Zara is very good with her hands—with anything she sets out to do," Rimonah said, her voice brimming with confidence. "But her future has been decided. She is betrothed to a fine young man."

"You were wise to plan her future, but why not allow her to embark on a fulfilling life now? Break the betrothal and allow her to live at the palace. She will be in good hands and will be given everything she needs. The girl will live in luxury. My wife is a kind mistress and does not beat her servants. She treated her former handmaid like a mother, and she would treat your child like a daughter."

A strangled sound issued from my mother's throat. "Plans . . . have been made. Zara is set to marry a shoemaker once she is of age. The contract has been signed and witnessed."

"Such contracts are easily set aside. Your daughter will bear no disgrace because she has been offered something far better. Living at the palace, she will walk the same halls as kings and princes. Think of it, woman! We have a Hasmonean queen, so the palace is not foreign soil. And I can assure you—I have known the king since his childhood, and he is not the monster some people have claimed he is."

"Our people are from the tribe of Levi," Aunt Rimonah said. "Ours is a fine family."

"I'm sure it is. I do not know what you've heard about the

king, but let me assure you he is a righteous man. He observes the Law and the Sabbath, he circumcises the male members of his family, and he fears HaShem. You need not worry about your daughter being tainted by any pagan religion."

I thought Rimonah would mention the betrothal again, closing the matter, but instead she shifted the conversation to practical matters. "Zara is so young. What would your wife expect her to do?"

Our visitor smiled. "Salome needs a handmaid—someone who can run errands in the palace, who can do her hair and help her choose her clothing. Salome is looking for a young girl who can be taught to drape a himation and arrange hair in the latest Roman styles. And she wants someone who can keep a confidence and work quietly."

"How long would Zara remain at the palace?"

"For as long as she pleases Salome—probably years. She would be free to marry and have children, of course, if HaShem wills. She could even marry someone from the royal household. She might remain with Salome for the rest of her life. But know this: Zara would be a servant, not a slave. She could leave at any time, if she chose to go . . . or if Salome thought it best to release her."

A moment of silence followed, and in it I could almost hear the pounding of my mother's heart.

"Please," the man finally said. "Think about my offer. I will come again on the morrow, and you may give me your answer then."

I crouched beneath the window, silent and still, and heard the creak of the courtyard gate. When the crunching of the man's footsteps had faded away, Aunt Rimonah said, "She could marry into the royal household."

"Hmm?"

"Pay attention, sister, and think of your daughter! The king's house is filled with couriers and ambassadors and counselors. Zara could meet all sorts of people, even princes and kings."

"He was probably thinking she might marry a stableboy."

"So what? Is that not better than marrying a shoe seller? The future will depend on Zara . . . and HaShem. If she decides to marry a stableboy, fine. But one of the king's sons might notice her, as well. She could marry a prince."

"The king's sons are babies," Ima scoffed. "But . . . she might marry the queen's brother. Young Aristobulus lives at the palace."

My mother's voice had gone soft and dreamy, and my heart began to beat at twice its usual speed. I did not know much about our new king's family, but I did know the Hasmoneans. I knew all about Mariamne, the beautiful daughter of Alexandra, who also had a son, seventeen-year-old Aristobulus. I had seen Aristobulus at the Temple, at the market, and riding by this house, and each time his beauty had left me breathless. Both of Alexandra's children were handsome, yet while Mariamne seemed aloof and distant, Aristobulus had always worn a friendly expression. His manner put everyone at ease, and the women of Jerusalem, even old women who had buried their husbands long ago, giggled like girls when they spoke about him.

If I lived at the palace, I might see Aristobulus every day. Perhaps even his beautiful horse.

"They might become friends," Ima went on, "and by some miracle he might feel fondness toward Zara. HaShem might give him a true love for her, and he might desire to take her for his wife. The king would surely allow it, because everyone knows Herod is trying to endear himself to the people of Jerusalem by aligning himself with Jewish royalty."

I bit my lower lip lest an excited squeal slip from my mouth.

"Ask yourself this," Aunt Rimonah said. "Would Zara be

happier as the wife of a shoe seller or the wife of a courier? Or even a prince?"

Ima sighed. "I can barely imagine her as a wife at all. She is still my little girl."

"She will not be your little girl much longer." Rimonah lowered her voice, so I moved closer to the window to hear her next words. "You know what the doctor has said. Your injury is not improving, and your days are numbered. I know you want what's best for Zara, but think, sister—is she better off with me or in the palace?"

A sob broke from my mother but was quickly muffled.

Finally, after a long moment broken only by the sound of sniffling, Ima raised her voice. "Zara?"

I hesitated, knowing a quick reply would reveal my hiding place. After a little time had passed, I stood and looked out the window. "Yes?"

"Would you like to live at the palace?"

What girl would not want to live in a house with princes and beautiful horses? Yet I had no idea how to answer, whether I should appear indifferent or eager, though I had no intention of squandering this unexpected opportunity.

I closed my eyes and considered my answer. Was this what HaShem had planned for me? Had He opened the door to the king's house? Last year I had no idea what my future would hold; today I could choose between being the bride of a shoe seller or living in a grand palace.

Of course, I could not know if my mother's dream would come true and I would marry a prince. But if I did not, the palace held other advantages, and being a royal lady's hand-maid could not be so difficult. Slaves did the hard work in any household—the carrying of water, scrubbing of floors, grinding grain, and cooking meals. Ladies' handmaids performed more genteel tasks—arranging hair, choosing garments, stringing pearls, light sewing. I could weave for the king's sister and embroider designs on her gowns. I could make myself useful, and if ever I grew tired of the work, or if I did not please her, I could always come back to help Aunt Rimonah . . .

"Surely there are other eligible men at the palace," Aunt Rimonah said. "Surely not all the king's men are Idumaean; some have to be Jews. One of them might notice our Zara, find her winsome, and want to marry her."

"Unless she remains at the palace too long," Ima countered. "If she comes home after twenty years, or thirty, when she is no longer of an age to have children, none of the men from this neighborhood will find her desirable. They would look on her with suspicion and wonder if her time in the Idumaean's palace has tainted her."

I lifted my gaze to the ceiling, where HaShem always seemed to hover above the roof tiles. *Is this opportunity a gift from you? Or is it a temptation to avoid the future you have planned for me?*

Adonai did not answer with a thunderclap, a mighty wind, or an audible voice, but when I opened my eyes, my heart had filled with a fierce and enthusiastic joy.

"Yes, Ima!" I called, leaning out the window. "Yes, I do want to live at the palace!"

CHAPTER SIXTEEN

Salome

I was in my bedchamber, fussing at the Egyptian slave who had just burned my ear with the hot *calamistrum*, when Joseph strode through the doorway wearing a cocky grin.

"Did your horse win," I quipped, "or did you wager on something else this time?"

Joseph dropped onto my bed and clapped his knees. "I've brought you a gift."

I waved the slave away, not caring that only half my hair had been curled. Better to wear it down than to have my ears burned by the latest instrument of torture from Rome.

"You've brought me flowers? Jewelry?"

"Neither. The king charged me with finding you a new handmaid."

"You?" I lifted a brow. "You know nothing of women's hair or clothing."

"I know what Herod wanted. He asked me to bring you a Jewish girl, someone Mariamne would accept. I was reluctant at first, knowing how you feel about our queen, but then I thought you might enjoy ordering around a Jewish girl, since you cannot command the somber old women who look with disapproval on their royal family."

I took a wincing breath. "Who have you brought me, husband?"

Grinning, Joseph lifted his hands and clapped. The door opened, and one of the guards appeared, his hand wrapped around the upper arm of a slender girl with wide, soft eyes.

"So young!" I stood and walked over to the girl. The top of her head barely came to my shoulder. She was a pretty little thing, though unadorned with cosmetics or jewelry. Her dark hair had been twisted into a single braid that ended at her waist. She wore a chemise of fine linen, and the himation draped over her shoulder had been dyed a lovely blue.

"Hello," I said, drinking in the unexpected sight. "Did you dress yourself?"

She blinked rapidly, nodded, and pointed shyly at Joseph. "The master took me to a room and said I might choose whatever I liked."

"You chose well. You are lovely—you look a bit like our new queen."

A blush darkened the girl's cheeks. "You are kind to say so."

"Do you speak Greek?"

"A little."

"What other skills have you? What are you accustomed to doing?"

She glanced uneasily at the waiting Egyptian slave, then returned her gaze to me. "I weave and sew. I can milk a goat. And I can braid hair in all sorts of ways."

"That is good, since that is chiefly what I'd like you to do. Did your family have servants?"

"We did . . . until my father died. Since then, Mother and I have done all the work."

"How did he die?"

"In the siege."

The siege. Would this girl hold me responsible for her father's death? Perhaps not, though she might blame Herod and the Romans. But she was here, which meant her mother had considered this opportunity and thought it would be good for her daughter. Yet would she be good for me?

I gave her a noncommittal smile, then looked back to Joseph. "She is so young. Perhaps too young."

"She is teachable," he said. "And the deal is struck. Her family nullified a betrothal so she could work for you."

"Really." I drew a deep breath. I had been hoping for someone older, someone who could serve as a confidante, but perhaps this girl would do. After all, even a tree stump could listen to my rambling thoughts, while a girl could make sounds of agreement and nod occasionally. For I needed no more than that.

"I think we shall get on very well together." I turned to the Egyptian slave in the corner. "Escort this girl to Nada's room. Make sure she has everything she needs." I then looked at my new handmaid. "Take some time to look around the palace. It will be your new home."

"And you, slave," Joseph added, fixing the Egyptian girl with a stern look, "do not fill this child's ears with gossip or treat her like your equal. You are a slave. She is free."

I gave the girl a warmer smile, knowing she had to be frightened. "Before you go, tell me, what is your name?"

"Zara."

"Your age?"

"Nine years."

"You *are* young."

The girl lifted her head. "I am old enough to know how to serve."

The unexpected display of confidence pleased me. "Good, Zara. I believe we shall get along very well indeed."

CHAPTER SEVENTEEN

Zara

The slave who had escorted me to the servants' building led me upstairs, then left me at the entrance to a small room, plainly but comfortably furnished. I stepped inside and dropped the basket containing my few belongings on a wooden chair, then ran my hand over a dusty table. A bed had been placed against the wall, and a bench held several empty baskets—storage, I supposed, for clothing or any goods I might obtain while living here.

I had brought very little from home. Only two tunics, an extra pair of sandals, four wooden hair needles, and a set of carved hair combs. If Salome wanted me to weave or sew for her, she would have to furnish the materials. But since she was the king's sister, surely she could get whatever she wanted. Everyone knew the king had amassed great riches by stealing the property of the Jewish families who resisted his authority. Ever since the Romans declared the Idumaean our king, even to speak against Herod meant placing one's life and family in great danger. Even now, my aunt warned me, the king had spies scattered throughout the city, and those spies were ruthless.

Some said the spies had grown wealthy themselves because of their work for the king.

I dropped onto the bed and tested the strength of the ropes beneath the straw mattress, then stood. What was I supposed to do now? An older woman might be content to sit and wait to be called, but I yearned to be active. And I was curious—where did Aristobulus live? And might I get to ride his beautiful horse?

Hadn't Salome said I should look around and make myself familiar with the palace, in case my mistress asked me to run an errand or fetch something from one of the other rooms?

I smoothed my braid, checked to make certain my tunic was still clean, and slipped out of my room. I yearned to explore everything but could not find the courage to venture out of the servants' quarters. Perhaps later when I had grown more confident of my mistress and her trust in me.

I quietly descended the stone steps and realized the servants' building was located next to the kitchen area. Across an alley, servants bustled in a large room that opened to the alley, and women wore knotted cloth around their heads to blot the perspiration streaming from their red faces. Two women prepared chickens at a long table, sending wispy feathers floating through the air as one of them plucked and the other chopped off yellow feet and sectioned featherless bodies.

One of the women jerked her chin toward me. "Looking for something, girl?"

I shook my head. "Just exploring."

The woman smirked. "Best explore elsewhere or you'll find yourself set to work."

Embarrassed, I left the kitchen and returned to the alley. A half-dozen chickens scattered at my approach, and beyond them I saw a building occupied by workers and horses. Three carriages stood near the building, and behind them shirtless men shoveled manure into the back of an open wagon. Nothing much to see there.

That left only the largest building, the palace. Perhaps I could tiptoe through it, moving quickly, staying in the wide public halls. I might see important people, even Aristobulus.

I lifted my skirt and stepped carefully through a series of puddles, not wanting to track mud or chicken dung into the king's house. I stopped at the end of the alley and looked around. An open courtyard stood in front of me, and the thought of crossing it to enter the king's house made a cold panic skip down my spine.

I would explore the palace some other day, I decided.

I woke the next morning when a chorus of roosters heralded the rising sun. For a moment I did not remember where I was, until I recognized the small room with its sparse furnishings. Salome. My mistress. Did she need me? How would I know if she wanted me?

Dressing quickly, I went downstairs in search of water. I found a woman filling buckets to water the horses, so I used the well water to splash my face. Then I followed the slaves until I found the privy.

Most of the morning passed with no word from my mistress. I went to her chamber and stood outside the door, but I never heard her voice or sounds of movement. I returned to my room and waited for a slave to summon me, yet no one came.

I grew hungry. Driven by hunger pangs, I walked downstairs to the alley and loitered near the kitchen doorway until one of the workers took pity on me and pressed bread and cheese into my hand. "Don't expect your mistress to feed you," she said, her eyes smiling above her flushed cheeks. "Whatever you need, you'll have to seek for yourself."

When at last a slave came to my room and said my mistress wanted me, I hurried to Salome's chamber, determined to perform my work—whatever it was—in a way that pleased her. I found Salome at her dressing table, which was covered with an assortment of cosmetics and jewelry.

"Good morning, Zara." She gave me a quick smile. "Did you sleep well?"

I nodded.

"Good. Every morning about this time I want you to bring me grapes, wine, and cheese. You can get them from the kitchens, and you may enter after knocking. Even if I do not answer, enter anyway and leave the food on this table."

I took a step toward the door.

"Not now! This morning I want you to watch so you can learn how I like to do things. Now." She gestured to the items on the table. "Do you know how to apply cosmetics?"

I shook my head. Neither Ima nor Aunt Rimonah had painted their faces.

Salome sighed. "Watch carefully as this slave applies my cosmetics. Tomorrow I will expect you to do it."

I nodded and moved closer, not wanting to miss anything.

The slave picked up a jar of what appeared to be crushed green stone mixed with oil. Flecks of gold shone in the mixture, and after the slave applied a thin layer to Salome's eyelids, my mistress's eyes shone like sunlight on moving waters.

"You must smooth it carefully," Salome said. "You do not want lumps, which might fall into my eyes."

"No lumps," I echoed.

I watched as the slave applied black kohl to Salome's eyelashes, olive oil to her unruly eyebrows, and a white powder to her face. When she had finished, she combed Salome's thick hair, then applied fragrant oil to her hands and worked it into the length.

"Now." Salome flicked the back of her hand toward the slave, who bowed and left the room. "You said you know how to do hair."

I nodded.

"Good. Let me see what you can do with this mess on my head."

I took a few deep breaths and stepped forward, my heart pounding against my ribs. What if my fingers forgot what to do? Salome's hair was thicker and curlier than Aunt Rimonah's or my mother's, so what if my favorite styles would not work on my mistress?

But as soon as I thrust my fingers into her silky hair, my fears vanished. My hands always felt at home in hair, and I realized that braiding Salome's might be easier than doing my aunt's or my mother's. My mistress's hair seemed easier to grip and less slippery.

"Look at this." Salome handed me a coin with a woman's profile engraved on it.

I blinked at the coin, having never seen one like it. We had coins in Judea, but none of them had images of people on them.

"That is a Roman coin," Salome said, smiling at the woman pictured there. "I want you to do my hair like hers."

"Who is she?" I bit my tongue, knowing I had spoken too freely. I did not look up, afraid I would meet a stern glance, but Salome did not seem to mind.

"According to Herod, she is a valiant Roman woman called Fulvia, and she was once married to Mark Antony. She may be dead now, but no matter. I would have you do my hair like hers."

I studied the coin more closely. The woman's hair had been made high over her forehead, and a braid ran from the highest point of her head to the center of the back where the length had been coiled into a bun. "I can do this," I said, returning the coin to my mistress. "But I will need time."

"Time I have." Salome leaned back in her chair and propped her feet on a low stool. "I am in no hurry."

While Salome hummed and studied her nails, I ran a comb through her hair and divided it into two sections, front and back. From the back section I made three braids, then pulled them together and curled them into a bun. A large wooden needle held it in place while I threaded another needle with wool the same color as Salome's auburn hair. I then sewed the bun and anchored it to the center of her head.

The front section would be trickier. I held the strands in one hand and ran my comb toward the scalp with the other, creating an airy mass atop her forehead. I pulled the ends together, divided them into three parts, and created a loose braid. I sewed this braid to the flat section of hair on her head and then tacked the end of the braid to the bun just above her neck.

I did not realize how tense I had been until I stepped back and felt my shoulders sag in relief. Whether or not she liked it, I had done my best. "All finished, mistress."

Salome, who could not have been as nonchalant as she seemed, sat up and beheld her reflection in the looking brass on the table. She turned her head left and right, running her fingers over the back of her head, testing the bun's solidity. "Very good," she murmured. "Very good indeed."

She turned to look at me, her brows rising in a delicate arch. "Today I would like you to go through the house and learn all you can about how it operates," she said, her voice smooth. "My brother plans to build his new palace soon. This house simply cannot hold all of us, so the new palace will be larger, grander, and far more suited to his station. While it is being built, Herod will rely on me for ideas and instruction. I, in turn, will rely on you. You must be my eyes and ears among the servants. So interview them, speak to the slaves, find out what they do and how they would change things to make the house run more efficiently. I suggest you begin with the older servants; they have been around the longest and know what works best."

I blinked at the enormity of my assigned task, then nodded. "I will do my best, mistress."

"I know this is a big job for one so young," Salome added, "but your youth may work in our favor, because your presence should intimidate no one. Remember, Herod's palace must be as grand as those in Rome. Your master—my brother—will not settle for second best, because the Romans will judge his ability by what he produces. Herod's palace should be amazing."

"I will do what I can to please you."

She eyed me a moment, looking from the top of my head to my sandaled feet. "You are a pretty girl, but you must improve your appearance if you are to represent me. Report to the women who sew in the work house and have them make you new tunics—at least one for every day of the week. I have some jewelry I will give you, as well. Nothing expensive, but far better than your being unadorned."

"Thank . . . thank you, mistress."

She dipped her chin in a curt nod. "I have given you enough to do today. Away with you now. You may begin your interviews. Remember what is good and make note of what is inadequate. Every day we will discuss these things while you do my hair."

I bent my knee in what I hoped was a respectful display of submission, then slipped out of the room.

CHAPTER EIGHTEEN

Zara

For the next several months I worked hard to understand my place in the king's household. I spent a great deal of time in Salome's chamber, of course, learning her tastes and quirks. I learned she liked sweets, red wine, and men who made her laugh. She did not like haughty women, giggly girls of any rank, and she most especially did not like her sister-in-law, the queen.

When I was not talking to other servants or helping Salome, I worked hard to hone my ability to arrange hair. I practiced braiding threads, strands of wool, and straw, and soon I was able to create braids without thinking. I studied Roman coins whenever Salome could procure them, especially those with images of women. Salome liked whatever the Romans liked and insisted her hair reflect their latest styles.

"We never know when Herod will be asked to visit Rome," she said. "So we must be able to travel with him, and I will not travel to Rome looking like a Judean peasant."

I also learned my way around the palace—which apartments housed the king, his wife and her entourage, including her mother and brother, which housed the king's brother and uncle, and which belonged to Salome. I learned which servants were responsible for which members of the king's family, which cared for the queen's three children—a number that seemed destined to increase every year—and which cared for the king's dogs and horses. I became friends with the girls who managed the flocks outside the palace kitchen, as well as the chicken girl and the shepherdess who kept the sheep and goats.

I felt more at home with the servants and slaves than I did the royal family, though I longed for the day when I would see Aristobulus and his horse again. Surely HaShem would arrange things so that my mother's dreams could come true. She was a good woman and deserved to have her prayers answered.

But I did not have much time for such dreams or prayers, because when I was not doing something for Salome, others in the palace were all too willing to find chores for me. I might have been able to refuse them—after all, I was not their servant—but when someone needed my help, I could not refuse to aid them, small though my effort might be.

As for my mistress, I cannot say I disliked her. Many of my servant friends ridiculed their mistresses when we talked together, but I did not want to mock Salome. She was kind to me, gently correcting me when necessary, and quick to praise when I learned from my mistakes. She understood my youth and inexperience, so she did not command me the way other members of the royal family ordered their servants about. Whenever Mariamne or Alexandra barked orders or openly insulted their servants and slaves, Salome would often look at me, her head shaking almost imperceptibly as her eyes narrowed in disapproval.

As I interviewed other palace servants, I met Mava, a young woman who served as handmaid to the queen. Mava was a freeborn servant, and from her bearing I could tell she had come from an influential Jewish family. Her nails were manicured, her hair beautifully braided, her clothing finer than what the sewing ladies made for servants. She had been chosen as Mariamne's handmaid when the queen was first betrothed to Herod, so Mava had been part of the queen's retinue for over six years.

But she was not so highborn she would not speak to a simple Jewish girl, so I found her a valuable friend and a reliable source of information. Whenever I needed to know something about how things should be done, all I had to do was ask Mava.

One afternoon, while Mava and I relaxed in the courtyard, I mentioned that Salome seemed more like an ordinary person than a royal.

Mava's eyes widened. "You do not know?" she laughed.

"Know what?"

She leaned against me and sighed. "Sometimes I forget how young you are. Salome and Herod *are* ordinary people, or at least they were until a few years ago. Their father, Antipater, was a servant in King Hyrcanus's household."

"Like a manservant?"

"At first he was in charge of the treasury. But the king was gentle and unassertive, so he allowed Antipater to control the soldiers, too. Antipater helped Julius Caesar in Egypt, and he rebuilt the walls of Jerusalem. So his sons—Herod and Phasael— were made governors of territories in Judea, and after that they became even more powerful."

I nodded, but only the name Herod meant anything to me. "I've never heard of Phasael."

"Probably because he's dead."

"Or Antipater."

"Murdered." She lowered her voice and leaned closer. "One of the Jews close to Hyrcanus did not like Idumaeans. So one night, while at dinner with the king, he had a servant put poison

121

into Antipater's wine. He died later that night . . . in your mistress's arms."

I gasped as my mind filled with the image of a frantic Salome with her dying father. "Who was that horrible man?"

Mava looked around before answering. "Malchus. He's dead now—also murdered—but no matter. After all that, the Romans gave Herod and Phasael the authority to rule, and now Herod rules Judea alone. So his family did not start out as royal; the Romans made them so."

I told Mava I had to go, as the hour was getting late. Climbing the stairs to my mistress's chamber, I felt nothing but sorrow for Herod's beautiful sister. She was about the same age as my mother, yet she had no children. Her brother had married her to an old man who rarely spent time with her, and though she lived in a house filled with people, she often seemed lonely. What sort of life did Salome want? Did it differ from the life her brother had arranged?

I did not know, but I found myself praying that somehow HaShem might use me to bring my mistress a measure of happiness.

CHAPTER NINETEEN

Salome

I propped my chin in my hand as I watched Joseph follow my handmaid out of my bedchamber. I was not certain what my husband had in mind when he engaged her. I winced to think he wanted to give me the Jewish girl to command because I could not command my sister-in-law. Regardless, I found myself liking the child. How could I not? Zara was still innocent, and thus far my heart felt nothing but tenderness toward her. She always seemed agreeable and willing to please, and what woman would not appreciate someone who honestly wanted to help?

I rose from my stool, wrapped a himation around my unsettled hair, and went in search of my brother. Despite Herod's brilliant renovations, the palace that had served several Judean high priests and kings seemed small and dilapidated, and I could not wait to be away from it.

Time enough for the new palace later. First Herod had to solidify his grip on the throne, make himself indispensable to Mark Antony, and father enough sons to ensure a dynasty. My job was to help him do those things by making sure no one stood in his way.

I walked to the wing that housed the king's apartment, climbed the curving staircase, and paused outside the door to Herod's bedchamber. Another woman stood there as well, and my spine stiffened when she turned—Alexandra.

"Salome."

Since she greeted me without a single extraneous word, I responded with the same economy of speech. "Alexandra."

"Today is a day for celebration." The woman brought her hands together. "Today my son will be anointed as high priest. Surely this will endear the king to all the people of Judea."

My mouth twisted in bitter amusement. "A day for celebration indeed."

The woman was right about one thing—the people would be thrilled to have Aristobulus as high priest because he was handsome, with curly dark hair, snapping eyes, and a well-formed body. The people were accustomed to seeing old men in the office of high priest, and to see a youth with only the merest suggestion of a beard . . .

"The people will be pleased," I admitted. "Though I'm not certain the Jews will love the king any better. Some might believe this was your idea."

She gave a soft laugh. "I daresay Mariamne suggested it to the king first, and he granted her request on account of his great love for her. Ananel is no longer high priest, and Aristobulus holds the post he should have inherited months ago." Her smile broadened. "Such is the power of love."

A sharp retort sprang to my lips, but at that instant the door flew open and Herod walked out of the chamber, his head down, his eyes intent on the stairs. He did not pause to speak to me or his mother-in-law but hurried down the steps, his sandals slapping the polished stone.

Leaving Alexandra to gloat with her daughter, I hurried after my brother.

CHAPTER TWENTY

Zara

Summer eased into fall, the farmers went into the fields to collect the harvest, and the Feast of Tabernacles began. The priests offered up seventy bullocks for the seventy known nations of the world, and on the festival's first night the Levites lit the four golden candelabra that stood on bases fifty cubits high. Each candelabrum had four branches, and each branch supported a large basin in which rested a twisted wick made from holy garments the priests had worn in previous years. When the great wicks were lit, the intense light brightened much of the city, including the courtyard of the king's palace.

I stood in the courtyard and pressed my hands together, remembering Sukkot celebrations with my mother and father. The city streets were always crowded at the Feast of Tabernacles, for Jewish pilgrims came from all over the world to celebrate with other Jews. Makeshift booths lined the streets, propped up by walls, sticks, and carts, all of us leaving our homes for temporary dwellings lest we forget how we once wandered in the wilderness.

Herod's household kept the commandment, but their tents

were nothing like the ones I used to make with Ima and Abba. My mother had used rough cloth or a lambskin, and Salome instructed her servants to create tents of colorfully striped fabrics and hang them from elaborate systems of poles and ropes. By the time they had finished, the tents were works of art, and even Mariamne was impressed. For a week the royal family moved their chairs and beds into the Sukkot tents, where they feasted on delicious fruits, roasted lamb, and the finest wines.

As the week of celebration drew to a close, my mistress said she would not need me on the last day of the festival, though I was welcome if I wanted to join her for a trip to Jericho. I bit my lip and considered briefly, then said I would like to visit my family while she was away. She nodded, apparently pleased with my answer.

I left the palace before sunrise on the last day of the festival and walked briskly through the cobbled streets until I reached Aunt Rimonah's home. I knocked on the door and let myself in, waking them. Ima and Rimonah were startled to see me, but after exclaiming over my fine clothes and my generally healthful appearance, they hugged me through happy tears.

"We have missed you," Aunt Rimonah said.

"But here you are," Ima added, pinching my cheek. "Growing tall and looking as rosy as a sunset."

The words seemed out of place in this house, for Ima did not look rosy or well. She was thinner than when I had last seen her. Her legs were like branches and her arms like twigs. Her skin seemed to hang on her bones, and when I looked up and saw Rimonah studying me with an intense expression, I realized my aunt was waiting for me to see what she did not want to tell me: Ima was dying.

"It was good of you to come," Rimonah whispered, bending close as she squeezed my arm. "You have answered your mother's prayers."

My heart had contracted so tightly I could barely draw breath to speak, yet I forced the words over my tongue, "I am glad I could come."

Ima would not want me to be sad on what might be our last day together, so I shoved my sad thoughts into a corner of my mind and determined to be cheerful on this festival day. Aunt Rimonah had procured the citron, palm, myrtle, and willow branches for the Sukkot celebration, so we bound the branches together for our visit to the Temple.

"You have come just in time," Rimonah said. "We are going to the water-drawing ceremony. This will be the first time we see the ceremony performed by our new high priest."

My heart began to race. "Aristobulus?"

Rimonah nodded. "We have not seen much of him. Either I have no one to carry your mother inside or the crowds are too large and we find ourselves in the back of the sanctuary. I am hoping things will be different today."

I nodded. "I might be able to help."

Rimonah tilted her head. "You?"

"My mistress . . . I could use her name. Perhaps we could go through another entrance."

Rimonah's eyes glowed. "We would be grateful if you would try."

Our neighbors, Rachel and Reuben, agreed to travel to the Temple with us. Reuben, whose broad shoulders and thick arms were used to carrying sheep, carried my mother as we joined the stream of worshipers on their way to the special service.

We knew what had already transpired on this holy day. Before daybreak, as I was walking to Aunt Rimonah's house, a group of Levites and priests had gone down to the spring of Siloam and filled a large golden ewer with fresh water. After the morning sacrifice, the high priest would pour the water on the altar to cleanse it. If we timed our arrival perfectly, we should enter the Temple about the same time as the Levites' procession. Aristobulus should be with them, so we might see him . . .

All around us, the people buzzed with happy congratulations and whispers. "At last! We will celebrate Sukkoth with a priest from the royal family!" "A true Jew, not a foreigner!" "Salome Alexandra must be smiling to see her great-grandson carrying the golden ewer!"

We did not see the Levites, but when we reached the Temple I pointed to a small door near the front of the sanctuary. While no crowds stood outside it, I knew it opened to an area near the altar. It would be a good place to observe the water ritual, and from there we would all see Aristobulus.

A Levite at the door frowned as we approached. "Who are you?" he asked, looking at Reuben.

"Please, sir," I said.

He looked down at me, a suggestion of annoyance marking his face.

"I am servant to Salome, sister to Herod the king. This woman is my mother, and she would like to see the water ceremony." I lifted my chin, daring to look directly at him, and something in my words or attitude must have worked on his heart. After only a moment's hesitation, he stepped aside and opened the door, allowing us—me, Ima, Rimonah, Rachel, and Reuben— to enter.

The area before the altar was already crowded. Reuben shouldered his way through, with the rest of us following in his wake. Finally we stopped at a place where we would have an unobstructed view of our new high priest, our *cohen gadol.*

We had just settled in our places when the trumpets sounded and the Levitical procession entered the Temple. The people burst into enthusiastic shouting, their lulavs waving as Aristobulus led the way to the altar, carrying the widemouthed pitcher of gold.

I knew I ought to appreciate everything—the musicians, the gleaming candelabra, the other Levites—and yet I could not tear my eyes from our handsome high priest. Never had such a beautiful man filled out those robes, I was certain of it. His cheeks glowed with youth, his curls clung to his forehead, damp with perspiration from his walk, and his teeth shone whole and white against his tanned skin. The crowd roared their approval as he came in, which only broadened his smile, and when he climbed the steps to the altar, the sound of the adoring people nearly drowned out the musicians, which were playing with all their might.

Then the high priest stepped forward, his eyes sparkling above his dark blue robes, his height making him easily visible over the altar. He offered the prayers, lifted the laver, and poured the water onto the sacred stone. But instead of responding with prayers of their own, the people chanted his praises: "Blessed be Aristobulus of the Hasmoneans! Blessed be the heir of Judah Maccabaeus! May HaShem make you fruitful as a tree planted by living waters!"

The young man responded with a smile that only enhanced his natural appeal. I gasped and studied his face, marveling that any man could appear so pleasing even from a distance. He looked very much like his sister, and no wonder. At only seventeen, his face had not yet developed the paunchy flesh and heavy jowls that marked most older men.

But his beauty was more than external. I had seen him up close, and from living at the palace where I talked with those who served him, I knew him to be kind and good, a student of the Torah, and a youth devoted to serving HaShem.

All things were still possible, and my mother's dream might yet come true. One day Aristobulus and I might meet. We might like each other. We might marry . . .

I lifted my voice and joined the chorus of praise that echoed against the timbers of the Temple ceiling. Only after Aristobulus departed, a train of jubilant Levites and priests following him, did the supportive shouting subside.

I turned, about to lead our small party home, when my eyes happened to glance at the balcony where the king and his family sat. They remained in place, their faces stiff and pale, and though Salome and the brothers wore awkward, unnatural smiles, the look on King Herod's face was anything but joyful or supportive.

Chapter Twenty-One

Salome

With one glance at my brother, I realized he had not been pleased by the events of the morning. He had hoped Aristobulus's appointment to the office of high priest would placate the people and help them love their new king, but their noisome praise at the Temple service was for Aristobulus alone. Their shouts were salt in an open wound. My brother wanted nothing more than to be loved by his people, who looked upon him with scorn while openly adoring the boy. And what had the boy done to merit such adoration? Nothing. Nothing but to be born handsome, tall, and Hasmonean.

We left the balcony where we had observed the water ceremony and walked out to where our litter-bearers waited. The king's guards kept the crowds away, and I was glad Herod would not have to hear the praise spilling from Jewish lips.

I looked up when someone nudged my arm. Alexandra, her face wreathed in a smile, was glowing as she walked up with Mariamne. "Did he not do an outstanding job?" she said, her voice pitched a note higher than usual. "Your brother seemed so at home next to the altar, Mariamne. HaShem obviously intended him to be our high priest."

She inclined her head toward Herod, who walked ahead of us. "You were wise, O king, to remove Ananel and appoint Aristobulus as our cohen gadol. And I am delighted to continue our celebration at my palace in Jericho. The pool will feel lovely in this heat, and my servants are preparing a grand feast."

Mariamne left her mother's side and walked to Herod, her eyes shining as she took his arm. "Please say you will ride with us, my husband. I would love to talk about Aristobulus."

Herod sighed as he glanced over his shoulder and caught my gaze. "What can I say?" Then he looked at his wife. "I will attend your mother's feast, Mariamne, and I will go to Jericho. But I will ride with my men."

I steeled myself for the afternoon to come. At Alexandra's house, which felt like enemy territory, I would have to pretend to have a good time while Alexandra and Mariamne flaunted their success, their wealth, and their family nobility. My brothers and I would bear their subtle barbs without comment, but by the end of the day, we would all be snappish and ready to return to Jerusalem.

Perhaps I would skip the feast and nap in my chamber instead. Zara could bring me something from the kitchen when she returned.

After all, what was it Solomon once said? "Better a meal of vegetables where there is love than a fattened ox where there is hatred."

~~~~~~

When I told Joseph I wanted to stay behind, he responded with unusual curtness. "You cannot," he said, giving me a look of disbelief. "Your absence would be noted, and we would never hear the end of it."

"What if I had a headache?"

He shook his head. "You did not have one this morning."

"They can come on suddenly."

"And they can fade away. Gird up your courage, Salome, and resign yourself to the journey. The sooner we leave, the sooner we can return."

I thought we would depart for Jericho almost immediately, but Herod had other plans. While Joseph and I waited in the entry, impatient to be under way, Herod decided to invite some Idumaean friends to join us in Jericho. He sent runners to fetch those young men, and once they arrived, breathless and sweating in the heat, he summoned them to his chamber for wine and food before the journey.

"He feeds them before we leave for a feast?" I asked Joseph, who was nearly as impatient as I. "Does he intend to spend the entire day in Jericho?"

Apparently he did, for the sun had reached its zenith by the time Herod and his friends left his chamber and headed for the stable. The men would travel on horseback, flanking Herod in his chariot. I would follow in my coach, accompanied by Joseph and one of the female slaves. I found myself wishing I'd asked Zara to return early, for her quiet company soothed me. She was still with her family, however, and it was too late to send someone to bring her back in time.

At least I would not be traveling with Mariamne, as she and her mother had gone ahead to oversee preparations for the feast. Herod might be missing his beautiful wife, but I was grateful for her absence. During the journey, at least, I would not have my ears burdened with excessive praise for the boy priest.

As I climbed into my coach, I realized the fledgling priest had probably already reached Jericho. With his head full of accolades, the lad was probably lapping up his mother's and sister's adoration. By the time we arrived, he would be sour with the stink of flattery.

Once Joseph climbed into the carriage and shut the door, I sank back on the cushions and closed my eyes, hoping the day would pass quickly.

Alexandra's winter home had been known as the twin palaces of Jericho, the two identical palaces Salome Alexandra built for her sons, Hyrcanus and Aristobulus. Her sons had been rivals in everything, and despite her efforts to deal with them evenly, the young men were never satisfied with what they received from her. Even at the queen's death, her chosen heir, Hyrcanus, was attacked almost immediately by his brother, who coveted the throne.

Now Alexandra ruled over the entire complex, the two palaces having been combined into one grand estate. The setting was lovely, and as I stepped out of the carriage I couldn't help admiring the stately two-story buildings. Joseph and I waited for Herod and his men to dismount and enter the complex and then we followed.

The first structure featured an inner courtyard with an open reception area at its southern end. Alexandra had prepared a feast in the reception room, where dozens of white-robed servants stood with heavy trays, waiting to serve. Several upholstered couches had been scattered about the room, with those near the center arranged in a semicircle. Herod naturally took the seat at the center, Mariamne sharing his couch. Aristobulus, now wearing a simple white robe that set off his olive skin and dark hair, sat across from them, his mother at his right hand.

While I did not like Mariamne, Alexandra, or this young priest, I could not deny the young man was handsome enough to awaken a carnal desire in any woman with a heartbeat. For an instant I wondered if Herod might be convinced to let me marry the boy. But no, for not even the Law would allow such a marriage. The high priest had to marry a virgin, and if by some miracle I could be proclaimed a virgin, another Hasmonean-Herodian coupling might produce an heir to rival Herod's children, and my brother would not tolerate a rival.

And I would not let him.

No, young Aristobulus would undoubtedly marry some devout Jewish virgin from an upstanding family. Alexandra would arrange everything.

Herod's noisy friends settled onto the outer couches, and Alexandra's nostrils flared as she studied the crew who had arrived with us. I was sure she wanted to rebuke Herod for bringing them. But they were the king's friends and who dared rebuke the king? Herod had invited them, and a good hostess could only welcome them, even as they indulged themselves at her expense.

The thought made my mouth curve in a wry smile. Perhaps that was why Herod invited them. If Alexandra wanted to flaunt her beautiful palace, her wealth, and her illustrious history, let her show off to a group of young men who knew little about her and cared nothing for her.

My gaze shifted to Mariamne, who said little and ate slowly, keeping her eyes downcast. She fairly dripped disapproval of the raucous men scattered throughout the room, and yet what could she say? Her brother, Israel's own high priest, was laughing heartily at their jokes, and his countenance was flushed and merry. The lad had to be relieved—he had pulled off his first water ceremony without any mistakes, the people had loved him, and his future success seemed assured. No wonder Alexandra's son was in high spirits.

"Aristobulus, have more wine." Herod took a pitcher from a servant's tray and offered it to the lad. "Drink up. You deserve it."

Aristobulus, his eyes shining, held out his cup as Herod sloshed wine into the vessel. I studied my brother. He had appeared as

sober as an executioner before we left Jerusalem, and I doubted
he had imbibed on the journey. How had he become inebriated?

I lifted a questioning brow when he caught my eye. He only
smiled and lifted the pitcher higher. "We drink today to celebrate the marvelous success of Aristobulus, my brother-in-law
and Israel's latest high priest. May his office continue forever!"

A half-dozen cups were raised in acknowledgment of the
king's wish, and a roomful of thirsty men shouted Aristobulus's name, though not as eagerly as the people this morning.

After we had all eaten our fill, after Herod had plied his
friends and Aristobulus with so much wine that not a man
among them remained steady on his feet, Alexandra sent the
servants away. "Thank you all for honoring my home with your
presence," she said, inclining her head toward the king. "Now
enjoy the pool and the courtyard while I take the ladies to rest
in the shade on the eastern portico."

I glanced at Herod—did I have to sit with those women? I
would much rather remain with the men than talk about servants and children and household matters.

My brother did not meet my eye. Instead he nodded to one
of his Idumaean friends. His cheeks flushed, the young man
stood and clapped Aristobulus's shoulder. "Come, my friend.
The sun is hot, and I believe the pool is calling our names."

"Go, go." Herod waved them off. "I am not much for rough-
housing. Go have fun, all of you."

I watched, still chafing at the thought of joining the women,
as the Idumaean led Herod's friends away. Aristobulus, unsteady
on his feet, draped his arm around another man's shoulder and
stumbled toward the courtyard.

When the sound of their voices had faded, I rose and went
to Herod, dropping into Mariamne's empty place. "It is not
like you, brother, to dismiss your audience. Why are you not
swimming with your guests?"

He gave me a distracted glance, then stared at the doorway through which they had disappeared. "I shall not swim today. Nor you, eh, Joseph?"

My husband, who had been snoring on his couch, jerked awake. "What? Did I miss something?"

"Nothing," I assured him. I looked back at Herod. "You are king, so do what you will. But please tell me I do not have to sit with those women. I have heard enough about the Hasmoneans today; I do not need them to tell me again how they are noble and highly esteemed."

Herod nodded and gave a half smile. "Then remain with me, sister, and let us talk about the future."

I snorted. "What have we to do with the future? It lies beyond our reach."

"Not always, little one." His hand fell upon mine. "Sometimes we can affect the future by taking action today."

"So you say." I pulled free of his grasp and moved to the window, which offered a view of the pool and courtyard. The men had pulled off their light summer tunics and were swimming naked, the sun burnishing their skin.

My eyes gravitated to Aristobulus, who would have been the center of attention in any gathering. He stood in the center of the pool, where Herod's friends had encircled him.

"I'm next!" one of the men shouted. While Aristobulus grinned like a drunken fool, the young man reached out and pushed down on the high priest's head, submerging him. The man held him under until Aristobulus's arms rose and smacked at the man's hand, freeing himself.

Aristobulus surfaced, openmouthed, dripping and gasping for breath. "I do not understand this game," he said, slinging water from his hair. "When do I get to hold one of *you* under?"

"Not yet," another young Idumaean said, striding through the water. His arm swung up, his hand planted firmly on the high priest's head, and his burly form rose to push Aristobulus beneath the surface.

"What sort of game is that?" I asked Herod.

"Hmm?"

"They are playing a game, but it makes no sense."

Herod waved my concern away. "They are drunk. Soon they will get out of the water and sleep like dead men."

I squinted to focus on the scene below. The Idumaeans shouted and splashed and cheered, not with the uncaring merriment of youth but with purpose in their expressions and manner. I waited, my concern rising, until Aristobulus's arms shot up from the water and slapped at yet another tormentor's hand. I expected Herod's guest to release him, but the fellow—the largest of the group—only shifted his weight and pressed harder, his biceps bulging as his other hand gripped Aristobulus's shoulder, pinning the priest against the bottom of the pool . . .

"Herod?" My voice squeaked.

The men gathered around the thrashing pair seemed to become frantic with merrymaking, shouting, counting, splashing. From the other side of the house, the Hasmonean women must have heard the noise and smiled, imagining their triumphant young priest having a good time, a well-deserved celebration after the stress of the Sukkot ceremony.

The large Idumaean youth lifted his hands and stepped back. The others stopped yelling, and silence as thick as fog rolled over the courtyard . . .

The body of Aristobulus sank deeper into the clear blue water of the pool and settled on the bottom.

〰〰〰

I could not find my voice. My feet had carried me outside on a flood of awful realization, and afterward I could not speak. Herod passed me in the hallway, and now he stood at the edge of the pool, his hands wound in his hair, tears streaking his cheeks as Joseph and the others lifted the pale body of Aristobulus and laid it on the pavement.

"An accident," one of the youths said, his voice flat and final. "It was a terrible accident."

One of the servants must have run to fetch the women, for at that moment a horrifying wail pierced the hot stillness.

"Aristobulus? That cannot be my son. He cannot be dead. He cannot be dead!"

Alexandra ran to her son's side and dropped to her knees, drawing his wet head into her lap. I watched the lad's hair curl on her lap like wet ribbons, saw the lips I had desired to caress. They had gone the color of a twilight sky.

"Oh, my son! How—how—?" Alexandra's eyes flew up like angry hornets. "You!" She fastened her hot gaze on Herod. "*You* did this."

Herod lifted his wet hands. "How could I? I loved him."

"You hated him. You cannot bear to share your glory with another, so you did this."

"Alexandra . . ." Herod spoke slowly, in a low and broken voice. "I loved the boy as you do. Is he not my brother by law? Would I harm the brother of my beloved wife?"

"You would kill your own son if it pleased you. You have no love in you, Herod. You have a rock where your heart should be—"

"Mother?" With wide, dazed eyes, Mariamne knelt at her mother's side and squeezed her arm, then looked up at Herod. "You must forgive her for the things she says. She does not mean them."

Herod sighed heavily, then sank onto a stone bench as if this sudden grief was too heavy to bear. "I am broken in spirit and heart," he said, beating his chest. "If any sort of mischief was wrought here, I will not rest until I discover it."

"No mischief," one of the Idumaeans said, a worried note in his voice. I recognized him—he was the largest youth, the one who held Aristobulus under at the end. His eyes had gone wide, and in that instant a cold reality swept over me in a terrible wave. It would be a simple matter for Herod to have this young man put to death. If Herod had ordered him to kill Aristobulus, an execution would wipe away the chief witness. Someone would pay for the crime, even if someone else had ordered it.

"It was an accident, my king." The young man's voice wavered with honest fear. "We were playing a game, holding each other under the water. He—I—we must have been drunker than we realized. But no harm was intended, especially to the cohen gadol."

Herod had closed his eyes as if he could not bear to look upon the corpse. Now he looked up and met the terrified gaze of the man who had drowned Aristobulus. "You swear," Herod said, carefully pronouncing each word. "You swear upon your life that this was an accident?"

The man fell to his knees and clasped his hands. "I swear it."

Herod glanced at Alexandra, then turned back to the young man. "Let us not double our burden of grief today. I believe you. You will not be punished."

The man looked as though he might collapse as Herod stood and walked to Mariamne. He held out his arms, waiting, until she rose and stepped into them. "My dearest love," he murmured, "I am so sorry this day has brought such tragedy, especially after such joy this morning. What can I do to ease your pain?"

Mariamne turned and stared at her brother's body. "Are we certain he is dead? Perhaps he is only cold and can be warmed . . ." She stepped forward as if she would warm him herself when Herod caught her arm.

"No, dear love. He is gone."

She turned wide eyes toward his, and in that moment she recognized the truth. She tipped her head back and screamed, and the sound of such primal agony elicited yet another cry from her mother. Herod embraced his wife and looked to me for guidance.

What advice could I give him? Surely my brother had a gift for arranging actions without taking thought for what came afterward.

"Leave them to their grief," I said, feeling suddenly weary and worn. "And let them voice their sorrow. Plan a royal funeral for the young man, and let all Judea mourn his untimely and accidental death."

Herod nodded, then hung his head and buried it in the curve of his wife's neck as he, too, lifted his voice in agonized wailing.

CHAPTER TWENTY-TWO

Zara

I heard the voices first. Voices in the distance, shouts heard over the steady *clip-clop* of horses' hooves, punctuated occasionally by screams. Mava and I stepped onto a balcony at the servants' quarters and stared at the courtyard gate as the sound grew louder. I looked at her, a question on my face, but she shrugged. "Sounds like bees," she said, her brows furrowing. "Angry bees."

The gate swung open and in rode the king's guards, surrounding a carriage. The carriage pulled up to the entrance, the door opened, and the king stepped out, extending his hand to Mariamne, who practically fell into his arms.

Behind the carriage came the king's chariot, driven by Joseph, and a rough wagon, with Alexandra sitting on the wagon bed.

Mava snorted softly. "That's a sight I never thought to see— the queen's mother sitting in a hay wagon."

As the conveyance drew closer, I could see that Alexandra sat next to a lumpy sheet, one hand pressed protectively to whatever lay beneath the fabric.

"What is—?"

"A body," Mava whispered, her hand going to her throat. "I think . . . I think someone has died."

Who? I looked at the carriage again and saw Salome step out, her face pale and her hair disheveled. So who was missing?

A moment later the king's physician came running. He climbed into the wagon, threw back the sheet, and I gasped. "Aristobulus!"

Trembling, I took in the scene with one horrified glance: the dead priest in a wagon, the king's guards silent and grave on their horses, the grieving king supporting his wife, the mother on her knees, her arms draped over the pale body of her beautiful son.

A ripple of dismay ran through the servants behind me while I remained frozen in place. My mother's dreams were dying in that rough wagon, her hopes for my future becoming as cold and dead as the corpse it carried.

"Is it the priest?"

"The king has killed him."

"Would the queen be with him if that were true?"

Mava called to a guard in the courtyard below, "What happened?"

The guard looked up at us. "The lads were playing a game in the pool," he replied in a hushed voice, "holding each other beneath the water. I thought it odd, though, that the high priest was the only one being dunked. But then all of them were addled in the head by their drinking."

"The king has gone and done it," a servant behind me muttered. When I turned around to identify the voice, no one would meet my gaze. No wonder. That sort of comment should not be owned by anyone.

But did he speak the truth? Surely not! Our king wept openly, beating his breast even as he clung to his grieving wife. Mariamne covered her face with a veil and slumped against the king, as if the weight of the world had just fallen on her slender shoulders.

Only Alexandra remained dry-eyed. As we watched, she gently covered her son's body with the sheet, then stood and regarded the king with a cold, passionless stare. Then, without a word, she pivoted and walked to the back of the wagon, where slaves helped her down. When she reached the pavement, she lifted her chin and strode away, a half-dozen servants running after her.

I brought my hand to my mouth to stifle a sob. How could this have happened to a youth with such promise? How could HaShem have allowed it? Aristobulus had been HaShem's chosen priest, and he should have led us in worship for years to come. But now he was dead, and he had not worn the high priest's robes for more than a few weeks.

I turned away from the troubling sight, unable and unwilling to speculate about what had happened. Along with Ima, I had hoped to meet Aristobulus, marry him, and bear sons who would serve HaShem as their father had. Now none of those things would happen, so why was I living in the palace? If I was not meant to marry Aristobulus, why had HaShem brought me to this place?

Tears blurred my vision as I staggered into a quiet corridor and pressed my hands to the stone wall. "Why, Adonai?" I whispered. "Why have you allowed this horrible thing?"

I lifted my wavering voice to heaven, but no one answered, nor did any sort of peace fill my heart. This grief was mine, but not mine alone. Aristobulus's mother, sister, and king would mourn his death, and all of Jerusalem would mourn with them.

CHAPTER TWENTY-THREE

Salome

Anyone who studied Herod in the days following Aristobulus's death would not doubt his deep and sincere grief. He arranged a magnificent funeral for the young man, built a tomb worthy of a king, and gathered so many treasures to place within the tomb that I worried about thieves. He hoped the people of Jerusalem—who mourned their high priest as if they mourned a member of their own family—would realize what great care and expense he had lavished on the Hasmonean heir. They *did* realize he was doing a great deal to honor one of the last Hasmoneans, but his actions did not soften their hearts toward him. When the people learned their young, healthy, handsome high priest had died among Herod's Idumaean friends, they spread the rumor that the boy had been murdered on the king's command. "The guilty purse spends freely," they whispered.

In the quiet of my own heart, I wondered if Herod could have been desperate enough, jealous enough, to have the youth murdered. Was the rumor true?

Alexandra certainly believed it. Though she would not dare publicly accuse my brother of murdering her son, she did not appear in the king's presence for weeks, claiming she would not leave her chambers until she had finished mourning. Her suspicions undoubtedly colored Mariamne's attitude, for although the queen could not refuse to come when the king summoned her, she no longer smiled at his jokes or blushed at his compliments.

She also refused to meet my eye. In the throne room, at banquets, and in passing, she remained a pale wraith at Herod's side, eating nothing, saying little, and smiling not at all. She took to wearing only white garments, which exaggerated her ghostly appearance, and let her hair tumble over her shoulders like a madwoman's.

I understood grief—I had lost two brothers and a father, so I was well acquainted with that state of mind. But I also knew Alexandra and Mariamne well enough to understand they would not mourn quietly but would take some sort of action against my brother. What would they do? What could they do from within the walls of the palace?

In private moments, after Zara had done my hair and left me alone, I sat and stared out my window, wondering if Herod had ordered his friends to kill Aristobulus. Given the circumstances— the sudden invitation to his friends, the free-flowing wine, the timing, the place—my brother could easily have arranged an unofficial execution. But Herod would not do such a thing unless he felt it absolutely necessary. He did not kill without reason. He had killed many men in war, and the situation with Alexandra was a war of strategy and necessity. If she had not insisted on forcing her young son to the forefront, if she had not insisted that Herod break tradition and dismiss Ananel, none of this would have happened.

Instead, like a commanding general, she planned her strategy, she made her move, and Herod had to respond.

I might never know if Herod had given the order for murder, but if he had, I could understand. He had been forced to act.

Weeks passed. Herod reappointed Ananel as high priest and began meeting with certain members of his court in his private chambers—meetings from which Joseph and I were excluded. "I do not want to bother you with everything," he replied when I caught him and asked about his reclusiveness. "In truth, I expect to make a journey soon, and I am making preparations for my time away."

My uneasiness swelled to alarm. "Where are you going?"

"I expect I will be going to Alexandria." Herod gave me a wintry smile. "Or wherever Antony is. I'm sure Alexandra's letter has reached him by now."

I caught my breath. Of course she would write Antony. She had written him before, begging him to force Herod to bend to her will, but this time she would demand justice for her dead son. Her letter would be filled with accusations, false reports, exaggerations . . .

"Will you take witnesses with you?" I asked. "Some of the men who were in Jericho that day?"

Herod glanced over his shoulder to make certain we were alone, then guided me to a secluded corridor. "I must not look guilty." He leaned against the wall and drew a deep breath. "I will go with a clear conscience and take gifts for Antony and his children. I have already gathered several hundred talents."

I gasped at the vast amount. A king's ransom, surely.

"I worry about you, brother. While you are away, we can do nothing to help you—"

"Do not worry your pretty head, sister. I am leaving Joseph in charge. I will not be gone more than a few weeks. But"—he lifted a warning finger—"if you must do something, keep a watchful eye on my bride and her mother. I have heard that Alexandra is so distraught that she has considered destroying herself. We cannot have that."

"Why not?" The question was callous and cruel, but still it

slipped from my tongue. "Wouldn't her death solve many of your problems?"

"Salome." Herod rebuked me with a stern look, then caught my hand. "Can you imagine your grief if something happened to *our* mother?"

My eyes welled with tears as the question hung in the space between us. My mother had always seemed as enduring as an oak. Though she was not as active as she had been in years past, she was always available to listen and give advice. I could not imagine losing her.

"I thought so." Herod's voice softened. "Even so, Mariamne loves her mother dearly, and I love my wife. So we cannot let anything happen to Alexandra."

I clasped his hand between mine and breathed a kiss onto his fingers. "Go, then . . . and return safely. I have already lost Father and Phasael and our brother Joseph—I do not want to lose you, too."

"Fear not," he said, giving me a relaxed smile with a great deal of confidence behind it. "I am not worried about facing Antony."

⁓⁓⁓⁓

Later that night, Joseph escorted me to my chamber and dismissed the servants. When we were alone, he sank to a stool and regarded me with bleary eyes. "Your brother asks too much of me," he said, attempting a weak smile. "I am getting up in years, and I cannot keep up with him."

"Reigning in his stead will not be too hard for you," I said. "Your chief concern will be keeping an eye on the queen and her scheming mother. Yet this arrangement will only last a short time. Herod will return, you'll see. He will not let himself be defeated by Cleopatra."

"Ah, Salome, you think everything is so simple." He gripped

his knees and drew a deep breath. "But that is not all Herod has asked of me."

I sank to a footstool and looked up at him. "What else has he asked?"

Joseph shook his head. "I should not say."

"Please, husband. If it is important, should I not know? Perhaps I can be of help."

He drew another ragged breath. "If Herod is killed while in Alexandria, I am to kill Mariamne. Herod says he loves her so much that he cannot bear the thought of being without her in the afterlife."

I listened, blinking, then laughed aloud. "Is that what he told you?"

"Of course."

"Herod does not believe in the afterlife—at least I've never heard him speak of such a thing. There must be another reason."

Joseph chewed his lower lip. "Perhaps you are right. He also mentioned how much he distrusts Alexandra. Apparently Antony's letter mentioned a portrait of Mariamne—an image commissioned and sent by Alexandra."

My shoulders slumped as the pieces of the puzzle came together. Of course! Alexandra was dangling her daughter before Mark Antony as incentive to execute my brother. *If you eliminate Herod, his wife can be yours.*

I closed my eyes to consider the situation. Cleopatra might like to know about the portrait Alexandra had sent Mark Antony . . . or did she know already? If she did know, she might want Herod to return to Judea alive and well, for not even the wealthy queen of Egypt would want Mark Antony to take another woman into his bed.

No, Cleopatra would not want to kill Herod, at least not now, so why would Herod want to kill Mariamne? He did not care about the afterlife. No, what he wanted was to possess

Mariamne and not share her with anyone else. With Mariamne dead, no one else would have her, sleep with her, or love her. Herod wanted to possess her, body and soul, and if he could not, he would make certain no one else could, either.

Especially not Mark Antony.

I patted Joseph's knee. "It would be a hard order to carry out," I said, softening my voice, "so we must pray Herod returns safely to us and his wife."

"He told me he has no hope of escaping with his life."

The words lit a hot ball of frustrated anger in my heart. I had taken a vow to protect my brother, but how could I do anything with him so far away? He should take me with him on this trip. He should let *me* face Mark Antony and Cleopatra. If someone had to pay for Aristobulus's death, I would do it.

But I could say none of these things to Joseph, who no longer had the energy for a passionate defense. Nor could I say them to Herod, who would think I was overstepping my role.

I drew a deep breath and looked into my husband's dark eyes. "Be on your guard with Mariamne and her mother—they bear us no love, I am sure of it."

Joseph gave me a look of weary indignation. "I am not a fool, Salome. If Herod believes I can rule in his place, I can certainly handle two women."

"I am certain you can, but be wary nonetheless." I pressed a kiss to his forehead, then patted his shoulder and made a small gesture of dismissal, sending him on his way.

CHAPTER TWENTY-FOUR

Zara

"You sent for me?" I bowed before my mistress, who was reclining on a couch while a slave offered her a tray of delicacies.

"Yes." She picked up a honeyed date, licked the syrup from it, and dropped it back onto the tray. "My brother is in Laodicea with Antony and his Egyptian harlot, and I believe Alexandra and Mariamne are plotting something. I hear them whispering, yet they fall silent whenever I enter the room. I would know what they are planning."

I frowned. "I do not believe they would tell me anything, mistress. They know I am your—"

A flare of irritation lit Salome's eyes. "You do not walk up and *ask* them what they're planning, silly girl. You find out in more subtle ways. You hide. You eavesdrop. You question one of their slaves. Use your wits, Zara—aren't you Jews supposed to be intelligent?"

Her words stung, but I told myself she was upset and worried about her brother. The king must be risking a great deal on this visit, perhaps even his life.

I bowed and left her chamber, then walked toward the building that housed the queen's luxurious apartment. Perhaps I could visit Mava. Perhaps, if HaShem willed it, while in the queen's chamber I could learn something that would satisfy my mistress's curiosity.

I slipped through the servants' entrance at the queen's apartment and headed toward the small room where the two young princes, Alexander and Aristobulus, slept. As I had hoped, Mava was with them. She looked up and smiled when I entered.

"Has the wet nurse come and gone?" I asked, trying to appear relaxed as I leaned against the doorframe.

"Yes, though I thought she would never leave. The babies go right to sleep when their bellies are full, and that's a good thing."

I peeked into the small baskets that held the young princes. I did not know much about babies, never having had a younger sibling, but these two seemed robust and healthy. The little one, Aristobulus—even *thinking* the name brought pain—had the dark curls of his namesake.

I turned toward the main chamber from whence came the soft sound of women's voices. "Your mistress seems content."

"The ladies are always calmer when the king is away. They spend most of the day lying on their couches, eating fruit and listening to music."

I forced a smile. "My mistress is likewise aimless. She tries to keep busy, but I fear her thoughts wander too much. She has a vivid imagination."

A flicker of apprehension flowed through me when someone else entered and walked directly into the ladies' chamber. Recognizing Joseph's robust voice, I pressed my back to the wall, not wanting to be discovered by my mistress's husband.

"I have to go," I whispered. "I do not want him to see me."

"Do not worry," Mava whispered back. "He never comes into this room."

"My queen." Joseph's deep baritone echoed in the spacious

chamber beyond. "And her lovely mother. How are you two ladies faring in the king's absence?"

I pressed my finger across my lips, warning Mava to keep silent. She shrugged, wordlessly reminding me that the important people in yonder room were not likely to call for her.

"Welcome, Joseph." Mariamne's voice flowed like oil, smooth and rich. "We are well. How do you like running Judea?"

Joseph released a deep sigh, accompanied by the creak of a couch. "Life continues to vex, the people continue to whine, and the priests continue to pray for a Messiah to deliver them from Rome. Meanwhile, I pray Herod will return safely."

"Do you doubt he will?" Mariamne asked.

"I do not," Joseph responded. "But a man's fate does not always lie in his own hands. And my brother has charged me with making certain you are well looked after in his absence. He loves you very much, you know."

"So you've said." Mariamne's voice went flat. "At least ten times a day you remind me."

"Do you not believe it?"

Joseph spoke in a light, joking tone, but I did not have to see Mariamne's face to know she was not in the mood for jests. "Since my brother's death, I do not know what to believe."

"I can assure you, Herod had no part in that horrible accident—"

"How does a strong young man drown in water barely up to his chest?" Alexandra's words sizzled with fury and indignation. "Anyone who expects me to believe the king's story must think I am a fool."

Joseph sighed. "The games of young men are often rough and unruly. Many a youth has accidentally injured another, especially when they have been drinking."

"Most youths do not make a point of playing rough games with Israel's high priest." I heard the swish of garments; Alexandra must have risen from her couch.

"I swear to you," Joseph said, his voice gaining strength, "you must not doubt my brother's love for your children. He needs the support of his queen in all things, especially now."

"You mean since Antony has summoned Herod to Laodicea," Mariamne added.

"Antony summoned him to account for my son's death," Alexandra said, her words clipped. "If there is any justice in this world, Antony will take Herod's life in exchange for the life Herod took from me."

From my hiding place in the nursery, I pressed my fingertips over my lips. Alexandra was speaking treason, and if Salome or Pheroras had heard her statement, she might be arrested for disloyalty to the king.

But Joseph possessed a more forgiving nature. "How can you say such things? Herod loves you beyond reason and would never purposely bring you pain. Why, before leaving he pulled me aside and told me he loves you so much that . . ." His voice broke off.

"So much that what?" Mariamne asked.

Joseph cleared his throat. "I should not reveal the confession of a lovestruck husband."

"Joseph, I am your queen. If you have any respect for me, you will tell me what he said."

"He told me something in confidence."

"Are confidences not freely broken when the king asks for them?" This came from Alexandra, whose voice had sharpened. "Your queen asks you to respond. If you have any respect for the king and his queen, you must answer."

Joseph sighed so loudly I could hear him from the nursery. Then he spoke slowly and clearly. "The king loves you so much that he cannot bear the thought of separation from you, even in death. If Herod does not return home, he has asked me . . . asked me to make it possible for you to unite with him."

"Unite with him? What does that mean?"

An unnatural silence flooded the room and overflowed into the small space where Mava and I sat with the babies. Even little Alexander seemed to sense something significant was about to be revealed, for he jerked awake and stared at the ceiling with wide, unblinking eyes.

"What did you mean?" Mariamne's voice had gone soft with disbelief. "Has he . . . has he asked you to take my life?"

Unable to resist, I leaned toward the thin curtain that separated the nursery from the queen's chamber. Through the fabric I saw Joseph shift his weight, his face flaming.

"Only if he dies. The situation sounds more dire than it is, my queen, because we know Herod will not die. I only mentioned his request because I wanted to assure you of the king's great love. He adores you so much that—"

"He would kill me." The queen looked at her mother. "Have you ever heard of such love?"

"I have not and cannot believe he would ask such a thing of our dear Joseph." Alexandra gave their visitor a wobbly smile. "Would he steal a second child from me?"

Stammering, Joseph stood. "The king loves you greatly, my queen—that is all I intended to say. Do not worry. I have every confidence in our king. He will have a productive meeting with Antony and return to us. All will be well, you shall see." He turned and quit the chamber, his garments whirling as he left the two women alone.

Realizing that I was about to witness an explosion of raw feminine outrage, I gave Mava a rueful smile. "I must return to my mistress," I whispered, moving toward the servants' door. "May HaShem keep us—all of us—safe."

It was not until I arrived at Salome's chamber that I realized I had forgotten to gather the information she requested.

CHAPTER TWENTY-FIVE

Salome

When my handmaid returned, the girl wore the look of a child who had just broken a precious piece of art. She gave me a perfunctory bow, then stood silently, her hands clenched at her waist.

"You went to the queen's chambers?"

She nodded.

"Was Alexandra with her?"

She nodded again.

"Speak, girl, or I shall be an old woman before I learn anything."

"They were together. They spoke of nothing really, until Joseph—your husband—entered the apartment."

I straightened. "Joseph was there? Why?"

A flush traveled from the girl's cheeks to the base of her throat. "He came to check on them—he said the king had charged him with making sure they remained well in the king's absence."

That news did not explain the stricken expression on my handmaid's face.

"Did they say they were well?"

"They said . . ." Zara lowered her gaze. "They are still upset about Aristobulus. Especially Alexandra."

"We are all upset about the lad. What else did they say?"

"The queen said something about . . . well, she does not think the king truly cares for her. And Joseph assured her the king loves her deeply."

I chuckled. "Is that the only matter disturbing our queen?"

The girl shook her head.

"What else, then?"

The girl's chest heaved. "Joseph said the king made him promise something before he left."

"He told them about his promise to the king?"

The girl's flush deepened as tears appeared in her eyes. "Apparently the king said that if he did not return, Joseph should . . . he should make sure Herod and Mariamne would be united in death."

I lowered my head and adopted a blank expression. Given Zara's consternation, perhaps it would be better if I pretended ignorance of Herod's order. I furrowed my brow. "Can you explain further?"

"From what I understand, the king asked Joseph to kill the queen, so she would be with him in the afterlife."

I looked away from the stammering child and focused on the wall. Had Herod given Joseph any other secret orders? Anything concerning his sister? I looked back at Zara. "Did Joseph say anything else?"

She shook her head. "He did not mean to reveal the king's secret, but the queen and her mother forced him. Afterward he left the room quickly."

"Of course he did. And how did the queen react?"

"She and her mother were quiet when I left, but I slipped away after Joseph left."

"Good," I murmured. "Thank you. You have given me much to consider."

After Zara bobbed her head and hurried out the door, I sank to my couch and pulled a pillow to my chest. Though Herod's request had surprised me when Joseph first told me about it, my brother's reasoning now made sense. He had couched his request well, speaking of eternal love and such, but I knew his true nature. His passion concerned more than the woman. Mariamne represented the royal line of Israel, and Herod did not want anyone usurping his sons' place in that line. If Herod died and Mariamne did not, Alexandra would marry her to someone else, and that man's children would sit upon the throne of Judea. Herod's sons by Mariamne would have to be set aside or die, and Herod's name, his progeny, and his immediate family would be wiped off the earth.

Herod had not asked Joseph to kill Mariamne out of love for her—he had done it out of love for his family, his children, and his future. He had not made his request to be cruel; he had meant it to be pragmatic. Practical. And protective.

I propped my chin on my hand and considered the future. If Mariamne had ever loved Herod, she certainly did not love him now. She had been cool to him ever since Aristobulus's death; now she would despise him utterly. The high-and-mighty Hasmonean princess had been put in her place. She belonged to Herod, who could cherish her or destroy her, and Joseph had unwittingly proved the point.

As for Joseph . . . I sighed heavily. Was there no end to his stupidity? Why had he told Mariamne about Herod's order? What sort of leader could be so witless? The man had outlived his usefulness, both to me and to Herod.

I moved to the window and looked out over the courtyard, where servants worked, horses whickered, and tradesmen plied their wares. For my brother's sake I would dearly love to eliminate Mariamne and Alexandra's constant meddling, but how? Send them into exile? Send *one* of them away? Either option would be difficult because Herod dearly loved Mariamne, and that lady dearly loved her mother.

Yet the situation was not entirely hopeless. Alexandra had already made trouble by attempting to sneak herself and her son out of Jerusalem in a coffin. Herod's men had caught them at the docks, yet he had demonstrated rare patience and not punished her.

But that night had revealed what a schemer she was. And as surely as evening follows sunset, I knew she would reveal her true nature again.

CHAPTER TWENTY-SIX

Zara

The sun rose hot the next morning, and the floor tiles gleamed as I hurried toward my mistress's chamber. Though Salome usually slept well past sunrise, I knew she had special plans for the day and would rise early.

I had just passed a pair of guards and entered the hallway that led to the queen's apartment when a slave signaled for my attention. I knew the woman; she belonged to the queen's mother. I stopped and gave her a polite smile. "Do you need something?"

"My mistress"—the slave lowered her eyes as if she were unworthy to look directly at me—"has asked me to find you."

"The queen's mother wants to speak to *me*?"

"Please." The girl opened the door wider. "She is in her bed-chamber."

Reluctantly I entered the richly decorated apartment and stepped inside the innermost chamber, where the walls shimmered with silks and other fine fabrics. The bed dripped with furs and linens, and in the middle of an overstuffed mattress

I found the queen's mother. I barely recognized her, for her graying hair was undone and her face completely unadorned.

"You." The woman lifted her chin. "You are Salome's handmaid?"

I nodded.

"What does she call you?"

"Zara."

"You are Jewish?"

"Yes."

"Then how can you stand to work for that woman?" Alexandra waved the thought away and swung her legs off the bed. "I have a request to make of you, Zara. I hope you will have mercy on me and grant what I ask."

I dipped my head in respect. "I will do my best."

"I hoped you would say that."

The older woman sighed and braced herself on the edge of the bed. "I do not know if you realize it, but I am being held prisoner here. Did you see the guard in the hallway? I am not allowed to leave. Any messages I send must go first to Salome, who reads every word. Any guest I receive must be approved by Herod's brother, Pheroras. I am held captive by my son-in-law."

I blinked, surprised by the woman's assessment. "I do not believe the king would—"

"You are a child. You cannot possibly know him as I do. He says he is protecting me from people who would do me harm, but who in Jerusalem does not love me? The only person who wishes me ill is Herod. And possibly that woman, his shadow."

"Who?"

Her dark eyes blazed up at me. "Your mistress."

I glanced toward the open window and wished I had the power to fly away. Listening to this woman made me feel disloyal. "I should get to my mistress—"

"Trust me, Herod intends to keep me a prisoner. So I find

myself in dire need of help. And who better to help than a young girl who serves the king's sister?"

My nerves tightened as my thoughts scampered like frightened mice. No matter what this woman asked of me, I could not do it. I did not want to disobey or displease my mistress, and no one who had any sense would want to come between Alexandra and the king.

"I have watched you," Alexandra said, leaning toward me, "and I know you are a virtuous girl, despite the woman you serve. I will not ask you to do anything that might put your life in danger."

The tension in my shoulders abated, but only a little.

"I have come up with a plan," Alexandra went on, "and it is stored here." She tapped the side of her head. "But I will need assistance, and you can give it." She reached beneath a fur blanket and pulled out a sealed scroll, then offered it to me. "I want you to take this to the king's reception room and look for Joseph. You will go up to him and deliver this message. He will recognize you as his wife's handmaid, so he will accept it. Will you do this for me?"

I stared at the scroll as if it were a poisonous snake. If I took it . . .

"No one would suspect you of carrying a message for me; no one would ever suspect Salome's handmaid."

"But suppose someone saw me come in here? If I came out carrying a scroll—"

"You are friends with my daughter's handmaid, are you not? Anyone who saw you would believe you came in to look for Mava. If you tuck the scroll into your tunic, no one will see it. You have freedom of movement, Zara, and I do not. And I have good reason to believe my life is in danger."

The statement startled me, for I could not believe the king would harm his mother-in-law. Had he not forgiven her many times? But then I looked down and saw honest fear in Alexandra's dark eyes, and her hand trembled as she offered me the scroll.

Was it not a sin to refuse to perform a good deed?

I took it, dropped it beneath the neckline of my tunic, and felt it fall to my belt where it rested against my bare belly.

"I will do this for you," I said, backing away. "But please do not ask me to be disloyal to my mistress again."

I did not carry the scroll to Joseph right away. I left Alexandra's apartment and hurried to Salome's, my heart thudding with every frantic step.

"You are a virtuous girl," Alexandra had said, counting on my piety and my desire to please HaShem. But I desired to please my mistress too and not because I hoped palace service would improve my station in life. I wanted to please her because that was a servant's duty, and I knew my place.

Yet was Alexandra truly in danger? I saw no signs of it. So which woman should I obey, my mistress or the queen's mother?

I greeted Salome with a stiff bow, brought her a bowl of fruit, and set about braiding her hair in a style she favored. Only six sections of hair were braided, the rest was left to flow down her back. Then two groups of three braids were sewn together, side by side, forming a wide band of braids. Finally the braid bands were pulled across the front of the head, from right to left and left to right, the bands secured in place with needle and more thread.

"Finished." I stepped back and let my mistress admire herself in the looking brass. "Do you need anything else, mistress?"

Salome smiled at her reflection, lowered the brass, and looked at me as if I'd lost my good sense. "Would you send me out with an unpainted face?"

"Oh! I am sorry. Let me get the applicators."

After painting her eyes, cheeks, and lips, Salome was finally ready to face the world. I helped her dress, then stood aside as she checked her reflection again and left the chamber.

I carried the scroll in my tunic for the better part of the day—as I tidied up, made her bed, and cut fresh flowers from the garden. Yet my conscience nagged at me, giving me no peace. So as the sun lowered and my mistress began to prepare for dinner, I stepped into her bedchamber and bowed low.

She was rummaging through a trunk, probably looking for a himation or hair ornament. "Come, Zara, let's be quick tonight. I am starving, and Joseph is entertaining guests from Rome."

Instead of replying, I pulled the scroll from my belt and set it on her dressing table.

My silence made her look up. "What is that?" She nodded to the scroll.

"Alexandra asked me to deliver it to your husband. She asked me . . . I was not to tell you about it."

"Really." My mistress's brows rose as she stepped forward and broke the seal. Holding the scroll close to the flickering oil lamp, she read the message, then carefully rewrapped the soft leather around the spool. "Fetch me wax and candle," she said, her eyes growing distant. "We will reseal this and then you will take it to Joseph. You should do it as soon as you finish here. Alexandra will be wondering why she has heard no response."

"Yes, mistress."

Salome did not speak of the scroll again, but when I finished helping her dress, I picked it up and delivered it as promised.

CHAPTER TWENTY-SEVEN

Salome

The talk at dinner that night was of the rumors circulating throughout Jerusalem. Herod had not been gone a full month, barely time for news to travel across the Great Sea, but we had no shortage of unofficial reports from Laodicea: Herod had stood trial before Antony and Cleopatra, he had been found guilty of plotting to murder Israel's high priest, and he had committed the murder through hired mercenaries. Our Roman guests had heard even darker stories since landing at the port. "We heard Herod confessed everything under torture," a man called Publius casually remarked as he reached for a piece of venison. "Then Antony had him beheaded, just as he beheaded Antigonus."

I gave the man a hostile glare. "You speak, sir, as if the subject on trial were a dog or a bull. Herod is my brother and my king. We do not find these false reports entertaining."

"Oh?" Publius smiled as he chewed. "I beg your pardon, lady, but the streets are full of such talk."

"Sir, this is the palace, not the street." I stood and pressed my hands together, addressing the guests. "Thank you for coming, but you have delighted us long enough. Good night."

A few brows shot upward in surprise; most banquets lasted half the night. Even Joseph, presumably the host, gave me a puzzled look, yet he did not protest as I moved toward the door.

"I am sorry," I murmured as I passed him, "but I could not endure one more minute of that man's insulting drivel."

Joseph came to my chamber later that evening, his face clouded with fear. He did not sit but paced at the foot of my bed, his shoulders stooped with anxiety. "What if the rumors are true?" he said, glancing over at me. "What should I do? The people will seize upon this news and revolt. They will find someone—probably Hyrcanus—and put him on the throne. If I stand in their way, they will kill me without hesitation."

"They would never choose Hyrcanus," I pointed out. "He is too old and was never a good king. No, they would allow Mariamne to act as regent until her eldest son was of age." I tilted my head, realizing that the same thought must have occurred to my brother. "What about your promise to Herod? Did he not ask you to kill Mariamne if he were executed?"

Joseph looked at me as if I had suddenly grown a second head. "Are you mad? She is a Hasmonean; the people would storm the palace if I executed her. If they believe Herod is dead—"

"That is why you must convince them he is *not* dead. Double the guards around the perimeter. Maintain a show of force at the towers. And warn the commander at the Antonia—he must be alert for signs of trouble."

Joseph kept pacing, but he did not mention the plan Alexandra had suggested. He did not know I had read her message, so I knew the thoughts crowding his mind.

How revealing his silence was! In her message to Joseph, Alexandra had suggested that he take her, Mariamne, and the royal princes to the Antonia for protection in case of revolt. *For it is coming*, she had written, *as surely as Antony will punish Herod for the unspeakable crime of murdering my son.*

I climbed out of bed, walked to my husband, and placed my palm against his chest, stopping him in place. "I know you are planning to take Alexandra and the Hasmonean heirs to the Roman commander. I find it interesting that you have made no mention of taking the king's brother or sister with you."

I said nothing as Joseph stammered and flushed, proving my suspicions. If a revolt broke out in the coming days, the Jewish royals would be saved but not the Idumaeans. Not Herod's kin. Except for my husband, of course.

Joseph, who had a soft spot for his beautiful queen, and who might like to spend his dying years as king.

"I would take the entire royal family," he said. "But it will not come to that."

"Indeed, it will not. Because how could these rumors be true? Herod is not the sort of man who confesses to crimes he did not commit. And if he were dead—" my voice caught in my throat—"if he were, I would feel it. I would *know* it. And I have felt nothing since he left."

Joseph lowered his head and moved to the door, where he paused and looked back at me. "I hope you are right—I hope Herod is alive and well. Because if the people *do* rebel, I am not sure we can hold them off."

"I'm sure you are correct," I told him, climbing back into bed. "I do not think *you* could hold off a wasp. But Herod will return, and then you will be ashamed of your cowardice this night."

～～～～～

Herod returned a few weeks later. He arrived in the heat of the afternoon, accompanied by his elite guards, and nothing in his demeanor led me to believe he had been chastised by Mark

Antony. He held his head as high as ever and was as firm with the guards who greeted him at the palace gates. And when the crowds outside the palace realized their king had returned, they did not shout or protest but remained silent and went about their business as if he had never gone away.

My brother entered the palace in a burst of energy and warmly greeted those who had gathered in the reception hall. Indeed, as I watched, I saw a man who was happy to be home, not a dog who had been whipped and kicked by his master.

Not until later, when Herod summoned me, Joseph, and Pheroras to his inner reception chamber did his smile fade. Even then, however, he did not speak of defeat but of victory.

"So?" Joseph asked. "How did Antony approach the matter of Aristobulus's death? Did he openly rebuke you?"

Herod leaned back in his chair and propped his dusty sandals on the table, then folded his hands across his belly. "He did not even mention the boy."

The three of us stared, mouths agape, until the somber look on Herod's face erupted into a wide grin. "I could not believe it myself," he said, reaching for the fruit bowl on the table. "In fact, Antony ate all his meals with me and allowed me to sit with him in judgment. Later he told me he had rebuffed Cleopatra and told her not to meddle in other people's affairs."

Pheroras guffawed. "Truly?"

"So it was all for naught," I said. "Antony told Cleopatra he would confront you about Aristobulus, but he was only trying to keep her happy. That's why he met you in Syria instead of Alexandria."

Herod winked at me. "Clever girl. I set sail convinced my run of good fortune had come to an end, but Antony had no wish to punish me. In my shoes, faced with a popular rival from a competing family, he said he would have done the same thing I did. I came away with the clear impression that Antony cares little about what happens in Judea, as long as the people are peaceable and our taxes are paid on time."

"Amazing." Pheroras shook his head. "He trusts you implicitly."

Herod shrugged. "He trusts me enough. He had heard about my deep mourning, the lavish funeral, and the ornate tomb. He also appreciated the many gifts I brought him—Antony has always appreciated rare and beautiful treasures."

The words *rare* and *beautiful* reminded me of Mariamne, but I would not mention her until I could catch Herod alone.

"How will Antony escape Cleopatra's ire?" I asked. "She has to be furious about this outcome. Many times she tried to take Alexandra and Aristobulus away from you, yet each time she failed. And I hear she is a woman who does not like to fail."

"I do not like to fail, either," Herod answered, scoring a pomegranate with his knife. "But Antony found a way to placate her. As soon as we met, he informed me he was giving Cleopatra Jericho and bits of other Judean territory, including the Beka Valley."

"But we have settlements there!" Pheroras protested.

"We shall have them still," Herod said. "We will pay rent to her, but we will keep our settlements, our groves, and our forests. The price will sting"—he shrugged—"but the woman wanted my head, so I am resigned to relinquishing some of our territory. Especially since she asked for *all* of Arabia and Judea."

He broke open the fruit, spilled the juicy seeds into his hand, and tossed them into his mouth. Chewing, he nodded at Pheroras. "You will send word to the overseers of the balsam forests and the palm groves. Let them know they must give a strict accounting of all profits and expenses. We have a landlord now, and we will pay Egypt's fee."

He went on, asking Pheroras about several building projects.

When finished, he smiled at me. "And how have you been, little sister?"

"I would like to speak to you alone," I said. "When you have a moment."

My husband and Pheroras, neither of whom could imagine me capable of an original thought, said farewell to Herod and left the room. After they had gone, Herod leaned across the table and grinned. "What troubles you, Salome? Has Mariamne snubbed you again? Or did Alexandra insult you?"

"Do you think I would care about such common things?" I strode over and closed the door. When I was certain we would not be overheard, I sank back into my chair. "It pains me, brother, to be the bearer of distressing news."

His grin vanished. "What is wrong? Is it Mariamne?"

I drew a deep breath. "I know you asked Joseph to look after her while you were away. He obeyed, brother, a little too well."

"What?" Herod's eyes narrowed to slits. "What do you mean?"

"We heard rumors of your death at Antony's hand. Shortly thereafter, my handmaid brought me a message—a scroll Alexandra had intended to reach Joseph alone. Zara is loyal, however, and she brought it to me first."

A tremor touched Herod's smooth lips.

"Alexandra wrote out a plan. She wanted Joseph to escort her and Mariamne and the little princes to the Antonia, where they would be safe when rioting broke out. Later, Joseph came to me, worried about the rumors, and I confronted him with what I knew about Alexandra's message. He did not deny her plan . . . or that he did *not* intend to include me and Pheroras in his flight. I asked Joseph if he had forgotten his promise to kill Mariamne if something happened to you, and he turned on me like an enraged beast. Clearly—and it pains me to tell you this—he intended to marry Mariamne and let her reign as regent until your son comes of age. He had no intention of fulfilling his vow to you."

Herod's face went pale. I expected him to scream or yell or pound the table. Instead he remained as motionless as a statue, silent except for the pinched sound of his breathing.

"I will kill her," he finally said, staring at nothing. "She must die, and Joseph too."

"I know this is hard for you," I said, leaning toward him. "Such an act—on both their parts—cannot be forgiven."

"Do not worry." Herod stood and pushed away from the table with such force that his chair toppled over. "This crime will not go unpunished."

***

I was not successful in my attempt to remove the twin arrogances known as Mariamne and Alexandra from the king's house, and yet my efforts did produce one desirable outcome.

Herod was furious with his queen when he learned she and her mother had plotted with Joseph during his absence, but when she denied the charges of conspiracy and adultery, he forgave her everything.

The next afternoon he called me to his chamber, where he fixed me with an unblinking gaze. "Did your husband have an affair with my wife?"

I could not move, stunned by sheer disbelief at his expression. I had already told him everything I knew, so why was he asking this pointed question? Did he doubt my report? Had he ceased to trust me? If so, all the years of my life, my work for him, my steadfast love had come down to this moment . . . and meant nothing.

I tried to control myself, but my chin wobbled and my eyes filled in spite of my efforts. "I cannot . . ." I began, then stopped when my voice broke. I drew a deep breath and began again. "I cannot believe the distrust I see in your eyes."

"Salome." Herod's eyes softened. "I am not doubting you—I am not—but you should know what your husband does, and you did not say if he had slept with the queen."

"How am I to know what happens in the queen's bedchamber?" Bereft, I fell onto my knees before my brother. "Joseph never sleeps with me, so I do not know what he does at night. I know he visited the queen and her mother regularly. I also know they conspired to leave the palace and seek shelter from the Romans. They were leaving *together*. So I ask you—what was I to think?"

A melancholy frown flitted across my brother's features. "Mariamne denies the charge of adultery. She swears she has been faithful to me."

I sniffed.

"But your husband—he failed me. He proved he would not keep his oath, even if I were dead." He crossed his arms and studied me with a calculating expression. "If you had made such an oath, Salome, would you fulfill it?"

I stared at him, searching for the meaning behind his words. Was this some sort of test? Was he doubting me again?

"Herod." I underlined the name with rebuke. "I have spent my life adoring you, and since you have been king I have spent my days serving and defending you. When you put me at Masada with your betrothed and her mother, did I complain? No, I endured them patiently and stood at the balcony every morning, searching the terrain for some sign of your return. When you were gone to see Antony, I safeguarded your interests, even though those who worked against you had already given up. I married Joseph for you. So yes, if I swore an oath to do something after your death, I would most certainly carry out my promise."

Herod grunted and looked away. "Would you be rid of your husband?"

I closed my eyes and sighed. Joseph, my uncle and my husband, had never been my lover. Due to his disinterest, I had no children. No one looked at me as Herod looked at Mariamne. I slept in an empty bed and shared my secrets with my ten-year-old handmaid.

And Joseph had become a liability. If I could not trust him, neither could the king. Herod could not afford to have an untrustworthy man in his inner circle.

I opened my eyes and met my brother's gaze. "Do what you will with Joseph. I will not mourn him."

Herod nodded and brushed his hands together. "Then it is time he left us. I care not if he is our uncle; he should never have been so cold to you. He will be gone by sunset, and we will find you a better husband. Someone more suited to your station."

My heart quickened. If I did not speak now, Herod might marry me off to someone as old and stultified as Joseph.

I flattened myself on the floor and reached for his feet. "Forgive me, brother, for asking for what I do not deserve."

He lifted a brow. "Has someone caught your eye?"

"Someone . . . has impressed me because I thought he might be of service to you. I would never have had the temerity to think of him for my own sake, though he is a pleasant-looking man. No, when I saw him at court, I thought he might be of great service to you, for he seems wise, wealthy, and confident. He is a good soldier—"

"Am I to know the name of this amazing man?"

I sat up, allowing a smile to curve my lips. "He is called Costobar, and I believe you know him. He is one of us, an Idumaean."

Herod's eyes glimmered with recollection. "Of course, the man I appointed governor of Idumea and Gaza. He guarded the exits during the siege of Jerusalem."

"He lacks a wife," I said, coming directly to the point. "I am still young, brother, and I would like to have children. I believe Costobar would make a good father—an Idumaean father."

Herod lifted a brow, and too late I realized my words could have been interpreted as an insult to him for marrying a Jewish woman.

I bowed my head. "I stress that our offspring would be Idumaean only because I would not want them to compete with your children in any way. Mariamne's babies are the union of Idumaean and Jewish royalty. My offspring will neither compare nor compete."

Herod rubbed the back of his neck, then nodded. "Tomorrow I will bring Costobar to court. If there is no impediment, I will arrange the marriage."

I stood in what I hoped was a suitably humble posture. "I only hope he will agree."

"Who would not want to marry the king's sister?" Herod laughed. "Go in peace, Salome. But if you have anything to say to Joseph, you should go to the dungeon straightaway. He will not live to see the sunrise."

"I have nothing to say to him."

Leaving Herod alone, I walked to my chamber, realizing that perhaps my life had not been wasted after all.

CHAPTER TWENTY-EIGHT

Salome

My chief mistake, I realized later, was underestimating the depth of Herod's passion for Mariamne. He had no such passion for Joseph, whom he dispatched despite my husband's frantic denials before the court. At my suggestion, Herod sent for Zara, who came and stood before him, trembling like a frightened mouse. Herod had only one question for the girl: "Did you, child, see your mistress's husband in the queen's apartment?"

The girl nodded, and the order of execution was carried out.

I expected Mariamne and her mother to be executed soon after, but Herod could not bring himself to kill either woman. I could not understand his reasoning. After Herod's return, Mariamne was cold and distant when he visited her room, demanding to know how he could love her when he had ordered Joseph to kill her. Herod found himself on the defensive, and so powerful was Mariamne's indignant anger that he became mere putty in her hands.

By the time he left her chamber, Mariamne had been forgiven and Herod was even more furious at Joseph for being foolish enough to disclose his secret order. "If they had not already removed his body," he told me later, "I would have executed him again."

In those few days I learned something about my brother—gaining the throne had changed him. Before becoming king, Herod had been ruthless and fearless, never afraid to attempt the unthinkable, never reluctant to challenge the status quo. His intrepid ambition had undoubtedly caught Mark Antony's attention, who saw that quality as a necessity for a client king.

Before becoming king, Herod had little to lose but his life, and he thought nothing of risking it. Our father had challenged all of us to be ambitious, clever, and perceptive, and the family loyalty he instilled always served us well. As he worked as adviser in the court of King Hyrcanus, we had loitered in the shadows and learned the value of being indispensable, dependable, and discreet.

Now Herod sat on the throne of Judea with no more mountains to conquer. He was not so foolish as to dream climbing the rungs of power in Rome, for he knew the Romans considered him too foreign, his religion too odd, and his people too backward.

At thirty-eight he had achieved the highest position open to him, and his only remaining challenge was in defending his throne from men and women who had been cast from the same mold—fearless, ambitious, clever schemers who would not stop until they had achieved the same pinnacle of power.

This realization elicited a new kind of fear in Herod, a vulnerability he took pains to hide. But I saw it nonetheless. Mariamne had the power to turn his fearlessness into insecurity, and I was unaccustomed to seeing weakness in my brother. *"A king,"* Father had always told us, *"cannot show fear, especially to his enemies. They will seize upon his weakness and devour him."*

Mariamne, I saw clearly, was Herod's weakness. And Alexandra lived to support her daughter.

Perhaps the most alarming lesson my brother learned after his trip to visit Antony was that his authority could be threatened and his confidence rattled by a woman . . . a possibility he had never considered.

But I knew the power a woman could wield. I also knew Alexandra of the Hasmoneans was determined to destroy my brother.

~~~~~~~

Costobar and I were married, not in a Jewish ceremony but, at the groom's insistence, in a traditional Roman rite. Herod, Pheroras, and our mother acted as witnesses as the Idumaean priest waved a pot of incense around us and we agreed to be married.

Herod was the first to step forward and clap the groom's shoulder. "Congratulations, brother!" He beamed as he took my new husband's hand. "Treasure and guard her well, for she is the only sister I have."

Costobar bore Herod's congratulations with grace and a good measure of patience, for he clearly wished to be on his way. We had no reception, no banquet, no festivities of any kind. When Herod and Pheroras had departed, taking Mother with them, Costobar grabbed my hand and led me out of the palace and through the streets until we reached his house. I caught a fleeting impression of finely chiseled stones, a wide entryway, and several startled servants who were apparently unaware they were about to welcome a mistress. Then Costobar swung me into his arms and carried me up the stairs and into his bedchamber, where he released me and let me catch my breath.

I smoothed my tunic and took a moment to look around. The room was decidedly masculine, dominated by a wooden bed piled high with furs and embroidered pillows. A brazier glowed in a corner, and several pieces of leather armor lay piled on a bench. A desk sat against the wall, covered with scrolls and parchments, and colorful fabrics spilled from an open trunk in the corner.

Costobar stood without speaking, his hands on his hips, until I had finished taking stock of my surroundings. Then he cracked a crooked smile. "Does my chamber meet with your approval? I hope so, for I am not changing it."

Was he hoping to intimidate me? He would find I was not easily cowed.

I lifted my chin and draped the train of my new tunic over my arm. "I see no place for me or my things, so I will keep my chambers at the palace. When I am here, though, I expect to have a place reserved for my handmaid, so she can be close enough to hear my call."

Costobar laughed. "There is no room for handmaids here. This house is simple—designed for a commander and his officers. This room has a desk only because your brother has set me over Idumea and—"

"I know your position," I interrupted, keeping my voice cool. "And if this is where you will billet your men, then I and my handmaid shall remain in the palace. You will come here when you need to work with your soldiers, and you will come to my apartment if you want your wife."

I gave him a smile and approached the bed, allowing my fingertips to trail over the pile of lush furs. "I do not know where you acquired these, but if they are filled with fleas, I will not sleep here. My bed, on the other hand, is perfumed with cedar and sandalwood, and the furs are clean. The sheets are as soft as a baby's cheek, and the air is altogether sweet. Would you not rather take your pleasure there than in a place like this?"

He did not answer but reached out and drew me to him, his arm like an iron hook around my back. I pressed my hands to his chest, about to resist, but his lips were surprisingly soft, his caress unexpectedly gentle. His lips probed and explored my face and neck while his hand rose to the back of my head. A moment later he had undone the clasp with which Zara had constrained my riotous hair, sending the auburn curls tumbling down my back.

"I will let you sleep in your palace apartment," he said, his breath heating my neck as he lifted me into his arms, "but not just yet."

He set me on his bed, and though the furs smelled of animals and woods and smoke, I forgot to protest.

CHAPTER TWENTY-NINE

Zara

In the summer of my tenth year, a servant woke me in my chamber and said I had a visitor.

I sat up and blinked until my eyes focused in the gloom. "Who would come to see me?"

"A woman. She says she is your aunt."

I slid out of bed and wrapped my shawl around me. I followed the slave through the servants' quarters and down the stairs, then paused in a small courtyard filled with the odors of manure, blood, and rotting food.

I peered into the predawn fog. "Aunt Rimonah?"

"Here, child." Rimonah stepped out of the shadows and smiled, the moonlight gilding her face with silver. The sight of her started a fountain of nostalgia flowing in my heart, so I hugged her, then searched her face. "What brings you to the palace, Aunt? And how did you get in?"

Her mouth twisted with irritable humor as she jerked her thumb toward a wagonload of bloody beef. "I slipped in with the butcher. That is why I had to come before sunrise. And that is why I cannot stay."

"Oh." Suddenly at a loss for words, I looked from her to the butcher, then back to my aunt. "Is something amiss?"

Sadness tinged her smile. "I am sorry to bring you sad news, but you should know—your mother died last week."

I had expected to receive such news one day, but expectation did not dull the sharp pang that stole my breath. To my girlish mind, my mother was immortal. She had always been there for me, and she always would be. Even after coming to the palace, I never wavered in my belief that Ima was just beyond the thick walls, thinking of me, missing me, and praying for me.

Yet Rimonah said she had been gone a week. How could I not have sensed her loss?

I hiccupped a sob, and Aunt Rimonah drew me close. "She knew she did not have long to live. I wanted to send for you, but she said she did not want to bother you in your new life."

"My new life?" I choked on the words. "The only life I have I owe to her. How could I do anything if she had never given birth to me?"

"Hush, child." Rimonah strengthened her grip on my shoulders and positioned me in a stream of moonlight. "You look well, Zara. You have put on some weight. It is time you did." The corner of her mouth rose in a gentle curve. "You are beginning to look like a woman."

My cheeks burned. "It is the darkness, that's all. I do not feel any different."

"You will, in time. Soon, in fact." She held me in a tight embrace, her chest falling as she exhaled. "I will never know if I did the right thing to send you away. Your mother wanted to keep you with her until the end, but I knew you would miss the opportunity of a lifetime if she did. So tell me"—she stepped back and looked into my eyes—"how is your mistress? Does she treat you well? Do they feed you enough? Do you ever see the king? Is he as horrible as they say?"

I lifted my hands against the barrage of questions. "My mistress is fine. I get plenty to eat. And I have friends among the other servants."

"And the king?"

I shrugged. "The king is the king. He has nothing to do with me."

I thought she might be disappointed to discover the king and I were not good friends, but instead she sighed in relief. "That is good to hear. They say no one is safe around the king, no one. So keep your distance, child, and honor HaShem in all you do. As He directed Daniel in Babylon, He will direct your steps."

I nodded.

Aunt Rimonah studied me for a long moment. "I see so much of your mother in you," she said, her chin quivering, then pulled me to her again. "She loved you so much."

Something within me gave way at those words. I wrapped my arms around my aunt's waist and quietly wept.

CHAPTER THIRTY

Salome

Careful!" I warned as Zara's fingers trembled on the reed she was using to outline my eyes. "Make the line thin and curved, not straight like the Egyptians favor it."

"I'm trying, mistress."

"Please try harder." I tried not to be cross with the girl, for we were all anxious. Even Herod, who always seemed unflappable, appeared ill at ease, and Mariamne had also been overly excitable. She was pregnant again, and every time I saw her, she was moaning about how she felt too fat to be receiving visitors, especially *royal* visitors.

I do not know how it came to pass, but Cleopatra was sleeping beneath our roof—one Egyptian queen, more than sixty slaves, and a dozen handmaids whose job, it seemed, was to follow her, perfuming the air she breathed with melting cones of scented wax. Apparently, Antony had asked Herod if he would show her the glories of Jerusalem and then escort her safely back to the Egyptian border. How could Herod refuse?

The royal lady had already spent six nights as our guest, and I was growing impatient to see her go. Not only did caring for her entourage overtax our household maids, cooks, guards, and horsemen, but they had also forced our servants to vacate their quarters. Zara and most of the others were sleeping on mounds of hay in the stable, yet Cleopatra's servants had the temerity to complain about the overcrowded conditions.

"Did you notice," Zara said, interrupting my frustrated thoughts, "how many wigs the queen has? I was expecting her to wear those long, straight wigs we see in Egyptian art, but she is as fashionable as any Greek or Roman lady."

"The world is one big family now," I told her. "We can't expect the Egyptians to dress like Egyptians anymore. Rome sets the standard for all of us."

"Except the Jews," Zara said, making a valid point. "The men, that is. The priests have looked the same ever since Moses and Aaron."

"Perhaps, but their women haven't," I countered. "Now, should I wear the gold chiton or the purple? Purple is the color of royalty, but gold—"

"The gold makes your hair shine." Zara applied the last stroke of kohl to my lashes, then stepped back and smiled. "I think your husband prefers gold."

I nodded in silent agreement. Costobar did seem to like the color—in fabrics and on coins, vases, platters, and jewelry. The man definitely had a taste for shiny things.

I stood and held out my arms as Zara fastened the chiton at my shoulders, then adjusted the flowing fabric until it puddled around my feet. She then found a gold belt and tied it at my waist, pulling the chiton up and over the belt until I was able to walk without tripping.

"Will there be many guests at tonight's banquet?" Zara asked as she moved to the jewelry case. "Will you want large pieces to be seen from across the room?"

I shook my head. "Herod wanted an intimate dinner tonight.

Cleopatra, her chief advisor, Mariamne, me, Costobar, Phero-ras, and his woman."

"Who will he invite?"

"I have no idea." I peered into the looking brass to check my reflection, then turned and pointed to a pair of earrings that would dangle almost to my shoulders. "Those. Cleopatra should certainly notice the stones in that pair."

Zara had just finished slipping the earrings into my ears when Costobar entered the room. He spread his arms, his face brightening, and proclaimed me the most beautiful woman in all of Judea.

"You'll have a hard time proving that tonight," I told him while on my way to the door. "Come, we do not want to be late."

An hour later, I looked around the crowded banquet room and realized that although we had given a banquet with an intimate setting, delicious food, and athletic jugglers to entertain, the queen of Egypt looked completely bored. And no wonder—I had heard tales of her extravagant dinners and elaborate entertainments and how she often invited her guests to take home sofas, slaves, exotic animals, and mountains of food. Mariamne had been flabbergasted when I told her about the banquet Cleopatra arranged to capture Mark Antony's attention, and I knew our feast had to seem paltry by comparison. Still, *she* had come to visit *us* . . . so perhaps she would accept us as she found us.

"Herod." Reclining on the arm of her couch, Cleopatra leaned toward my brother, her lashes fluttering. "I have been so comfortable beneath your roof, I wish I could stay longer. But I must ask that we begin our journey back to Egypt."

"Really?" Herod dropped the chicken bone he had been gnawing and glanced at Mariamne. "Perhaps we should set out soon.

My wife's time is fast approaching, and I want to be back in Jerusalem by the time my next son is born."

"You have a lovely wife." Cleopatra gave Mariamne a perfunctory smile. "But surely you have not confined yourself to one woman? Is that a Jewish regulation?"

Costobar had lifted his cup to drink, but the audacity of the queen's question made him sputter, which resulted in a coughing fit. Patting him on the back, I could not tear my gaze from Cleopatra and Herod.

"I love my queen," Herod answered, for once taking the diplomatic approach. "Though it is not unusual for a king to have concubines or other wives."

Cleopatra picked up her golden goblet and smiled. "Then you will have no problem visiting my room tonight."

Herod's expression did not change for a moment, and then her words fell into place. "What?"

"Lie with me tonight," Cleopatra said, practically purring the invitation. "Surely you are not embarrassed by my straightforwardness. I have heard that you appreciate people who speak directly to the point."

Costobar began to cough again, and Mariamne's face went the color of pomegranate seeds. I swallowed hard, closed my eyes, and prayed Herod would not accept Cleopatra's proposal—not now, not ever.

What was the woman thinking? She knew Herod answered to her lover, and surely she felt some sort of loyalty to Mark Antony . . . or did she? Did the marital bed mean nothing to the Egyptians, or was this sort of promiscuity confined to Cleopatra alone?

Herod's mouth curled and rolled as though he wanted to spit. "If we are to leave for Egypt tomorrow," he said to Cleopatra, his voice calm and indifferent, "then I would prefer to sleep tonight. If you need a man in your bed tonight, I suggest you find someone from your retinue to keep you company."

"Very well." Cleopatra released a three-noted laugh. "But do not ever deny that I gave you this opportunity."

Costobar and I had just reentered my bedchamber when I turned to Zara and abruptly dismissed her.

"But, mistress, do you want me to help you—?"

"I am not retiring right away, so run along. Costobar and I must meet with the king."

Zara bowed and departed straightaway, which left my husband and I alone for the first time that night. "Did you hear . . . ?" I began.

"Of course! I thought I was imagining things."

"How could she?"

"They must do things differently in Egypt. And she *did* have a son by Julius Caesar."

"I'm sure his wife wasn't happy about it."

"Mariamne looked as if she wanted to slap—"

"She might have slapped Herod if he had not refused."

"He will want to talk about this. Will he summon us tonight or tomorrow?"

"He's probably trying to calm Mariamne now. If he wants to talk, we'll know soon enough."

The moon had scarcely risen above the horizon when a messenger knocked on the door. "The king asks for you and your husband to—"

"We're coming."

Costobar grabbed a lamp and I followed, moving silently along the halls until we mounted the stairs to Herod's private reception room. We found him inside, not pacing as I had feared but sitting calmly at the table, a loaf of bread and a block of cheese in front of him.

"Come," he said, gesturing to a pair of empty chairs. "Have

something to eat while we discuss what we should do with the queen who has made herself too much at home."

"I thought you were taking her back to Egypt," I said, sinking into the chair. I looked at the cheese and frowned—the notion of food suddenly turned my stomach.

"She needs to leave," Costobar said, taking his seat next to me. "And on the journey you would do well to place guards around your abode. A woman that forward would think nothing of slipping into your tent during the dead of night. And what would Mariamne do then?"

"I do *not* want to sleep with that woman," Herod said, his voice flat. "She does not interest me."

"I know you do not want to offend Antony—"

"My reasons have nothing to do with Antony. Cleopatra is not beautiful, Mariamne is. Why would I sleep with a short little woman who talks too much, plots with Alexandra behind my back, and would happily kill me if she could arrange it? We know she covets Judea. I cannot see how she would profit by sleeping with me, unless it was to turn Antony against me. But I am not a man who would willingly give her pleasure."

I blinked, surprised by the vehemence of my brother's words.

"Then what do we do with her?" Pheroras asked as he came into the room. He nodded to Herod, broke off a hunk of bread, and dropped into an empty seat. "If you travel with her to Egypt, you had better double the guard around your tent. She's the sort who would pay handsomely to have someone stick a knife in your back as you slept."

"I've already advised him on that account," Costobar said. "For an entirely different reason."

Herod snorted. "I do not want to take her back to Egypt. I want to kill her."

For a moment I thought I had misheard, but then I looked at the others and realized they were as stunned as I.

"Kill her?" Pheroras shook his head. "Antony would surely kill you."

"Would he?" Herod fingered a bit of bread, working it into a small ball. "I would be doing it for Antony's sake. That woman has made him weak. She will be the cause of his destruction, mark my words. The Romans covet her lands because Egypt feeds Rome with its grain. The Senate no longer trusts Antony because they believe he has fallen under her spell—and he has. If I killed her, the Senate would be grateful and so would Antony . . . in time."

"But she is descended from a long line of kings and queens," Costobar argued, his hand on his chest. "It is one thing to kill a common man; it is quite another to kill a noble ruler."

"Is it?" Herod flicked the ball of dough at the wall, then grinned. "Have we not seen how a common man can be made a king, while a king becomes a common man? If a man with courage and daring can become a king, surely he has the right to stop a queen from ruining another courageous man."

Resting his chin on his hand, Pheroras studied our brother. As much as I loved both my brothers, I had never been able to read Pheroras as easily as I read Herod. Pheroras had a diplomat's face—almost anything could be going on behind those dark eyes and that large forehead, and he did not easily share his thoughts.

At least not with me.

"You might consider waiting," Pheroras said at last. "I can see your reasoning: by ridding yourself of Cleopatra, you would regain the lands Antony asked you to surrender to her. Antony might place you over Egypt itself, if Rome would allow it. But regicide . . . you might find your Roman overseers looking at you as though they wonder if you would ever decide to kill *them*."

"You cannot kill a woman," I said. "You might kill another king in an act of war, but to kill a woman? The Romans have odd ideas about women. They pretend to esteem them even while they keep them in a lower estate."

"You cannot kill anyone who has been entrusted to you for their safety," Costobar added. "Antony asked you to escort her to Egypt. If you kill her, not only have you killed a ruler, your master's lover, and the mother of his children, you have violated every law of hospitality. She came to you because she trusted this to be a safe place—"

"She trusted my position as one who fears Mark Antony," Herod interrupted. "What she does not realize is that my esteem for Antony involves more than fear. I admire him, I want to serve him, and killing her would be the greatest service anyone could perform for the man."

Costobar and Pheroras looked at each other, then turned to me. I shook my head and saw agreement in the faces across the table.

"Herod." I reached out to him. "Do not do this thing. See her to Egypt as soon as you can, and be done with her. Let Antony do what Antony will do, but do not insert yourself into their situation. Let Rome deal with them. Then, afterward, you can deal with Rome or Antony, whichever holds the upper hand in the end."

Herod looked around the table and slowly dipped his chin in acquiescence. "You have convinced me," he said, a note of regret in his voice. "Yet we may have to revisit this discussion again. If that time comes, unfortunately the woman is not likely to be within our grasp."

CHAPTER THIRTY-ONE

Salome

In the fifth year of Herod's reign in Jerusalem, Mariamne gave birth to her fourth child, her first daughter, whom she named Salampsio. The girl joined her three brothers— Alexander, Aristobulus, and Herod—in the nursery, which had to be enlarged to accommodate my brother's growing family. I thought Herod might be disappointed to welcome a daughter, but he doted on the little girl, constantly inquiring about her health and endlessly speculating about which prince she might marry when she came of age.

Life in Judea was never uneventful, and I counted every year Herod maintained his position as a victory. My brother was involved in disputes far and near. He was at war with Malichus, the second Nabataean king of that name, and every year he grew more concerned about the disintegrating relationship between Octavian and Mark Antony.

I was not privy to the many meetings Herod had with visitors from other kingdoms in the Roman Empire, but from what he told me, I learned the agreement between Octavian and Antony had frayed beyond repair. Antony spent nearly all his time in Egypt, and members of the Roman Senate worried that Antony intended to proclaim himself and Cleopatra co-rulers of the Empire. The fact that Antony and Cleopatra were raising four children—the eldest, the son of Cleopatra and Julius Caesar, and three who had been sired by Antony—did not help the situation. Were they, the senators speculated, trying to create a dynasty to overthrow the Roman Republic?

Antony and his lover had already declared their children kings and queens and given each of them territories to rule. At a bizarre ceremony in Alexandria, Antony dressed as the god Dionysus-Osiris while Cleopatra portrayed herself as Isis-Aphrodite. They sat on golden thrones, where Antony affirmed Cleopatra to be queen of kings and ten-year-old Caesareon her co-ruler as king of kings. Caesareon was also affirmed to be Julius Caesar's true heir, a direct rebuttal to Octavian's authority. Alexander Helios and his six-year-old twin sister were awarded Armenia, Media, Parthia, Cyrenaica, and Libya. And two-year-old Ptolemy Philadelphus had been proclaimed master of Phoenicia, Syria, and Cilicia.

Octavian wanted Antony and his lover to disappear, but the Roman army revered Antony as a soldier and commander. So how could Octavian quell the threat?

Herod proffered the question one evening as my brothers joined Costobar and I on one of the balconies, enjoying the evening breeze.

Pheroras leaned forward. "Get rid of Antony and Cleopatra? He should send an assassin."

Herod shook his head. "Too risky, particularly if the assassin is captured. Public opinion might turn against Octavian, and he needs the support of the military legions."

"He could have one of them killed," I suggested, though I did not feel up to playing this game. "The two-headed monster is reduced to one. If their love is genuine, perhaps the remaining lover will be too distraught to wage war."

Herod shook his head again. "I would be distraught if I lost my beloved Mariamne, but I would never be too distraught to fight. I would be bent on vengeance."

He glanced at Costobar, and my husband only shrugged. "Perhaps we should have killed Cleopatra when we had the opportunity."

Herod acknowledged the remark with a wry smile, then folded his hands. "The answer is simple—the legionaries will not make war against Antony because he is one of them, a true Roman soldier. But Cleopatra is not Roman, and the legionaries would enthusiastically make war against a woman accused of luring Antony away from Rome. So Antony will be drawn into the fray, and he will end up fighting his own men—*if* his men will fight against fellow Romans."

"Those are important considerations," I said, realizing just how formidable a challenge Antony would face. "What will you do? I know you are beholden to Antony, but if he is not able to win . . ."

"I do not know." Herod's mouth twisted, bristling the whiskers above his upper lip. "But I will give him my best advice and hope he will take it."

I lifted a brow. "And that is?"

"I will tell him to have Cleopatra killed and take Egypt for himself. He is the father of three heirs, so the people will accept him. Then he can approach Octavian with his hands outstretched, offering Egypt, breadbasket of Rome, as a prize. Octavian will be pleased, the Roman Senate will proclaim Antony divine, and the people will be solidly on his side."

"Good advice," Pheroras said. "But will he take it?"

Herod scratched his beard. "I do not know. All will depend on whether Antony is willing to be ruled by his head instead of his heart."

Nine months after my marriage to Costobar, Zara attended me while I gave birth to my first child. The royal midwife caught the child, announced that I had given birth to a healthy boy, and handed the baby to Zara.

"Give him to me," I cried, extending my arms toward the squalling infant.

Zara made a face. "Would you not prefer that I clean him first?"

"No, just give me my son."

Zara leaned in and passed the baby to me. I beheld him— the dark eyes, the wet hair, the white covering on the skin, the smear of blood on his arms—and I thought I had never seen anything more beautiful.

"Are you sure he is healthy?" I asked the midwife. "Is everything in the proper place?"

The woman looked up from the afterbirth she had just delivered. "You have a fine baby boy. He will grow up to make his father proud." She looked around. "Where is the father? Surely he would like to see his son."

"He is . . . away." I held out my hand, and Zara instinctively gave me a damp cloth. I used it to wipe my son's skin, cleaning him even as he wailed and clenched his tiny fists.

"I do believe he has strong lungs," I laughed. "Wait until Herod sees. And Costobar—he will be so happy."

The midwife gave me a pointed look. "Are you sure your husband did not want a daughter?"

"He will father a daughter next year or the year after. But this little boy is his heir." I pressed a kiss to my babe's tiny forehead, then handed him to Zara. "Please swaddle him. I will nurse him in a moment."

I waited until the midwife finished her ministrations, then gently waved her from the room. I had things to say, but I did not want a woman I barely knew to hear them.

Zara wrapped the baby in soft linen and helped me settle him at my breast. She stood back and smiled. "Look how strongly he nurses! He is a most unusual newborn."

My heart overflowed as I studied my son. "He is the son of a governor and the nephew of a king. Not at all common, no matter what Mariamne says."

"Have you decided on a name?"

"I will name him Alexander, of course. He will share the name with many great men."

"I have always thought it a fine name."

"He will be the first Alexander in Costobar's line." I smiled down at my beautiful boy. "And his father will take great pleasure in him."

Zara began to clean up after the midwife. Watching her work from the corner of my eye, I asked a question that had been weighing on my mind for some time. "What think you of your new master?"

Zara lifted her head, her eyes widening. "Which master do you mean?"

"Costobar, of course. I have never heard you give an opinion. Do you like him?"

From the astounded expression on her face, I might well have asked what she thought of Octavian or the Roman Senate. "He is . . . admirable," she answered, her voice unsteady. "He is good to me."

I lowered my voice to a whisper as the baby's eyelids closed. "He is his own man. Though I love my brother deeply and would do anything to protect him, I am glad Costobar does not depend on Herod for everything. He has plans of his own. He was reluctant to tell me about them at first, but once he learned to trust me—" I paused, then smiled—"I like a man who can think for himself. His clan did not capitulate when John Hyrcanus required the Idumaeans to become Jews, and

Costobar does not pretend to be Jewish by going through the motions at the Temple. He comes from a long line of men who were priests of Quas. He is proud to be Idumaean."

Zara nodded but showed no sign of genuine interest. Still, I needed to tell someone what I had learned, and who else in the palace could I trust? Zara would not breathe a word of my secrets.

"Costobar has gone to Alexandria," I continued, lowering my voice even further. "He is going to ask Cleopatra to ask Antony to restore her control over Idumaean lands. If she agrees, Costobar will swear allegiance to her, and in return, she could—she *should*—declare him ruler over Idumea." I looked down at the sleeping baby in my arms. "If this comes to pass, I am hoping this child will be a prince, son of the king of Idumea."

Zara froze, giving me a warning look that put an immediate damper on my spirit. "Would your brother approve of your husband's request? He would lose control of lands he possesses—"

"Why shouldn't Herod approve? Idumea would remain in the family. Besides, if Antony is not inclined to transfer Idumea to Egypt, nothing will come of it and Herod need never know." I forced a laugh, yet it sounded artificial even to my ears. "Herod wants to tell Antony to kill Cleopatra, but I do not think the man can be convinced. If he wanted to be rid of her, he would have left her years ago."

Zara said nothing. Instead she ducked her head and continued cleaning.

I would have appreciated some sign of agreement, some assurance that I was doing the right thing by supporting my husband, but my handmaid knew little about politics or international affairs.

No matter, for my happiness did not depend on Zara's enthusiasm. I had a husband who loved me, a beautiful son, and my brother was secure in his kingdom. All was well with my world.

CHAPTER THIRTY-TWO

Salome

I expected the birth of my second child to go as easily as the first, but apparently my body had forgotten what was required in order to bear fruit. Once again, Zara attended me with the midwife, but this time Costobar paced outside my chamber, cursing and sweating as I groaned and screamed.

A full day after the birth pangs began, the midwife finally pulled the baby from me and announced the arrival of our second son. My husband immediately poured drinks for any man who passed in the hallway, and a few moments later he disappeared, presumably to share the news with Herod and others in the royal court.

Zara admired the baby as she bathed him. "He's a fine, fat boy, with all his fingers and toes. Have you decided on a name?"

"Herod." I pushed my sweaty hair from my forehead. "After my brother."

"Along with Mariamne's son?"

"I do not care. Have we worn out the name Alexander?"

Zara wrapped linen around the baby and handed him to me. "No one is likely to confuse your lad with the other. Mariamne's

197

son is thin and pale. Yours is ruddy and handsome—a perfect combination of your beauty and your husband's strong features."

I ignored the insult to my nephew—no one had ever described Mariamne's third son as handsome—and studied my baby with an analytical gaze. Zara was right. This child was attractive, with a heart-shaped face, long lashes, a perfect nose, and a strong chin. He looked more like a king than Mariamne's third son ever would.

Such a pity, then, that neither of my sons would sit on a throne. Nothing had come of Costobar's trip to Alexandria, because Antony refused to grant Cleopatra's request. Costobar would never be king of Idumea, and that was probably a good thing.

I had decided we were fortunate Herod did not learn about my husband's attempt to win a throne of his own. I hoped my brother would not care, but as the months passed and I thought more about it, I realized he would be furious if he knew Costobar had acted without his knowledge. I hoped they might work together with Idumea as a shared kingdom, but since that time I had learned that some men, including Herod and Costobar, did not like to share. Herod would not be happy to lose a single cubit of territory, and Costobar would not be willing to yield his authority.

Men. I did not always understand their stubbornness, but when I heard that Antony refused to grant Cleopatra's request for Idumea, I realized Herod would likely refuse me if I asked him to surrender that territory to Costobar. While love might be strong enough to bind a king's heart, it was far too weak an inducement to relinquish one's power.

A week after I gave birth to Herod III, Mariamne had a baby girl, whom she named Cypros in honor of my mother. Since she could barely endure being in the same room as my mother, I knew Herod had named this infant.

Another year passed in relative peace, though all did not go well for my brother. Though the women in the palace managed to maintain an unspoken truce—perhaps because Mariamne and I kept busy having babies, and our mothers kept busy doting on them—life was not peaceful outside the walls of Jerusalem.

The sixth year of Herod's reign brought great darkness to Judea. The one bright light in the king's life was the birth of my daughter, Berenice. He stopped by my chamber to congratulate me and take a peek at his new niece. "She is lovely," he said, peering at the infant's pinched face. "Her face will smooth out after a while, right?"

I resisted the urge to frown and gave him a sisterly smile instead. "Your babies looked very much like this, brother, and all of them are handsome now."

"Especially the third boy, Herod." He grinned at me and clapped Costobar on the shoulder. "Congratulations to both of you. Now, if you will excuse me, I have to meet with my generals."

Octavian and Antony were earnestly at war with each other, and Herod was preparing to send soldiers to aid Antony's cause. But Antony told him to deal first with Malichus, king of the Nabataeans. Malichus had grown weary of renting territory he considered his own, but after Antony placed Herod over it, Malichus stopped paying rent. Herod and Malichus went to war while Cleopatra supported the Arab king. If he won, she would gain control of Judea, Samaritis, and Galilee, areas currently under Herod's authority.

My brother had always been a good soldier and skilled commander, so I was not surprised when he defeated the Nabataean army at a place called Dium. He should have won the second battle with the Arab chief, but just when Herod had the Nabataeans on the run, Athenion, Cleopatra's general, reinforced the enemy army and brought about a turn in the situation. My brother suffered a staggering loss and had to send messengers to sue for peace.

Success made the Nabataeans foolish and bold. Buoyed by their success, they murdered my brother's envoys and had the temerity to invade Judea. Herod pulled his troops from outlying areas and reinforced the walls of Jerusalem. Those months were among the darkest since the day he had taken Jerusalem.

I thought Herod's outlook could sink no lower, until one morning when the earth shook and tremors bumped me out of bed. At first I thought Costobar had jarred the bed frame, and then I realized the chamber walls were trembling. I called my husband and glimpsed his form through dust pouring into the room, and together we ran into the open courtyard.

The entire household—servants, slaves, children, guards, even Herod and Mariamne—stood beneath a darkening sky and watched the trees at the gate sway, their branches thrashing as if HaShem had taken hold of them. Then, after an interval woven of eternity, the rumbling slowed and stopped. We stepped over fallen stones and branches and walked back inside to assess the damage.

Forty-five people died in the palace alone, most by injuries from falling stones or bricks. Thousands more died throughout Jerusalem, and several buildings collapsed. During the following week, we learned that vast amounts of property and livestock had been destroyed. The monastery at Qumram, home to the Essenes, had been severely damaged and had to be abandoned.

Herod knew we could rebuild, of course, yet we would need months to recover from the destruction. His new palace, the three beautiful towers—all had suffered damage and would have to be reinforced and repaired.

I had never seen my brother so defeated. His kingdom had been devastated, and his people were suffering from severe emotional and physical losses. His military campaign, which had begun with such promise, ended in defeat, with Antony's Egyptian lover having acted against him. Antony probably did not even know that Cleopatra had betrayed his client-king. Yet Antony was embroiled in a battle with Octavian, so no help would come from that quarter.

My brother's ambitions and dreams suddenly seemed ephemeral, as insubstantial as dust.

As desperately as I wanted to help Herod, neither Mother, Pheroras, nor I knew how to encourage his state of mind. Mariamne was no help either, for although he might have been comforted by her beauty and the children she had given him, she cared nothing about political or international affairs. She was content as long as she felt admired and loved, and had always left the political maneuvers to her mother.

As for Alexandra, she should have remained quiet during those dark months. Her greatest ally, Cleopatra, had no time for her, and our resident schemer should have felt eclipsed by the crucial matters threatening the Egyptian queen. But Alexandra was not the sort of woman who could rest, surrender, or forget. Her desire for revenge had not been slaked, and her deathless ambition had not been satisfied. But with her son gone and her daughter content, what pawn could she use to reclaim the throne?

She turned to the only remaining Hasmonean—her father, Hyrcanus, whom Herod had welcomed back to Judea and given a safe place to live. Hyrcanus had been a gentle king, which undoubtedly led to his downfall, and he did not have a warrior's nature. His daughter, however, had more than enough determination for the two of them. Later I learned that she began to visit him during the time of Herod's troubles. She encouraged her father to fight for his throne and reclaim the kingdom that had once been his as king and high priest.

But the former king was over seventy years old and had been deformed—someone had purposely ripped off his ears—so he could no longer qualify as a high priest. He had no heart for making the hard decisions a king must make, but he could not ignore the dripping refrain coming from his stubborn daughter.

During her frequent visits to his home, Alexandra begged Hyrcanus to write Malichus, king of the Nabataeans, and ask for asylum. After some time, the former king reluctantly agreed and sent a message to Malichus by Dositheus, a trusted friend. At Alexandra's bidding, Hyrcanus asked the Arab king for a safe escort from Jerusalem to the Dead Sea.

Yet Alexandra did not know that Dositheus was loyal to Herod, so instead of delivering the message to Malichus, he took it to the king. Rather than order Hyrcanus's and Alexandra's immediate execution, my brother instructed Dositheus to deliver the message to Malichus. When Dositheus returned with Malichus's reply—which granted Hyrcanus's request—Herod brought the correspondence before his council, a group consisting of our mother, Costobar, Pheroras, and me.

Herod read the letters to us, then dropped the scrolls on the table and waited for our reaction.

"I do not think you have a choice," Pheroras said, his gaze intent on the documents before us. "He has spurned your offer of a home and sided with your enemy."

"I am well acquainted with this Hyrcanus," Mother said, a quaver in her voice. "And he has no stomach for war. This is that woman's doing."

"The implication is clear," I added. "And Mother is right—Alexandra is behind this. If Hyrcanus goes to Malichus, Alexandra will urge him to gather an army to unseat you."

"I hate to execute the old man." Herod sighed and propped

his foot on a stool. "If he were not such a genial king, my father and I would not have risen to the stations we achieved under his reign. He allowed we Idumaeans to accomplish great things, where another king would have kept us under his thumb."

"A stronger king," I interjected. "You were able to rise because Hyrcanus refused to lead."

Costobar shook his head. "Still—"

Herod cut him off with an uplifted hand. "I know. He has committed treason, and he must die. So be it."

"But make no mistake," I said, forcing the words through a tight throat. "Alexandra is set against you, brother, and certainly you can see it now."

I thought he would agree and order her execution as well, but Herod only lifted his head and gave me a weary smile.

"My son is in love," Mother said, "and he had better be careful. The love that makes him strong can undo him just as easily."

In later years I often wondered how our fates might have been different if we had killed the queen of Egypt. Antony might have become emperor of Rome. Herod might have been placed over Judea and Egypt, and the world would have been coming to *him* for bread. Cleopatra would have been a mere name in a long list of Egyptian kings and queens, while Herod would be remembered in a far better light.

But because we did not harm her, the saga of Antony and Cleopatra unfolded in tragic fashion, and the entire civilized world felt repercussions from their unfortunate love affair.

The news reached us before Cleopatra had been entombed— the Egyptian queen was dead, a breathless messenger told Herod's court, by her own hand, and Antony had predeceased her.

The report from Alexandria ushered a dark cloud of grief

into Herod's palace. The king retired to his chamber, and for several hours he would not admit anyone save the messenger, not even his beloved Mariamne. When I voiced my frustration, Zara suggested the king might be praying, but I knew better. My purely pragmatic brother would not turn to God at a time like this; he would draw upon his wits.

At sunset, Herod sent for me. I went to his chamber alone and found him sitting at his desk, his face lit by a single candle. "I am going to Rhodes to see Octavian," he said simply. "While I am gone, Soemus will be in charge of the government. I want you to observe everything that happens while I am away, and I will expect a full report when I return."

"*Will* you return, brother?" My voice cracked beneath the pressure of repressed emotion. "You were Antony's most loyal man. How will Octavian receive you—if he receives you at all?"

Herod gave me a lopsided smile. "What was it our father always said? '*Whatever your hand finds to do, do it with all your might.*' I am going to offer Octavian my friendship. I hope he will find it an acceptable gift."

"Does Mother know?"

"I will let you tell her after I am gone."

Of course he would. Mother was the only woman in the world who made Herod nervous.

I pressed my lips together, not needing to point out the inherent dangers in his position. Octavian needed Herod as much as he needed Antony, which was not at all. What Octavian needed was Egypt, and he had won it and its riches, ensuring that the grain basket of the world would flow at his command. What did Judea have to offer Rome? We had no treasures, no grain, no politicians save Herod, who had sided with Antony against Octavian up to the moment of Antony's death.

Herod was walking into a viper's pit, and he knew it.

"In case things go wrong," my brother added, speaking more

slowly, "I am sending you and Costobar, our mother, and your children to Masada. You will be safe there and under guard."

I tilted my head, as something seemed . . . wrong. "What of your wife and children?"

His mouth curved in a rueful smile. "I think it best to send Mariamne, her mother, and her children to the fortress of Alexandrium. Pheroras will take care of them."

He was making preparations for the near-certain probability that he would not return. Costobar and I would be safe at Masada, Mariamne and Herod's heirs would be under Pheroras's protection at Alexandrium. If Herod died, Pheroras would serve as regent until Alexander, the oldest boy, came of age, who would then rule in Herod's stead . . . unless Octavian decided otherwise.

Alexandra would win, and her grandson would inherit the throne of Judea. I could do nothing to stop a Hasmonean victory . . . at the cost of my brother's life.

I closed my eyes, resisting the truths he did not speak, as images flashed before me. I saw Herod at thirteen, stumbling over Hebrew words as he read from the Torah; at sixteen, showing me how to string a bow; at twenty, kneeling to look into my eyes and assure me that even at twelve, I was a beautiful girl with nothing to fear from anyone. I smelled the fat in the fire from the wild venison he cooked, tasted the sweet cakes he sneaked away from Hyrcanus's banquet. I saw Herod at twenty-six, awkward and shy, marrying Doris, holding baby Antipater a year later, a look of thunderstruck awe in his eyes. I saw Herod's tear-streaked face when our father died, his stuttering shock after learning that our brother Phasael had committed suicide, Herod's satisfaction when he arranged his betrothal to Mariamne, his boundless joy when he held Alexander, his firstborn from his Jewish queen. Was he thinking of these same moments? Was he ready to leave this life?

I fell to my knees in front of him. "Be careful, brother. You have always been there for me, and I do not know what I would do without you."

"Truly?" Herod's voice rasped. "Are you sure you would not prefer your husband over me?"

I blinked in confusion. "What do you—?"

"In these past few hours I have heard several reports out of Egypt, including news that your husband convinced Cleopatra to ask Antony for Idumea, which is as much my homeland as it is Costobar's. Apparently your husband wanted to serve a queen instead of his king."

My thoughts spun as I lowered my head. The faded images of the past vanished as Herod's words dredged up a memory I would rather not recall. His spies had been thorough.

"I should execute him for his treachery," Herod said, his voice deadly quiet in the darkening room. "Did you know about his ambition?"

"Herod, you cannot kill him—he's the father of my children." I clasped my brother's feet in desperation. "He made a mistake, true, but he has not pursued the matter. Nothing became of his visit to Alexandria. If Cleopatra *had* regained Idumea, she might not have chosen Costobar to govern it. She made him no promises, and he has done nothing to incite men against you."

"Should I let such treachery go unpunished? Idumea is mine. It is my homeland."

"Of course it is. Herod, I admit—and I would never lie to you—that my head was turned when Costobar spoke of ruling Idumea. I loved him deeply, for he was my husband, and he had just given me a son. A son, Herod! A son who could become a prince! But as I thought about it, I realized you would not want to lose even a small portion of your kingdom. And though I love my husband, he is not blood to me, as you are. You are my brother, and you and Pheroras come before everyone else. I would sooner die than disappoint you."

The door opened with a complaining screech, and a servant appeared holding a tray. Herod snapped his fingers and gestured toward the door, and the servant disappeared.

"You did disappoint me. I cannot believe you knew."

Herod stared at me, a watchful fixity to his face. I would have despaired of my life had I not remembered his speaking of Masada, where he was sending us to safety. Surely he did not intend to kill either Costobar or me . . . but he had also said we would be under guard. And those guards, at some predetermined time or event, could easily execute us.

Knowing I had not convinced him to spare our lives, I cast about for some reason, however trivial, to banish the cold gleam from his eye. "Mother will be upset if you kill my husband. Costobar is family, and you know how she feels about family."

That remark, born out of despair, seemed to cool Herod's anger but did not vanquish the frigid glint in his eye. Faced with the threat of our mother's formidable wrath, my brother would spare Costobar and might one day consider pardoning him, yet he would never again trust my husband.

If Herod survived his trip to Rhodes . . . and Octavian's judgment.

CHAPTER THIRTY-THREE

Salome

I did not stand with Herod when he spoke before Octavian, of course, but I heard a full report from the guard Eurus, who routinely traveled as part of the king's escort. The friendly Idumaean came to see me at Masada and said he would be among the soldiers who would escort my family back to Jerusalem.

I could see the man was about to burst with news from Rhodes, so I asked him about the trip.

"Should we wait until your husband returns?" Eurus asked, ever mindful of his manners.

I waved his concern away. "Costobar is out touring his farms and will not return today. So please, I would love to hear what happened in Rhodes."

"You would have been proud of the king," Eurus began, gratefully accepting the chair I offered. "Herod was brilliant in his planning and his approach. Even Mark Antony would have been impressed."

"Indeed." I sat opposite him and rested my chin on my hand, eager to hear more. "Do tell me everything."

The guard returned my smile in full measure. "We sailed into the harbor of Rhodes and caught the legionaries by surprise; they had no idea we were coming. And when the guards confronted us, Herod stepped off our ship like an ordinary commoner—without his diadem, his royal robes, or his sword. He told the captain who met us that he was king of Judea and was seeking an audience with Octavian, if that great man would agree to see him."

"Go on," I urged, a grin tugging at the corners of my lips. "I see the story so clearly when you tell it."

Warming to his role, Eurus leaned forward, resting his elbows on his bare knees. "Not long after we went ashore, the summons came. And when we walked into Octavian's tent, Herod bowed, then stood upright and firmly proclaimed his allegiance—not to Octavian, but to Antony. He confessed he owed all to the man, and he had given all to Antony, whatever his master needed, including a large amount of food, auxiliary troops, weapons, and other supplies. He also mentioned that he and his army had not been with Antony at Actium because they had been detained by a conflict with the Nabataeans. 'Even after Antony's defeat,' the king said, 'I remained by Antony's side to counsel him, but he was too infatuated with the Egyptian queen to rid himself of that fatal monster of a woman. I have come here now to rest my safety on my integrity,' he said, standing before Octavian as bravely as any man alive. 'I am not ashamed to declare my loyalty to Antony. But if you would disregard the individual concerned and examine how I requite my benefactors, how staunch a friend I prove, then you may know me by the test of my past actions. I hope the subject of inquiry will be not *whose* friend but *how loyal a friend* I have been.'"

I sank back in my chair, both stunned and impressed by Herod's insight. He could not have hidden his friendship with Antony, so he made the most of it, offering the same rich friendship to Octavian.

I brought a hand to my mouth to hide my smile. Father would have been pleased.

"And that's not all," the guard said.

"There is more?"

"I haven't told you what Octavian said in reply."

"By all means." I chuckled. "Don't let me stop you."

The guard leaned forward, resting one elbow on an armrest while he peered at me over his clenched fist. "Octavian looked right at King Herod—just like this—blinked, shook his head a bit, and said, 'So staunch a champion of the claims of friendship deserves to be ruler over many subjects . . . Antony did well in obeying Cleopatra's behests rather than yours, for through his folly we have gained you.'"

"And then," Eurus said, his face brightening, "Octavian ordered an official decree to be written up and given to the king. So that all might see where Herod stood in his affection, Octavian ordered Herod to ride beside him across Syria on his way to Egypt. On entering Herod's own kingdom at Ptolemais, our king had a lavish banquet prepared and had Octavian ride next to him when he reviewed his troops. And if that were not enough, our king had eight hundred talents put in a chest and taken to Octavian's tent as a personal gift." The guard slammed his fist on the arm of the chair in a burst of enthusiasm. "*That* ought to seal the deal with Rome!"

"Indeed." I stared at the man in dazed agreement. Eight hundred talents? I did not know Herod had so much, if the gift truly had come from his own coffers. Most likely he had confiscated the money from someone or someplace else.

"So . . . the friendship between Herod and Octavian is official, but is it genuine? Did this new Caesar seem to *like* Herod, or will we forever have to doubt his loyalty?"

"I would say it's genuine." The guard leaned back and grinned, revealing a wide gap where two front teeth should have been.

"Before they parted, Octavian agreed to return the territories annexed by Cleopatra, and Octavian also gave the king Samaria and Strato's Tower. Herod was so pleased that he declared Strato's Tower would be rebuilt and renamed Caesarea in honor of Caesar." The guard motioned me closer and lowered his voice to a conspiratorial whisper. "Everyone knows Octavian's best friend is Marcus Vipsanius Agrippa, but everyone with us kept saying Herod had become Octavian's second-best friend. The bond is strong, my lady, and will certainly last as long as Herod wishes to occupy his throne. Caesar all but guaranteed it."

"So Herod is coming home."

"Soon, I'd say."

"Good." I sat back and savored the news, then reached for my purse, determined to give the guard a coin or two.

Eurus thrust out his hands and shook his head. "I would not think of accepting payment for sharing good news, my lady. I am happy to fight for our king. Only in this case, I was glad we did not have to fight at all. Octavian said if our king had been fighting with Antony at Actium, well, he would have been forced to treat Herod differently. But thanks to HaShem, your brother did not lift his sword against Rome, so his future is assured."

Was it? After dismissing the guard, I sat and pondered what I had just heard. Had God ordained my brother's future by sending him to battle Malichus instead of Octavian? Or was Herod simply the most fortunate man who ever lived?

Either way, he had won a great victory when he should have been executed. Best of all, Alexandra's dream had been vanquished . . . without any help from me.

~~~~~~~

By the time my children and I arrived back at the palace, I had realized the full implications of what transpired between

211

Herod and Octavian. I knew the meeting with Rome's new Caesar had fortified Herod's position and that of our family. No longer would my brother have to handle the Hasmoneans with careful diplomacy, no longer would he have to scrape before his supercilious mother-in-law. Alexandra had lost Cleopatra as a confidante, and she would no longer be able to send images of her handsome children to entice Antony's lusts.

I also realized my husband was playing a dangerous game he was not likely to win. One day I looked through his farm reports and saw names that rang a distant bell in my memory. By the time Costobar arrived home that night, I confronted him with the reports and demanded an explanation. I received one, and as a result I could not sleep that night. Soon I would have to take action.

Zara was still unpacking my trunks when my mother entered my apartment. Ignoring Zara, she sat on the edge of a chair and gripped her walking stick. Her eyes gleamed as she regarded me, and I knew she was eager to discuss something. But she would speak to me only in private.

"Zara"—I smiled at Mother—"would you leave us now? You can finish unpacking later."

Zara left the room without a word, leaving Mother and me alone.

"Mariamne and Alexandra," she finally said, each word a splinter of ice, "are due to return tomorrow."

I shrugged. "We should not be surprised. I'm sure Herod sent for them at once."

"This is our opportunity, Salome. We must not let it slip away."

I sank to the edge of my bed. "Perhaps I could better understand, Mother, if you explained yourself. Why should we worry about Alexandra now? Hyrcanus is dead. Aristobulus is dead. There are no more mature male heirs."

Mother snorted. "Do you think such an insignificant fact would stop a woman like her? She will invent heirs if necessary. She will declare herself queen regent until Mariamne's sons are old enough to reign."

I fell silent, for Mother had a point. I had once imagined a similar situation, with Pheroras as the boys' guardian.

"Herod commanded Soemus to look after Mariamne in his absence," Mother went on. "And he gave Soemus the same order he gave Joseph the last time he had to go away."

I swallowed a choking cough. "*That* order did not sit well with our queen."

"Nor did it this time, I am sure. Mariamne will be furious when she returns, and she will not welcome her husband with loving arms. Herod's prospects are higher than they have ever been, and he deserves to be celebrated. When his wife proves unwilling, we must do all we can to point out her unfitness to be queen. How can she deride and debase the man who charmed Octavian? How can she not see that her husband is more clever than any Hasmonean who dared call himself king? Mariamne is not to be tolerated, Salome, and all we have to do is point out her unsuitability. Herod will see it—surely this time he will."

Would he? Thus far he had proved remarkably blind when it came to Mariamne and Alexandra. Still, my mother was usually right. She had a gift for seeing a situation more clearly than anyone else.

I had vowed to do whatever I could to protect my family, my brother, and his throne. How could I do that as long as Mariamne and Alexandra were free to wreak havoc whenever they chose? And for all I knew, they were already at work, perhaps even involving my husband in their nefarious schemes . . .

I looked at Mother and nodded. "Whatever you do, I will support you. You have my word."

～～～～～

Mariamne's homecoming drama played out as Mother had predicted. Herod had been anxiously waiting to welcome his wife back to Jerusalem, but upon her arrival, Mariamne behaved like an offended virgin when he approached her on the stairs and tried to kiss her. He asked why she was upset; she said he had treated her as a possession, not a wife, by insisting that Soemus kill her upon news of the king's death. This time Herod responded in anger, roaring that she had no right to question his decisions and insinuating that she must have fallen in love with Soemus in order to think such a thing.

Mariamne, full of sauce and spite, replied she did not have to obey a man who had murdered her brother and father.

From where we stood in the downstairs vestibule, we heard more angry voices and slamming doors. The queen's return, apparently, was not as loving as Herod had hoped.

I later learned that while they waited in Alexandrium, Mariamne and Alexandra had showered Soemus with presents and attention, flattering and enticing him until they learned the king's instructions regarding their fates. I do not know why they were surprised by what they learned. Herod had not changed since he gave the same orders years before, so either they were the stupidest women to ever walk the earth or they enjoyed enticing vulnerable men who could not resist their charms.

When Herod heard from servants who reported the flatteries and gifts, he publicly accused Mariamne of being unfaithful. Standing before his assembled court, he threatened to put his queen on trial. In response, Alexandra, proving to be a greater opportunist than my mother, showed her true self. As a suddenly humbled Mariamne knelt to beg the king for mercy, Alexandra strode forward, grabbed her daughter by the hair and screamed that Mariamne's impudence had ruined her. I expected Mariamne to react with similar hysterics, but to her credit she remained silent and bore her mother's accusations without comment or tears.

For betrayal and having divulged the king's request, Herod had Soemus executed immediately. So inflamed was his temper, he would have immediately executed Mariamne as well, but Pheroras and I urged him to wait and grant the queen a trial for the sake of the people. We knew how the people of Jerusalem loved Mariamne, and she would always be the mother of the king's heirs.

Reluctantly, Herod agreed.

I attended the trial but remained in the shadows, determined to keep out of sight. I never wanted to do anything that might lead people to think I was jealous of my sister-in-law. Though she was beautiful, I was attractive in a different way; though she was Jewish, I was proud of my Idumaean heritage.

I must admit that I never cared for Mariamne's constant name calling and harping on my background. After years of marriage to my brother, she persisted in calling me "common," her way of implying my family did not deserve the throne. How could she forget that my brother, her husband, was highly favored by Rome? And was he not king of Judea? Was he not more talented and more clever than the Hasmonean kings who had squandered and rioted and murdered on their path to power?

Yet, truthfully, I wanted Mariamne to vanish from our lives. Her children were still young, but I could not forget what Mother had warned against—at some point, Alexandra could find some reason to discredit my brother. She would then proclaim Alexander or Aristobulus king, and she would reign as regent until they were old enough to rule. Such things had happened before. Such things could happen again.

Mariamne stood alone before the members of Herod's court at her trial. No one defended her. No one spoke on her behalf.

Herod stood before the members of the court and repeated the long list of charges: she hated him, she planned to poison him with love potions and drugs of divers types, and she had been unfaithful to the king. Herod's voice rose in volume and pitch as passion made him tremble, and by the time he had finished, every member of the court knew they would be committing a grievous folly if they decided against the king.

To a man, they voted to execute the Hasmonean queen. Later I learned that some of them had entered the chamber thinking they would imprison her indefinitely, but clearly the king wanted her to disappear. The cause of a Hasmonean queen unjustly accused and imprisoned could fuel a rebellion, so Mariamne would have to die.

I sat in a back row as Mariamne walked calmly to the stand where she would meet her fate. Some would later describe her as a queen distinguished for her continence and magnanimity of character, but they would never be able to deny that she was also excessively quarrelsome. She had beauty, grace, but a saucy, sharp tongue. Lacking the power to control it, she would never be able to please the king or be the wife she should have been. She treated her husband imperiously, one judge stated, and tended to forget she lived under a monarchy. In the end, she had succeeded in making enemies not only of me, my mother and Pheroras, but of Herod himself, the person she should have trusted to do her no harm.

After the panel of judges rendered their verdict, Mariamne lowered herself to her knees and pulled her hair over one shoulder, baring her neck. The executioner stepped forward, lifted his sword, and swung. The blow neatly severed her head, but the sight of the bloodletting did not rattle me nearly as much as the feral howl that lifted the hair on my arms as the head rolled onto the floor.

The king—my brother—had come undone.

CHAPTER THIRTY-FOUR

Zara

I settled into a chair at the back of Herod's throne room, content to linger in the shadows where I could see but would not be noticed. Upon greeting my mistress earlier that morning, Salome had let me know she would be spending most of the day with the king, so I should go to court in case something unusual happened, something that deserved the king's attention.

"I know you find it difficult to sit and do nothing." She gave me a distracted smile. "But the king has not been well, so I need to help him. Today Pheroras will receive the king's visitors, so you may take a bit of sewing or other quiet work to occupy your hands. If anyone disturbs the proceedings or attempts to take control, come to me at once. I will be in the king's chamber. Or, if he will not let me inside, I will be waiting outside his door."

Everyone in the palace knew how badly the king had reacted to Mariamne's death. I could not understand how a man could accuse her of unfaithfulness in one hour and grieve her loss in the next, but I had never been married. Marriage appeared to hold a great many mysteries, and the only royal marriages

217

I had closely observed were Salome's. Her marriage to Joseph seemed more like friendship than love. Her marriage to Costo-bar brought her great pleasure for a while, but he often seemed distracted when they were together.

Yet I was a maid of only fifteen, so what did I know of men?

I opened my sewing basket and took out a bit of embroidery, then threaded my needle the way Ima had taught me. In truth, I did not mind long hours at court. I had grown familiar with the faces of the king's friends, and newcomers always interested me. Foreigners often came to visit the king of Judea, while merchants vied for Herod's interest in their wares. Some presented him with fabulous gifts in hopes of winning his approval or even his notice. The last time I visited, a man from Lebanon had brought airy glass spheres and presented them to the king with a great flourish. Herod was transfixed, as was Mariamne, and the visitor explained that they were created by heating the glass until it could be blown into almost any desired shape. A pity Mariamne's character could not be shaped into a form the king would find more pleasing.

A pain squeezed my heart whenever I thought of our queen. Some said she was not guilty of the deeds for which she had been accused; others said her arrogance toward the king was more than enough reason to put her aside. But *kill* her?

I focused on my embroidery in my lap lest someone spot the tears in my eyes. We servants had been instructed to carry on as though nothing had changed, when in reality Mariamne's death had shaken everyone.

Especially the king.

On this morning, Herod remained in his chamber while Pheroras supervised the grand reception hall, sitting not on the throne but on a bench several feet away from the king's gilded chair. Word of the king's illness must have been made public, because in the back of the room I saw no merchants or foreign dignitaries, only a group of dark-robed Temple scholars. I had never been terribly interested in listening to boring interpretations of Torah teachings, so I considered taking my basket and retreating to the silence of Salome's chamber. But because I had promised to fulfill this duty, I kept my head down and my eyes and ears alert for any unusual circumstance.

A moment later, the king's brother stood to greet the scholars. They walked forward, the oldest of them moving as if weighed down by the dignity of his vast learning. Their long gray beards flowed over their robes, and their eyes seemed frozen in a perpetual squint, the result of years spent peering at ancient texts.

The oldest scholar, who apparently had been chosen as spokesman, stopped in the center of the room and announced that they had come to voice their objection to Mariamne's execution.

Pheroras sat on his bench and sighed heavily. "Let us hear it, then."

The spokesman unfurled a manuscript and began to read. His manner of speaking reminded me of an old and dusty scroll, and his message contained references to several sections of the Torah and the Law of Moses.

Of course the scholars would object. To remain silent would imply approval, and these men would never approve the execution of a Hasmonean princess. Their appearance here would be recorded, their message saved in a bin, and tomorrow they would return to their work. Nothing else would change.

I might have been able to put the scholars completely out of my mind, but movement from a man in the back row caught my eye. He was one of the younger teachers, for his beard was still black and his skin unlined. I found myself studying him, for whether he knew it or not, his body drew attention to itself with constant motion. As the elder scholar continued reading his statement, this tall, thin man bounced on his heels, his head bobbing above the other Torah teachers. When the men folded their hands to wait for Pheroras's response, the young man laced his fingers too, though his knees moved beneath his tunic, animating the fabric. He would tip forward, as if trying to see over the men in front of him, and then he would sigh and tip backward as if exasperated by having to wait.

Was no one else noticing this odd man?

I scanned the room, searching for a familiar face. Finally I spotted Mava, who sat by the back door with red-rimmed eyes and a somber countenance. And no wonder—since the Torah teachers were discussing the execution of her mistress, she had likely come here to support them.

I picked up my embroidery and basket and moved quietly to her side, then reached out and touched her arm. "I'm sorry," I mouthed, acknowledging her grief. I leaned closer and nodded toward the fidgety man in the last row of scholars. "Have you ever seen that Torah teacher before?"

She shook her head. "I do not know him. But I am glad he came. I am glad they all came. While their words cannot bring her back, at least the world will know a great injustice has been committed in the king's court."

Knowing it would not be proper to carry on a conversation in this place, I waited until the Torah teachers had finished and left the reception hall. Only a handful of visitors remained, who had come to pay their respects to the grieving king.

When Mava slipped out of the chamber, I followed her into the vestibule. "I am sorry," I repeated, giving her a sad smile. "I can only imagine what you must be feeling."

"Can you?" Her tone had gone chilly and her eyes cold. "I should not even be speaking to you. Your mistress and her mother conspired together to destroy our queen."

I gasped. "*My* mistress? I will admit there was no love between her and Mariamne, but Salome had nothing to do with the way your mistress behaved." I lowered my voice as others entered the vestibule, then grabbed Mava's arm and drew her into the courtyard.

"My queen was not unfaithful!" Mava hissed. "I would have known if she had entertained men—*any* man—in her chamber. She never did, not while she was in Alexandrium, and not before."

"Did she not insult the king? Did she not insult his family? She alone is responsible for her death, Mava. If she had been more gentle, if she had been kind, she and Salome might have been as loving as sisters." I caught her arm again and softened my tone. "What happened between them has nothing to do with you and me. I suppose it is natural we should defend our ladies, but we are not royals. We are only servants, and I am glad of it."

Mava closed her eyes as her expression darkened with unreadable emotions. Then she drew me into a tight embrace and burst into tears. "I have no one to talk to," she said between sobs. "They have set me to work for Cypros, but I cannot serve her. She acts as though nothing has happened, while our queen, our beloved Mariamne, is dead, leaving behind four children . . ."

I patted her back and made shushing sounds, leading her to a bench beneath a tree. The poor girl needed to release her grief, and she certainly could not do so in the presence of the king's mother.

"We do not know why HaShem allows such things to happen," I said when she had calmed herself. "Still, we can trust Him to have everything under His control. He has purposes we cannot understand."

She sniffed. "Is that what some Torah teacher told you?"

"It is what my father always said—what I learned when he died and my mother was injured during the war for Jerusalem. And when I found myself working in the household of the same king who brought that war."

I dropped into a well of memory so deep that at first I didn't realize I had left the present. I was nine again, standing alone in a palace corridor, terrified of a scolding or worse, horrified to find myself lost in the twisting hallways where Israel's kings and high priests had walked. I wanted my father, but he was gone; I wanted my mother, but she had sent me away. And why? So I could find my future, a husband, a life in a palace rather than a hovel.

Mava sniffed, and the sound brought me back to my present self. I squeezed her arm, not to comfort her so much as to anchor myself in reality.

"It was difficult at first," I admitted. "My mother told me it would be. But when I cannot understand, I must trust HaShem all the more."

Mava swiped her tears away. "I'm sorry I—"

"I know it has been hard for you. These past few days have been hard for all of us, but especially for you."

She drew a quivering breath and looked toward the doorway. "Why did you ask about the man in there? The jiggly one?"

I laughed. "I do not know. I just thought he was . . . different."

"My friend has a brother in the Sanhedrin; he knows everyone. I can ask about him, if you like."

I bit my lip. "I . . . I am curious to know why he cannot stop moving."

"Perhaps he sat on a bed of ants," she said, and we leaned on each other, convulsing with silent laughter. When we finally regained control of our emotions, we stood in time to see Cypros walking through the courtyard and heading toward the throne room, a frown on her austere face.

"There goes my mistress." Mava sighed and gave me a wavering smile. "I will see you later."

"You will," I promised. "And we will talk again."

"His name," Mava told me when we met in the hallway a week later, "is Ravid."

I frowned. "Who?"

"The wiggly worm who caught your attention when the Torah teachers visited the palace. You asked me about him."

"Oh. I'd forgotten."

"Liar." Grinning, she drew me aside so we could converse privately. "What else do you want to know? My brother told me more."

Despite my awareness of the vast difference in our ages and situations, something in me wanted to know everything about the young man. "How much more do you know?"

"Much more. Though Ravid is young, he is a Torah teacher. He is from the tribe of Judah and spends most of his time at the Temple. He teaches Torah to the younger boys—as soon as they leave their fathers' knee, they go to study under Ravid."

I closed my eyes, imagining a roomful of active six-year-olds in the care of this young man. In that context, his mannerisms made sense. "Is that all you learned?"

Mava shook her head, a smile ruffling her mouth. "Are you sure you want to know? If knowledge will only make you yearn for the impossible?"

"I am not yearning, I am only curious. Please, speak."

She gripped my hands. "Ravid married young, a girl from his village. She was pregnant when Jerusalem fell to Herod and the Romans. Ravid fought with those on the wall, so he was not home when the Romans killed his wife and unborn baby. Ravid survived the battle, but barely. He could not teach for many months, so burdened was he by his wound and his grief."

I blinked away fresh tears. Even after eight years, memories of that battle still elicited a pain deep inside. "I am sorry to hear it. I . . . I lost my family, as well."

"Many of us carry scars from our introduction to the man

who now calls himself our king. But though Ravid teaches the young boys, he is most interested in the teachings of the Essenes. When he is not at the Temple, he often visits with them in meetings scattered throughout the city." She lowered her voice. "They keep their meetings secret so as not to attract attention. They do not know how Herod feels about the Essenes, and they do not want trouble."

I frowned. "I do not think the king dislikes the Essenes. I have seen him dine with Pharisees, Sadducees, and Essenes."

"He is cordial to them, yes, but Ravid and several other scholars are concentrating on a particular teaching from the Prophet." She lowered her voice again and moved closer to whisper in my ear, "It concerns the coming king."

I blinked as my throat went dry. "Coming king?"

She shook her head. "I will say no more. If you are still curious, perhaps you can meet with my brother and Ravid. My brother says Ravid is passionate about this future king and constantly searches the prophetic writings to uncover clues about his coming."

In a sudden burst of insight, I understood why Ravid and his friends met secretly. Herod and his family were constantly worried about maintaining his position. He feared opposition from the people, from Rome, from rivals, even from his wife. Herod did not seem to mind HaShem sitting on the throne of heaven, but if for one moment he thought Adonai wanted to sit on the throne of Judea, Herod would mount a war against heaven itself.

Yet the prophets had long written about a coming king, a Messiah, and a priest from the order of Melchizedek. This king had not come, however, and surely he would not arrive anytime soon. For what sort of king could step onto the scene with Herod in power and Rome ruling from the west? How could such a man fight them both? He couldn't. So this king, whoever he was, was certainly not coming in the foreseeable future, no matter how much Ravid and his friends longed to welcome him.

I smiled, grateful to have a new topic to discuss with Salome on the morrow.

CHAPTER THIRTY-FIVE

Salome

My brother had executed dozens of men and women, but none of those deaths affected him like Mariamne's. In the days following her burial he remained locked in his chamber, drinking. Neither banquets, parties, hunting, nor other women could entice him to shake free of his melancholy and grief.

Mother came to me several weeks after the funeral, and even though she tried to maintain her composure, I could see how worried she was. "He keeps telling the servants to fetch the queen," she said, her voice trembling as she sank onto a chair. "And today he could not get out of bed. I sent for the physician, but he could find nothing wrong, though he is clearly worried. Herod will not eat or drink, and if we press him, he asks for his sons. But none of us want him to see his sons right now—I do not believe Alexander, Aristobulus, and Herod know their mother is dead."

"They don't know?" I asked. "Where . . . where have they been?"

"With Alexandra." Mother finally met my gaze. "And I can

only imagine what she has told them. If they do not hate their father now, they will soon enough."

I turned away to consider the situation. Someone would have to tell the boys the truth, and soon. That someone should be their father. If not Herod, then Pheroras or me. We should not leave this responsibility to Alexandra.

I faced my mother again. "Alexandra will still be a problem, and she should not have so much time with Herod's sons. Has she done anything we could bring to Herod's attention? If not, perhaps we could invent a story . . ."

Mother harrumphed. "We will not have to invent anything. That woman will commit treason on her own, wait and see. She is as distressed as Herod is now but in far less control of her reason. Give her time, daughter, and she will be the architect of her own undoing."

"Good." I managed a smile and rubbed my pregnant belly. "Because when Alexandra falls, the fault must be her own—not Herod's."

As always, my mother was right—we did not have to wait long.

Within days of Mariamne's death, I gave birth to my second daughter. But Herod did not visit his new niece. Instead he remained locked inside his chamber, reportedly sick and in bed.

Costobar visited him one afternoon and returned with sad news. "His affections for Mariamne are kindled anew, even more outrageous than before." He sat on the bed so he could hold his new daughter. "His love for her was never of a placid nature."

"Like yours for me?" I asked, testing.

He gave me a smile. "It is exactly as you say. But now he feels he is suffering the pangs of love as divine vengeance for taking her life."

I bit my lip, at a loss for suggestions about how to help him. But someone had to do something—a king afflicted by this sort of weakness would not remain king for long. Had not we learned that lesson from Hyrcanus? I looked at Costobar. "Did you try to help him?"

"I suggested he try to distract himself from his troubling thoughts—have a feast, convene an assembly, those sorts of things. I reminded him that he must see to the administration of public affairs. He cannot afford to remain locked in his room, calling for a woman who will not answer." Costobar sighed. "And the pestilence is not helping matters."

Alarm spurted through my bloodstream. "What pestilence?"

"Ah, you have been confined, so you would not know. A pestilence has come over the city—a disease that has already claimed many, including some of Herod's most esteemed friends. When he comes out of hiding, he will be shocked to discover how many supporters he has lost."

I glanced toward the window, where Jerusalem stretched from the sill to the hills beyond. "What kind of disease is it?"

"The people die quickly, and the doctors cannot stop it. Many are saying this is HaShem's punishment for the injustice done to Mariamne."

"That's not good. Herod must not hear that."

"He will hear it. As soon as he begins to go out among the people, he will not be able to escape the reports."

"Then . . . let us take him to Samaria. The air is sweeter there, and my brother has always liked the city. He can recover in Samaria."

I made plans for our immediate departure. I thought Herod would protest, unwilling to leave the palace where Mariamne had lived, but he did not protest. The next morning our retinue left Jerusalem and the epidemic spreading through the city. Once we reached Samaria, Herod went to his room and closed the door. I gestured to Costobar, urging him to persuade Herod to rejoin the land of the living.

Over the next few weeks, I watched as Herod tried to follow Costobar's advice. He held elaborate feasts for nobles and the leading families of Samaria, yet the atmosphere at these feasts was anything but festive. He held public assemblies to discuss his plans for the region. Sadly, a noticeable lack of enthusiasm for his ideas hampered his presentation and left the people confused.

One afternoon I went in search of my brother and found his chamber empty. "Where is the king?" I asked a servant. "Has he gone riding?"

The man shook his head. "He says he's gone hunting, though I do not think he will get anything."

I frowned. "Why not? He is good with a bow—"

"He went hunting in the desert, lady. And he took only one servant with him."

"Why is that so odd? I know the king's hunting parties are usually large, but if a man prefers solitude—"

"If a hunter kills a deer, how is one servant supposed to carry it *and* the king's gear?"

How indeed?

I worried for the next two days, afraid Herod intended to stop beneath a tree and command his servant to kill him. Had he become so unhinged that he cared nothing for his life? Had some dark spirit taken possession of him? Or perhaps he imagined himself haunted by the sharp-tongued ghost of Mariamne . . .

My brother finally returned, with nothing to show for his efforts but a sunburn. The next morning he woke in great pain and commanded his servants to call the physician, who then summoned me.

"What is it?" I asked, rushing to my brother's room. Herod lay on the bed, his eyes closed. I could not tell if he slept or was only pretending to sleep.

The physician stepped away from the royal bed and drew closer to me. "He has an inflammation," he whispered, "and a pain in the back part of his head. Combined with the madness, it is a most severe condition."

"What madness?"

The physician shot me a look of disbelief. "Surely you know, lady, that the king calls for his queen several times a day. And when she does not come, he breaks down and weeps bitter tears."

I waved the comment away. "This will pass. Give him medicines. Make him well again."

"We have tried, but the medicines cannot conquer a disease of the mind. And he is not eating. He says he is not hungry, but he cannot get well until he takes sustenance."

I paced the room, thinking, then stopped and looked at the oblivious man on the bed. "Then we will wait until his appetite returns," I said. "For as long as it takes, we will wait."

CHAPTER THIRTY-SIX

Zara

I was surprised when my mistress told me I did not have to go to Samaria. She wanted me to remain in Jerusalem and keep her children safely confined to the palace. I was not to allow them to venture into the city, where the pestilence held full sway, but to keep myself and the children healthy at all costs.

So I found myself in charge of Alexander, Herod, Berenice, Antipater, and the newest baby girl, who had not yet been given a name. Because I wanted to call the baby *something*, I called her Phebe, Greek for *sparkling*. She was a sweet infant, whose eyes sparkled when she smiled, and she smiled nearly all the time.

Mava remained at the palace as well, because Cypros had charged her with keeping an eye on Alexandra. "I have become a spy," Mava told me when we met outside the kitchen.

"And I a nursemaid." I shifted Phebe in my arms. "I'm only grateful Salome's children are small and fond of sleep. The wet nurse cares for them several hours a day." One of the cooks handed me a basket of bread and cheese, which I slipped over my arm and turned toward the stairs. "What is Alexandra doing while Herod is away?"

"I haven't seen her," Mava replied, falling into step beside me, "but she has been receiving guests. At first I thought they were friends coming to console her, but yesterday the captain of the Temple fortress came to her apartment. Why would she need to see him? I still don't know, but he did not look happy when he came out of her chamber."

"Have you heard her say anything . . . disloyal?"

Mava shook her head. "She will not speak when I am in the room. She is always sending me out on errands when she receives guests."

I nodded while sorting through the possibilities. Alexandra could be up to anything, arranging a monument for her dead children and father, asking for news about old friends, or planning a revolt. I couldn't read the woman—few people could.

"Mava, will you send word to Cypros?"

"When I know something certain." Mava bit her lip and looked through the open window at the city beyond. "The air around Alexandra feels heavy, like a summer day before a storm. If the storm breaks, keep your young charges safe. You might have to hide or disguise them."

She did not need to explain herself. Both of us knew that if Alexandra attempted to spark a revolution, the first thing she would do was have her army kill the king's family and his heirs. Herod had killed hers, but only after he had been provoked. Alexandra, however, would strike as swiftly as an adder.

CHAPTER THIRTY-SEVEN

Salome

I had just come in from breaking my fast on the balcony
when I saw a messenger standing near the doorway of my
apartment. I groaned, annoyed that my servant—an infe-
rior handmaid compared to Zara—had granted him entrance.
But the sight of a scroll in his hand piqued my curiosity.

I gestured to the scroll. "Is that for me?"

The man bent forward in a bow. "From the lady Alexandra,
in Jerusalem. She bade me bring it to you with all haste."

I accepted the scroll, then made a shooing gesture. "You
may leave me now."

"Should I wait for a reply?"

I shook my head. "I can't think of anything I would say to
that woman."

When he had gone, I sat on a nearby bench and broke the
seal. I unfurled the parchment and immediately recognized Alexandra's handwriting.

Salome,
   *I have been entertaining loyal guests in the king's ab-
sence, among them several sons of Baba, who have been*

*loyal to the Hasmoneans since the time of Judah Mac-
cabaeus. Knowing that at one time the king sought their
lives, I asked how they had managed to remain safe. When
one of them mentioned the noble man who had given
safety and protection not to him only but to his entire
family, I was delighted. I am certain the king will not be
delighted, for the sons of Baba have been protected by
someone dear to his heart, and yours as well. Their savior
is none other than your husband, Costobar.*

*If you wish this secret to remain safe, you will not
hinder me in the coming days. For the time has come for
me to protect the legacy of the Jews' royal family, and I
will stop at nothing to accomplish my purpose. So if you
wish to save your husband's life, you will remain silent
and at peace.*

My hands trembled as I lowered the scroll. What had Costobar done this time? I knew little of the sons of Baba, but the
name evoked a sense of familiarity. Something about the fall
of Jerusalem, and Herod's frustration in not being able to find
the men who had garnered quite a reputation for courage and
loyalty to the Hasmonean cause.

Alexandra's intent was clear—she was about to take action,
and if I warned Herod, she would bring his wrath down upon
my husband, even perhaps upon my children and me. Would
Herod believe I had been unaware of Costobar's activity, or
would he believe I had placed my husband's welfare above his?

He would remember Costobar's foolish attempt to persuade
Cleopatra to set him over Idumea. I had said nothing about it,
because I foolishly believed that two men could share authority.
Herod might believe I had been so in love with Costobar that I
had agreed not to reveal his involvement with the sons of Baba.

I rested my elbow on an armrest and chewed my thumbnail.

If Alexandra was to set a revolt in motion, I would have to decisively counter it. But how could I when I had no idea what she was planning?

I went to the desk in the room and pulled parchment from a drawer, determined to write my mother.

~~~~~~

Once again, my mother proved prescient. She had remained in Jerusalem to keep an eye on *that woman*, as she called Alexandra, and a week after we left for Samaria her instincts proved true.

After hearing about Herod's illness, Alexandra realized her time had come. She wrote me, then sent for the commanders of the two fortified towers in Jerusalem—the Antonia Fortress adjacent to the Temple, and the Phasael tower attached to the city walls. She told the commanders they had the power to control the entire city. "Especially you," she told the commander of the Temple fortress, "for the people would be more willing to lose their lives than to leave off the daily sacrifices."

She then told the commanders it would be right and proper for them to deliver the fortresses to her and Herod's sons, lest someone else should seize the government upon Herod's death. "And if the king does not die," she said, smiling, "who could keep the fortresses safer than someone from his own family?"

She must have expected the Jewish commanders to obey her without question, but both men soothed her and departed without committing to her demands. Both were loyal to Herod, and both thought it distasteful to predict the king's death while he was still alive. One of them, Achiabas, sent messengers to Samaria and relayed Alexandra's request.

I learned about Alexandra's actions later, though I was sitting with my brother when he received the report from the Antonia's commander. By that time Herod was better, but far from well, still sorely afflicted in mind and body.

When he heard what Alexandra had done and how she intended to involve his sons in her treasonous maneuver, he gave the order to have her slain. "And I," he said, throwing the covers off his pale, inflamed skin, "must get back to Jerusalem. The palace needs a good housecleaning."

CHAPTER THIRTY-EIGHT

Zara

For at least a year after the queen's execution, those of us who lived in the palace felt as though we walked atop a sharp, thin blade. Lean too far toward either side and you were likely to be injured.

Once the king returned from Samaria, still weak but having regained the fire in his soul, he executed anyone he had ever suspected of disloyalty, including some who had proven their faithfulness time and again. Alexandra was the first to die, followed by others, even men from the king's court. Those Herod did not kill had to swear a loyalty oath, and rumors of secret spies abounded. "They wander through the streets of Jerusalem," Mava told me in a frightened whisper, "and report those who speak against the king."

I had heard such things before and wondered why Salome, who counseled her brother in all matters, did not try to soothe his temper. But after returning from Samaria, she kept a careful distance from him, preferring to spend her time with her children or her mother. Because I did not have to dress and do her hair nearly so often anymore, I had time to pursue interests of my own—a luxury I had not known since childhood

Spurred by curiosity and an urge I could not define, I asked Mava to go with me to a Torah study in the city. Grateful for any opportunity to escape the palace, she agreed at once. Her brother told us the location of a home meeting where women were welcome, so we went together. The Torah teacher, I was thrilled to learn, was Ravid.

After we arrived at the modest house, I nodded politely at Mava's brother, then moved a little closer to my friend. Except for our host's wife, we were the only women present, and our hostess did not seem exceptionally friendly. She kept her head down as she welcomed us, offering cups of cool water for the thirsty and a basin for washing dusty feet.

By the time the lamps were lit, everyone had found a place to sit. Mava's brother sat on a pillow at her right, leaving me on her left. I was thankful Mava's brother was present. Mava had a tendency to talk, so if she whispered to her brother, I would not be distracted from Ravid's teaching.

"Welcome," he said, bouncing on his feet as he stood before us. "I am glad you have come to learn more about the time that is coming." His gaze swung across the room, lingering for a moment on me and Mava. "I am happy to see two women have joined us," he added, the corners of his eyes crinkling as he smiled. "The Word of God is available to anyone who has a heart to hear it."

He bowed his head and led us in an informal prayer. When he finished, he sat on a stool and opened a scroll. "What I am about to tell you comes from the Teacher of Righteousness," he said, glancing up at us. "We believe he is a prophet who has been given truth and insight into things to come. Listen and let his words speak to you."

Heads nodded across the room as Ravid gripped the scroll

and began to read. "'We are living in a time of great turmoil,'" he began. "'And Israel will be delivered by two Messiahs. We have seen what happens when a man is high priest and king; the power of the king corrupts the holiness of the high priest. But we look for a royal Messiah, a son of King David; and a priestly Messiah from the line of Aaron. He will bring us back to God while the Son of Man rules the nations and brings them to judgment. He has always existed, even from the time before time, and He is the Son of God.'"

I lifted my head, startled. I had never heard such teachings—not from a Torah teacher and certainly not from my father. From where did such ideas come?

"'Our warrior king,'" Ravid read on, "'will gather the scattered people of Israel into their Promised Land and rule them in innocence and justice, subduing all other nations. But our priestly Messiah will reconcile us to God and forgive our many sins.'"

Murmurs of agreement rippled throughout the room.

"You all know," Ravid continued, looking up from the scroll, "how HaShem chose to enter into a covenant with Israel. But years later our fathers disobeyed HaShem, and He sent our people into exile, rejecting them because they broke covenant with Him. But HaShem has always preserved a remnant, and even though Judea is now filled with the children of Abraham, most of them do not live in covenant with Adonai. They mind the sacrifices and follow the Law with great zeal, yet their hearts are dark and rebellious and do not seek to love and obey Adonai. Even so, the remnant remains, and God will create a new covenant with them. All those who hear His voice will be the circumcised of heart, and we will recognize the Messiahs when they come."

I glanced at Mava. Was she as bewildered as I? I had never heard such things. Was Ravid a rebel or was he one of the few teachers who actually spoke the truth? I had no idea, but my father used to say that many of the religious leaders, even the priests, did not follow the commandments of Adonai.

I looked around the room and wondered if Ravid's madness was contagious. Most of the men appeared to be listening intently, while skepticism gleamed in two or three pairs of eyes. The sight comforted me. I would not want to remain if these people were following a false teacher.

"When our earthly lives come to an end"—I looked up and focused again on what Ravid was saying—"we do not disappear. Our bodies turn to dust, yes, but our souls live on. A bodily resurrection will occur after the final war has been settled by HaShem. Then a new kind of communion with Him and the angels will begin. We will worship HaShem in a new Temple in a new Jerusalem, and death and its shadows will disappear, never to torment us again."

My thoughts drifted to my last memory of Mariamne, who had quietly, stoically surrendered to the executioner. Of my father who sacrificed his life to a losing cause. Of my mother who had wasted away, her body but a shell of the strong woman she had once been before the fall of Jerusalem. How wonderful to think death could be defeated! Herod might even welcome a new king, if it would mean the end of parting and pain.

But Ravid said the end to death would not come until after a final war. I did not know when that would be, yet such bliss would probably not come in my lifetime. Like so many others, I would have no choice but to live and wait and hope for this better future.

Ravid lifted his hand and swayed in the rhythm of his closing prayer. After he finished, I took Mava's hand and firmly pulled her out of the house and into the night.

"Why are we in such a hurry to go?" Mava asked, irritation in her voice. "I wanted to ask my brother about something."

"Ask him next time," I said, my heart nearly beating out of my chest. "I am not sure about this teacher. I have never heard such things, and his ideas seem . . . dangerous."

"All the more reason why we should go again. Perhaps we will begin to understand."

"Understanding will not help us if Herod hears we went out searching for a new king." I released her hand and felt my shoulders relax. "I will go with you again, but I will not take these teachings to heart."

Mava frowned and drew her cloak over her head. "Do not worry—I will not ask you to."

My mistress sat on her dressing stool, facing the looking brass, as I heated the calamistrum.

"So," Salome said, studying her nails, "is anything happening in the servants' quarters? Any gossip I might find interesting?"

I pulled the calamistrum from the fire and, careful not to let my fingers touch the heated rod, wrapped a strand of Salome's hair around it. "Not about the servants. But I met an interesting man yesterday."

One of Salome's brows shot up. "My young handmaid has met a *man*?"

My cheeks heated beneath her gaze. "He is a Torah teacher at the Temple. He has unique views about HaShem, and about the future."

Salome stifled a yawn. "They always do. What does this one say?"

"He says"—I pulled the cylindrical rod away and let the steaming curl dangle freely—"the Teacher of Righteousness has prophesied that we are to expect two Messiahs in the future: one who will be our high priest and reconcile us to God, and another who will be a king from the line of David."

Salome lifted her head at the word *king*. "The line of David no longer exists, so why would he say such a thing?"

I used a comb to smooth another hank of hair. "Because the Teacher of Righteousness says the Messiah will be born into the House of David, but he will not be born until the House of David has returned to the poverty it experienced during the days of David's father, Jesse. The Messiah will be born in lowliness but will have the sevenfold fullness of the Holy Spirit."

I wrapped the hair on the calamistrum, then released it. When I glanced at my mistress again, her eyes had gone cold and sharp. "Zara," she said, an edge to her voice, "if you value your life at all, you should guard your tongue when you speak of a coming king."

For an instant my blood chilled, but then I forced a laugh. "Oh." I smiled as if I had been prattling foolishness. "This Messiah will not come for generations, mistress. How could he? The coming king will rule the earth, and how could anyone do that with Herod on the throne of Judea and Octavian ruling the world? Do not pay any attention to my rambling thoughts. People like the Teacher of Righteousness have been making such predictions for years."

"I know about the Essenes and their prophet," Salome said, relaxing in her chair. "They were calling for the advent of the Messiah when my grandfather served Alexander Jannaeus and Salome Alexandra. She studied the Scriptures and looked for the coming Messiah too, but she died without ever seeing him."

I set the calamistrum on the glowing coals and combed out another section of my mistress's hair. "Would you like me to prepare another henna rinse? The color is fading, and you might want it freshened for some special occasion."

"Remind me when I must attend a special occasion," Salome replied, and when her eyes met mine I knew she'd seen through my attempt to change the subject.

I returned my attention to the curling instrument, but beneath my calm exterior my heart was beating as fast as a bird's. I should learn to keep quiet. Sometimes, especially when I was feeling relaxed and content, I trusted my mistress far too much.

I should know better than to trust King Herod's sister.

⁓⁓⁓⁓⁓⁓

Mava and I went back to the Torah study. The second time we visited, another man taught the lesson, and he was not nearly as provocative as Ravid. On our third visit I was delighted to walk in and discover Ravid standing in the center of the room. As I sat with Mava and our hostess, I hoped he would not notice the blush heating my cheeks.

"Consider our nation from the beginning," he said, his gaze catching mine. "HaShem made a covenant with Abraham, to bless him and make a great nation out of him. Indeed, many nations have come out of Abraham, through Ishmael and Isaac. Isaac had two sons: Esau, father to the Idumaeans; and Jacob, father to the Jews. And Adonai wrestled with Jacob, and blessed him, and promised his seed would be as the dust of the land, and he would burst forth to the west and to the east and to the north and to the south. And in him all the families of the earth would be blessed—and in his seed. And so our people have come from Jacob, and from us will come a priest and a king who will rule the world."

I glanced at Mava, who seemed more interested in a man across the room than in Ravid's teaching.

"And God made a covenant with the people under Moses," Ravid went on. "He gave us the Law and promised blessings if we would keep it. But if we disobeyed it, He promised curses, warning us that we would be forced from the land He had given us. These things came to pass when our forefathers followed after other gods and married foreign wives, who turned the hearts of the men from the worship of Adonai. After seventy years, when HaShem brought us back to our land, He said, "'Do not remember former things, nor consider things of the past. Here I am, doing a new thing; now it is springing up—do you not know about it?'"

The owner of the house stood and interrupted, declaring that the hour had grown late. Ravid bowed his head as other men stood and began moving toward the doorway.

But I remained where I sat, my heart stirring with unexpected and unfamiliar longing. Once again I had been astounded by the words that poured from Ravid's mouth. I had never met a teacher who claimed to get his information from a prophet who spoke to HaShem. Everyone else spoke of the Law and tradition.

When I turned to look for Mava, Ravid stood behind me, his dark eyes studying my face. "Do you plan to stay all night?"

I drew a breath to answer, but then I saw the dancing light in his eyes. He was teasing.

My cheeks burned as I scrambled to my feet. "I was . . . thinking."

"About your friend?"

"About what you said." I forced my stubborn feet to turn toward the door, even though I wanted to remain exactly where I was.

Ravid walked with me. "You live at the palace, do you not? Let me escort you and your friend to the palace gate. Two women should not be alone on the streets at this hour."

I looked away, afraid to let him see how much his offer pleased me. I thanked him, then found Mava and tapped her on the shoulder. "Come, it is time we were away."

She bade our hostess farewell, smothered a yawn, and gave Ravid a look of weary resignation. "I'm sorry I did not listen better. I was up before dawn with one of the princes. Royal toothache."

Ravid gave her an understanding smile, and soon we were

all making our way down the street. Mava trudged behind us, blaming her tired feet, while Ravid and I walked side by side. "Tell me, Zara—"

"You know my name?"

He chuckled. "I asked Mava's brother. He said you were handmaid to the king's sister."

"I am."

"Then I will continue to pray for you. That job cannot be easy."

"You have been praying for me?"

"Of course." His answer was so natural that I wondered how many other girls he mentioned in his daily prayers. After all, he was a Torah teacher and so had an interest in his students.

"I have seen you at these meetings," he said, "and wondered why you were coming. It is unusual to see a girl of your age studying Torah."

"I am not so young."

"Yet you are not so old." He grinned. "I have wondered— who is HaShem to you?"

I blinked, startled by the question. "Who is HaShem? Don't you know?"

"Of course. But I want to know who He is to *you*."

"He is the Creator of the Universe. He is our God."

"Yes, but that is what He is to everyone in Jerusalem. Who is He to you, Zara?"

"Why . . . the same as He is to everyone, I suppose."

His smile deepened as he looked down at the cobblestones beneath our feet. "Moses called him *friend*. David called him *Lord*. What do you call Him?"

My confusion grew by the moment. "I call Him HaShem."

I did not know how he wanted me to answer but sensed I'd missed the mark. Yet I saw no disappointment in his expression, only an odd eagerness.

"Too many of our people," he continued, "see HaShem as the God who wrote the Law, the Judge we must please by counting our steps, tithing our herbs, and giving to the poor. But though we must always respect the Law, HaShem wants more than our obedience to a set of rules. He wants to know us personally; He wants us to love Him as Moses and David did."

I stopped in mid-step, almost causing Mava to collide into me. She muttered something under her breath, then walked around me and continued toward the palace.

"I cannot know God as Moses did," I whispered, afraid to speak such presumptuous words in a normal voice. "Moses was a holy man, while I am only—"

"Moses was a man like me," Ravid said. "And his sister Miriam was a woman like you. They knew HaShem and were not afraid to speak to Him. Your prayers should not be formal words you recite like a blessing; they should flow from your heart as naturally as water flows from a brook. He wants to know your honest thoughts, Zara, and He wants to speak to you."

"Does He speak to you?"

"Sometimes."

I staggered backward, convinced I was conversing with a madman. "I cannot speak to HaShem. I am only a girl."

"Not so very young, though, right?" He smiled. "Give yourself time. Study the Scriptures with me, and you will see I am showing you the truth. God is doing a new thing, and He is doing it among us. Please keep coming to our meetings and study Torah and the prophets along with me. I am certain your eyes will be opened."

I did not know how to answer him. Something in me realized Ravid was dangerous and that allying with him likely meant trouble, but still he fascinated me.

And though I suspected he was leading me toward an uncertain and perhaps perilous future, I also knew I wanted desperately to go with him.

Chapter Thirty-Nine

Salome

I could avoid Herod no longer. I had tried to remain distant, telling Pheroras I did not wish to attend the king's nightly banquets because my children needed me, but in truth I had been terrified by my brother's temper, and by what he might have learned from those who executed Alexandra. Did she speak of me and Costobar before the executioner took her life? Did she leave a letter for Herod? Had she entrusted her secrets to a favorite slave?

My brother's moods had been so unrestrained and unpredictable since Mariamne's death that merely being in his presence unnerved me. He might be watching, like a cat watches a mouse, waiting to see if I would confirm that my loyalties lie with my husband instead of my king.

I knew he had heard rumors and wanted an explanation as to why my husband had stopped visiting my chamber at the palace. Since our return from Samaria, Costobar had been spending his nights at his house in the city or on his farms, where he employed workers to tend his fields. He had not slept with me since before Phebe's birth, and though my bed was lonely without him, I had come to realize he was a threat to me and to my children.

So when Mother told me Herod was beginning to seem like himself again, I knew I should go to him at once. I had grown tired of being imprisoned by fear, and Herod's successful encounter with Octavian had inspired me to commit a similar irrevocable act—an act I'd known was inevitable ever since the moment Herod asked about my husband's dealings with Cleopatra.

Costobar, I concluded, was a liability and posed a danger to our family, and I had been foolish to fall in love with him. By allowing myself to be charmed by a handsome, strong, clever man, I had violated my vow to protect Herod from any threat.

I once admired Costobar for being independent, but by the time Herod recovered his senses I knew only one man could rule in Judea, and that man was Herod. Costobar was twice guilty of treason, and though for my sake Herod had forgiven him once, he would not be so gracious again.

So I did what the Jewish Law forbade any woman to do: I issued my husband a writ of divorcement. With the document firmly in hand, I had Zara dress me in my finest garments, then walked into the king's reception hall and waited for Herod to recognize me.

When Herod finally turned and greeted me with a warm smile, I stepped forward and declared that I was taking an unconventional step solely out of loyalty to my king. In the writ, which I read in front of several witnesses, including Costobar, Pheroras, and our mother, I proclaimed what I had learned from Alexandra and others: Costobar had been sheltering the sons of Baba, a pro-Hasmonean group of rebels. During the siege of Jerusalem, Costobar had been assigned to watch the city exits. While guarding the gates, he protected the rebels and smuggled them out of the city. He had been sheltering them ever since.

My brother's face contorted with shock and anger as he listened to my written condemnation, leading me to believe that this was the first time he had heard such news. When I finished, he shifted his attention to Costobar, who did not look in my direction. "Does your wife speak the truth?"

Costobar was no fool; he knew he had been defeated. He stood and lifted his chin. With a confidence born of courage, he nodded. "She does."

"Eight years?" Herod's face flushed. "For my entire reign you have sheltered rebels?"

Costobar crossed his arms. "I have."

"Where have you hidden the sons of Baba?"

"On my farms." Costobar turned, his dark, impassive eyes raking my face. "Those loyal people live there still, along with their families."

Herod turned to the captain of his guard and made a swift gesture; even I could interpret it without words. The captain hurried away, and I knew that neither the sons of Baba nor their family members would live to greet the sunrise.

Herod gripped the gilded arms of his throne and leaned toward the man he had once trusted. "Costobar, governor of Idumea, your honors and wealth are stripped from you. You will die at sunrise tomorrow. Salome"—I steeled my courage as Herod looked at me—"your divorce is granted."

Costobar said nothing but stepped back, his eyes wide and blank.

With difficulty, I tore my gaze from the father of my children. Leaving all formality behind, I focused my attention on the brother I had not spoken to in months. "Herod, I am so sorry. I should have seen the truth sooner. I should have understood he was not loyal when he went to see Cleopatra. I failed you when I meant to protect you . . ." I hiccupped a sob and hung my head, broken. "I didn't know what he was planning, but it pains me to think I have been a fool. He knew everything about us, and I understood nothing of his plotting until Alexandra threatened me with the news—"

"Salome." Herod's voice softened, and he looked at me with a smile behind his eyes. "Forget the past. I have missed you more than you will ever know. You have not been disloyal. And I would never call you a fool."

His mercy and forgiveness—which I did not deserve after being so blind and foolish—broke my heart. I covered my face and wept quietly, ignoring the whispers behind me. Let them talk and murmur. Let them say I broke the Law. Let them call me an idiot.

I deserved their scorn and Herod's ire.

But my brother had softness in his heart. Once he saved me from a stranger. Now he was saving me from myself.

"My dear sister," he said, a muscle quivering at his jaw, "you have five children by this man. What shall be done with them?"

"My king." I fell to my knees in gratitude. "My children, all five, are nieces and nephews to the king of Judea. Let them be sheltered in your court, and let them live among your sons, so that all the world may know they are from your royal bloodline. Let them be called Herodians and nothing else."

The words pleased Herod, as I hoped they would. "So be it. I shall find you another husband, if you like."

"Thank you, my king, but I am in no hurry to remarry. It is enough to live in your house, inhabit your court, and be of service to you."

"Welcome back to court, Salome."

I gave him a grateful smile, then turned toward Mother, who watched us with approval and relief in her eyes.

As time passed, the tumult Mariamne and Alexandra caused faded into unpleasant memories. Herod married again—and again—but though he could never seem to find a woman who excited him as much as Mariamne, he did not stop searching for a wife who might fill the emptiness in his heart. After Mariamne, he married Malthace, a Samaritan beauty. Two years later he married Cleopatra of Jerusalem, the daughter of a priest. He had scarcely climbed out of his marriage bed with Cleopatra when he married another Mariamne, the daughter of Simon, son of Boethos.

Malthace gave him two sons, Archelaus and Herod Antipas, and a daughter, Olympias. Cleopatra gave him two sons, Herod Philip and Herod. The second Mariamne also gave him a son named Herod Philip.

I did not know if any of his new wives made him happy, but I did know they could never compare to his memories of Mariamne the Hasmonean princess. Those memories did not fade with time, for in them she seemed to become more rarefied, more beautiful, and more regal.

The love he could no longer lavish on his beloved wife he now lavished on her sons, Alexander, Aristobulus, and Herod. With a secure grip on his kingdom, he looked toward the future and decided to name Mariamne's sons as his heirs. But first they must be prepared to rule, and who better to see to their education than his friend Octavian, now known as Augustus, emperor of Rome?

In the fourteenth year of Herod's reign over Jerusalem, when the boys were thirteen, twelve, and eleven, he wrote Augustus and asked if he could send his sons to Rome and entrust the emperor with their care. The emperor responded with enthusiastic approval, and all three boys sailed straightway to Rome, where they were welcomed by Herod's friend Pollio, who arranged for them to stay in his home. Occasionally, as we learned when the boys sent letters, they resided with Augustus and his wife, Livia, in the imperial palace.

"What an honor!" Herod beamed every time he read such reports. "My sons, guests in the emperor's home—Father would be so proud."

"He would," I agreed. "Even Mariamne would be impressed." Why did I mention the wife I had detested with every ounce of my being? Because I knew my brother. Mariamne had constantly reminded all of us that we were common, not royal, and not as Jewish as she and her family. But now the only remaining Hasmoneans were Alexander, Aristobulus, and young Herod, and they were Herodian . . . and royal.

I could not help approving of Herod's plan to have his sons educated abroad. In Rome they would receive an education appropriate for their rank. In Jerusalem they would have learned about the Torah but would not enjoy Greek theater or observe the workings of Roman law or study artistic statuary. Furthermore, those handsome young men would be maturing in the light of the emperor's approval. Augustus took pleasure in having them around, if only for ornamentation.

While his favorite sons lived in Rome, Herod began to dream of a glorious future for Jerusalem and Judea. He had always had an eye for outstanding architecture, and his visits to foreign cities had convinced him that Judea needed splendorous buildings of its own. He began to oversee and plan additional palaces, fortresses, theaters, amphitheaters, and harbors. But his greatest project, the one into which he poured his hopes and dreams, was rebuilding the Temple.

His first mention of his Temple plans made me smile. "Do you remember the prophecy?" I asked. "I told you about it years ago. 'He who restores it to the glory of Solomon's Temple will have the blessing of HaShem to the fourth generation.'"

"Then I shall be blessed forever," Herod said, grinning. "For my Temple will surpass the glory of Solomon's, and the people will finally bless my name and love their king."

My heart warmed to see Herod's excitement. For months after Mariamne's death he had not been able to garner such enthusiasm for anything, not even for his new wives. Now the fire had returned to his eye, and without the Hasmonean thorns in his side, I thought the people might finally learn to love their king.

"And so," he explained to me one afternoon, "these building projects have several purposes. First, Judea needs strong fortresses where the king and his family can be safe in case of a revolt. Second, I want to increase commerce by creating a port at Caesarea, a station large enough to handle seagoing merchant ships. Third, I want to solidify my standing with the emperor by establishing his name in as many locations as possible. And finally, there is the Temple . . ."

To my great surprise, the Jews of Jerusalem did not enthusiastically support the Temple project. When I asked Zara why they murmured, she said many Jews worried that Herod might pull down the existing structure and run out of supplies before completing the new one.

"That concern is easily remedied," I told Herod. "You must assemble all the supplies in advance, so the people will not worry. Then you must appoint priests and Levites to oversee the design and execution of the building program. Let them be responsible for the sacred objects and holy places, and let them be accountable to the people."

Though Herod was reluctant to release authority to the priests and Levites, eventually he agreed. And when his builders completed the main sanctuary in only eighteen months, the people celebrated with a great ceremony at which their king sacrificed three hundred oxen.

Herod also ordered other building projects that did not involve the Jews. He built a more defensible royal palace, a home that far surpassed the old, and an amphitheater and hippodrome, both of which were designed to cater to Jews who had acquired Greek tastes. He built a fortress named Cypros to honor our mother, and a city called Phasaelis to honor our brother.

Not far from Jerusalem, just southeast of a small village called Bethlehem, Herod erected the Herodium, a fortress designed to house a theater, a dining room, and the king's tomb.

Yet Herod's grand plans did not enjoy an auspicious beginning. A famine struck the land as he commenced his building program, and the people hungered. Many in Jerusalem interpreted the famine as HaShem's judgment on Herod. It seemed every unfortunate event was blamed on the king. But Herod saw the trial as an opportunity. Eager to win the love of his people, he converted all the gold and silver ornaments in his palaces into coins, then purchased food from Egypt to feed his people in Judea and Syria. After losing a pair of golden candlesticks and several silver apples to this confiscation, I was dismayed to learn that even though Herod had made a great personal sacrifice to feed his people, still they did not love him.

To the Judeans he was still the man who had replaced—some would say *usurped*—the Hasmoneans. And even though that year he forgave one-third of the people's tax debt to help them recover from the famine, they did not love him any more or hate him any less.

PART TWO

20 Years Before the Common Era

CHAPTER FORTY

Zara

B y the time I entered my twenty-fourth year, I had decided that marriage would not be part of HaShem's plan for me. Everyone around me was marrying—in the house of Herod, multiple marriages were common—yet I had no family to find me a suitor, and the handsome prince my aunt hoped I'd meet in the palace never materialized.

The king, however, added another wife to his harem—Pallas, who gave him a son named Phasael.

My mistress fell in love with Syllaeus, prime minister of the Nabataeans. I watched, bemused, as Salome behaved like an infatuated young girl, and when Syllaeus asked to marry her, I hoped she would finally find happiness.

But the king was appalled at the man's request. He had fought the Nabataeans not so many years before, and he refused Syllaeus, but then relented save one condition: "You may marry my sister," he told the prime minister, "if you are circumcised and adopt the Jewish faith."

Salome watched in horrified dismay as her lover shook his

head and left the palace. The king had asked too much, demanding a price Syllaeus was not willing to pay.

I tidied my weeping mistress's room that night, then sank onto a stool by the bed where she watered her pillow with tears. "Mistress," I said, lightly touching her arm, "perhaps this is for the best. How strong could his love be if he was not willing to adopt your faith?"

Salome looked up, pulled unraveled hair from her eyes, and stared at me. "How would you know?" she asked, her voice breaking. "You have never been in love, nor have you been married. So how could you understand?"

After that, I left her alone and retreated to my room.

What did I know about marriage? Not much. But she was wrong about my being in love. I had been in love for nine years, though I had nothing to show for it.

~~~~~~

After meeting Ravid, I had begun to attend any meeting where he would be teaching. In many ways he reminded me of my father—he was kind, clear in his instruction, and seemed wholly devoted to HaShem. Stories from the Torah and the prophets came to life when he related them, filled with majesty, humor, and awe, and every week I came away with a deeper appreciation for HaShem and for His love of Israel.

Mava did not always go with me to the house meetings, and when she did not, I always found her in the palace and shared what I had learned. After a few months, she touched my arm and stopped me in the middle of the tale of Abraham and Isaac on the mountain. "I know the story," she said, a sly smile twisting her mouth. "And all the others. I have only been listening because your growing love for the Torah teacher fascinates me."

"Love?" I blinked at her. "I think he is a good teacher, that is all."

She shook her head. "If you do not love him, why do you not visit some of the other meetings?"

I opened my mouth to answer and found myself speechless. None of the other teachers was Ravid, that was why. But my attendance had nothing to do with love.

Or did it? I began to notice my reaction to his presence. I had been fascinated with him since the first time I saw him bouncing around in the king's hall, and he had not lost the ability to hold my attention. I was happy in his presence, even if I had to sit on the floor or skip the evening meal, and I could pick out his voice in a crowd of men. I knew the back of his head, the curve of his cheek, and the pattern of hair on his forearm . . .

Perhaps I *did* love him. So what? A woman could not walk up and choose a man as easily as she plucked fruit from a tree. More important, Ravid certainly did not love me.

We had become friends, if an unmarried man and woman can be considered as such. After every Torah class, he would walk me back to the palace, conversing on the way. He told me about his family; I told him about mine. He told me about his siblings; I told him about my mistress and her children. He even told me about his wife and son who had died in the war for Jerusalem, and I listened with grave sympathy and remained silent, not wanting to compare my losses with his.

After a year or so, he asked me if I knew Judith, a girl in our Torah class. I replied that I did not know her well, and why did he ask?

"I have decided to marry again," Ravid answered, locking his hands behind his back, "and think she may be a suitable bride."

I experienced a blank moment when my head buzzed with words. Then all my yearning and confusion united in one spontaneous exclamation: "You can't marry her!"

Ravid lifted a brow. "Why not?"

"Because—because she is too young."

"She is your age, is she not?"

"Yes, but . . ." I shook my head and walked faster. "Marry her, then, if that is what you want."

But he never mentioned Judith again. Some weeks later, when I brought up the dreaded subject, he replied that Judith had been betrothed to someone else.

Not knowing how to respond, I launched into a detailed description of the new garments Salome had ordered.

Several months later, he asked me about Rachel, the daughter of a Levite. Again my heart rebelled against the notion, but that time, at least, I was able to wish him well on his upcoming betrothal. Still, Ravid did not marry Rachel. I do not think he even approached her father.

Every few months for eight years Ravid would mention some girl in his Torah class, and while I tried to respond with support and affirmation, my base nature could not contain itself. I always found something to remark on—the girl's appearance, her manner of speech, her laugh, her feet—yet usually I finished by wishing Ravid well in his new marriage. Afterward I would change the subject, talking about Salome, explaining the latest hairstyles from Rome, or describing the antics of the royal children.

I never realized that by talking so much about my mistress, I was giving Ravid the impression that my life—past, present, and future—revolved around my service in Herod's palace.

If I had been more transparent in my words and actions, I might have saved myself a great deal of heartache.

After nine years of friendship, Ravid and I were walking back from a Temple service when he halted abruptly on the street.

"Stop," he said, turning to face me. "I am tired and growing old. I must speak my mind, and I would have you speak yours."

I was not in a listening mood, for my thoughts had been occupied with sad news from Rome. Young Herod, Mariamne's third son, had been taken with a fever. Despite having the best physicians and care, the young man died. Because the disease disfigured the youth, Augustus convinced Alexander and Aristobulus to entomb their brother in Rome until he could be taken back to Judea.

The king and his family were deeply shaken by the news, and my mistress was particularly bereft. "We should have kept him in Jerusalem," she had told me. "A king does not need three heirs, so why did we not keep Herod with us?"

I stopped and squinted at Ravid. "I'm sorry, I was thinking about the young prince. What did you say?"

"Your thoughts are always centered on the palace." Ravid released a sigh. "Clearly you love your mistress, but must you give Herod's family all your love?"

I resisted the urge to scowl at him. I could not deny that I had strong feelings for the people I served. Though I would never be part of the royal family, I cared deeply for them and mourned the young prince as if he were one of my own relatives.

"What is love," I countered, "if not a choice to serve someone and put their interests above your own? It is not wrong for me to care about my mistress."

"Of course not. But is there no room in your heart to care about me?"

I could not have been more surprised if a handful of pearls had slipped from his tongue. "What?"

"I have tried to imagine a home with someone else, but I cannot. Nor can I be content knowing your heart is given to the king's sister. So make me a happy man, Zara, and marry me. I know I will have to ask your mistress to free you from

261

her service, but if she is willing, I will marry you at once. Live with me as my wife before we are both too old to enjoy each other's company."

I stared, all thoughts of the royal family slipping from my head. Marry him? What about Judith and Rachel and Miriam and all the others? And after so many years of friendship, why would he think I did not love him already?

"Why me . . . and why now?" I knew this was not the response he wanted, but if he desired honesty, I had to know why he would ask when I was twenty-four and no longer a young maiden. As an esteemed Torah teacher, he could marry a sweet virgin of fifteen or sixteen, a girl who could easily be molded into the sort of wife he wanted.

"I want to marry you because I love you as Jacob loved Rachel," he said, taking my hand. "I have waited for you even longer than Jacob waited for Rachel, but I can no longer stand to watch you devote yourself to the palace. I want to marry you because two are better than one. I want to marry you because I want to be with you always. I want to know what you think about things, and I want you to bear my children should HaShem grant us that blessing. Please, Zara—let me go to Salome and ask her to release you from your service as her handmaid."

I shook my head. "Why have you waited so long? I did not think you cared for me in that way. You asked about all those other girls . . ."

"Ah." He crossed his arms, tugged on his beard, jiggled his knees. "How do I explain? I did not think you wanted to give up your position at the palace. Whenever I mentioned marriage, you could only talk about Salome and the children and the king. I thought you had pledged your life to them, for you seemed so devoted to your mistress."

"I am," I admitted. "We've been together a long time. But,

Ravid, why do you think I search out your Torah classes? I have loved you for years."

He leaned forward as if he would take me into his arms—on a public street!—and I lifted my hand and stepped back. I looked at him with skepticism, the result of having loved him for so long without a shred of hope that he loved me, as well.

"I cannot give you a final answer now," I told him truthfully. "Let me go to my room and pray about this. I must also speak to Salome. I will give you my answer tomorrow."

I thought he might be angry, or at least irritated, yet when he nodded I glimpsed assurance in his eyes. And as he squeezed my hand to bid me farewell, I saw his confident smile.

The man had always been too self-assured as far as I was concerned.

I slept little that night, but the fault did not lie with my mistress. The thoughts that kept me from sleep were my own concerns, and they involved Ravid, Salome, and the entire royal family. When I first met Ravid, I would have burst from happiness had he asked to marry me. I would have abandoned Salome without a second thought.

But the intervening years had brought me closer to my mistress. Indeed, I had come to see her for exactly what she was—a determined, clever woman who would do anything to protect her brother and his throne. I could never hate her as some people did, for I knew her determination sprang from love. Like me, she loved her family and was particularly defensive of Herod. I could not say the king acted from the same motivation. After spending fifteen years in his palace, I had concluded his determination was fueled not by love but by fear.

Yet I could also understand fear. I had known loss and terror, so I could appreciate why Herod might be terrified by anything that threatened what he had strived so hard to achieve.

Salome and I had been together a long time, and I could not simply walk away. Though she would not want to admit it, she depended on me and I understood her. We had formed a unique bond, and when—if—she found someone to replace me, she might never find a handmaid who could interpret her moods like I could. Especially since she was now forty-five and feeling the advance of passing years.

What if she did not give me permission to go? What if the king forbade me to leave his sister?

I could always escape, but Salome might be angry enough to search for me. If she refused my request, I could remain at the palace, but Salome would always remember I had wanted to leave and she might hold that desire against me.

She would ask why I wanted to go. If I cited love as a reason, she would mock me, because all she knew of it was the irrational obsession Herod demonstrated for Mariamne and the frustrated passion she felt for Syllaeus, the man she could not marry. She would urge me to love Ravid in private, to become his mistress if necessary, but to remain at the palace because she needed me.

And that, no matter how much I might desire it, was something I could not do. Ravid could not take a mistress and remain the righteous man he was. If he were not a man completely committed to HaShem, I would not admire and love him as I should.

So perhaps I should not even mention marriage to Salome, but instead should simply continue as I was. Yet if I ignored Ravid's question, I would lose him. He would stop seeing me, saying the pain was too great, or he might disappear into the desert and join the Essene community. Or he might decide to forget me and look for a wife who would accept his request.

And I would feel terrible, for not only would I be denying myself happiness but I would shutter a light that shone through me in a palace where most people walked in darkness, not knowing that HaShem yearned to speak to them . . .

I closed my eyes and watched memories play on the backs of my eyelids—Ravid smiling at me over a meal with friends, passionately explaining HaShem's love for individuals, his eyes finding me when I entered a room. His voice echoed in my thoughts, booming one instant, tender in the next. I recalled each time our hands touched as I handed him a parchment or a scroll, each time my shoulder brushed his, how the brilliance of his smile warmed my heart on a chilly night.

Ravid had revealed truths I had never heard at the Temple, insights even my father had never shared. I understood him well enough to know that the grief over his wife and unborn child had abated, and perhaps I had something to do with that healing. He laughed at my paltry jokes, something not even my mistress did, so perhaps I brought him some measure of joy . . .

By the time I opened my eyes again, I had made my decision.

Salome did not send for me until almost midday. She had slept late, and with dark circles beneath her eyes her face reflected every one of her accumulated years.

She leaned toward the dressing table, resting her head on her open hands as though she lacked the strength to hold it up. "Zara," she groaned. "Please, something to drink. Wine, if you can find any."

I was afraid I would have to go down to the kitchen, but beyond the bed, on the floor, I found a nearly depleted wineskin. An overturned cup lay beside it, so I set the cup on the table and carefully poured the wine. My hands trembled in anticipation of the request I had to make, and Salome noticed my nervousness.

Her sharp eyes flew to my face when I handed her the wine. "What's this?" She brought the cup to her lips. "My handmaid has a secret?"

"Not a secret." I thought about making up an excuse for my trembling, but Salome had always appreciated directness. "A request."

She sipped the wine, then closed her eyes and sighed. "Ah. Last night has left me quite exhausted. New lovers always do."

"Syllaeus? I thought—"

"We have decided not to marry. That does not mean we cannot enjoy each other."

She turned back to the looking brass and regarded me in the reflection. "Do you wish to have a day to spend with your Torah teacher? You may go. I will not be entertaining anyone this afternoon."

I caught a breath. "I wish for more than a day, mistress. Ravid has asked me to marry him. I told him I would have to think about it, but really I knew I would have to decide whether or not to leave you. Years ago I promised to serve you, but the time has come—I am now asking you to free me from that promise."

A glimmer of confusion entered her eyes. "You promised . . ." She frowned. "Tell me, how much do you remember of your coming to the palace?"

"I remember arriving here, meeting you, going to my room—"

"Not those details." She shook her head. "Joseph made the arrangements for you to become my handmaid. Do you remember him?"

I searched my memory. I had been so young and so easily intimidated. I remembered a man escorting me to the palace, but the image of his face eluded me. "I am sorry, mistress, but I cannot picture him."

Salome sighed. "No matter. He told me about the deal he struck with your family. They agreed to let you come to the palace, but only if you could be free to leave anytime you wished. I will honor that agreement, of course. Because you have served me well, young friend, and I want you to be happy."

At the conclusion of her speech, she lifted her cup and drank deeply.

"Mistress?"

She held up a finger, silently urging me to wait. When she had drained the cup, she lowered it and looked at me with heavily lidded eyes. "You have always been free to depart, yet I do not want you to go. So let us strike another bargain. Marry your Torah teacher, live with him, but come to the palace every morning. Continue as my handmaid, because skilled handmaids are difficult to find."

A flicker of hope stirred in my breast. "I would like that, mistress, but . . . what if I have a child? I could not possibly care for a child, a husband, a home, and a mistress."

"Then let us negotiate a truce. Marry your scholar and work for me until you have a child. After that, you may go, and I will find another handmaid. But you will have to train her."

I closed my eyes, wondering if I should feel guilty for the wave of relief washing over me. The thought of marrying so late in life, of leaving everything I found comforting and familiar—this would be a welcome compromise. I would spend my evenings with Ravid and my days with Salome. He would spend his days at the Temple and his nights with me. Surely such an arrangement would make both of us happy—all three of us, if I included my mistress.

"You can go home every day after you dress me for dinner. If I need you after sunset, I will call"—she gave me a tipsy smile—"someone else."

"Thank you, mistress." My heart sang with delight. "Thank you for being more generous than I expected."

"Go find your man, give him the good news." She waved

me away, then held up her hand. "Wait! Before you go, more wine. Please."

My heart pounded as I took the cup, ran to the wineskin, and emptied its contents. I pressed the cup into Salome's hand. "May I go now?"

"Go." Her fingers curled around her drink. "God go with you."

"He does. Oh, He does!"

The last thing I saw before leaving her chamber was her melancholy reflection in the looking brass.

CHAPTER FORTY-ONE

Zara

I opened my eyes to the light of a new morning and turned to look at my husband. Moving carefully so as not to disturb him, I felt like a child with a new toy. I had a man now, a husband of my own. An intelligent, righteous, handsome man.

I smothered a smile when I saw his nose smashed into the pillow, bent at an awkward and possibly painful angle. His beard lay like a dark shadow on his throat and chest. His face had been tanned by hours spent in the sun, while his shoulders were nearly the color of the linen sheet over us.

Ravid. My husband. My love.

One eye opened, staring at me with deadly concentration. I managed a trembling smile, and then his hand caught mine and squeezed it. "Are you sorry?" he asked as he slid his face closer to mine.

"Why would I be?" I replied.

He shrugged. "You've slept alone for so many years, but now there's someone taking the blanket."

"And snoring." I moved closer to him. "I don't mind sharing the blanket. And now you will say I snore, too."

"You don't. At least I didn't notice."

He kissed me, then relaxed, his arm coming to rest casually across my bare shoulder. "So, what shall we do today?"

"I will prepare a tray for you to break your fast," I said, pulling away. "Then I must get to the palace. Salome will be up before too long."

"Will you ever get a morning when you do not have to run away from me?" Ravid asked.

"Yes." I pulled my tunic over my head, then grinned. "Salome has promised I can leave her when we have our first baby. I will be free to stay home with you then."

As my husband sat up, folded his hands and smiled, I began pulling bread and cheese from a basket. Marriage, I realized, had turned out to be unexpectedly pleasant.

CHAPTER FORTY-TWO

Salome

During the summer of my mother's seventy-sixth year, the king's physician sent for me. I hurried to Herod's chamber, afraid my brother had been stricken with some sudden disease, and found him pale and trembling.

"It is Mother," he said, his eyes filling with tears. "The physician says she will not live to see another sunrise."

My hand went to my throat. "Is she . . . able to speak?"

"She is, and she is calling for you. I have already met with her and said my farewells."

I tried to sort through my scrambling thoughts. "Have you sent for Pheroras?" The year before, with Augustus's permission, Herod had named our brother tetrarch of Peraea, an area east of the Jordan and north of the Dead Sea. He and his wife now lived there.

Herod dipped his chin in a reluctant nod. "I have, but I doubt he will arrive in time." For a moment I thought he would collapse in my arms, but we were not alone. Malthace was in the room, and I knew he would not show weakness before one of his wives.

I drew a deep breath to calm my pounding heart and hurried to my mother's chamber. The room had been closed up, the curtains drawn over closed shutters, the space lit only by a flickering oil lamp. Mava, my mother's handmaid, greeted me with a deep bow, then touched my arm. "She is weak, lady. The doctor says we should not overtax her."

Or what? The irreverent thought niggled at my brain as I strode toward Mother's bed. She lay on her back, her head and shoulders propped on pillows, her hands folded over her belly.

"Mistress," Mava said, "your daughter Salome is here."

Mother's eyes flew open, and she scowled. "I have but one daughter—I am not so far gone I would not know her name."

I sank onto the edge of Mother's bed as the handmaid backed away. "I came as soon as the physician sent for me."

"Good." Mother's eyes had paled over the last several years, but now they gleamed with determination. "There are things you must do for me since . . . since I will not be able to finish."

"Anything, Mother. What is it?"

With an effort, she lifted her head and motioned for me to lean closer. "Your brother will not live forever. You will likely outlive him, being the youngest."

My throat tightened at the thought of losing yet another brother. "Perhaps."

"You must swear you will do all you can to prevent Herod from naming Alexander or Aristobulus as his heirs."

I blinked. She had mentioned his two favorite sons, and if truth be told, I had always liked the boys. They were charming, attractive, and bright, even as children.

"Why?" I asked. "They are the sons Herod favors most."

"*Because*"—Mother's eyes sparked as she hissed the word—"if either one of them becomes king, Alexandra has won. Do you not see it? The entire time she lived with us, Alexandra schemed to have her descendants put back on the throne of

Judea. So if Herod places the crown on either son's head, all our struggles and suffering will have been for nothing."

I patted her hand, desperate to calm her. "I do not think—"

"You *must* think," Mother rasped. "Imagine the reign of a King Alexander. The people will rejoice and say the glory has returned to Israel. He would appoint his brother high priest, and together they would mirror previous Hasmonean families. In a generation, people will have forgotten us . . . forgotten Herod. Your brother will become a vague memory while the Hasmoneans continue their murderous dynasty. And somewhere beyond the grave, Alexandra will celebrate."

I fell silent, realizing she was right. I had been so focused on my new lover and my children of late that I had not thought much about the Hasmoneans. All those who could be king were gone—except for Mariamne's sons.

"I was a princess in my family," Mother said, her voice a broken whisper. "My father was a chief among the Nabataeans. Then Herod betrothed himself to Mariamne . . . and those women entered my life . . . and they never missed an opportunity . . . to call me *common*."

I studied the crimson spider webs beneath the delicate skin of her cheeks. My mother had never been common. She had nerves of iron coupled with innate grace and a fierce, protective way about her. And here she was dying, yet her thoughts were centered on protecting her son.

Her eyes pinned me in a long, silent scrutiny, and I knew what she was asking. She would not ask this of Herod, because she knew how he doted on those boys. But she would ask it of me, her only daughter, because I was a mother and I understood.

"Swear to me," she said, her trembling fingers tapping my wrist.

"I swear it, Mother. I will do all I can to keep Mariamne's sons from the throne."

Mother closed her eyes and leaned back, her face relaxing into the mask of death. "Do not fail me . . ." she murmured. She drew another halting breath and exhaled slowly.

I waited, tears streaming over my cheeks, but my mother did not breathe again.

CHAPTER FORTY-THREE

Zara

Life for me settled into a different but pleasant pattern. After spending time with Ravid every morning, I went to the palace and attended Salome, who never rose until midday. I did her hair, listened to her many complaints about Judea and its people, and helped her dress. Sometimes I listened to her children, who were growing up all too quickly. Alexander and Herod were already young men, and not fond of visiting with women, but Berenice, Salome's eldest daughter, was seventeen; her son Antipater, only fifteen; and her youngest daughter, Phebe, a tender twelve.

Salome had never seemed particularly close to her children, preferring to consign them to the care of nursemaids, so perhaps it was only natural that they began to confide in me. Berenice told me she wished to marry a king one day, Antipater confessed to being terrified of battle, and young Phebe crawled into my lap and said she hated living in the palace. I did not betray their secrets but listened intently, nodded in the appropriate places, and promised to pray for them. That promise always caught them by surprise, but soon they began to return to me, asking if I would take other requests to HaShem.

"I don't know why," Phebe said, "but I think HaShem listens to you." I assured her that HaShem listened to anyone who spoke to Him, but as long as she needed me to add to her prayers, I was happy to do it.

I knew Salome would learn of her children's trust in me, and she did. But instead of being jealous or hurt, she seemed amused that her royal offspring would choose to confide in a handmaid with no authority or influence of her own. Clearly she placed no confidence in the power of my prayers, though I did not care. What mattered was her children—that they had someone to talk to, someone who would not take their secrets and use them as currency in political power plays.

Yet as I listened to Salome's children, I could not help but yearn for children of my own. I knew Ravid wanted children very much. He had been thrilled to hear he would be a father when his first wife conceived, but he had lost both wife and child. Now he had another wife, though I was far from young, and I knew he was praying for a son.

I prayed, too. I often read the story of Hannah at the Tabernacle, of how she prayed so fervently that the high priest thought her drunk. As time passed and I did not conceive, I began to understand Hannah's frustration. I longed for a child like a starving tiger longs for food, but I did not dare make Ravid feel guilty about not doing his part to answer my prayers. He did everything he should—he treated me with kindness and loved me with tender consideration, yet month after month I remained barren.

In the first months of our marriage, we often stretched out and talked about what our children would be like. "They will have your eyes," Ravid said, his thumb caressing the back of my hand. "And it would be nice if they were tall like me."

"I hope they inherit your love of the written word," I said. "And I hope you will promise to teach our daughter to read."

"You have my promise." Ravid kissed my cheek. "I will read to her every night."

"I hope our daughter doesn't have long feet." I sighed. "I have always been self-conscious about mine."

"'How lovely are your sandaled feet, O nobleman's daughter,'" Ravid quoted. "'The curves of your thighs are like jewels, the work of a craftsman's hand.'"

I laughed, imagining my feet and thighs on a king's wife. "You are too funny, my love."

"And you are beautiful." He kissed my ear, my neck, and the hollow between my breasts.

And as he made his intentions clear, I clung to my husband and prayed this would be the night Adonai worked a miracle and gave us a son.

CHAPTER FORTY-FOUR

Salome

"Antipater!" I strode toward my nephew with open arms, but his disgruntled expression did not soften. I gave him a hug, then stepped back. "How you have grown! How is your mother?"

His smile was as thin as barley water. "She is well."

"It is so good to see you. I am glad you accepted my invitation—I have been wanting to introduce you to your cousins. And my new husband."

"You have married again?"

"For two years now. The marriage was your father's idea. I was opposed at first, but now I am glad of it. Alexas is a good man."

"I hear—" Antipater paused and looked around—"that Pheroras's wife died."

"She did. I'm sure he is still grieving her loss."

"I also heard Father offered him my sister Salampsio as a wife, and Pheroras refused her."

I drew a deep breath, not wanting to wade into troubled waters so soon. "Pheroras has a mind of his own. Perhaps he is not ready to remarry."

"Is that why he also turned down my sister Cypros?"

"I cannot read my brother's mind, nephew. As I said, perhaps he is still grieving."

The young man's mouth dipped into a frown. "He is brave, turning down the gift of a king's daughter."

"Pheroras is your uncle. Surely he deserves a measure of understanding."

Antipater sighed, then glanced over his shoulder. "Has Father . . . does he care that I have come?"

"Of course he cares! But he is away now, off with his engineers to discuss one of his many building projects. I thought it would be good for you to meet my children while we are together. Later you will have time to meet your father's new wives and children. Come, let me take you to my chambers."

I babbled thoughtlessly as we walked through the palace courtyard, speaking of my children and their mediocre accomplishments and talents. In truth, I had summoned Antipater to the palace for his sake, not for the benefit of my children. My offspring, lovely as they were, were not the sons of a king, yet Antipater was. As long as Herod lavished his love and attention on Mariamne's sons, I would focus on Antipater. If neither Alexander nor Aristobulus could inherit Herod's throne, then Herod's firstborn ought to be king.

I linked my arm through my nephew's, and for the first time I realized I was not speaking with the boy I remembered but with a man of twenty-seven years. And what a man he had become! He had finally developed his mother's good looks, and his shoulders had broadened since I last saw him.

"How you have grown! The last time I saw you, you barely came up to my shoulder. But now you are as tall as I am."

"Taller." He gave me a tight smile. "I believe I am the tallest of Father's sons."

I did not think he was right, but I did not want to invite

comparisons. So I smiled and changed the subject. "What do you hear from your brothers in Rome? Surely Alexander and Aristobulus write you on occasion."

"They do not. They have never written me."

"Really?" I pressed my hand to my chest, feigning horror. "I would have thought they had better manners. Their mother was always adamant about the way things should be done."

"I still do not understand why they live with the Roman emperor while I live in exile with—"

"Your mother?" I finished his sentence with a sweet smile. "Think no more about it, Antipater. Your father never sat for lessons in Rome and look how clever he is. He enrolled in the school of life, and his natural abilities helped him rise. You have those same abilities and will rise, as well. As for being in exile, are you not in the palace now?"

"Am I?"

"You are, and I am going to make certain you stay. It is only right. You are the firstborn, after all."

He stopped and turned. "Father has probably forgotten I exist. He has not sent for me in years, and yet he sends Mariamne's children to Rome. He does not write my mother or inquire after her health—"

"You must be patient." I looked him directly in the eyes and lowered my voice. "These things must not be rushed."

He stared at me, an almost imperceptible note of pleading in his expression, and for a moment I glimpsed the little boy inside him.

A wave of maternal feeling swept over me. "Did you know you have always been my favorite nephew?" I patted his arm. "Come, let us find your cousins and my husband. Then we will talk about your future."

I smiled at Zara, who bowed before Antipater, and I breathed in the aroma of the roasted chicken and vegetables she set on the table. "Ah, that smells wonderful. Thank you, Zara. You may go now; Antipater and I will take care of ourselves for the rest of the evening."

Zara gave me a quick smile, then hurried to grab her head covering and depart.

"Your servant leaves every night?" Antipater asked, reaching for a chicken leg.

"She is married now. Rather than lose her, I asked her to stay until she has her first child. After that, I will have to find another handmaid, though good servants are hard to find."

"If you say so." Antipater took a bite of chicken and looked around as he chewed. "Must be pleasant to live in the palace."

"You could live here too, but you cannot be so contentious." I leaned forward, determined to talk sense into the young man. "I'm glad you have come, Antipater. But you must understand— the invitation came from me, not your father. He is infatuated with his sons by Mariamne, but I do not believe it is fair for him to ignore you. So I want to bring you back to court, perhaps with your mother. Before I do, I need you to promise you will make a genuine effort."

Antipater's face twisted. "What makes you think I would not?"

"Your countenance, for one thing. You have grown into a respectable young man, strong and attractive, yet your face sours every time your father's name is mentioned. You will have to work hard not to let your countenance reveal your bitterness. And you will have to learn how to get along with Alexander and Aristobulus . . . for a while, at least."

At the mention of those names, his face twisted in a scowl.

"See? Anyone who saw you at this moment would know you despise your brothers."

"*Half* brothers."

"Brothers. For your sake, you had better learn to see them as close kinsmen. Right now your father is surrounded with babies and young wives, so I am sure he would welcome the sight of his mature firstborn. You have an advantage—Mariamne's sons are in Rome, but you are *here*."

Antipater chewed slowly, his eyes narrowing as he considered my words. After swallowing, he folded his hands. "You really believe you could restore me to favor?"

"Everything will depend on you," I said. "But yes, this was your grandmother's dying wish. She made me swear I would do all I could to prevent the throne from falling back into Hasmonean hands."

His brows lifted while a trace of softness came to his eyes, and for the first time I saw hope there. "Grandmother always loved me."

"She did. And given time, I know I can persuade Herod to invite you to resume your place at the palace. After that, you must win his heart and his confidence."

Antipater chewed the inside of his cheek for a moment, then smiled. "Then, dear Aunt Salome, plead my case before the king, and I will do all I can to be a model son."

"That is all I ask." I leaned back and felt tension leave my shoulders. The promise I gave Mother had been weighing on me for months, and at first I had no idea how to weaken Herod's love for Mariamne's sons. Then I remembered Antipater—if he rose to the challenge, he could sway the king's heart and ensure a Herodian dynasty.

"There is one thing you must do to prepare for your future," I said, studying his expression. "You must marry a suitable wife."

"And who decides who is suitable?"

"I do, for I know how your father thinks."

Antipater's lips curved in a sour smile. "Do I have no say in the matter?"

"Not if you want to be king of Judea."

He blew out a breath. "Have you found a suitable candidate?"

"I have. She is not yet old enough to marry, but we could arrange a betrothal. Her royal father is dead, and her mother will be eager to make a good match."

Interest flickered in Antipater's eyes. "Is she beautiful?"

"You are *so* much like your father."

"But is she?"

"She is. And her name is Mariamne, the third of that name in her family. Her father was Antigonus, the Hasmonean king your father defeated when he took Jerusalem."

Antipater made a moue of distaste. "You want me to marry one of *them*? I thought you despised the Hasmoneans."

"Your father will be charmed by the girl's name, and you will appreciate her beauty. The Hasmonean connection will win the approval of the people. Besides"—I reached for the pitcher and poured more wine—"the king rules the kingdom, not the queen. Never forget that."

Antipater held out his cup. "You have done a great deal of thinking about this."

"Of course. I had hoped Mariamne's sons would do something to displease their father, but they have been in Rome and out of reach. Still, the king is growing older, so it is time to make preparation for the future."

"How old is Father now?"

"He is fifty-five, but life is a fragile thing. One must always be prepared." I picked up my cup, held it aloft, and smiled at my nephew. "Let us drink to Judea's future king. May he be true to his father and his father's heritage."

CHAPTER FORTY-FIVE

Salome

Antipater proved as good as his word. Over the next several months he met and married Mariamne, daughter of Antigonus, and wrote his father often, stating his willingness to serve in any way, no matter how humble the service. While Herod approved of this, he did not invite his firstborn to live in Jerusalem, despite my urging him to. His head and heart were too full of Alexander and Aristobulus, for they had finished their Roman education and were ready to come home.

Herod invited me and Alexas, my husband, on the journey to bring the young men back to Judea. We would travel with the king's retinue, which now included a new wife, Elpis. I was allowed to bring my children, who were delighted to finally visit Rome.

Alexander and Aristobulus had been away only five years, yet those years had been formative. Mariamne's sons were now educated, steeped in Roman and Greek culture, and far more sophisticated than even their father. They were wealthy, intimate with the emperor and his family, and known for being of royal blood.

Five minutes after I greeted them, I felt the first frisson of fear. Standing on a marble portico with Augustus and his wife, these two young men outshone their father and all their siblings. Anyone who spent more than three minutes with them would see it. Though Augustus and Livia took great pains to make us feel welcome, I felt like an unpolished schoolgirl in their presence, and Herod seemed a blustering and bellicose pretender.

Mariamne's sons, on the other hand, seemed to have been born into nobility. They laughed easily with the emperor, joked with Livia, and spoke of hunting with Marcus Agrippa, now co-regent with Augustus. They treated Herod with respectful civility and embraced me as a beloved aunt, yet my skin crawled at their touch. The six of us exchanging pleasantries and greetings felt wrong somehow.

I sighed with relief when we boarded the ship that would ferry us back to Judea. We carried not only Mariamne's two living sons but also her third son, Herod, who had died in Rome. We would bury him in the same tomb where his mother and grandmother lay.

I stood on the deck and stared at the sun-spangled sea, which slapped rhythmically against the barnacle-covered timbers of the docks. I knew I would feel like myself again once we were away from Rome and I would no longer have to worry about the appropriateness of every word and gesture. But would I have to worry about my nephews?

Mariamne's sons had been only six and seven when their mother died, but they were older now, and surely they had asked Augustus about their mother's trial. They must have learned about Herod's breakdown after her death, and they might have heard rumors that my mother and I were instrumental in seeing her brought to trial.

Now that they were older and on the verge of attaining power, would they seek revenge? Did I need to worry about them? Did Herod?

~~~~~~~

The illusion of peace in our family began to fray as soon as we stepped off the ship at Caesarea. As Alexander and Aristobulus walked through the streets, people stopped and cheered, just as they had shouted praise for Alexandra's son Aristobulus after he conducted the Water Ceremony at the festival of Sukkot.

A thrill of fear rattled me, carrying me back to that dark day. I could almost hear Alexandra laughing in anticipation of the revenge that would be hers when Mariamne's sons held the reins of power in Judea. With Herod gone and Augustus as their friend, what wouldn't they be able to do?

I did not see much of Mariamne's sons once we returned to Jerusalem, but I could not help but wonder what they were about. Herod embarked on his plans for them. First on his agenda was marriage, so he arranged the marriage of Alexander to Glaphyra, the Gentile daughter of the king of Cappadocia. He married Aristobulus to my daughter, Berenice.

I had mixed feelings about becoming mother-in-law to one of Mariamne's sons. Did Aristobulus secretly hate me? Would he make my daughter suffer on my account? I would have begged Herod to find Aristobulus another wife, except Berenice was thrilled by the thought of marrying her handsome cousin, and Herod had made up his mind. "The best for the best," he had said.

And my brother, once set on a course of action, did not waver.

As time passed, however, Herod's joy over his sons' return faded, replaced by uneasy trepidation. Though he had appeared confident when he welcomed his sons home, he began to ponder what action the young men might take to avenge their mother.

Insistent rumors did not help, as his spies reported that certain people were predicting his newly arrived sons were merely waiting for him to display a moment of weakness. Then they would turn against their father because of what he had done to their mother.

While Herod spoke of his concerns to me, he did not speak of them publicly, nor did he share them with Pheroras, of whom we saw little in those days.

Herod's affection for Mariamne's sons began to wane. Not everyone could see it, but I certainly could. This stirred odd feelings in me, for while I wanted Antipater's star to rise, I did not want Mariamne's sons to suffer unnecessarily.

When I suggested that perhaps it was time we brought Antipater and his wife to live at the palace, Herod quickly agreed. "I would like to get to know my firstborn son," he said, his countenance brightening. "And why not invite Doris to return to Jerusalem, too."

I bowed my head. "Antipater would love to have his mother close. They have become quite attached through the years."

"Hmm." Herod's eyes grew thoughtful. "I haven't seen her in so long . . . do you think she has changed?"

"We all change," I reminded him. "But she was a beautiful woman. I'm sure she is still lovely."

That night at dinner I nearly dropped my wine when I heard Herod tell Alexander and Aristobulus to beware—their succession was not certain.

Alexander gaped in bewilderment. "But, Father, I have seen your will. You named me as heir and promised another role to Aristobulus."

"Augustus has given me the power to name my own successor," Herod said, hunkering over his dinner as he stared at his son. "I will write as many wills as I choose."

Alexander cast a worried look at his brother, while Glaphyra, his bride, appeared close to tears. Berenice glanced at me, her face a study in confusion, and I shook my head slightly. *Do not worry, love.*

"Brother," Pheroras said, unsteadily holding his wine cup, "I heard something disturbing in the street today."

Herod lifted a brow. "What did you hear?"

Pheroras turned to Alexander. "I heard that this one has employed a man to interview all who were present at Mariamne's trial."

Herod's face went ashen. "Why . . . why would you do such a thing?" he stammered, glaring at Alexander. "What is on your mind? If you have a question, you have only to ask me."

"I did not employ anyone." Alexander's square jaw tensed. "If I am lying, may HaShem strike me—"

"We know you would never do such a thing," Antipater interrupted, standing. "You are a noble son of a noble father. You would never resort to such dealings."

Alexander frowned and nodded. "You are right."

I stared at Antipater, perplexed. Later, when we had finished eating and the king had retired to one of his wife's chambers, I caught Antipater in the hallway.

"Why did you defend Alexander?" I asked. "If he has employed a man to uncover the details of his mother's trial, this could be just the thing we need to turn your father's favor—"

"He did not hire anyone." Antipater grinned. "I know he did not."

I blew out a frustrated breath. "Have you spies of your own now? How do you know this?"

"Because I started the rumor." Antipater's eyes danced. "I paid a man to talk to Pheroras and two or three of the king's other spies. In the days ahead my father will be hearing all sorts of things about Mariamne's sons. Each time they are confronted, I will emphatically defend them."

I stared at him in bewildered wonder, and for a moment I couldn't speak. Then I finally found my voice. "You have your grandmother's spirit in you. She might have done the same thing, if she were here."

Antipater smiled and tossed a grape into his mouth. "Sleep well tonight, Aunt. You said the future would depend on me."

"I did."

"Well then, do not worry. As you can see, I have the situation well in hand."

I did not know how to feel about this new Antipater living in the palace. I had told him to comport himself like a prince, like his father's son, but the zeal with which he rose to the task unsettled me. I meant he should be responsible and win his father's trust, but Antipater's methods more closely resembled Alexandra's than those of a noble king. If he thought nothing of paying a man to falsely accuse his rivals, what sort of king would he be? And even more troubling, what sort of behavior—if any—would he consider unthinkable?

I told myself he would learn; he would be better in the future. He would watch his father and learn that one resorted to certain tactics only when nothing else would do.

When he was not plotting against his brothers, Antipater helped his father and was particularly active in the king's construction program. Now that Judea was at peace with its neighbors, Herod began to build. He loved building the way other kings loved war.

His first project, begun when he served Mark Antony, had been the Antonia Fortress, remodeled and renamed after his benefactor. The fortress had been known as the Baris, but Herod added apartments, cloisters, a bath, and porticoes to connect it to the Temple.

His palace was a marvel. Even our cosmopolitan travelers,

Alexander and Aristobulus, were impressed with it. Herod's new palace consisted of two main buildings, the Caesareum and Agrippeum, with banqueting halls, one hundred guest rooms, cloisters, courtyards, and several pools. Along with the three observation towers named Phasaelis, Mariamne, and Hippicus, he built our family tomb north of the Damascus Gate. He also built a theater, an amphitheater, and a hippodrome near Jericho.

Not all of his projects were designed to glorify his benefactors; many were designed to aid the people. Solomon's pools, located south of Bethlehem, had aqueducts that carried water to Jerusalem and Arrub. The Pool of Mamillah serviced western Jerusalem, as did Hezekiah's Pool and the Sheep Pool. The Antonia Fortress had the Struthion Pool, and the Pool of Israel lay outside the north wall of the Temple Mount.

Nor did Herod confine his building program to Jerusalem. Alexandreion, Hyrcania, and Masada received new structures, fortifications, barracks, baths, and cisterns. The old city of Samaria, where Herod married Mariamne and recuperated after her death, was renamed Sebaste in honor of Augustus, and there Herod built walls, gates, fortifications, and colonnaded streets. There he constructed a public forum and two temples, one to the goddess Roma, and the other to the divine Augustus.

With endless enthusiasm Herod went on to build in Phoenicia, Syria, Greece, and Asia Minor. He might have been trying to turn Judea, particularly Jerusalem, into a marble edifice to equal the glory of Rome. Though an impossible task, given our climate and history, he was determined not to be ashamed of Jerusalem when Augustus came to visit.

Day after day I watched my brother work with his architects and travel to the various building sites, usually with one of his sons by his side. I did not know what Alexander and Aristobulus were learning on these journeys, but I hoped Antipater would watch, listen, and learn how to be a good king.

CHAPTER FORTY-SIX

Salome

Any man ought to spend his latter years in peace, enjoying the fruits of his labor, but as Herod entered his sixtieth year, family dinners became a battlefront, complete with traps and combative warfare. With all his sons and wives present, meals were fraught with tension. As Herod tried to pretend all was well with his household, the sons and wives watched the aging king as if counting the days when he would take his last bite, his last breath.

I could see what they were doing, yet I was powerless to stop it. I attempted to talk to Herod, to convince him to choose Antipater as his heir and end the suspense, but he refused. "I will write as many wills as I choose," he repeated for what was surely the hundredth time. "And my sons will wait until I am gone before they survey their kingdoms."

One night at dinner, Alexander whispered something to Aristobulus and made him laugh. Herod noticed. "Something funny, Alexander? Perhaps you would like to share your thoughts with all of us."

Alexander tossed a pheasant bone over his shoulder and smiled. "No, Father. It was a private joke."

"Even so, I would like to hear it." Herod's eyes hardened. "Please share it with the family."

Alexander glanced at his brother, then let his gaze rove over the assembled wives and their offspring, ranging from mature men to toddling children. "I said—" Alexander hesitated—"I said the king's hair has turned alarmingly black. It now matches his boots."

The room swelled with silence. The younger children wore puzzled faces, unable to comprehend the meaning behind Alexander's statement. But those of us who understood sat like stones, amazed by Alexander's brazen tongue. Mariamne's saucy spirit had definitely passed to her sons, because no sooner had Alexander spoken than Aristobulus began to laugh.

I stared, wanting the floor to open and swallow both of them. My brother was sensitive about his appearance, and he had asked me to have Zara mix up a dye to cover his gray hair. He had refused any experimentation, insisting that black was black, and Zara's concoction had left Herod's hair a shade darker than was natural for any man.

I saw a flash, like light caught in water, when Herod's gaze crossed mine, and I knew he was deciding how to respond. Should he let the brothers see the royal temper fully unleashed, or should he respond with humor to lessen his embarrassment?

Antipater decided the matter for him. Glowering at Alexander, he stood and faced the king. "Father," he said, his eyes fixed on Alexander, "I wanted to say that you are looking very well today. I have never seen a man so fit, not even among the Olympic champions we saw in Rome. They did well to name you perpetual Olympic President. You are an example of fitness to us all."

Herod's expression softened as the memory sank in. "Thank

you, Antipater." He gave his firstborn a broad smile. "We will have to go to Rome again—as soon as it suits the emperor. The two of us will go, as I believe Augustus would like to spend more time with my firstborn."

I glanced at my husband and heaved a sigh of relief. Thanks to Antipater, Herod had defused a tense situation and still managed to put his impertinent sons in their place.

Later that night, as Alexas readied for bed and I sat at my dressing table, he came up behind me and rested his hands on my shoulders. "Was your brother really an athlete?"

I lowered my hair comb and smiled at his reflection in the looking brass. "In his youth, few could match his accuracy with a javelin or a bow and arrow. He has always been interested in athletic games."

"I did not know." He pressed a kiss to the top of my head, then squeezed my shoulders. "We were fortunate tonight. I saw the look on the king's face—for a moment I thought he might have Mariamne's sons arrested."

"I would not have been surprised." I caught his hand and pulled it to my cheek. "The tension between them grows more palpable every day."

Alexas nodded. "I am sorry to say it, but I have heard that . . . Alexander has been cavorting with some of the eunuchs who attend the king."

Was he teasing? I turned to examine my husband's face. "Cavorting?"

He flushed to the roots of his hair. "They have been pleasuring him."

I grimaced. "Surely not. That sort of thing should not be done in Israel, and especially not in the king's palace."

"But they have been influenced by the Romans, and everyone knows the Romans think nothing of such things—"

"We are not Romans. We are Jews."

"Are we?" His question was curious, not spiteful, but I had no answer for him. In Jerusalem we were Jews—we worshiped at the Temple, we observed the festivals and the Sabbath—but in other cities Herod built temples to Roman gods and furnished citizens with gymnasia and theaters and other entertainments many Jews frowned upon.

"I hope—" I swallowed hard—"I hope that story does not reach Herod. He would be furious."

"You are right," Alexas said. "But you know that Herod hears everything these days."

I did not respond, yet I knew very well what he meant. Herod heard everything, because Antipater made sure of it.

CHAPTER FORTY-SEVEN

Zara

In the seventh year of our marriage, around the time of Sukkot, I did not bleed at the appointed time. For the next few mornings I woke with anticipation in my heart and remained overly aware of my body as the day progressed.

Was that a wave of nausea or simply the smell of rotten eggs? Did my breasts feel tender? Was the bulge at my belly a sign of new life or gluttony? Perhaps, I told myself, this was the month Adonai had chosen to bless me with a child.

I counted three days past the usual time, then four, then five. I did not speak of my hope to anyone, especially not Ravid, because he had been wounded by false hope far too many times. Neither did I mention my hope to my mistress, who conceived as easily as a cat. She would not understand.

Six days past my time and no sign of blood. I looked at the tidy cotton rolls in my basket and prayed I would not need to use them for at least a year. Maybe HaShem would bless us with a second child soon after the first. I would not mind having two children close together, and neither would Ravid. Or—a wave of giddiness swept over me—perhaps HaShem would bless us with twins! Like Jacob and Esau, two babies would grow in my belly. They would become men in this amazing time of waiting for the Lord's anointed king, and perhaps they would walk with our future Messiah.

On the seventh day, I decided I would tell Ravid at sunset. I had never gone a full week past my appointed time, and he might be wondering why I had not observed the traditional rites of niddah. Soon he would ask why I had not remained at home instead of going to the Temple. Or perhaps he would casually remark that I had not taken my mikvah, so did I have some unusual news to share?

At midday I took a nap, for expectant mothers needed their rest. When Salome's voice woke me, I got up and noticed a tight feeling at my center. I slipped off the couch and walked to the jar in the corner of a back room, then squatted to relieve myself. Once I had finished, I reached for a cloth, cleaned, and stared at the blood blooming like a flower at its center.

I drew a deep, shuddering breath, struggling to inhale air that had gone thick with the heaviness of despair. I had seen blood before—in the streets, when Jerusalem fell to Herod and the Romans. On my mother, when she suffered from the blow that ultimately killed her. On Mariamne's neck. On Costobar's . . .

And every time it signaled the same thing—an end.

My plans for a joyous announcement vanished like the morning dew, and my heart contracted in silent anguish.

No child lived within me. We would not be having a son. Not this time. Perhaps not ever.

CHAPTER FORTY-EIGHT

Salome

"You sent for me, my king?"

I bowed before my brother, because something in the messenger's posture had warned me that this would not be a casual meeting. Herod was sitting in his chamber, alone except for his adviser, Nicolaus of Damascus, who had only recently come to court. The man had once been tutor to the children of Antony and Cleopatra, and I hoped he was wise enough to give my brother good advice.

"Yes, sister. I have questions and need answers."

I straightened and wondered what had spurred this sudden need for a meeting. No one could predict the direction of Herod's thinking these days, not even me. Over the years I had watched him turn against so many he loved—Mariamne, Alexander and Aristobulus, even Pheroras. Would he one day despise me, as well?

I forced a smile. "I will do my best to answer, brother."

I hoped he would gesture to the empty chair in front of him, for I would feel a great deal more relaxed if I were sitting, but he did not.

When he began with "I have heard," a suffocating sensation tightened my throat. What had he heard this time, and from whom had he heard it? I hoped he would not ask me to ascertain the truth of a matter, because I had no way of knowing what was true and what was one of Antipater's falsehoods. The palace had become a den of liars and schemers, and no one felt safe anymore.

"I have heard a great many things," he repeated, his faint smile shrouded in sadness. "Some things are unfit for a woman's ears. But this one thing concerns me, and I wondered if you have seen any evidence to support or disavow it."

I spread my hands. "When you tell me what it is—"

"I have heard that Alexander and Aristobulus are plotting to kill me in order to avenge their mother's death." Without warning, his gaze rose and locked on mine. "Have you heard the same rumor? Have you harbored the same suspicion?"

In truth, I had heard that rumor for years, but nothing had ever come of it. So why was he asking about it now?

"If I thought you were in danger, brother, I would have done everything in my power to protect you. I always have."

"But what of Mariamne's sons? Do you know any reason why I should fear them?"

What to do? Wavering between the vow I made my mother and what I knew of Antipater's falseness, I took the safest option available—I told the truth.

"Brother, I admit that I worried about reprisals when the boys returned from Rome. Their mother and I did not get along, and everyone knows I bore her no love. I was relieved when you made Antipater your heir, because I dreaded to think what Alexander or Aristobulus might do when—if—one of them became king."

Herod's brow wrinkled, and something moved in his eyes. "It distresses me to think you would have any cause to fear my own sons. I would not have you worry even a single hour, so

I have decided to take them to Rome and accuse them before Caesar. Augustus is wise, and he will be the judge of their fate."

I swallowed hard, wanting to protect my brother, but not wanting to punish innocent men. "Are you certain this is what you want to do? Do you have evidence of their plotting together to harm you?"

"How can we have peace in Judea when the king's palace is filled with such dread?" He lifted his head, and in the hard light of the winter sun I saw the face of a fearful, aging king. "Yes, I have decided. We will leave matters in the hands of the emperor."

CHAPTER FORTY-NINE

Zara

Herod's palace did not lie far from the Essene Quarter where Ravid and I lived. Depending on how many wagons crowded the streets, I usually managed to walk through the upper city in less than an hour.

But now that the king and his sons were away, life had slowed in the palace, and Salome had not been in a mood to entertain. She fretted in her apartment, took long walks through the courtyards, and frequently wept into her pillow. I did not know what troubled her, and she would not tell me. Her husband seemed unable to ease her mind, and not even the jeweler and dressmaker could distract her from her troubling thoughts.

One afternoon I left the palace early and walked east toward the Temple. Though the sanctuary had been completed for ten years, the forecourts had only recently been finished. Artisans, masons, and stonecutters still clustered around the structure, adding porticoes, streets, shops, gates, even a bridge to the upper city. On all days but the Sabbath we had to ignore the sound of chisels and grinding stone.

Whenever I visited the Temple, I thought of Hannah—of

300

how she wanted a son so desperately she made a promise to HaShem: if He would grant her request, she would dedicate her son to Adonai's service. The Lord heard her prayer and gave her a son, Samuel, who served as high priest in the time of King David.

I was not Hannah, but perhaps I, too, could bargain with Adonai. I had certainly prayed as long and fervently, perhaps even longer. I had wept and fasted, pleaded and begged, and thus far HaShem had chosen not to answer. Ravid said HaShem always answered, but not always in the way we wanted Him to. If I pressed my husband for an answer as to why we were childless, he would say HaShem had answered my prayer with *no*, or in an attempt to be gentle, *wait*. But my heart could not be content with either of those responses.

I felt like Rachel, who clutched at her husband, Jacob, and said, "Give me sons. If there are none, I'll die!" I had not yet been driven to clutch at Ravid and make the same demand, yet he probably saw the same desperation in my eyes and heard it in my voice.

I walked along the ancient wall that once marked the boundary of Jerusalem until I reached the new stones surrounding the mount on which the Temple rested. I skirted the area where workers carved and polished stones, then clambered over a pile of rubble and found a path leading to the Temple courts.

I walked through the Court of the Gentiles and entered the new Court of the Women. I breathed deeply of incense-sweetened air. I studied the trumpet-shaped chests along the wall. Ravid and I regularly deposited tithes and offerings into those chests, but I would give anything, even my life, if HaShem would answer my prayer.

I walked to the center of the open space and knelt, then spread myself on the floor, arms outstretched, forehead to the dusty stones. *I cannot believe*, I prayed, *that you brought me to the palace to spend my life in service to the king's sister. I have plaited her hair, helped her dress, and listened to her complaints, but what does that do for you? How can I be useful if you keep me in a palace where no one is happy and no one seeks after you?*

If you care for me as a woman, as a person, then use me, Adonai. Take my life and let it be something more than it is by giving me a son who will do great things for you.

I would die now if you wanted my life. Ravid says I should speak to you as a friend, but what sort of friend would ignore my earnest prayers? I have asked only for a child, Adonai, a little son to love. If you want my life, take it now; but if you want me to live, give my life meaning by giving me a son. If you do, I will raise him to honor you in everything he does. And I will give you the glory for all things, even if I live only long enough to see my son's birth.

I waited for several moments, expecting to hear something— thunder, a voice, perhaps a rushing wind—but I heard only muffled footsteps approaching. When I lifted my head, a Levite stood near me, his head tilting as he studied me.

I sat up. "I was praying," I said, rising. "And now I will be going."

"Good." The Levite dipped his head in an emphatic nod. "I would not make a habit of praying like that."

CHAPTER FIFTY

Salome

I should have slept well, but I did not. I should have been
buoyant with relief that Herod, Antipater, Alexander, and
Aristobulus had returned home, at peace and reconciled,
but the snake of anxiety still coiled in my belly.

Antipater gave me details as soon as he returned to the palace. "You should have seen it, Aunt," he began, dropping onto
a couch in my chamber. "The emperor heard our case in his
home because he said he considered us family. Friends." Antipater grinned. "I am now a friend of the emperor. I'm sure my
brothers never expected to hear *that*."

"Go on." I forced myself to sit across from him. "Tell me
everything."

Antipater leaned forward, propping his elbows on his knees.
"Father spoke first, of course, telling Augustus that Alexander
and Aristobulus had been plotting against him. He cited reports
from servants and friends—"

"Whose friends?"

"Mine." Antipater gave a lopsided smile. "They were well
paid to deliver reports to the king. I only wish they could have

come on the journey, for they might have enjoyed meeting the emperor."

"Did you speak?" I asked.

Antipater's smile faded. "I did not need to, as I wasn't the accused. Alexander spoke next, delivering an apology for disturbing the emperor and his father the king. He denied plotting to murder the king and blamed everything on me."

"He blamed *you*?"

"But he had no evidence." A grin winked in and out of Antipater's thin beard. "I wish I had studied oratory like Alexander. The way he held them spellbound . . . truly an amazing experience."

"What happened next?"

Antipater leaned back, plucked a pomegranate from a bowl, and rubbed it against his tunic. "The emperor spoke. He talked about peace and family and how we all need to get along for the sake of Judea and the Republic. When he had finished, Father embraced all three of us and said to go home in peace. And upon his death, all three of us would be kings, but I would be the chief power, the primary heir." He pulled a knife from his belt and cut off the pomegranate's crown. "As you can imagine, Augustus was the only person pleased with *that* arrangement."

I brought my hand to my mouth and looked away. I might have been content with that settlement, but Mother would not have been satisfied. Neither would Mariamne or Alexandra.

I did not believe the strife between our two families could be settled by diplomacy.

"I pretended to be delighted by Father's judgment, of course," Antipater said, scoring the pomegranate along its ridges. "Alexander and Aristobulus were clearly displeased, however, which only made me look like the better prince. Soon I will prove myself the better son. I have put plans in motion that should result in my brothers being stripped of their titles, if not worse."

I watched in fascinated dread as Antipater thrust his thumbs into the top of the fruit and split it, revealing a bounty of crimson seeds. He offered one of the juicy segments to me. "Would you like some?"

His thumb, which had burst some of the seeds, dripped red juice onto my carpets. I forced myself to look away from his stained fingers. "What are you planning?"

"I have been speaking to Pheroras and some of Alexander's servants. When the time is right, you will understand everything."

He tossed back a handful of pomegranate seeds, stood, and gave me a kiss on the cheek before departing. I went to my dressing table and stared at my reflection in the looking brass—a bloody smear marred my cheek, stained by Antipater's kiss.

I looked up as Zara came in, her face pink from her walk to the palace. "Good morning, mistress. You are up early."

I lifted my chin and studied the girl. No, not a girl any longer, but a mature woman. "Zara, how old are you now?"

She turned, startled. "Mistress?"

"I forget how much time has passed. You were nine when you first came to the palace, so how old are you now?"

She hung her cloak on a hook. "This will be my thirty-second year."

"Still . . . so young."

She laughed. "I wish I felt young. I feel like an overripe fruit, always waiting—"

"Waiting for what?"

She shook her head. "I shouldn't bother you with my personal problems."

"You have a problem? You always seem so . . . calm."

She gave me a tight-lipped smile and came to stand behind

me. "I am your servant. I am supposed to be calm. Now." She dropped her hands to the back of my chair. "Do you have any special events today? Now that the king has returned—"

"How do you do it?"

"Mistress?"

"I have just realized—you were going to work for me until you had a child, but you've been married . . . how long now?"

"Eight years." Her tone was clipped.

"I am sorry." And I was. Though I had never experienced the heartbreak of a barren womb, I had known other sorrows. The grief of not being allowed to wed Syllaeus, the premature deaths of my father and two brothers, and now the constant tension between Herod and his three oldest sons.

"How do you cope?" I turned to look directly into her eyes. "You have obviously been carrying a burden for some time, yet I have never seen evidence of your struggle. I would assume you've worn a false face in my presence, but you have always been honest with me."

"The Torah commands us to speak the truth," she said, looking away to rummage through a basket of combs and hair needles.

"What else does the Torah command? Does it tell you how to cope with a family that seems bent on destroying itself?"

The question caught her by surprise. She turned, her mouth falling open, and stammered an answer. "I could never tell you what to do, mistress."

"I'm asking about the Torah. If you were in my situation—" my throat clotted, but I pushed out the words—"if you were pinned between one evil and another, what would you do?"

She took a deep breath, then tried on a smile that seemed far too small. "All I can tell you, mistress, is what the prophet Micah wrote. 'He has told you, humanity, what is good, and what Adonai is seeking from you: only to practice justice, to love mercy, and to walk humbly with your God.'"

Justice . . . mercy . . . humility. Attributes that might benefit a common family, but not a king's.

I sighed and turned back to the looking brass. "I have to attend the king's banquet tonight," I said, straightening in my chair. "Let's wear my hair in curls, shall we?"

CHAPTER FIFTY-ONE

Zara

Two more years passed—long years in which I served my mistress, my husband, and Adonai, though my heart no longer took pleasure in serving any of them.

Though Salome guessed my secret grief that long-ago morning in her chamber, I knew she had put the memory from her mind when she invited me to accompany her on a visit to Berenice's chamber. "She will be eager to show you her new baby." Salome bent to peer in the looking brass, then patted her hair. "After all, she spent many happy hours of her childhood with you."

I murmured something about congratulations and silently followed Salome through the winding halls of the new palace. Berenice and Aristobulus had been given lavish rooms adjacent to the outer wall, where the wide windows offered views of the sprawling vista outside the city.

When we opened the door, we were greeted by a chorus of children's voices. "Grandmother! Savta!" Salome bent to embrace her grandchildren, all except the new baby, who lay swaddled in his mother's arms.

I stood near the wall and counted heads: Mariamne, age six;

Herod IV, age five; Marcus Julius Herod Agrippa, age three; and the newborn, Aristobulus II. After hugging the three older children, Salome moved immediately to the bed and held out her arms. Berenice gently handed over her infant son, and together they cooed at the baby and compared chins and noses.

I watched as long as I could, then quietly turned and left the room.

I was happy for my mistress, truly I was. I was happy for Berenice, who had grown up to be a lovely and kind young woman. But with each child born into the king's household, my heart shriveled a little.

Why did HaShem allow those women to prosper when they cared so little for the things of Adonai? Why did HaShem quicken their wombs year after year and bless them with children? Why?

I knew the stories of Rachel and Rebecca and Sarah, barren women who conceived after a struggle because HaShem heard their prayers. But those stories did little to ease the twisting of my heart when I lay beside a husband who had lost a child and desperately longed for another. Once, before we were married, Ravid had been teaching when he remarked, "The first mitzvah in the Torah is 'be fruitful and multiply.' One who does not intentionally fulfill this mitzvah is akin to a murderer, for he is depleting life and minimizing God's presence in the world."

Was it my fault? Ravid could father children; he had already done so. So was I guilty of depleting life? Was I being disobedient to Adonai?

At night, as I lay next to my husband, I stared at the ceiling and asked HaShem why Salome and Berenice should be so blessed and my portion so meager. And then, closing my eyes and drifting off to sleep, I often thought I could hear Him reply, *Wait a little while, my child, wait a little while.*

But how long was a little while?

CHAPTER FIFTY-TWO

Salome

For the next two years, Antipater kept up his slanderous campaign against the sons of Mariamne. He continued to pay spies to spread false stories until finally, when the king had heard enough, he had several of Alexander's friends arrested. When they would not speak against Alexander, Herod had them tortured.

The news horrified me. I had never heard of free men being tortured, only slaves, for everyone knew slaves could not be trusted to voluntarily reveal the truth. I pressed Pheroras for details, and he quickly pulled me into a quiet hallway. "Herod would not like me to tell you this."

"Why shouldn't you? There should be no secrets between us."

"But you are a woman, and women do not . . ." He glanced at my indignant face and sighed. "They begin with first-degree torture."

"What is that?"

"Beating of the soles of the feet, perhaps beating of the back. If that does not elicit the desired confession, they move to second degree."

310

I crossed my arms and lifted a brow, waiting.

Pheroras sighed again. "Second degree involves the breaking of bones or the pulling of teeth. They have devices that can crush a man's knees and feet."

I closed my eyes and forbade myself to shudder. After all, I had asked for this. "And if that does not obtain the desired information?"

"You do not want to know."

"We've been through this, brother. I want to know what Herod has been doing to Alexander's friends."

"Third degree." Pheroras lowered his voice to a hoarse whisper, as if the words were too horrible to speak in a normal tone. "This involves spikes, blades, boiling oil, and fire. Most men do not survive third degree, if it persists."

The walls around me began to sway, so I reached for Pheroras's arm and steadied myself. "And Alexander's friends?"

"Several of them have already died. One of them, however, did confess that Alexander was planning regicide. That confession, I'm afraid, has irrevocably turned the king's heart against Mariamne's sons."

"But so many of those young men died *without* making a confession. They were willing to give their lives rather than confess to something false!"

"Antipater was with the king when the jailer brought that news, and when our nephew observed that the king grew thoughtful, he praised the dead men's loyalty. 'To have such friends,' he said, 'men who would die rather than betray your secret!' He then produced a letter from Alexander to Aristobulus, a letter listing details of how the king would be murdered by poison."

I covered my mouth and turned away—I had heard enough. Leaving Pheroras, I walked toward my apartment with a thickly beating heart, my shoulders weighed down by grief.

I understood—and so did Antipater—why the threat of

poison so alarmed Herod. Poison, administered by a so-called *friend*, killed our father. He had come home from a banquet with Hyrcanus and fallen to the floor in a seizure. I wrapped my arms around him, begging him to calm himself, to breathe, but to no avail. The physician, who arrived too late, said I could not have saved him.

At the end of the hallway I turned back and saw that Pheroras had moved to a window. "Brother," I called, "what has the king done about this?"

Pheroras shifted and regarded me, an aura of melancholy radiating from his lined face. "He has put Alexander in prison."

The old feelings of grief and loss overwhelmed me, just as they had when our father died. Antipater had woven his web, and I could do nothing to save Alexander.

Over the following weeks, Alexander wrote a long document outlining his defense. Herod might have softened after reading it, but in his letter Alexander named me and Pheroras as guilty parties, claiming we had spread stories and forged letters. He even claimed I had entered his bedroom and forced him to sleep with me. I was shocked speechless when I heard that report, because until that moment I had believed Alexander to be a lover of truth.

Had Herod's sons gone mad, or had they been driven to these extreme behaviors by desperation?

I was bereft, convinced matters would proceed to the inevitable bitter end, until King Archelaus of Cappadocia arrived in Jerusalem to seek after his daughter, Glaphyra, Alexander's wife. Apparently she had written her father with news of our troubled household. After spending an afternoon with her, he went to the prison and appeared to be furious with his son-in-law. He demanded an audience with Herod, where he declared he would have the marriage set aside so that he could take his daughter home to Cappadocia.

The man was as devious as Antipater, only for far more noble purposes. As Herod heard Archelaus denounce and ridicule Mariamne's eldest son, his slumbering love for Alexander awakened and he began to defend the young man. By the time the meeting had ended, Herod had released Alexander from prison and Glaphyra had fallen to her knees and thanked her father with grateful tears.

As for me, I was glad Alexander had been restored to his wife, yet nothing had really changed. Antipater, Alexander, and Aristobulus were still caught in a triangle of resentment from which none could escape unscathed.

And I was still bound by a deathbed promise to keep the Hasmoneans from the throne.

In the twenty-eighth year of Herod's reign in Jerusalem, my brother stumbled into a situation from which no one could protect him. For several years Nabataean raiding parties had been crossing into Judean territory and terrorizing villages. Herod's generals attempted to subdue the raiders, but when two new Roman officials, Saturninus and Volumnius, took control in Syria, Herod informed them of the raids and demanded the offenders be punished.

To placate Herod, Saturninus and Volumnius gave him permission to attack a Nabataean town called Rhaepta. When Herod's attack was successful, he reported the outcome to Rome.

But Syllaeus, my former lover, went to Augustus and exaggerated the devastation. While 25 Nabataeans had been killed, Syllaeus reported it as 2,500 deaths. Augustus asked a blunt question: did Herod cross the border with a military force? The answer, of course, was yes.

Herod's action infuriated the emperor who had once been

his friend. Augustus wrote Herod, declaring that my brother was no longer a friend but a subject. Devastated by the misunderstanding, Herod immediately sent envoys to explain what had happened, but Augustus would not grant them an audience.

I had not seen Herod so low since the days following Mariamne's death. His loss of the emperor's friendship not only saddened but terrified him. Although Augustus loved peace, he had no qualms about ridding his kingdom of men who ventured beyond their authority. Herod's political troubles, combined with the constant quarrels of his wives, his failing health, a falling-out with Pheroras, and the tumultuous relationship with his sons all left him paralyzed with indecision.

I visited him several times, promising my support and attempting to help him recognize his many successes, but my brother had become completely paranoid. I was glad he welcomed my company—indeed, he seemed to prefer my company to any of his wives'. Yet my heart ached to see my once-strong brother reduced to a state of anxiety.

One afternoon, as we sat together on a sunny balcony, he turned to me. "Did you know Pheroras is in love with a slave? That is why he would not marry Salampsio or Cypros. Can you imagine? A *slave*! A man once married to Mariamne's sister, a Hasmonean princess, now sleeps with a slave woman."

I stared at him, my heart pounding. "I . . . I had no idea."

"He meant to keep the news from us, of course, but I have spies in his palace. In a few months, his slave will give birth to his child."

I said nothing but covered my mouth, grateful that our mother was no longer alive to hear this news.

"I do not know—" Herod's voice broke as he looked toward the horizon—"I do not know what to do, Salome. You are the only person in this house who understands and supports me.

My wives squabble all day, shoving their children in my face as if they could replace my firstborn." A tear trickled from the corner of his eye. "Mariamne's sons, the boys who were once the apple of my eye, now wish me dead. And Augustus, who had proved to be as steadfast as he is generous, now refuses to meet with me."

I reached across the space between us and placed my hand on his arm. "This, too, shall pass," I whispered, watching the golden light of sunset play across his lined face. "Wait a while, Herod, and you will see. You are an athlete, a competitor, and your race is not yet finished."

In less than a year, Herod and Augustus reconciled. Nicolaus of Damascus, Herod's adviser and philosophy teacher, traveled to Rome and met with the emperor. He confronted Syllaeus with his distortions, then explained to Augustus that Herod had acted under the oversight of Roman officials. Augustus realized he had been deceived by the Nabataean and that Herod's actions had been correct. He reinstated my brother's status as a friend of Rome.

Finally, my brother's spirits began to rise. With the emperor's friendship restored, the king's confidence returned. Armed with fresh determination, he set out to investigate his household and put an end to the intrigues and rumors about his sons.

Under torture, three eunuchs in the king's service confessed that Alexander and Aristobulus had hatched a plan to kill their father in a hunting accident, and afterward sail to Rome for the emperor's confirmation as Herod's heirs. Herod had their quarters searched for evidence to confirm this plot, but nothing was found save a letter from Aristobulus to Alexander about Antipater's growing influence and income.

"No wonder you found nothing," Antipater told the king.

"They are too clever to leave evidence behind. They only speak of their plans; they do not write them."

Herod had Alexander arrested. When the torture of the prince's friends began again, other plans were confessed—one plot to use poison and another to go to the emperor and accuse Herod of secret agreements with Parthia.

Archelaus of Cappadocia returned and again acted as peacemaker, wisely pointing out that Alexander had no reason to kill his father. If Mariamne's sons killed the appointed king, Augustus would never allow them to assume the throne.

But then another man came to court, Gaius Julius Eurycles, a friend of the emperor. I distrusted him from the moment I saw him, and my reaction had nothing to do with the arrogant way he carried himself or his reputation as the son of an executed pirate. I distrusted his eyes, which seemed as remote as the ocean depths, even when he smiled. I could never trust a man whose soul did not shine through his eyes.

This wily worm ingratiated himself with Alexander and began to tell the prince that he, his brother, Mariamne, and Glaphyra were of royal blood, yet a commoner sat upon the throne. Warmed by the flattery and commiseration, Alexander and Aristobulus unburdened themselves, admitting a litany of complaints against their father.

After memorizing the men's grievances, Eurycles went to Antipater and gave him all he needed to stoke the fire of Herod's fury. Leaving Antipater, Eurycles went to Herod himself, saying that in order to repay the king's many kindnesses toward him, he had come to save the king's life. He explained that Alexander and Aristobulus were conspiring to kill the king by running him through with his own spear, then making it look as though he had pierced himself with his spear by falling from his horse. The two men had also been suborning Herod's generals. As Herod seethed in fury, Eurycles went on to praise Antipater as a loyal son.

Herod put the Hasmonean brothers under house arrest. I had been more than willing to watch from a distance, but when I heard that Aristobulus was threatening to tell Herod I had conspired with Syllaeus to jeopardize Herod's relationship with the emperor, I went directly to my brother. "According to the gossip being spread by your son Aristobulus," I said, my chest heaving with indignation, "you are planning to kill me."

"Kill the only person who is truly loyal to me?" Herod's face went purple, and veins stood out in his throat. "They will both die."

I remained quiet, knowing that Herod could change his mind yet again. Because the boys were close friends of the emperor, he would not execute them immediately. In time, he might soften enough to let them live out their lives as princes, enjoying their wives and children in the palace.

Antipater could win. For my mother's sake, I hoped he would.

CHAPTER FIFTY-THREE

Zara

"Why, HaShem, would you allow such things to happen?" I had developed the habit of praying as I walked to the palace, and lately my prayers had been a continuous refrain of questions. "Why would you allow the king's family to develop such hatred for one another? Where there should be love, there is hate; and where there should be joy, there is only bitterness."

I stepped over a puddle and continued along the cobblestone street. Silence hung over the city, for the hour was yet early, and the only people stirring were those who made deliveries or tended hungry livestock.

And me, who cared for the king's sister.

Salome was away from the palace, and for the past several months she had not been herself. Though she took pains to pretend that nothing was amiss, I often caught her staring into space, her eyes vacant and her lips pressed into a straight line. Streaks of gray had appeared in her hair, and not even frequent applications of henna could hide them.

I knew what had happened with the princes—everyone in

318

the palace knew, though no one spoke of it openly. Herod had written the emperor, who had told him to bring his accused sons to a court in Berytus. The princes would stand trial, the evidence would be presented, and the court would rule.

Salome and Pheroras went with Herod to Berytus, as did some Roman officials from the area. We had not yet heard the outcome of the trial, but I hoped for the best. I had been impressed with Archelaus of Cappadocia, who had urged peace and reconciliation, while the king's advisor, Nicolaus of Damascus, seemed only to reinforce whatever the king was feeling. And the king's emotions vacillated like those of a young girl.

I stopped to let a donkey and cart pass by, the smell of donkey urine assaulting me. Overcome by the stench, I clutched my stomach, bent over and vomited in the street. Trembling and embarrassed, I spat the vile taste out of my mouth and stood. No one had seen me but an older woman, who was setting up her vegetable cart.

"Aye," the woman said with a grin. "How many will this make for you?"

I blinked in confusion. "What do you mean?"

She stopped sorting vegetables and gaped at me. "Could this be your first, then?"

"My first . . . ?" My mouth dropped open as realization bloomed in my chest. My first. Could it be, after so many years?

"Give it time," the old woman said, cackling as she returned to her work. "If you're still losing your breakfast next week, better start gathering your swaddling cloths."

I shook my head. No. She had to be wrong. After praying so hard and for so long, why would HaShem answer my prayer now? Why did He not let me conceive when I had strength and energy? Why would He not let me bear a child when I was struggling with jealousy over Salome's fruitfulness? Why now when I was thirty-seven years old and tired?

I hurried to the palace and sat on the edge of a bed, one hand on my belly. My stomach did not feel distended, but unless I was mistaken, my breasts had swollen. Was the old woman right?

I said nothing about my suspicions until a month later when the full moon rose and I still had not bled. But neither had I experienced what other women called "the heat." My stomach had become a small mound, barely visible beneath my tunic.

When Ravid came home from the Temple that night, I silently caught his hands and led him to the bed. I pulled him down to sit beside me and placed his hand on my growing belly. "I thought I had entered the final stage of womanhood," I whispered, my voice husky, "but HaShem has touched my womb and I have conceived."

My husband's eyes filled with wonder. He pulled me into his arms, kissed me, and murmured that HaShem had been good to us and all would be well.

<hr />

I soon learned that carrying a child at thirty-seven was nothing like carrying a child at twenty. On my walks to the palace or to the well, I frequently spotted other expectant women, and few of them struggled as I did. The larger my baby grew, the more difficult I found walking, and when I returned home at night, I could barely summon the strength to prepare our evening meal.

Fortunately, Ravid took pity on me and asked our neighbor Rachel for help. She invited us to dine with her family, so we ate at her table every night. While I appreciated her hospitality, I longed for the day when I would be alone with my husband and our child, free to enjoy the motherhood for which I had prayed so long.

Salome did not notice I was pregnant at first. I do not blame her for being unobservant. Since her return from Berytus, her mind and heart had been occupied with dreadful things.

The sons of Mariamne had been tried and found guilty of plotting to kill the king. Without being allowed to speak for themselves, and without proof of their crime, they were found guilty. Of their judges, Volumnius argued for a harsh sentence, and though Saturninus thought the young men guilty, he did not believe the crime worthy of death. He said he had three sons of his own and believed that killing any one of them would be the greatest tragedy he could imagine for himself.

I did not hear how Salome or Pheroras voted or even if they had a say in the matter. The judges were present only to advise; the sentence was entirely up to Herod.

When Herod and his party returned to Caesarea, several soldiers and the king's barber tried to intervene on the princes' behalf. Herod ordered the barber and three hundred soldiers arrested and beaten to death.

The sons of Mariamne were taken to Sebaste where Herod had married their mother, and they were executed by strangulation. Their bodies were buried at Alexandreion, where Herod had buried Mariamne, Alexandra, and the son who had died in Rome.

Now they were gone, along with the threat, real or imagined, they had presented. Knowing my mistress had never liked Mariamne and had always been wary of the brothers, I thought their execution would ease her mind, but she did not smile for weeks afterward. Neither did the king. I saw him one afternoon, shuffling along a hallway with a cane, his back bent, his head lowered, and his legs swollen. He did not see me, and even from a distance I could tell he suffered from some sort of malady.

When I mentioned the king's appearance to Ravid, my husband pressed his lips together and nodded. "'There is no health in my flesh because of Your indignation,'" he quoted. "'There is no wholeness in my bones because of my sin. For my iniquities are on my head—like a burden too heavy for me.'"

"One of the prophets?" I asked.

"A psalm of David," he answered. "When he cried out to Adonai."

I doubted that Herod was crying out to the Lord, but how was I to know?

I was nearly seven months with child when Salome finally realized I was moving more slowly than usual. "I see you have finally conceived," she said, arching a brow as she studied my reflection in the looking brass. "Yet I cannot help noticing that you are struggling. I know we agreed you would stay until you gave birth, but perhaps the time has come for me to find another handmaid."

My hands froze in her hair as I struggled with conflicting emotions. After so many years of faithful service, was she planning to dismiss me so abruptly? Was I simply to disappear without so much as a farewell?

Somehow I managed to finish the braid and fasten it with thread. "I will always be grateful for what you have done for me," I said, taking pains to keep my voice light. "And you are right—it has not been an easy time."

"It is I who should be grateful . . . for you." With uncharacteristic tenderness she reached out and caught my hand. "You must think me the coldest and most unfeeling woman in the world."

I stepped forward and sank to a bench near her chair, wanting to see her face. "You are my mistress; it matters not what I think of you."

"Doesn't it?" She cast me a sharp look, then lowered her gaze to her lap. "I did not want the princes to die. If Herod had asked me, I think I could have convinced him to exile them or send them and their families to Rome. But his mind had been poisoned by Antipater and that awful Eurycles. Now my

322

daughter has no husband and Glaphyra is a widow. The only good thing to come out of this is that Herod has determined to be a better grandfather than he was a father. He will arrange excellent betrothals for the lads' children. He will dote on them . . . until his dying day."

I did not know what to say. So I listened without speaking, and when she looked up, I obeyed a sudden impulse to reach out and squeeze her hand.

She flinched at my touch, and no wonder. Though for years I had smoothed makeup on her eyes and cheeks, and though my hands knew her hair better than my own, I had never taken her hand. The gesture was warm and human, an unspoken bond between women, and I was not sure anyone had ever touched her in such a way.

I thought—feared—she might shake me off as if I were a pestilent fly, but she did not. "I may not always have shown my appreciation," she said, staring at my hand, "but I have learned a lot from you. Whenever I wanted to know how a Jewish . . . how a *righteous* woman would react, or what she would think, I had only to look to my handmaid. You were my looking brass. And though I thought you would begin to reflect my manner over time, I can only hope that in the future I will reflect you."

She placed her free hand over mine for a moment, then pulled away and put on her no-nonsense expression. "I know you need time to prepare for your baby, so I am going to release you from service. Please finish out the week with me, and then you may go home. But you will not go empty-handed. I want to make sure you and your husband will want for nothing. I will be giving you a house, yet I will wait for you to tell me where you want to settle. Please let me know after you have spoken to your Torah teacher. This is the least I can do for you."

Her offer—and the sincerity of it—caught me by surprise.

With great difficulty I stammered out my thanks. With tears blinding my eyes, I stood and backed away.

Ravid had always thought my mistress cold and scheming, but he was wrong. Like most people, Salome was not what she appeared to be.

CHAPTER FIFTY-FOUR

Salome

On Zara's final day, I looked up and saw her hesitating at the threshold of my chamber. "Come in." I gestured to her. The new slave, an awkward girl of a dozen or so years, stood behind me with a comb and threaded needle in hand, ready to learn. "Uru is eager to begin, so teach her well. I suspect I will not be seeing you again."

Zara pressed her hand to her back and waddled into the room, then nodded encouragement as the slave began to run the comb through my hair.

"Ouch!" I winced as the comb encountered a tangle. "Careful at the back of the head, please. My hair often tangles there."

I watched in the looking brass as Zara guided the girl, instructing her about how to section the hair, how to braid it, how to work the colored thread through the braids and secure them. "Always make sure the anchor braid is strong," Zara said, tugging on a braid at the back of my head. "It will not be seen, so it doesn't have to be pretty, but without it your mistress will not be comfortable."

"Indeed." I sighed, then smiled at Zara. "I have been waiting for your reply, so do not think I have forgotten. Have you and Ravid decided where you want to live?"

A blush crept into her cheeks. "Ravid would like to return to the home of his fathers. He would like to open a new school."

"So you would leave Jerusalem? He will no longer teach at the Temple?"

"He wants to remain close so he can help with the baby," Zara said, her eyes shining. "And he has family in Bethlehem."

"I have heard of the place. Herod built several pools south of that little town."

I smiled at her in my looking brass, grateful my handmaid would be able to enjoy a measure of happiness. That golden emotion had certainly been in short supply within the palace, especially of late.

"Then it shall be done," I said. "I will send a representative to find a suitable house, and you shall take possession before the baby comes. When it comes I hope your travail will be easy, and your future filled with joy."

I do not know if Zara expected more ceremony, more affection, or some sort of blessing, but I had no more time for formalities. "Thank you." I stood and adjusted the himation at my shoulder, then turned to face the two servants. "Now I must meet my husband and the king."

CHAPTER FIFTY-FIVE

Zara

Never having lived anywhere but Jerusalem, I found the quiet simplicity of Bethlehem a dramatic change. The walls of the town were neither exceptionally wide nor tall, for what did Bethlehem have worth stealing? The houses were built close together with shared walls, and each house had a small gated courtyard housing a sheep, goat, or several chickens.

Bethlehem might have been small, but it was old and had a rich history. As we had walked beside the wagon that held our few belongings, Ravid reminded me of Bethlehem's historic significance. "Rachel was buried here," he said, lifting his eyes as though he might spot her tomb by the road. "And Naomi and Ruth lived here."

"I know David kept sheep here," I said, grateful that I could add something to his list.

"Aye." Ravid nodded. "And the prophet Micah said the Messiah will be born here."

"Truly?"

Ravid smiled. "'But you, Bethlehem Ephrathah—least among the clans of Judah—from you will come out to Me One to be

327

ruler in Israel, One whose goings forth are from of old, from days of eternity.'"

My hand went to my bulging belly. "Do you believe that?"

"Of course. But only HaShem knows when He will come."

I patted my belly and kept walking, grateful to know that Ravid wasn't expecting *our* son to be the Messiah. After waiting so long to conceive him, I wasn't sure I would be ready to surrender him to the Lord's work. How had Hannah managed it?

Salome kept her promise. The house she bought us was larger than I would have expected and had belonged to a merchant who sold sheep at the Temple. The merchant recently died, my neighbor Huldah explained, and his wife had gone to Jerusalem to live with family.

"It is good to see a young couple moving in," Huldah said, her eyes fastened to my bulging tunic. She laughed. "But you are not so young, are you?"

I hoped my grimace would pass as a wry smile. "Not so young as you might think," I said, leaning on the courtyard wall to take weight off my swollen feet. "But not as old as Sarah when she gave birth to Isaac."

"Oh, yes." Huldah nodded. "When your time comes, have your husband fetch me. I have helped birth at least a dozen babies, and I will take good care of you."

Ravid and I soon realized an unexpected benefit to living in a large house. Since the village had no synagogue, he could begin his Torah school in our courtyard.

"I hope our baby can sleep through your classes," I said, stretching out on our mattress. I pressed my hand to my belly and smiled when the baby stirred beneath my skin. "I think he is almost ready to meet his parents."

The baby came a month later, earlier than I had expected—on a spring night, at sunset as the shepherds gathered their flocks and the farmers trudged homeward from a long day's work in the newly plowed fields. I braced myself for the pangs of labor while Ravid went next door to get Huldah. A moment later he came back, telling me that Huldah had gone out. "I left word with her husband," he said, taking my hand. "She will come when she can."

The first pale hints of sunrise had already brightened the eastern sky when Huldah rushed in, breathless and perspiring. "What a night! Babies coming everywhere, even out in the stables." She dropped to her knees and examined me. "You are ready. Push, Zara, and let us welcome your child!"

Our son entered the world just moments later. Huldah cackled with joy as she caught him and wrapped him in a swaddling cloth. "Another boy!" she said, a grin overtaking her features. "This is a night for boys, praise HaShem!"

Holding my baby in my arms, I marveled that an ordinary night could produce such a miracle. I had been present for all of Salome's births, but as much as I appreciated the joy a new baby brings, I had never realized the *depth* of that joy. I looked at Ravid, searching for words to express my feelings but could not begin to describe the sense of completion that flooded my heart.

For this I had been created. For this man, for this child, for this place.

My soul magnifies you, Adonai! I will praise you as long as I have breath to speak.

Ravid, never at a loss for words, must have been feeling the same emotions. He smiled at me, his eyes shining with unshed tears, then pressed his lips to my forehead and settled on the bed next to me, where we could both wonder at the beauty of our much-loved son.

CHAPTER FIFTY-SIX

Salome

Life in Herod's splendid new palace took a somber turn after the executions of Alexander and Aristobulus. The morning sunlight that used to pour through the windows and spangle the polished floors now seemed overly bright and painful to behold. When Herod entered the throne room at midday, the shimmering dust motes that drifted upward reminded me of dust stirring from the opening of a tomb. And at night, when we had time to sit alone exploring our memories and motivations, the dozens of torches and lamps barely pushed at the gloom, turning the high ceiling into a canopy of foreboding shadows.

As much as I had wanted Mariamne's sons gone, I had to admit that without them the atmosphere in the palace seemed darker, duller, and more fraught with tension. Now Antipater was the undisputed chief prince, and with every passing day he took on more of Herod's responsibilities. But he could not help noticing that Herod, acting out of guilt and a recommitment to his paternal duties, had turned his attention to his younger sons, sending Philip and Archelaus to Rome to be educated, just as he had Alexander and Aristobulus.

Herod also kept his promise to care for his grandsons, and those five boys were maturing before our eyes. Herod was not shy about displaying his fondness for them, and he often lamented their fathers' deaths, openly declaring he should not have killed them. On these occasions I watched with alarm, remembering his remorse after Mariamne's death. I did not want my brother to slip into madness as he had in those dark days, for Antipater waited like a hawk, watching his father for any sign of weakness. He had realized that Herod often changed his mind, and with every passing year, Herod was more likely to consider one of his younger sons for the throne.

Antipater had once been my ally, but I came to see him as an adversary once I realized he wanted his father to die. Herod was not well—he had been feeling the effects of advanced age for some time, and his servants whispered that he suffered from sores and worms in his private parts, along with fever, sore muscles, and aching bones.

Herod did not want anyone but his physician to see his weakened condition, so he tried his best to appear robust, though he would often leave meetings or abruptly send people from his chamber when he could no longer disguise the pain. Still, I knew my brother so well that he could not hide his infirmities from me. I saw pain in his bleary eyes, in his tenuous step, and in the odd way his eyelids quivered when he was overtired.

I also noticed an increasing tension between Pheroras and Herod. We had been united for so long, all of us pulling one yoke, that I could not believe either of them would allow anything to cause a rupture in our relationship.

One night I waited until everyone but my brothers had left the banquet room, and then I held up my hand. "We are going to talk," I said, looking from Herod to Pheroras. "I have noticed that you two are no longer close. At times you seem barely able to endure each other's company, so I would know what has happened between you."

Herod looked at Pheroras, then turned to me. "You know the problem, so do not pretend you do not."

"What problem?" I stared at Pheroras, who had crossed his arms and was facing the wall. "Pheroras?"

Finally he turned and met my gaze. "Herod will not accept my wife, and I will not put her away. We have a child together."

I lifted a brow—I had not heard about the marriage. "Congratulations," I said, wishing I could sound more enthusiastic. "Are we talking about the slave woman?"

"Her name is Panphila," Pheroras said, "and she is now my legal wife."

"And your slave," Herod interjected.

Pheroras shook his head. "I issued manumission papers years ago. She is a free woman and so is our daughter."

"You were married to Mariamne's royal sister," Herod said, leaning on the arm of his chair as if he no longer had the energy to stand. "She gave you three children. Yet after she died, you refused to marry two of my daughters. Men would kill for such an honor, but you refused my gifts as if I had offered slaves instead of my own offspring!"

"Your daughters would not want to marry an old man," Pheroras said, the corner of his mouth drooping. "They would have been wasted on me."

"So you marry a slave instead?"

"I came to love her." Pheroras's expression softened, and he looked at me as if I might understand. "I love her the way he loved Mariamne."

"You once promised me to be rid of her," Herod said. "Yet a few months later you were with her again."

Pheroras gave me a lopsided smile. "What can I say? I cannot deny love."

"Can you deny treason?" Herod clenched his fist, then glared at me and pointed a trembling finger at Pheroras. "Perhaps you have heard that the Pharisees refused to take the oath of loyalty to me and Augustus. I treated them gently, imposing a fine on them instead of something more stringent, and what happened? His woman—his slave—pays the fine for them!"

I caught my breath. "That explains it."

"Explains what?"

I glanced at Pheroras, hoping for some help, but his face remained impassive. "I have heard," I said, carefully choosing my words, "that the Pharisees have publicly predicted that your reign will soon end . . . and that Pheroras and his wife will sit on the throne of Judea."

The muscles in Herod's face tightened into a mask of rage. "You?" His eyes blazed as he stepped toward our brother. "Did you encourage this?"

I approached them, my fists clenched. "Stop it, both of you! You have forgotten what Father told us time and time again. We must pull together or we will fail. We are a *family*. We will not survive if we do not maintain our unity."

"Family?" Herod's voice dripped with disdain. "Family? This one"—again he pointed at Pheroras—"does not behave like *family*."

"Herod, stop. You have done so well of late." When he did not snap at Pheroras again, I continued, hoping to calm him. "You have done your best to bring this family together again. You sent Glaphyra back to her father in Cappadocia. You married my Berenice to Theudion, a noble man. You have provided for the upbringing and support of Alexander's and Aristobulus's seven children. You betrothed Aristobulus's eldest daughter to one of Antipater's sons. You betrothed Aristobulus's second daughter to your own son. You have done so much for so many."

I caught his outstretched hand, still pointed accusingly at

Pheroras, and gently lowered it. "You understand that a family united in marriage and bound by a love of our mutual children will hold your dynasty together. What does it matter if Pheroras refuses to participate in your plan?"

"I am sorry," Pheroras said, giving Herod a sad smile. "For years I have watched dangerous intrigues play out beneath this roof. I have seen wives pitted against each other. I have seen brothers fighting brothers, sisters plotting against wives, and husbands turning against children. I will have no part of it, not anymore."

Herod's gaze hardened. "If you side with your wife instead of me, you are no brother of mine. Leave this place and do not return."

"I am happy to go." Pheroras turned to me. "Farewell, sister. May HaShem bless you. Herod—be at peace. I will not return to this palace until you are dead."

I stared, amazed at the words that had just spilled from Pheroras's lips.

Without another word, Pheroras pulled his mantle over his shoulder and left us alone.

⸏⸏⸏⸏⸏⸏

"Pheroras, wait!" I called as loudly as I dared while hurrying to catch my brother before he departed.

He waited, then smiled as I stood before him, breathless and upset. "You can't talk me out of leaving, Salome. I should have walked away from Herod years ago."

"What—how? You can't leave a family. We are bound by blood, by a heritage."

"And that is part of the problem. Our heritage has been far too bloody." He tilted his head. "Do you know what I heard the other day? Apparently the emperor mentioned Herod in a public forum."

334

My pulse quickened. "What did he say?"

Pheroras snorted. "He said he would rather be Herod's pig than his son."

For an instant I stared at Pheroras, uncomprehending, then the words fell into place. Due to Jewish dietary laws, a pig would live out his natural life in peace here. Not so a son of Herod.

I closed my eyes. "Has Herod heard that?"

"I do not believe anyone has had the courage to tell him." He cupped my chin and lifted my head. "And if I were you, I would not be the one. Let it go."

"Pheroras." I caught his sleeve. "Please, do not leave. Herod will forget all about this if you meet him halfway. Keep your slave wife, but tell Herod you are willing to marry any woman he chooses. All he asks is that you obey your king."

Pheroras gently pulled his sleeve from my grasp. "I promised to love my wife, and I will. She would not want me to take another."

"Why?" The word ripped from my throat, borne on a tide of anguish. "Why are you doing this? You have always been so cooperative."

"Why?" His eyes lit as an odd smile lifted his mouth. "Salome, when Herod murdered Alexander and Aristobulus, I was forced to consider why we have done the things we have done. You and I have done everything to protect Herod and his throne, but those boys were no threat to him. They had no armies, and they would not have the support of the emperor if Herod did not choose them as his heirs. Yet Herod wanted them dead. Because, I think, the sight of them bothered his conscience. Guilt nearly drove him mad once, and he worried he would slip into madness again."

I carefully considered Pheroras's words. He could be right . . .

"You know Antipater's true nature," he said, his brown eyes narrowing. "But I do not think you know what Antipater has

335

been up to of late. He has confided in me because he knew I was unhappy with Herod."

Pheroras proceeded to tell me about his conversations with Antipater, conversations that made my talks with the young man seem mild by comparison.

"We say we are a family of Jews," Pheroras went on, "and though we observe the parts of the Law we find convenient, we do not take the Law to heart. We do not meditate on the Scriptures or pray apart from the rituals. We are too busy planning, plotting, and preparing for whatever Herod wants us to do."

"We are Idumaean. Father would not want us to—"

"Father did not apply the writings and the prophets to his heart," Pheroras interrupted. "But I have begun to study, and I am no longer the man I was. I was not a righteous man before, but I want to be righteous now. I want to love Adonai with all my heart, soul, and strength. Can you understand that?"

In truth, I could not. I felt as though my brother had suddenly begun to speak a foreign language and I could not understand a word. Had he forgotten who he was?

Pheroras moved closer, draped an arm around my shoulder, and pressed a kiss to my forehead. "Give my regards to your husband and children. Know that I will be praying for you. And may HaShem have mercy on Herod's house."

I stood in the hallway, bothered and bewildered, as my brother turned and walked out of the palace.

~~~~~~~~

For the next several weeks, I felt as though I walked the sharp blade of a knife. Though Pheroras had been living in Peraea for some time, knowing he would not come back to Jerusalem left a gaping hole in my heart. I mourned him as if he were dead.

Antipater seemed not to notice that his favorite uncle had disappeared from court. Instead he made broad hints to his father about a trip to Rome. He claimed he wanted to see the sights and pay his respects to Augustus, yet I knew he had more than that on his mind. He wanted to cultivate a friendship with the emperor, and then he would tell any lie and bribe any rumormonger in order to convince the emperor that Herod had lost his grasp on Judea and Antipater ought to be named king instead. The man could be charming when he wanted to be, and though he had never been as handsome as Mariamne's sons, his attitude of self-command and studied relaxation suited him well. Herod finally agreed and sent Antipater off to Rome.

Several weeks later, we heard that Pheroras had taken ill and was near death in Peraea.

I hurried to Herod's chamber, uncertain how he would take the news. To my great pleasure and surprise, Herod immediately sent his physician to Peraea to look after our brother, then made plans to travel to Peraea himself. I went with him, but by the time we arrived, our brother had succumbed to his illness.

Pheroras's wife, Panphila, stepped out of the room when Herod and I entered Pheroras's bedchamber. We stood by his body, then Herod clung to me and wept bitter tears. What could I say? I patted his back and murmured consoling words as he wept. Finally he straightened and wiped his face.

He gave orders that Pheroras's body should travel with us back to Jerusalem, where he would be buried with great honor in our family tomb.

Herod did not want to spend the night in Peraea but gave instructions to the servants of the household: in the coming weeks he wanted to interview them in Jerusalem, to learn what his brother had been doing during his last few weeks.

We rode back to Jerusalem under the cover of darkness.

CHAPTER FIFTY-SEVEN

Salome

The first sign of our unusual guests were the camels in the courtyard. We were used to camels—the Nabataeans frequently rode them, but their camels were equipped for speed, with light saddles and long legs. The dozen or so camels gathered at the watering troughs the morning after our return from Peraea were thickly furred and stout, bred for difficult journeys. They wore heavy, padded, and decorated saddles with tassels and fringe in riotous colors. Other camels in the caravan carried deep baskets packed to the brim, probably with supplies for a long journey.

Who had come to see us . . . and from where had they come?

I called for Uru, who had become a capable handmaid, and told her to dress me in a simple tunic and a wig. I wanted to see my brother as quickly as possible.

~~~~~~~~~

I found Herod in the central reception hall, where several people waited for an audience with the king. They bowed as I walked past, but I paid them no mind. I focused instead on the group of men standing before the throne. They wore gleaming jackets and dark, pointed beards, and their faces were deeply tanned by the sun.

"Ah, my sister Salome." Herod stretched out his hand to me, and the men bowed.

I stood at Herod's side and gave our visitors a polite smile. Then, from between clenched teeth, I pushed a quiet question to my brother: "Who are they?"

"Wise men," Herod said, lowering his voice. "From the East. They have come with an interesting story. They have traveled many miles in search of a king."

"A king." I frowned. "Well, here you are. They have found you."

"It is not me they seek—they are seeking one they call the King of the Jews."

"And are *you* not the king of the Jews?" I tilted my head and smiled again.

Herod nodded at the man who seemed to be the leader. "Please," he said, raising his voice. "Tell my sister who it is you seek."

The man nodded. He spoke Aramaic, but carefully, as if it were not his native tongue. "We have been traveling many months. We have come seeking the one who has been born King of the Jews. For we saw His star in the east and have come to worship Him."

"Worship?" The word slipped out on a tide of incredulity. I hesitated, then leaned toward Herod. "Are you divine already? It took Augustus years to be proclaimed a god."

Herod shushed me. "Mind your tongue and listen."

The visitors' representative continued, "We are familiar with your people. Years ago, a Jew called Daniel served a king called Belshazzar. He shared some of your holy writings with our people, including a prophecy." The man closed his eyes and recited: "'I see Him, yet not at this moment. I behold Him, yet not in this location. For a star will come from Jacob, a scepter will arise from Israel.'" The man opened his eyes. "We have seen His star, and we have come to meet the mighty King."

Herod threw me a warning glance and cleared his throat. "I am glad you have come." He smiled, though his eyes had shuttered into slits of annoyance. "And I will offer you hospitality here, in my palace, while I make inquiries. Let me summon my wise men, and I will ask them to search the Holy Scripture and the writings of the prophets. When I have an answer, I will share it with you."

The wise men conferred in their own language. Afterward the leader bowed. "Thank you for your generous hospitality. We will wait to hear from you."

They backed away from the throne and, at an appropriate distance, turned and left the reception hall.

I shifted my position so that those watching from a distance could not see my expression. "What do you make of it?" I asked, searching Herod's face. "I have never heard of this prophecy."

"Nor I," Herod replied, his voice dry, "but I have never studied the prophets. I will have to summon the *kohanim* and the Temple's best Torah scholars—"

"Why alert the entire Sanhedrin?" I asked, grateful to be of service. "Zara is married to a Torah scholar. I will send for him."

"Do so at once," Herod said, scratching his chin. "For if there is a new king in Judea, I would find him first."

~~~~~~~~

Herod was not a patient man. By the time Ravid appeared at the palace with the escort I had sent for him, Herod had already summoned several Torah scholars from Jerusalem. Those men did not appear happy to be yanked from their homes at the time of the midday meal, but they had come nonetheless. They were crowded into Herod's council chamber, where he sat at a table covered with every ancient manuscript he could find in the palace.

"Salome!" Herod's face brightened when I appeared in the doorway. "Have you brought someone who can help?"

I gestured to Ravid, who stood beside me, looking pale and uncertain. "This is Ravid, the Torah teacher I mentioned."

The Temple scholars stared at Ravid as Herod clasped his hands and nodded. "Good. My visitors are seeking a king of the Jews."

"But *you* are the king of the Jews," one of the Temple teachers said. "May you live long and—"

"Not me," Herod snapped. "They are seeking a new king. A powerful king, one who will crush foreheads and skulls."

The Temple teachers looked at each other, their faces twisting in bewilderment.

Ravid stepped forward and gave Herod a quick bow. "I am pleased to be of service, but I'm not sure what you require."

"I need an answer to a simple question," Herod said and glared at the scholars around the table. "A group of wise men have come to Jerusalem to seek a king. They say the prophets spoke of him in the time of Daniel, and now he has been born king of the Jews. What can you tell me about him?"

Ravid glanced at me, then cleared his throat. "If he *has* been born, He will come from the tribe of Judah."

"Aha!" Herod pounded the table in delight. "Now we are getting somewhere. You know about this king?"

Ravid nodded.

"You are from the tribe of Judah, are you not?" I smiled. "I believe that is what Zara told me."

"I am. If you recall the deathbed blessing Jacob gave Judah, he said, 'The scepter will not pass from Judah, nor the ruler's staff from between his feet, until He to whom it belongs will come. To Him will be the obedience of the peoples.'"

341

Herod nodded as if he were familiar with the prophecy, but I had never heard it.

"All right, then," Herod said, his face going somber. "So where is this king? How do I find him to pay my respects?"

Ravid drew a deep breath. "The prophet Micah prophesied that He would be born in Bethlehem."

"Bethlehem." Herod's voice went soft with disbelief. "The shepherd's village?"

"So said the prophet."

Herod leaned back in his chair, contemplating Ravid's answer, then nodded. "You may go!" he shouted at the men around the table. "All of you."

The scholars stood and shuffled out of the room. I caught Ravid's sleeve before he followed the others. "I would like to see you before you go," I whispered. "Please wait for me in the courtyard."

When the room had emptied, I sighed and moved toward the door. "The hour grows late," I said, "and I want to ask Ravid about Zara before he leaves."

Ignoring me, Herod shouted for a guard. A soldier appeared in the doorway, his eyes wide and his hand on the hilt of his sword. "Fetch the captain of my elite guard," Herod said. "At once!"

As the soldier hurried away, I gaped at my brother. "What has alarmed you?" I asked.

Herod smiled, a look of purposeful intent on his face. "When have I ever allowed a contender for the throne to live? Tomorrow I will find out exactly when this star appeared, and then I will eliminate the threat. As I always have."

I should not have been surprised, but I was. If a supposed king in Bethlehem was preparing to challenge Herod's throne, we would have heard about him. Unless the king was still a baby.

But how could a newborn child threaten an aged king?

I walked in the shadowy hall, pacing back and forth, clenching and unclenching my hands as my thoughts raced. Years ago I took a vow to protect Herod no matter what, and I had committed many regrettable acts in the defense of his throne. But how could I condone the murder of a child? This would not be an act of war; it would be an act of vanity for an aging king, one who had only a few years remaining, even if all went well. We had just lost Pheroras. Why did defending Herod involve so much bloodshed? And why had Ravid told Herod the king would be born in Bethlehem? He and Zara lived there with their baby.

My mind stuttered over an unexpected thought: what if *their* baby was this prophesied king? Could their son grow up to sit on the throne of Judea? Ravid was a devout man who would undoubtedly teach his son the Law of HaShem.

But if Herod had his way, Zara's son would die tomorrow. Not some nameless, faceless baby, but the son for which Zara and Ravid had waited and wept and prayed.

The thought chilled me to the marrow, yet what could I do? Herod was nothing if not stubborn, and he had already made up his mind about what to do.

Perhaps I was being foolish. Zara's baby was no king, surely not. And even if he were, would it not be better for him to die than to grow up to become king? Being king of the Jews had not brought Herod happiness. The throne had brought conflict and strife and stained his hands with the blood of his loved ones. His power had been limited, his wealth stolen, and he had never received the love, appreciation, and gratitude he sought from his people. What good was a kingdom if it came at such a high cost?

What was Herod thinking? He would not live long enough

for a baby to grow to manhood, so he must be thinking of his children. He wanted to kill a baby in Bethlehem in order to preserve his Herodian dynasty. That was why he wanted the Hasmonean sons of Mariamne to die. That was why he would kill an innocent child. His ambition was horrific, but what could I do about it? I could not stop him. I did not dare try. Over the years I watched Herod turn on his beloved Mariamne, on his sons, and on Pheroras. He might turn on me if I tried to oppose him, and then I might die under mysterious circumstances. Even though I had devoted my life to serving my brother, all my efforts would come to nothing if I tried to stop him from saving his posterity from this newborn king.

So what would I tell Ravid, waiting for me in the courtyard? Would I tell him to go his way and be at peace, or . . .

I stopped in the hallway where I had stood with Pheroras not so long ago. Outside an open window, the city lay like a colorful blanket as flickering lights began to seep through cracks in shuttered windows. If only I were a Jewish woman who lived in one of those houses, an ordinary woman with problems like what to cook for Shabbat dinner . . .

I realized I was weeping only when I tasted the salt of my tears. "Adonai." The name was the only one available to me; no one else could help. "Adonai, I am powerless. I cannot stop what is about to happen."

A soft wind blew through the open window, brushing my cheek. I swiped my tears away, not wanting to appear forlorn or defeated in front of Ravid, and then I heard Pheroras's voice as clearly as if he were standing next to me: "*I was not a righteous man before . . . I want to be righteous now. I want to love Adonai with all my heart, soul, and strength. Can you understand that?*"

I didn't understand, but with desperate clarity I knew I wanted life, not death. I wanted Herod to be known for his mercy, not his ambition. Why did a sixty-eight-year-old king need to defend his throne from a baby?

Then, from someplace I could not identify, I heard another voice:

When Israel was a youth I loved him, and out of Egypt I called My son.

I had never heard such words, and for a moment I wondered if the rumbling voice came from my own head. Was I losing my mind? But no—I had no reason to say those phrases, and I had not thought about Egypt in years.

Then, in a breathless moment of clarity, I understood. I had called out to Adonai, and He had answered . . . but at first I had been too dull of hearing to understand.

I sniffed, palmed the remaining tears from my face, and hurried to the courtyard to find Ravid.

<center>~~~~~~</center>

"Egypt?" Ravid stared at me as if I'd lost my mind. "You want us to go to Egypt?"

"As soon as possible," I said, moving toward a set of woven storage baskets the gardeners had left behind. "Here." I picked up a basket, dumped a mountain of dead leaves and spent blossoms on the ground, and handed the empty basket to Ravid. "Take this, go home, pack your things, and leave at once. It is not safe for you to remain in Bethlehem."

"Why?" Ravid stood like a statue, holding the basket with a blank look on his face. "Why would we leave? We have our school, and we have students. They will be waiting for us in the morning—"

"You must not be there." I dumped another basket, then halted in mid-step. "How old is your baby?"

Ravid frowned. "Nearly two years."

345

I shoved the second basket into his arms. "Go home, get your wife and baby, and leave Judea."

Ravid set the basket on the ground. "I still do not understand—"

"Ravid." I walked over and firmly held his gaze. "Today I asked Adonai for help. I received an answer. I heard something about 'out of Egypt I called my son.' That is why you must go to Egypt, and you must leave before tomorrow."

A tiny flicker of shock widened his eyes, and he blew out a breath. "The prophet Hosea," he said. "Those are the words of Adonai."

"Why are you still here?" I thrust a smaller basket into the container at his feet, then pushed his shoulder toward the gate. "Go. The escort is waiting with a cart outside. Be safe."

Something I said must have convinced him, because he picked up the baskets and strode toward the gate. But before leaving, he turned and met my gaze. "May Adonai bless you," he said, his dark eyes glittering with conviction. "Until the next time we see you."

I watched him go, and as he turned the corner, with pulse-pounding certainty I knew we would never meet again.

⁓⁓⁓⁓⁓

I sat as still as a statue as the scene I had dreaded unfolded before me. Because the wise men were waiting for darkness in case the star reappeared, Herod summoned the wise men at sunset and told them to look for the child in Bethlehem. Before sending them off, he asked when they had first seen the star that led them to Jerusalem. The leader of the group replied that they had been traveling for nearly two years, always moving west, where the star had first appeared on the horizon.

"Thank you." Herod smiled. "When you have found this king, return here and let me know where he lives. I would like to visit him myself."

The wise men bowed and left the reception hall, their voices blending into a masculine rumble as they went to the courtyard to assemble their caravan.

I had done all I could. I knew nothing about a coming king; I knew only that Zara and Ravid had a baby less than two years old and they lived in Bethlehem. But now they should be on their way south. They were righteous. So perhaps I could be counted as righteous for saving their baby's life.

I hoped—I prayed—they had believed me.

CHAPTER FIFTY-EIGHT

Zara

I had been napping, but Ravid woke me with a story that drove the last lingering wisps of sleep from my head. The escort that had driven him from Jerusalem left the cart with us and said Salome had instructed him to walk back. "That was good of her," I remarked, and Ravid looked at me as if surprised that goodness could exist in Herod's palace.

Ravid tossed belongings into baskets and trunks while I lifted our son into my arms. Just before we left, Ravid wrote a note to his students and tacked it to the door. He did not say where we were going or why. In fact, I wasn't sure of the *why* myself.

The night sky had begun to brighten in the east when we climbed into the cart and woke the sleepy donkey. My heart pounded when the animal protested with an ear-shattering bray, but no one stirred as Ravid slapped the reins and we set out, wheels creaking as we drove through the village gates and looked for the road that led south.

We stopped by the well to fill a water jug and were surprised to find another couple in a cart. Their donkey was older and even more recalcitrant than ours, and I said as much to the young woman as the men hauled up the bucket.

She smiled, and as the first rays of morning lit her face I was startled by her youth. Only a girl, really, though she held a baby to her breast. "What a sweet baby," I said, glimpsing a shock of brown hair. "A boy?"

She nodded.

"We have a son, too." I gestured to the basket behind me. "He tends to sleep through all the excitement."

She sighed softly. "I am hoping this one will sleep. He is a good baby, though."

"How old?"

"Almost two."

"Ours is the same age." I peered through the morning fog to check on the men, then looked back at her. "Are you going south?"

"I think so." She glanced at her husband. "Joseph did not say. He only said we had to go at once."

"We're traveling to Egypt." I sighed. "Though I am not sure why."

She laughed softly. "My husband is a carpenter. He says he can work anywhere."

"Mine is a teacher. I suppose he can teach anywhere, as well."

I glanced into her wagon, which, like ours, had been packed with baskets and rough wooden trunks. But her wagon also held several ornate jars, the sort of containers I had seen only in the king's palace.

When I looked up, I realized she had seen my curious glance at the contents of her cart. "We had unexpected guests before we left," she said, tossing a rough blanket over the beautiful jars. "They were generous with their gifts."

I smiled to reassure her. "You don't have to worry about us, but covering those is a good idea. Far too many thieves would be attracted by such things."

The men returned carrying an earthen water jar between them, and Ravid placed his hand on my shoulder. "We are going to travel together," he said, nodding to the young man. "There is safety in numbers."

"Good idea." I smiled at the girl. "My name is Zara."

"I am Mary," she answered. "And I am glad the Lord has made sure we will not be alone."

CHAPTER FIFTY-NINE

Salome

I spent most of the next day in the courtyard garden, watching the sun sail across the sky and waiting for the sound of a camel caravan. I hoped—I prayed—that if Zara's little son was the prophesied king, the wise men would find only an empty house when they reached Bethlehem.

Occasionally I heard an impatient roar coming from Herod's chamber. He was waiting too, and as one hour slid into the next, I knew he had realized the truth: the men from the East were not coming back. Somehow they had intuited my brother's intention and chose to leave Jerusalem behind.

Did they find their baby king, or did they simply ride away after a fruitless search? I thought about sending someone to ask Bethlehem villagers if anyone had noticed a camel caravan—surely it would not have gone unnoticed—but then decided to let the matter rest.

The sun was on its way down the sky when the doors of the garrison flew open and a squad of armed riders burst forward, spurring their horses through the gate. My hand flew to my throat at the familiar sound. I ran up the stairs and hurried to

351

the balcony built into the western wall. A moment later I heard footsteps and spun around to see Herod standing behind me, a look of stern satisfaction on his face as he watched the riders churn up clouds of dust on the road to Bethlehem.

Had Herod sent someone to search for news of a caravan?

"Did you find the king?" I asked.

He shook his head. "I do not need to find him. The star of this so-called king appeared two years ago, so I have given my swordsmen orders to eliminate every boy less than two years old. The threat will be eliminated by morning."

I felt my stomach drop and the empty place fill with a horrifying hollowness. "*Every* boy?" I whispered. "Every boy in Bethlehem?"

Herod nodded.

I felt the wings of calamity brush past me, stirring the air and lifting the hair on my forearms. I staggered toward the stairs and somehow made my way back to my apartment where not even Alexas could convince me that Herod had only done what was necessary for a king.

For three days I remained in my chamber with the windows shuttered and a sheet drawn over my head. Alexas stayed away out of respect for my dark mood, and Uru had learned enough to know not to disturb me.

In the past I defended Herod's hard actions because I understood how precarious his position was. But his position was no longer uncertain; he enjoyed the full support of Augustus, and while the people of Judea did not love him, their hatred had cooled to a point where they were not on the verge of revolt. Many grudgingly appreciated the things he had done for them—the buildings, the improved aqueducts, the restoration of the Temple, the relief from taxes during famine, his provision after the earthquake. A king did not have to be so generous, but Herod had done such things in an effort to win the hearts of his people.

And whether he wanted to admit it or not, Herod was nearing the end of his life. His health was not good, and he had outlived all his brothers. Why did he still feel the need to assert his authority with an iron fist?

When I woke on the fourth morning, I knew I could not spend the rest of my life in hiding. If Adonai had some purpose for me, it certainly was not to warm a mattress in Herod's palace while my brother veered from depression to madness in the winter of his life.

I got out of bed, rang for Uru, and squinted toward the light fringing my shuttered window. When the handmaid appeared, I told her I needed to look my best, for I was going to see the king.

⌇⌇⌇⌇⌇⌇

Once my handmaid had finished dressing me, applying cosmetics, and arranging my hair, I stood before the looking brass to check my reflection one last time. Like Herod, I had also entered the final season of life, and I suspected that no meeting with the king had ever been as important as the one I would have today. For the first time in my sixty years, I was going to tell him the truth about his firstborn son.

Though Herod's disavowal of Pheroras had shaken me, his late change of heart had reinforced my opinion of his best quality—Herod had always been as faithful as a dog. He had remained loyal to Mark Antony, to Augustus, and he had always respected Hyrcanus, even when he had to execute the man for treason.

So perhaps he would remain loyal to me when I brought news he would not want to hear.

I found him in his chamber and did not let myself appear

surprised to find him still in bed. His physician sat in a corner of the room, reading a scroll, while Nicolaus of Damascus sat in another corner, hard at work on Herod's biography, a work he had begun several months before.

I ignored the writer and the physician, just as I had ignored all signs of Herod's illness for the past few months. "Good morning, my king." I bowed before him.

With an effort, Herod pushed himself upright, propping himself on pillows. "What brings you here so early?"

"The truth." I rose and folded my hands. "May I sit?"

Herod nodded at an empty chair near his bed. I sat, grateful for something to support my quivering knees. "This brings me no pleasure, brother, but I feel I must tell you the truth about your firstborn."

I told him all I knew about Antipater and about how I had abetted him in the early years due to a vow I made our mother. I told him that Antipater had become close with Pheroras and had confided to our brother that he hated his father and complained that Herod was living too long, keeping him from power while devoting too much time and attention on younger sons who were not destined to be king.

I told him what Pheroras had told me about Antipater procuring a poison disguised as a love potion, and how he intended to give it to Herod. Pheroras had taken custody of the potion, and when he became ill, he was so touched by Herod's concern for his health that he destroyed the poison.

"Furthermore," I finished, "Doris has been advocating for her son, working behind the scenes to advance him to the detriment of your other sons. You were gracious to bring her back to court, and she has used your graciousness against you. The young man and his mother have been false-faced since they returned to Jerusalem. Even now, as Antipater is in Rome, I am certain he is working against you."

I stopped, having run out of things to say. The effort of unburdening had exhausted me, but when I looked over at Herod, I realized my words had a far different effect on him. His face had gone the color of a thundercloud, and the veins in his neck were throbbing. Had I gone too far?

"Herod—" I began.

"Enough, Salome. You were right to come to me. Now go, for I must speak to my physician."

Swallowing my protests and my regrets, I stood, bowed, and quietly left the room.

I did not see Herod for several days after my meeting with him. He remained in his room with his biographer and his physician. When I asked a servant if he had any other visitors, the man nodded. "He has been speaking with many servants from Peraea. And people from Jerusalem, as well."

I lifted a brow as understanding dawned. Herod was investigating, diligently confirming everything I and others had told him. Perhaps he had heard rumors of Antipater's activities before I unburdened myself, and my words had fanned the flames of his suspicion.

Herod wrote his firstborn a friendly letter, urging him to return to Judea at once, advising him to make haste in case his health should worsen and leave the throne vacant. Smelling victory, Antipater boarded a fast ship and arrived at Caesarea, where he was not greeted with the pomp due the heir presumptive but made to wait while his father greeted Quintilius Varus, who had arrived on the same ship. Varus, Antipater was shocked to learn, was the new Roman governor of Syria and would head the tribunal convened to conduct his trial.

The next day Herod assembled the tribunal. Before Herod's associates, informers who had been promised immunity for their part in Antipater's machinations told their stories of conspiracy, deceit, and bribery. In the end, Antipater was charged with parricide and engineering the execution of Mariamne's innocent sons.

I found the trial difficult to watch, yet the experience was akin to torture for my brother, as the trial was an indictment of his fatherhood. How could he have been so wrong, so blind to what was good and what was deceitful? Though he knew what the testimonies would involve, he was so grieved by the hard truth that he broke down and wept bitter tears. Unable to continue in the role of accuser, Herod stepped aside and Nicolaus of Damascus stepped into his place, charging Antipater with planning "such a sort of uncommon parricide as the world never yet saw."

The final condemnation came from Quintilius Varus after one of Pheroras's servants stated that he had not destroyed the poison meant to kill Herod but had hidden it. When he produced the flask, Antipater insisted it was a love potion. Then Nicolaus of Damascus commanded that the potion be given to a condemned criminal. The criminal was brought forth and forced to drink from the bottle. For a brief instant I wondered if Antipater had spoken the truth, but then the prisoner collapsed and died on the floor.

After his death sentence was pronounced and written, Antipater was taken to prison. The official record was sent to Augustus by messenger.

We could do nothing but wait for the emperor's approval.

CHAPTER SIXTY

Salome

In tremendous pain, suffering from fever, itching, agony in the colon, swollen feet, lung disease, convulsions, and eye problems, Herod sought relief with a paring knife. He tried to cut his wrists when his cousin Achiab, who was with him, wrestled the knife from his hand. My brother roared with pain and frustration, and that scream—thought to be beyond what a dying man could produce—echoed through the palace.

I heard it. The sound jolted me from sleep and propelled my feet to the floor. I flew to Herod's chamber, where a crowd had gathered outside the door. I walked past the guards, servants, wives and children, and entered to find my brother weeping on the floor, covered only by a thin blanket.

I told Achiab to help the king get back into bed, then instructed the physician to give him more pain-killing herbs.

I did not know that the sound of the king's scream had also traveled to the detention chamber, where Antipater was being held prisoner. Upon hearing the scream, followed by rushing footsteps and a general outcry, Antipater assumed the king

357

had died. He leapt to his feet and called the guard to his door, offering the man a bribe if he would release him at once.

The jailer did not reply but turned and strode to the king's chamber, where I was helping Herod settle in his bed. Both of us listened to the jailer's report, and then Herod ordered Antipater's immediate execution. He would not wait for Augustus's permission.

Afterward, my brother rewrote his will yet again. While he wrote, I begged him to go to the palace in Jericho where the warm springs might ease the pain of the lesions on his skin. Once he had finished the revisions on his will, Herod agreed.

Later I learned that trouble of another sort was brewing at the Temple.

As news of the king's imminent death spread through Jerusalem, Matthias the son of Margalus, and Judas the son of Sepphoraeus, both Torah teachers, told their students that the hour had come to rid the Temple of the one object that profaned it—a great golden eagle that had hung over Agrippa's Gate for more than twenty years. The Law of Israel, they said, forbade likenesses of living things, and even if the students should die for their action, they should pull it down.

At midday, in front of great crowds in the streets, the students climbed up to the roof, lowered themselves by ropes, and hacked off the golden eagle. Forty students, along with their teachers, were promptly arrested by Temple guards. They were taken to Jericho to stand before the king.

Though he was weak and in terrible pain, Herod sat on his throne in the reception hall, where he accused the Temple students and raged against them for their ingratitude. Did he not restore the Temple to greatness? Had he not made Jerusalem the center of the world? Why were the people not grateful for his brilliant construction and improvements?

When the students did not answer, he separated the teachers from the students. The students were to be executed by the sword, but the leaders—Herod winced as his tunic brushed the inflamed skin on his arm—were to be burned alive.

I closed my eyes, horrified by the severe sentence, which would be carried out immediately. As the Torah teachers were dragged from the hall to be immolated, Herod stood and staggered toward me. "If I must suffer this agony," he said, his face twisting, "so must they."

I gently took his arm and helped him to the baths, where I hoped the waters of the spring would ease his suffering.

As we walked I could not help seeing the eagle as a portent of things to come. No one had complained about the eagle in years, but because Herod was near death, rebellion had reared its head. What sort of traitorous displays would we see once Herod was gone?

The next day, my brother called me to his bedchamber. I thought he might want to assure me that he was ready to pass into the next life, but instead he gave me an order: I was to gather Jericho's elite Jews and hold them in the hippodrome. "Once you have all of them, particularly the leaders," he rasped, "have the guards close the gates. Have the people wait until they hear the news."

"What news, brother?"

The corner of his mouth went up in a half smile. "The news that I have died." His eyelids drooped, half closing. "Then you command the guards to kill them all."

"Why?" Once again my slippery tongue betrayed me. "Why, brother, would you kill so many of your people?"

His eyes closed, but he was not sleeping. "Let all of Judea and every household weep for me . . . whether they will or not."

I turned to Alexas, horrified by the order, but as long as Herod lived, I had no choice but to obey him. The captain of the guard had heard the command and already left the room, probably to send his men throughout the city. Before sunset, they would take the men, women, and children from their homes and herd them toward the hippodrome, the only structure large enough to hold so many people.

What was their crime? Not adoring their king?

Now I understood why the Jews had never loved him as he wanted to be loved—they loved HaShem above all. To love anyone more than their God was idolatry, and while Herod did not mind being a lesser power than Antony or Augustus, he had always wanted to be first in the hearts of his people.

My heart constricted in pity for my dying brother. Had anyone ever loved him enough?

"Brother." I moved closer to his bed, lifted his hand, and pressed it to my lips. "I have always loved you."

Then Alexas and I turned and left him with his courtiers.

~~~~~

"How is he?"

Alexas looked at me and shook his head. "He breathes still, but he has not spoken in several hours."

For two days I had been sitting on an upper row of the hippodrome, staring at the Jews waiting on the field of competition. The people had brought nothing with them, so at sunset of the first day I commanded the guards to bring them bread, water, and blankets. But now the children were crying, the adults frightened, and I had no answers to offer them.

Herod would have thought me silly, feeding and comforting condemned Jews, yet the people below me had done nothing wrong. Occasionally they shaded their eyes and stared up at me, and I hoped the distance was too great for them to see my expression.

I would not have them see the dread and fear on my face.

The captain of the guard had placed armed soldiers along

the front row of seats; they faced the Jews on the field. I could not know what the guards were thinking, if they were pleased or indifferent to the prospect of killing so many innocents only to mark a king's death.

I did not know many people in Jericho, but women like Zara were surely among the group on the field. Men like Ravid. Torah teachers and students like the ones who perished for ridding the Temple of a desecration. People who believed in something, in someone higher than themselves. Higher than an earthly king.

I turned to Alexas, who had been studying me for several minutes. "What are you thinking?" he asked.

"I am thinking," I said slowly, "how I have spent a lifetime protecting, defending, and pleasing my brother."

"No one can dispute that."

"Years ago, Joseph refused to carry out an oath he had sworn to the king. I told Herod that if I had sworn an oath to do something after his death, I would most certainly carry it out."

Alexas picked up my hand and gently held it. "Every situation is different."

"That's what I thought." I cleared my clotted throat. "Perhaps it is time I began to please someone else."

"The next king?"

"No—HaShem."

"Your brother is not yet dead." Alexas's voice held a warning note.

"I know. But now, in this moment, I have the power to right one of his wrongs." With resolve I pulled my hand from Alexas's and faced the captain of the guard. "Release those people at once—all of them."

The captain sucked at the inside of his cheek for a moment. Then he struck his breastplate with a fist and shouted to his men, "Release the prisoners at once!"

I looked out over the playing field, where the assembled families began to embrace each other and shout praise to HaShem. Did they know how close they had come to death? Surely some of them suspected. Why else would a dying king force so many into one place?

Herod had never understood his people. He had craved their love and loyalty, but he never received more than grudging gratitude on the few occasions he opened his purse and fed the hungry.

At least they would remember him for the Temple. For hundreds of years, he predicted, people would admire it and think of him.

Epilogue

Five days after he executed his firstborn, and four days after he executed the Temple teachers and students, Herod the Great died in Jericho in the year 4 BCE. He was sixty-nine years old.

His last will stipulated that nineteen-year-old Archelaus would be king of Judea. Antipas, at seventeen, was to rule Samaria, Galilee, and Peraea. Sixteen-year-old Philip was to be tetrarch of several territories north and northeast of the Sea of Galilee. Those stipulations, however, had to be approved by Augustus.

Before Augustus could confirm the terms of Herod's will, the Herodians began to fight among themselves. Finally they all appeared before Augustus, who decided to approve Herod's will but with certain modifications:

Archelaus would rule Judea, Samaria, and Idumea, but he would be ethnarch, not a king, until he had proved he deserved a crown.

Antipas would be a tetrarch and would govern Galilee and Peraea.

Philip would be tetrarch of Batanaea and Trachonitis, as well as the Golan Heights.

Salome would receive the cities of Jamnia, Azotas, and Pha-
esalis. Augustus also gave her a royal palace in the town of Ash-
kelon, and cash from the financial gift Herod had bequeathed
to Augustus.

Archelaus, who ruled Judea, never received a crown. When
unrest threatened the peace, he responded with mass slaughter,
causing both the Jews and the Samaritans to complain to the
emperor. Augustus called him to Rome to explain himself, then
exiled Archelaus to Gaul, where he lived out the rest of his life.

After Augustus vacated Archelaus's position, Judea was given
a procurator, Coponius, who claimed Caesarea, not Jerusalem,
as his official residence. He was the first of several procurators,
which eventually included Pontius Pilate, who presided over the
trial and execution of Jesus Christ.

In 10 AD, Salome died at age seventy-five.

In 2007, Israeli archeologist Ehud Netzer uncovered and veri-
fied the location of Herod's fortress tomb, where he had been
buried with great ceremony.

Interview with the Author

Q. In most versions of this story, Mariamne is the tragic hero-ine and Salome the villain. Why did you reverse their roles?

A. I have learned that no man or woman is completely good or evil. Perspective changes everything. Even "bad" people often have good reasons for doing what they do, whereas "good" people can do terrible things on occasion.

So I asked myself, Why did Herod massacre the innocents at Bethlehem? Why did he execute his wife, his mother-in-law, and his sons? Why did he gain a reputation for being ruthless and bloodthirsty?

He did those things to achieve his goals, to eliminate all threats to his position. He also wanted to be loved by his people, and yet no matter how hard he tried, he always fell short. Meanwhile, he resented the people who *were* adored, such as young Aristobulus the high priest, and later his sons by Mariamne—because he longed for adoration but never achieved it.

Salome, whom history records as a devious schemer, only

began to scheme and manipulate after Alexandra had been doing the same thing for years, so Salome learned from a master. Herod's court was filled with meddling women who formed cliques—mothers against mothers, daughters-in-law against daughters-in-law. I imagine there were also children pitted against children, but history doesn't go into those details.

It's safe to say, however, that with ten wives and at least fifteen children, most of them living in the palace at the same time, Herod's harem was one of the least peaceful places on earth, with plenty of mischief-making on both sides.

Q. Was it difficult to find enough historical information to write this novel?

A. My challenge was that there's almost too much information. If I'd included everything we know about Herod's buildings, his acts, his family, his wars, his wives, and his conquests, the book would have weighed twenty pounds and taken me years to write. I constantly had to reduce information to narrative and skim over periods of time in order to get at the bits of the story I wanted to tell—the story of Salome and her relationships with Herod and her handmaid.

Q. Is Zara a historical character?

A. No. Although I'm sure Salome had handmaids, Zara is a product of my imagination. Yet the key incident at the conclusion of the novel is true. When faced with what to do regarding the people in the hippodrome, Salome chose to do something she would never have done earlier in her life. Something caused her to change her ways, and I thought it would enhance the story if I could fictionalize that motivation.

Q. Where did you get the information about hairstyles?

A. Fascinating, isn't it? I discovered the work of Janet Stephens, an expert on ancient hairstyles, and watched her assemble some of these styles on YouTube videos. I learned that hairbrushes and hairpins had not yet been invented in the first century before Christ, so I had to make adjustments in the story.

Q. How much of the novel is fiction and how much is fact?

A. Nearly all of the events are factual. According to the historian Josephus, Aristobulus's drowning and Alexandra's letters to Cleopatra and her attempts to leave Jerusalem (in a coffin, no less!) are true. Of course, not even Josephus was privy to the prime characters' dialogue and thoughts, so those are fictional. But I always strive to be logical and stick to the facts when they're available.

Q. Did Cleopatra really proposition Herod?

A. If historical sources can be trusted, yes.

Q. Did Nicolaus of Damascus really write a biography of Herod?

A. Yes. He was a prolific writer, and researchers believe Josephus referred to Nicolaus's biography of Herod when he wrote his own history. Sadly, no copies of the biography of Herod have survived.

Q. Did Herod really disguise himself and eavesdrop on the streets of Jerusalem?

A. He did. Incidentally, though Rome was famous for its sewers and aqueducts, it wasn't until after the first century that the sewers were designed to keep standing water out of the streets, rather than move filth out of the city. While private homes may have had toilets, they were not connected to the sewer lines.

Q. According to your timeline, Jesus was born in 7 BC?

A. There's an ongoing debate taking place among biblical scholars concerning the exact time of Jesus's birth. In fact, those who hold to a later year would place the massacre of the innocents during the reign of Herod Archelaus, an idea that is plausible. But when writing historical fiction, a novelist has to choose a time and stick with it so the story's events will remain consistent. I went with the earlier date because it best suited the story.

Q. Is this the last book in THE SILENT YEARS series?

A. Yes. In *Egypt's Sister*, *Judah's Wife*, *Jerusalem's Queen*, and *King's Shadow*, we have covered all the major events during the four hundred years between the Old and New Testaments: the Seleucid occupation, the Hellenization of the world (including Judea), the Maccabees, the Hasmonean dynasty, the rise and sweeping influence of the Roman Empire, and finally the events leading up to the birth of Christ in Bethlehem.

I found it interesting that Josephus and other secular historians do not mention the slaughter of the innocents in Bethlehem, which has led many modern scholars to conclude that it did not happen. But I trust the biblical writers who both prophesied it (Jeremiah 31:15) and recorded it (Matthew 2). I don't know why Josephus and others didn't write about this slaughter. Bethlehem was a small city, so perhaps the event wasn't well known outside certain circles. Because an event was omitted in the historical record, however, does not mean it didn't occur. No source is exhaustive.

Q. What's next for you?

A. I'll begin work on a new series about women in the New Testament, women we haven't yet read about in novels. I'm looking forward to it.

References

Bateman, Herbert W. "Were the Opponents at Philippi Necessarily Jewish?" *Bibliotheca Sacra* 155, 1998.

Charles River Editors. *The Kingdom of Herod the Great: The History of the Herodian Dynasty in Ancient Israel During the Life of Jesus*, 2015.

Connolly, Peter. *Living in the Time of Jesus of Nazareth*. London: Oxford University Press, 1983.

Criswell, W. A. et al., eds. *Believer's Study Bible*. Nashville, TN: Thomas Nelson Publishers, 1991.

Elwell, Walter A., and Philip Wesley Comfort. *Tyndale Bible Dictionary*. Carol Stream, IL: Tyndale House Publishers, 2001.

Fruchtenbaum, Arnold G. *The Messianic Bible Study Collection*. Vol. 31. Tustin, CA: Ariel Ministries, 1983.

Gelb, Norman. *Herod the Great: Statesman, Visionary, Tyrant*. New York: Rowman & Littlefield Publishers, Inc., 2013.

Graf, David F. "Aretas." David Noel Freedman, ed. *The Anchor Yale Bible Dictionary*. New Haven, CT: Yale University Press, 1992.

Harrop, Clayton. "Intertestamental History and Literature." Chad Brand et al., eds. *Holman Illustrated Bible Dictionary*. Nashville, TN: Holman Reference, 2003.

Hoehner, Harold W. "A Chronology of the Life of Christ." *Holman Christian Standard Bible: Harmony of the Gospels*. Nashville, TN: Holman Bible Publishers, 2007.

Horbury, William. *Messianism Among Jews and Christians: Twelve Biblical and Historical Studies*. London; New York: T&T Clark, 2003.

Ilan, Tal. "Salome." *Jewish Women's Archive*. https://jwa.org/encyclopedia/article/salome, accessed July 27, 2018.

———. "Herodian Women." *Jewish Women's Archive*. https://jwa.org/encyclopedia/article/herodian-women, accessed July 27, 2018.

Josephus, Flavius, and William Whiston. *The Works of Josephus: Complete and Unabridged*. Peabody, MA: Hendrickson Publishers, 1987.

Marshak, Adam Kolman. *The Many Faces of Herod the Great*. Grand Rapids, MI: William B. Eerdmans Publishing Company, 2015.

Mowczko, Marg. "The Intrigues of Salome I, Herod the Great's Sister." https://margmowczko.com/salome-i-herod-the-greats-sister, accessed June 22, 2018.

Myers, Allen C. *The Eerdmans Bible Dictionary*. Grand Rapids, MI: William B. Eerdmans Publishing Company, 1987.

Negev, Avraham, and Shimon Gibson, eds. *Archaeological Encyclopedia of the Holy Land*. London: Bloomsbury Academic, 1990.

Netzer, Ehud. *The Architecture of Herod the Great Builder*. Grand Rapids, MI: Baker Academic, 2006.

Pelser, G. M. M. "Governing Authorities in Jewish National Life in Palestine in New Testament Times." *The New Testament Milieu*. A. B. du Toit, ed. Vol. 2. Johannesburg, S.A.: Orion Publishers, Halfway House, 1998.

Richardson, Peter. *Herod: King of the Jews and Friend of the Romans*. Minneapolis, MN: Fortress Press, 1999.

Robertson, A. T. *Word Pictures in the New Testament*. Nashville, TN: Broadman Press, 1933.

Stephens, Janet. "Ancient Roman Hairdressing: Fiction to Fact." https://www.youtube.com/watch?v=B5bfRkomVkg, accessed August 2018.

Swindoll, Charles R., and Roy B. Zuck. *Understanding Christian Theology*. Nashville, TN: Thomas Nelson Publishers, 2003.

VanderKam, James C. *The Dead Sea Scrolls Today*. Grand Rapids, MI: William B. Eerdmans Publishing Company, 1994.

Vermes, Gaza. *The True Herod*. London: Bloomsbury Academic, 2014.

Vos, Howard Frederic. *Nelson's New Illustrated Bible Manners & Customs: How the People of the Bible Really Lived*. Nashville, TN: Thomas Nelson Publishers, 1999.

Angela Hunt has published more than one hundred books, with sales over five million copies worldwide. She's the *New York Times* bestselling author of *The Tale of Three Trees*, *The Note*, and *The Nativity Story*. Angela's novels have won or been nominated for several prestigious industry awards, such as the RITA Award, the Christy Award, the ECPA Christian Book Award, and the HOLT Medallion Award. Romantic Times Book Club presented her with a Lifetime Achievement Award in 2006. She holds both a doctorate in Biblical Studies and a ThD degree. Angela and her husband live in Florida, along with their mastiffs. For a complete list of the author's books, visit angelahuntbooks.com.

Sign Up for Angela's Newsletter!

Keep up to date with Angela's news on book releases and events by signing up for her email list at angelahuntbooks.com.

More from THE SILENT YEARS

When her father and sister are killed, a distant relative invites Salome and her mother to live with his family in Jerusalem. Quickly betrothed to a pagan prince half her age, Salome questions God's plan. But when she suddenly finds herself being crowned queen of Judea, she learns that a woman committed to God can change the world.

Jerusalem's Queen: A Novel of Salome Alexandra

More Biblical Fiction from Baker Publishing Group

◈BETHANYHOUSE

You May Also Like . . .

When his evil father plots to sacrifice him, Hezekiah's mother, Abijah, searches frantically for a way to save him. But only two men can help her, and neither of them seems trustworthy. In a time and place engulfed by violence, treachery, and infidelity to Yahweh, Abijah and her son must discover the one true source of strength if they are to save themselves and their country.

Gods and Kings by Lynn Austin
CHRONICLES OF THE KINGS #1
lynnaustin.org

In this powerful novelization, the apostle Paul, bound in chains in Nero's bleakest prison, awaits his execution. Luke, a friend and physician, risks his life to visit him. Resolved to write another book, these two men race against time and history—and an emperor determined to rid the world of Christianity—to bring the gospel of Jesus Christ to the world.

Paul, Apostle of Christ by Angela Hunt
angelahuntbooks.com

◊BETHANYHOUSE